I0682407

Disciple's Quest II
The Adventures of Jeremiah & Zeal

Walter F. Cantrell

Copyright © 2015 Walter Cantrell

All rights reserved. No part of this book may be reproduced or transmitted in any form or by any means, electronic or mechanical, including photocopying and recording, or by any information storage and retrieval system, without permission in writing from the publisher.

ISBN-13:978-0692603369

ISBN-10:0692603360

Cover Design by Tyson Roberts

Editing by Rebecca LuElla Miller

All Scripture verses are the Author's own wording or taken from the New King James Version. All direct quotes are listed at the back of the book.

Scripture taken from the New King James Version®. Copyright © 1982 by Thomas Nelson. Used by permission. All rights reserved.

Published in the United States by Grace and Truth Publishing

:

DEDICATION

I would like to dedicate this book to my mother, Kay Cantrell. She has sacrificed so much over the years, and her help to both me and my children has been invaluable.

Table of Contents

1

TOWN OF RATIONALISM

In a small corner of the world, a mighty warrior is about to be called forth, whose name is Jeremiah. As our story begins, he is living a very simple and plain existence, but all of that is about to change with the visit of a stranger.

Jeremiah was a dark-skinned man of African heritage, approximately six feet tall, with short hair and just enough stubble on his face to look as if he had gone a day without shaving. His body was naturally muscular while not being overly bulky. Jeremiah carried himself with a quiet and sincere demeanor, putting everyone at ease the moment he greeted them. He was a humble man, always willing to give others the benefit of the doubt.

Jeremiah lived in the Town of Rationalism where everyone spent a great deal of time seeking new knowledge in the areas of mathematics, science, philosophy, and other intellectual subjects. Small groups would often gather to discuss different theories and to argue different points of logic and reason. Jeremiah owned a sandwich eatery, called Food for Thought, which was known for being the best place to go for intellectual conversation.

On one particular evening, as Jeremiah was closing up, an older man appeared outside the main entrance. The stranger gazed through a window, then knocked on the door to get Jeremiah's attention. Jeremiah shook his head and pointed to the "Closed" sign hanging on the door.

The older man nodded and talked loud enough so Jeremiah could hear him through the glass. "I know it's late, but I've traveled a long way, and your eatery was the only one that looked like it was still open. If it isn't too much trouble, may I please come in and get something to eat? I'll take whatever you have."

Jeremiah felt compassion for the man, so he approached the door and opened it. "I've got a turkey sandwich that I made about an hour ago. If you can eat it quickly, you're welcome to it."

"Thank you so much," said the older man as he stepped inside.

After Jeremiah seated him at a table, he handed him the sandwich and poured him a glass of lemonade. The traveler was also dark skinned like Jeremiah but had a little more hair on his face, and a little less hair on his head. He was a few inches shorter than Jeremiah but also carried a few more pounds around the midsection.

Jeremiah cleaned the counter and put away the last of the foodstuffs. He then sat down with the traveler. "My name is Jeremiah."

The man quickly wiped his hand with a napkin. "Nice to meet you, my name is Pastor George."

Jeremiah noticed he was carrying a large backpack. "You said you had traveled a long way. What brings you by here? Are you a salesman?"

"Oh no," said Pastor George, "I travel around and talk to people about God."

Jeremiah was not sure what to think about this. He had never met anyone who traveled for the purpose of talking about religion or God. These were not subjects that were discussed very often in the Town of Rationalism, and when they were, it was to make fun of them.

Jeremiah had always been curious about the kind of person that believed in such nonsensical things, so he thought he would ask the traveler a few questions.

"What makes you think there is any such thing as God?"

Pastor George took out his Book and held it up. "This Book I carry tells me that God is real, and I believe it."

Jeremiah shrugged and appeared unimpressed. "I've heard of that book, although I've never read any of it. Why should we accept what it says as proof of anything? There are many different religions with many different books, so why is yours special?"

Pastor George said, "This Book is special because it's the very words of God Himself."

Jeremiah sort of smirked because he felt this Pastor George character had just made a fatal error in his logic. Jeremiah was used to engaging in debates, and he conducted his discussions like he executed his moves in a chess game. He let his opponent make the mistakes, and then he would capitalize.

Jeremiah grinned, as he leaned back in his chair. "Do you not see the problem with your own reasoning? You say that you know God exists because your book says so, but the only proof you have that your book is authoritative is that it claims to be God's word. This is a circular argument, and it proves nothing. Anyone could write a book that claims to be God's words and then define God based on what that book said."

Pastor George ate another bite of his sandwich, acting as if none of this bothered him. Usually, at this point in a debate, Jeremiah would see his opponent start to squirm. He had just made a good point, and yet the man was not fazed at all.

Pastor George took a drink of his lemonade. "When it comes to questions about whether or not there is a Supreme Being, all arguments are circular except for one."

"And what is that one exception?" asked Jeremiah.

Holding up his hands, as he smiled, Pastor George said, "Well, the one that is actually true of course. If this Book is God's words, then God exists, and He exists as defined by the words in this Book."

Jeremiah shook his head and rolled his eyes. "You are speaking of a matter of faith. I believe in what I can see and what can be proved by scientific observation."

Pastor George shrugged. "Everyone puts their faith in something. The most common scientific theory of the origin of the universe cannot account for how physical matter originally came into existence. Even if there was something like a big bang, there had to be some kind of existing matter to begin the process."

Jeremiah leaned forward. "Well there are theories for that, and just because we can't know for certain what the answer is, that's not a reason to go about inventing a solution such as God."

"I agree," said Pastor George, taking another drink of lemonade. "We should not invent solutions to solve problems we cannot understand, but that's what I believe you're doing."

Jeremiah was not used to being on the defensive. He was quite annoyed that this traveler would challenge his intellectual capabilities with myths and superstition.

Jeremiah crossed his legs and turned to the side. "I don't have to invent anything. There's lots of scientific proof to back up what I believe."

Pastor George held out his hands. "There's lots of scientific proof which backs up many things, but when it comes to the original origin of all things and the initial process that started it, then it's all a matter of faith."

Jeremiah paused. Did Pastor George realize he had trapped himself in his own words? "So even if I accepted what you've just said as true, at best, you can only present what you believe as a competing theory. I choose to put my faith in what I believe the bulk of scientific evidence can prove, and you choose to put your faith in what a book says. I don't see how you can believe your argument is more persuasive than mine."

Pastor George finished another bite of his sandwich. "Oh, there's much more to it than just competing intellectual theories. You see, when I look around at nature, I see the handiwork of God. I see everything operating in an ordered way with a purpose, and I believe behind all of this is a cause. God's word declares that He is the one that created all things."

Raising his voice a notch, Jeremiah said, "But you STILL have to keep coming back to the words of your book as the only real proof of what you believe."

Pastor George pointed at his Book. "It isn't just that these words claim to be God's words. They demonstrate that they're God's words."

Now Jeremiah was ready to pounce because he thought for sure this man had just trapped himself again. Adopting a slightly condescending tone, while giving a half-smile, he said, "How can words demonstrate anything unless there's scientific proof to back them up?"

Pastor George grasped his Book. "These words prove themselves to be God's words, because as I read them, I experience God himself. I can sense the presence of the Holy Spirit teaching me things through them, and I see real changes in my life as I live by them. This may not be proof to you, but for me it is undeniable evidence that I live every day. I don't just read about God, but I have a personal relationship with Him. I am just as convinced that God exists as I am that you exist."

Jeremiah was astonished at this stranger's way of thinking. Becoming more agitated, he said, "Do you not see that you're appealing to feelings and superstitions? Do you not know that other religions claim the same experiences with their own writings?"

Pastor George said, "Oh yes I do know that, but there is only one Book that consists of the very words of God and produces an authentic experience with Him."

Jeremiah was extremely frustrated with the reasoning of this man. He could ask Pastor George once again why he could claim his book was the only one that was real and authentic, but by now he knew that this fanatic would just respond that it was the only source of truth because it said so. How could he win a debate with someone who was delusional?

Jeremiah wanted to try one more question. "I see that you feel very strongly about what you believe, and I can respect that. But if all you have to offer as proof is what your book says, then how do you expect to convince anyone who doesn't believe in your book?"

"Oh, you have me all wrong," said Pastor George as he sat back and drank some more lemonade. "I don't try to convince anyone of anything. This Book says that everyone already has the knowledge that God exists on the inside of them. The question is, what are they going to do about it?"

Jeremiah pointed his finger at Pastor George's book. "This knowledge is not on the inside of me."

Pastor George leaned forward, looking more serious. "This Book says that some have suppressed this knowledge, and while they know what is true, they choose to worship something else. You may worship logic, reason, science, or philosophy, but whatever you hold as supreme that is what you worship, and that is your god."

Jeremiah had never had a discussion go like this. There were rules for this sort of thing. A person was not supposed to act as if they had all the answers. The purpose of debate was to put all the ideas on the table, and then the best one would be declared the winner. This Pastor George didn't seem to understand how things went in the Town of Rationalism.

By now Jeremiah was just looking for a way to get out of the conversation and go home. He thought he'd ask one more question and then let the man know it was time to leave. "So if you're not trying to convince anyone, and you believe everyone already has the knowledge they need, then what is it exactly that you do?"

Shaking his head, Pastor George said, "I don't mean to imply that everyone already has all the knowledge they need, but they have enough to know there's a problem. What I do is provide them with a solution."

Jeremiah crossed his arms. "And just what is this problem you believe everyone has?"

Pastor George finished his sandwich and sat back in his chair. "The problem is that we're not perfect, and we fall short of God's moral laws. His moral laws are just like the physical laws He created. They exist whether people choose to believe in them or not. In addition to the fact that the knowledge of God exists in all, there's also a knowledge that we fall short of what God expects. The biggest moral dilemma in the universe is how do we deal with that problem? That is where this Book comes in. It tells us how this problem came to be, and what the solution is."

Jeremiah said, "I don't believe I have a problem. Sure, I'm not perfect, but who is? I live my life in a way that is honest and respectful."

Pointing toward Jeremiah, Pastor George gently said, "Unless you believe you have a problem then you will not seek a solution. That's why people suppress their knowledge of God."

Pastor George drank the last bit of his lemonade, then wiped his mouth with a napkin. "Jeremiah, you don't believe what you believe because it's more reasonable. You believe it because it's more convenient. If you admit there's a God and that you fall short of what He expects, then you will have to find a solution."

By now Jeremiah was exasperated with this traveling stranger. He had invited him into his eatery even after he was closed and ready to go home. And on top of that, he had been courteous enough to participate in a discussion which he thought was meaningless. Now this man was telling him that *he* had a problem and was in denial?

Jeremiah pushed his chair away from the table. "It's late, and long past when I needed to close up."

Pastor George stood up. "I do thank you for your hospitality. In addition to paying my bill, please let me offer you my Book. I have another one, and I'd like you to have this one."

Holding up his hand, Jeremiah said, "Thanks for the offer, but I already have many books I need to read."

"I understand," said Pastor George as he held out his Book, "but please take it, and if you don't have time to read it then that's okay."

Jeremiah thought it might get him out of there quicker if he just took the book, so he smiled and accepted it.

Pastor George was about to walk out the door when he turned back around. "I know you don't believe any of this right now, but if you're ever convinced that there's a problem, you can find more answers at a place called the Building of Reflection. I live in a home that's not too far from there, and if you're ever by that way, I'd love for you to stop by and visit."

Jeremiah smiled and nodded, not wanting to take the chance of getting into any more conversation. After Pastor George departed he locked everything up and left.

2

THE BOOK

When Jeremiah arrived home, he placed Pastor George's Book on a table, then headed to his favorite chair. It had been a long day, and he was ready to sit down and relax.

Jeremiah lived in a small house by himself. There wasn't much furniture, but he had what was needed. Next to his chair was a small couch for guests to sit on, with a coffee table in front. Two bookcases stood against the wall, filled with many different volumes on a variety of subjects. Some of his books took him on wild adventures while others transported him back to a period of history. Some books served to increase his knowledge, and others were strictly for entertainment.

As Jeremiah sat in his chair, with his feet comfortably placed on the footstool in front, he picked up his book on the history of philosophy. But as he read, Jeremiah noticed that his attention was somewhere else. His mind drifted back to his conversation with Pastor George. He had never stopped to question his beliefs on the origin of the universe or how man came into being. He had always felt comfortable in his conclusions based on the prevailing theories of the day.

Setting his philosophy book in his lap, Jeremiah stared out into space. Of course, there was no creator, right? The more he thought about the beginning of all things, the more he realized how much there was to consider. If the origin of the universe happened the way he had assumed, then essentially everything came about as some random, cosmic accident. This would also include his own existence. Was he the result of an accident? Was all life just the result of random mutations, with the fittest surviving? And more personally, did he himself have meaning? Did he have a purpose? Was there something greater out there that was the cause of all this, and if so did he have any responsibility to this being?

Jeremiah shook himself as if he was trying to wake from a dream. How could he be thinking such things and asking such questions? He knew the answers he would normally give, but those explanations didn't seem to be as conclusive as they once did. Jeremiah had an answer for everything as long as he kept things within a neat little box where he was in control. But his conversation with Pastor George had opened up possibilities he had never considered. After all, no one in the Town of Rationalism thought of such things so why should he?

As Jeremiah sat there wrestling with his thoughts, he remembered the Book that Pastor George had given him. He set the philosophy book down on the small table beside him and walked over to get the Book. After sitting back down, he opened it up. He saw that Pastor George had placed a few bookmarks in it, so he turned to the first one, which was a letter written to the Romans. Starting at the beginning, Jeremiah read where it said that everyone had the knowledge of God within them, even though some had suppressed this knowledge. He concluded this was what Pastor George had been referring to in their conversation earlier.

Jeremiah continued to read. The Book went further, stating that people had suppressed this knowledge of God because of their own ungodliness and unrighteousness. The passage even said that although these people claimed to be wise, they were actually fools. Was this Book accusing him? Was it saying this was true of all the inhabitants of the Town of Rationalism?

The next bookmark pointed to just one verse. Jeremiah read that what we could see was not made out of things which could be seen, but everything was formed by the word of God. A note in the margin gave a reference to the beginning of the Book, so Jeremiah turned all the way back and read about the creation of all things by God.

The last bookmark pointed to a story about someone named Paul who was speaking with philosophers in Athens. Jeremiah was interested to see how this encounter would turn out, so he continued to read. Apparently, these men from Athens looked down on Paul as some kind of idiot who was babbling strange things. Jeremiah could identify with how they felt because he was sure he would have thought the same thing.

As he continued to read, Jeremiah was surprised because this Paul was declaring to the philosophers that they were the ones who were ignorant. He told them that it was God who created all things, and it was God who was responsible for their very existence. He then explained that it was in God that they lived and moved and had their being. From Jeremiah's study of philosophy, he recognized that Paul was actually taking a quote from one of their own philosophers and using it to prove his point.

Then Paul did something that was really shocking. He told all of these learned philosophers that this God who created them was now calling all men to repent. Paul was not just presenting an alternative philosophy, but he was presenting his beliefs as *the* truth. Then he proclaimed to them that they were now responsible to this truth.

Jeremiah closed the Book and set it down. His encounter with Pastor George was unlike any conversation he had ever had, and now the words of this Book challenged everything he thought he knew. Perhaps his brain was just getting tired from the long day. He decided to get some rest, hoping things would be clearer the next day.

Waking up the next morning, Jeremiah got ready to go to his store as he usually did. Once there, he went about his normal routine to prepare for the day's customers. They would start arriving around lunch, and there would be a steady stream until the close of dinner. He baked all the bread and sliced the most requested kinds of meats.

By lunch, his eatery started to fill up, and lively conversation continued throughout the day. Jeremiah would usually take the time to sit and discuss different topics with his customers, but on this day he stayed busy until near the end of the dinner hour. It was at this time that his closest friends would gather, and after he served the last customer, he would sit with them for what he considered to be the best conversations of the day.

Only a few customers remained to be served, and all of Jeremiah's friends sat in their favorite spots in a small room off to the side. His last orders were all take-out, so Jeremiah served them their sandwiches and then locked the door behind them. At last, he joined his friends.

One of them named Scott noticed that there was something different about him. "Jeremiah, you've been quiet since we got here, and you look as if you're trying to solve some difficult mathematical formula in your head. What's going on?"

Jeremiah took a deep breath and then told them about his conversation with Pastor George the night before, as well as everything he'd read in the Book Pastor George had given him.

"Jeremiah," said Scott, "why is all of this troubling you? We've discussed these subjects hundreds of times. We all know what science says, and we know that most of the learned men of the day agree."

Looking around the table, Jeremiah replied, "Yes I know, but have we ever stopped to think about the outcome of what we believe?"

"What do you mean?" said Jane, a young woman who worked at the Farmers Market next door.

Jeremiah held up his hand. "If the existence of the universe is one big cosmic accident that just happened to happen, then our very lives are merely accidents. We live, and then we die. Is there any purpose?"

Jane chuckled, nodding her head. "Oh, you want to know the answer to the age-old question, what is the meaning of life. We've already covered that. Yes, we live, and we die, but what's important is how we live. We live in a way that is in harmony with the universe and our fellow man. When our time is up, we die knowing we lived the best life we could."

"And then what?" asked Jeremiah.

"That's it." Jane shrugged her shoulders. "Isn't that enough? What answer are you looking for? You've seen what happens to bodies after death. All that's left is a skeleton. That's part of the cycle of life. We live, and we die, and then the next generation comes along."

Jeremiah sat back in his chair, noticeably in deep thought.

Sitting across the table was Jeff, who often spent time with Jeremiah at his home. Jeff was known for being more easygoing, but his opinions were well respected by all.

Jeff leaned forward. "What's wrong Jeremiah? You're asking questions that you already know the answers to. Are you going through some kind of personal crisis?"

Shaking his head, Jeremiah said, "I don't think so. I was just fine until last night. I guess I never stopped to think about what if. What if there's more to life than just existing and then dying? What if there's a greater purpose?"

Jeff smiled as he sat back, putting his hands behind his head. "Now you're starting to sound like one of those superstitious types."

Jeremiah leaned forward and placed his hands on the table. "But we all know that science can't explain everything. We don't know where matter came from. We can't explain how something came out of nothing."

"Come on Jeremiah," said Jeff, shaking his head, "we may not be able to explain everything, but that doesn't mean we invent something to fill in the gaps."

Jeremiah had said almost the same thing to Pastor George. It sounded so logical at the time, but now it didn't have quite the same degree of certainty.

Jeff continued, "Jeremiah, you know that throughout history there are things that people couldn't fully explain. That's how myths, superstitions, and religions got started. There was a time when no one understood weather patterns, so they made sacrifices to the gods of the sky to make it rain. People who are weak invent things to make up for what they can't explain. We've progressed past all that. We don't need superstitions or a belief in some make-believe God."

Jane said, "From listening to you Jeremiah, it seems like this Pastor George guy just got you all confused because he didn't discuss things like we do. He stated his view as if it was the final truth. That's how any religious fanatic would present their beliefs. It could have been a representative of any religion, quoting from their particular sacred book, and they too would have approached you as if they were right and couldn't possibly be wrong. You can't argue with someone like that."

Jeremiah paused and took a deep breath. "But, what if?"

"What if what?" said Jane, shaking her head with an annoyed look on her face.

Holding out his hands, Jeremiah blurted out, "What if we're wrong? What if there's a creator? What if there's a God? What if we're not an accident? What if our lives have a deeper purpose?"

"Hold on," said Scott, grinning, as he grasped Jeremiah's shoulder. "Now you're just talking crazy. You've let this Pastor George guy, and his book get to you. I'm not sure why because you know the answers to all of this better than we do."

"I know," said Jeremiah, as he turned sideways in his chair, "and that's what bothers me. I do know all these things that you're saying, and I'm upset with myself because I seem to have lost my ability to think clearly."

Scott patted him on the back. "It's okay Jeremiah. We all have times where we need to be reassured. You've just run into someone who caused you some confusion. I know you'll get it together soon, and things will be back to normal. I would suggest you not let anyone else into your store after closing though."

Everyone laughed, and Jeremiah smiled as well. The rest of his friends went on with their conversations as usual, and he did his best to convince everyone that he was getting back to his old self. After another hour of conversation, everyone left.

When Jeremiah arrived home, he sat in his chair again, and there staring at him was the Book Pastor George had given him. At first, he started to put it aside. No! He had to get over this. He'd read it again with a clear head, with logic, and with reason. This time he would not let the conversation with Pastor George dominate his mind.

Jeremiah again opened the Book to Romans and read through the first chapter. This time though, when he reached the end, he kept reading into the second chapter, and then into the third. But it was here that Jeremiah became concerned.

The Book said that all mankind had sinned and everyone fell short of the expectations of the One who created them. Jeremiah plopped the Book down in his lap. What if not only there was a God, but this God was angry with him? What then? Instead of disproving what he had read the night before, Jeremiah felt the words of this Book convincing him that they were right all along.

This Book did not present a list of theories or suggestions. This Book stated what was true and demanded that everyone be accountable to it. If there really was a God, and he fell short of what this God expected, then this was a major problem.

Jeremiah didn't know what to believe, but he knew he needed to find out more. He was going to have to go where Pastor George had directed him, and he was going to have to discover some answers on his own.

3

THE ADVENTURE BEGINS

The next day Jeremiah went to see his friend Scott, who owned a coffee shop. Scott did most of his business in the mornings, serving up fresh coffee, doughnuts, and a variety of pastries for his customers. As Jeremiah walked in, he saw Scott hurriedly working behind the counter.

Scott heard the bell on the door jingling and looked up. "Jeremiah, what brings you here? You're usually busy getting things ready at your own place by now."

Jeremiah approached the counter. "Were you serious when you said you wanted to buy Food for Thought if it was ever for sale?"

Scott emptied a bag of coffee into a large pot. "Well yes, but I always thought that would be a long ways off, if ever. Why? Is something wrong? Are you in financial trouble?"

Shaking his head, Jeremiah said, "Oh no, nothing like that. It's just this whole thing that we talked about last night has me bothered, and I feel I need to find some answers. I'm going on a journey, and I'm not sure when I'll be back."

Scott pushed a tray of doughnuts into a large brick oven. "I wish you didn't have to go. I truly believe you already have the answers, but I suppose there are many people that need to go on a journey at some point in their life. My cousin set out to 'find herself' a few years ago and ended up spending a year with a group of Tibetan monks. I tell you what, I'll buy your store, but if you return within four weeks I'll sell it right back to you, and we'll just call it a vacation. You haven't taken time off in a while, and you need some rest and relaxation."

Jeremiah nodded. "Thank you. I could return by then or even

sooner."

Scott peeked into the oven to check on the doughnuts, then turned around. "No problem. I'll get all the paperwork ready and bring it by tonight as you're closing. We'll settle up, and then you'll be all set to head out the next day. We'll let the whole group know tonight what you're doing, and we'll make it a going away party."

Jeremiah thanked him for doing all of this on such short notice, then left for his eatery to get ready for the day.

That evening everyone gathered together, and Jeremiah told them what he was going to do. Just like Scott, they tried to talk him out of it, but he was determined. Once it was clear to them that his mind was made up, they all wished him well, letting him know they hoped he would be back soon. They assured him they would keep up the ritual of gathering together at closing time to talk about the topic of the day. As the night was winding down, a few random conversations took place, and then everyone left, leaving Jeremiah alone.

Preparing to leave, Jeremiah looked around and wondered when he would be back. Just a few days ago he could see himself in this business for the rest of his life, and now he wasn't sure when he would see it again. What was happening to him? Was he indeed going through some kind of personal crisis?

Pastor George had not brought up any new ideas or concepts. Jeremiah and his friends had discussed such things many times, and they always had convincing answers. But the Book Pastor George gave him, claimed to be the very words of God Himself, and they challenged him like he had never been challenged before. It was no longer as if ideas or theories were confronting him, but it was more like a person was confronting him. Was he imagining all this? What he knew for sure was that he needed to find out one way or the other.

Jeremiah went home and immediately picked up the Book again. He sat down in his chair, re-reading everything he read the night before, looking for some way to dismiss what it said. But after reading for a few minutes, he realized that if this Book was the truth, then it didn't matter what he thought about it. But was any of it true?

He was determined not to be one of those that accepted some new idea based on emotions. If God truly existed, and if He had created an ordered universe, then He must be consistent with logic and reason. Jeremiah was not going to throw away his mind or his intellect in order to embrace something new.

It was getting late, and there was still a lot to do to prepare to leave the next morning, so he got started. After putting his home in order, Jeremiah packed just enough of his belongings that he could comfortably carry. He then got ready for bed and went to sleep.

The next morning he awoke, knowing this was the first day in several years that he wasn't going to Food for Thought to get ready for the day. Feelings of apprehension swirled inside him. He was about to leave behind everything that was safe and comfortable, but he knew there would be no peace until he found the answers he was looking for.

Jeff was going to stay at his place and keep an eye on it. When he arrived, Jeremiah went over everything Jeff would need to know while he was gone. Finally, he told him that he would write to let him know when he would be coming back. As he threw his backpack over his shoulders and headed out the door, Jeff wished him well.

As Jeremiah ambled through the town, everyone else was busy starting their day. Horses and Buggies rumbled through the streets, while others were making their way to the various markets and stores. Many stopped to ask him where he was going. Not wanting to take the time to tell each one a long story, Jeremiah told them that he was going on vacation and that Scott would be running his eatery for him while he was gone. They all wished him well and told him to have a safe journey.

When Jeremiah reached the edge of the town, his decision to leave became more real to him. He had not been outside the Town of Rationalism in a long time. What kind of people would he meet? Would it be dangerous? He didn't know the answers, but he kept going.

There weren't many others moving along the road Jeremiah was on. Very few people ever left the Town of Rationalism. After traveling for most of the day, he came upon an inn. Jeremiah knocked on the door, and a nice gentleman dressed in a suit greeted him. Jeremiah inquired about a room, and after learning they had space available, he paid for a night's stay. The gentleman showed him to his room, then informed him that breakfast would be served at 7:00 am. Jeremiah was tired, so he got ready for bed and went to sleep.

The next morning Jeremiah came down for breakfast and sat at a small table by himself. As thoughts raced through his mind about what would happen next, a well-dressed, scholarly-looking man stopped at his table.

"May I sit down?" he asked.

Jeremiah wasn't looking for company, but he didn't want to be rude. "Sure," he said, removing the Book from the other chair.

The man sat down and extended his hand. "My name is Witness."

Shaking his hand, Jeremiah said, "It's nice to meet you. My name is Jeremiah."

Witness pointed to the Book, sitting on the table. "There's no better way to start your day."

Jeremiah glanced over. "I haven't read very much of it, and I'm not even sure it's true."

Witness ordered some coffee and a bagel from a waitress, then turned back toward Jeremiah. "If you're not sure it's true, how did you come to start reading it?"

Jeremiah told Witness about Pastor George coming to his town, and how he gave him this Book to read. Witness could tell that Jeremiah didn't want to engage in a lot of conversation, but he did want to ask him a few questions.

Witness took a drink of his coffee. "Since you left the Town of Rationalism where are you heading?"

"Pastor George said that if I wanted to find more answers, I would need to travel to a place called the Building of Reflection. Do you know where that is?"

Witness ate a bite of his bagel, and then wiped his mouth with a napkin. "Yes, I do. It's about a half a day's journey from here. Just keep going on the road past this inn, and you'll see the building back off the road a little ways and near a hill. I'm sad to say that most people traveling in that direction do all they can to avoid it."

Looking concerned and curious at the same time, Jeremiah asked, "Why is that?"

Sighing, Witness replied, "That building shows people what they do not want to see."

"What do you mean?"

Witness took off his glasses to clean them. "You'll understand when you get there."

Jeremiah picked up his Book. "If you don't mind, may I ask you a few questions?"

Finishing another bite of his bagel, Witness said, "Well sure, I love talking about God's word."

Plopping his Book down on the table, Jeremiah asked, "If God is perfect, then why did He create a universe that has so many problems? And why does He condemn man for not being perfect when it is He that created man? Isn't God the one responsible for how things are?"

Witness was a little surprised at the directness of the questions, but at the same time, he could tell Jeremiah was searching for answers. "When God created the universe, everything was very good. All of creation was perfect, including man. It was man that rebelled against God, bringing sin and destruction into the world."

Jeremiah shrugged. "But a perfect God would have known that man was going to rebel, so why create him in the first place?"

Witness took another drink of coffee. "Yes, God knew from the beginning that man was going to rebel, and He had a plan to provide a solution even before creating man. He was going to send His Son to suffer and die, paying the price for our sin, so He could restore what man had destroyed."

Jeremiah waved his hand around. "Things don't look restored to me. There are some terrible things going on in parts of this world."

"That's correct," said Witness. "But God's plan was not to restore everything at that time, but He was going to do a work in the people who received His Son. He would not bring total and perfect peace around them, but He was going to give His people a perfect peace on the inside of them."

Jeremiah sat back in his chair. "If what you've said is true, then it's man's fault things are so messed up. So why then did this Son of God have to pay the price to make things better? Why not make man clean up his own mess?"

Witness glanced around the room. "Because, we are not capable of cleaning up our own mess. When man became sinful, even the good things he would try to do, fell short of God's perfection. So even in trying to do good, man would just make the problem worse."

"But," said Jeremiah, raising his index finger, "if all that's true, then reason would seem to dictate that man should be punished, and not someone else. Logic would suggest that if man cannot fix his problem, then he must suffer the consequences."

"You're right," said Witness, nodding. "Mankind deserves to be punished, and God was in no way obligated to provide an answer. But even while we were sinful, God showed His love toward us by sending His Son to die for us. The Son of God took all the punishment that we deserved because of how much He loved us."

Jeremiah crossed his arms, shaking his head. "That's something else that makes no sense. I read in this Book that there is no one that does good, there is none that seeks after God, and in fact, there is nothing in man to love. So if this Book is true, then why did God love a creature in which there was nothing worth loving?"

Witness sighed. "God doesn't answer that question in a human kind of way. He loves us because He loves us. We have to receive His love, knowing that there's nothing that we ever did or ever could do to deserve it. It's just love that God freely provides."

Jeremiah looked away, shaking his head again. "You see, that's the kind of thing that makes this Book hard to believe. In the Town of Rationalism, everything made perfect sense. Every problem had a logical solution."

"God is very logical," said Witness. "He is the source of all wisdom and knowledge. His thoughts are far above our thoughts, and His ways are far above our ways. We as humans look at everything from a fixed point of view. We sit here on one small planet, looking out at the universe around us, as we measure all things based on what we've learned and experienced. God looks out over all things, all at the same time, seeing everything perfectly from beginning to end."

Jeremiah sighed. "If that's true then how are we supposed to understand things from God's perspective?"

Witness tapped on his Book. "He has provided us with all that we need to know about Him in His word. Answers do not come by us demanding that God explain Himself to us, but we receive answers when we align ourselves with what He says in this Book. When we accept God's word as truth, then we start to see things from God's perspective, and things start to make sense."

Jeremiah reached for his Book. "You've given me a lot to think about. I'm still not sure any of this is true, but I know I have to find out one way or the other. I believe I'll stay an extra day here at the inn and read some more before I travel on. Do you have any suggestions on where I should start?"

Witness received Jeremiah's Book from him. "Yes, I'll place a few bookmarks in it. I'll be leaving after breakfast, but I'm glad I got to meet you. I travel around these parts, and I enjoy meeting and talking to people."

Jeremiah said goodbye to Witness, then went outside to read.

4

FOR GOD SO LOVED THE WORLD

It was a beautiful sunny day as Jeremiah strolled around the inn, looking for a good place to read. Within a few minutes, he found a bench underneath a huge tree that would shade him from the sun. After sitting down, he took out his Book and opened it to the first bookmark, which was placed at the beginning of the Gospel of John.

After flipping ahead several pages to see how much there was to read, Jeremiah got comfortable and began. The opening stated that something called the Word had existed from the beginning, and in fact, this Word *was* God. But this Word existed with someone else that was also called God.

This seemed confusing, but he continued to read and discovered that the Word spoken of in the first verse was in fact, Jesus. With this in mind, he started back from the beginning. So if Jesus was God and someone else was also called God, then how could this be?

Further down, Jeremiah read that it was through Jesus that all things had been created. He paused for a moment, reflecting back on what he had read about the creation of all things in Genesis. He remembered noticing that God referred to Himself in the plural when He said: "Let Us make man..." Was more than one person called God?

Picking up reading where he left off, he came to the place where it was revealed that the Word became flesh. How did the One who created all things become a part of His creation? There was a reference to the Gospel of Luke, so Jeremiah flipped back and forth through the Book trying to find Luke. When he found it, he located the place that talked about the birth of Jesus. Luke said Jesus was born as a human being to a young virgin named Mary.

Looking up from his Book, Jeremiah thought, what kind of story is this? Jesus is supposed to be God, but He's being born as a man, from a mother who is a virgin. This entire concept would have been considered completely crazy in the Town of Rationalism. The idea of God being born as a small human baby seemed like something out of Greek Mythology. What other strange things was this Book going to say?

Reading further, he came to the story about a man named Nicodemus visiting Jesus at night. Nicodemus appeared to be an educated man and was a member of a group called the Pharisees. Jesus told him that he must be born again. Nicodemus was confused by this statement, and Jeremiah understood his confusion. Jesus seemed to be talking about a different kind of birth, a spiritual birth.

This introduced an entirely new concept to Jeremiah. He had always thought of different belief systems as things you adopt through your intellect only. From his perspective, a person could choose a different philosophy or religion based on making a rational decision to start following that belief system. But Jesus was saying that something new must happen on the inside of a person. Without this new birth, they would not be able to understand what He was teaching.

This concept was a lot for Jeremiah to take in. He set his Book down on the bench and ambled around the yard. As he watched different people interacting with one another, he wondered how someone could be so radically transformed on the inside, that it changed everything they believed.

He returned to the bench, picked up his Book, and continued in the Gospel of John. He came to the place where Jesus miraculously healed the man lying beside the pool. Jeremiah expected everyone to be happy about this, but instead, the religious leaders became angry and jealous. Then they became even angrier when Jesus made a statement which made Him to be equal with God the Father. Pausing for a moment, Jeremiah thought, was this what John meant when he wrote that Jesus was God? Yes, it was a very bold statement, but if it was true, then it was true.

What was going on, Jeremiah thought to himself? Was he starting to believe this stuff, or was he just following the logical flow of what he was reading? He once again laid his Book beside him and paced through the yard. If someone were watching, they might have thought Jeremiah was perplexed about some great difficulty in his life. He trudged back and forth, shaking his head and mumbling to himself. He wondered if this is how people become involved in strange religions. One day they were one way, and then after reading some religious literature, they start to buy into some bizarre and different ideas. He was determined not to let that happen to him.

Jeremiah returned to the bench, took a deep breath, and firmly grasped his Book. As he read further, he learned more about the Pharisees. They were the intellectuals of the Jewish community and were determined to oppose Jesus whenever possible. These Pharisees would angrily confront Him, but Jesus was not bothered by their opposition. In fact, it appeared to Jeremiah that Jesus became even bolder, declaring that they should honor Him just as they would honor God the Father.

Jesus was aware that the Pharisees wanted to kill Him, but He continued to make strong declarations about who He was. He even went further and confronted them for not believing He was who He claimed to be. These were the foremost Jewish religious leaders of that time, and Jesus was publicly confronting them.

As Jeremiah paused from his reading, a question formed in the back of his mind, and started to push its way forward. If he had been around at the time of Jesus, would he have been like the Pharisees?

Hesitantly, Jeremiah found his place in the Gospel of John and continued reading. There was more conflict with the religious leaders, and Jeremiah could feel the tension building. Time and again Jesus declared that He had been sent into this world by the Father, and the more He said it, the more agitated the religious leaders became. Then Jesus made another statement that caused them to want to kill Him. He said, "Most assuredly I say to you, before Abraham was, I AM."

Jeremiah shook his head. That line did not make sense. Wouldn't it be more proper to say, "Before Abraham was, I was?" There was a reference to an earlier part of the Book, so Jeremiah kept his place in John and turned toward the front to read of a person named Moses who saw a burning bush that was not consumed.

God talked to Moses and said His name was "I AM that I AM." Jeremiah thought he understood the logic of the statement. God was declaring that He was self-existent with no beginning and no end. When Jesus declared Himself to be the I AM, He was telling the religious leaders that He also was self-existent with no beginning and no end. That assertion prompted them to take up rocks to stone Him. They felt a mere man should not make such a claim. Yet Jesus had constantly told them that He was not a mere man, but they would not believe.

Jeremiah read about other times when Jesus healed someone, and the Pharisees became angry. Why did those religious leaders feel so threatened because people were being healed? Why did this make them so hostile? Then he thought about his conversation with Pastor George. What had made him so hostile at that time?

Pushing his questions aside, he continued to read and came across something that really challenged him. Jesus told those religious leaders that they did not believe in Him because they were not one of His sheep. His sheep believed on Him, and He gave them eternal life. How did someone become one of His sheep? Why weren't those religious leaders a part of His flock?

Further into the story, the Pharisees became even angrier when Jesus declared, "I and My Father are one." Again they wanted to kill Him for making Himself out to be God. Jeremiah set his Book down and began pacing in front of the bench. He was frustrated with those Pharisees. Even if they didn't believe Jesus' claim to be the Eternal Son of God, why couldn't they just be happy that someone was trying to do some good in the world? What was so wrong with that?

Shaking his head, Jeremiah sat down again. He returned to his reading and discovered that the way the Pharisees treated Jesus was actually a fulfillment of a prophecy by someone named Isaiah. In fact, the next verse stated that Isaiah prophesied those things when he saw Jesus' glory.

In the margin of the Book was a reference to where the prophet had written these things, so Jeremiah turned to it. Isaiah saw the LORD God sitting upon a throne, and John was saying that this was Jesus that Isaiah had beheld. Now the beginning of the Gospel of John made sense. Jesus had always been the LORD God, even as God the Father was also addressed as LORD God.

A feeling of awe and reverence came over Jeremiah. Up to this point, he viewed Jesus as a historical figure who made great claims about Himself. But now, he was starting to see Jesus as the Almighty Creator of the Universe.

He kept reading and came to the story of Jesus raising Lazarus from the dead. Jeremiah was moved by the emotion Jesus showed as He wept over his friend. Jeremiah then rejoiced as Lazarus came forth from the grave. But not everyone was happy. Some went to tell the religious leaders in an attempt to create even more conflict.

How strange that the same event caused some to become believers in Jesus and others to become more hateful. Was this discrepancy because some were sheep and others weren't?

Letting his Book collapse on his lap, Jeremiah stared out into the distance. In that moment, all of his strength seemed to leave. He felt nervous, even fearful, as a distressing question formed in his mind. Was he one of Jesus' sheep? He rapidly shook his head. Why was this Book having such an impact on him?

He returned to his reading and reached the story about Jesus and His disciples at the last supper. Jesus knew He was about to be betrayed, but His concern was not for Himself but for His disciples. He taught them many things, and let them know that He was going to die. Then Jesus made a startling statement; after three days of being in the grave, He was going to rise again.

Jeremiah read about Jesus and His disciples departing for the garden of Gethsemane. He could feel the anguish as he read of Jesus praying to the Father. Then the awful moment came when one of His own men betrayed Him into the hands of the religious rulers. Clearly, He was letting this happen, since Jesus could have easily avoided arrest if He had wanted to. Next came the trial. First, his enemies accused Him of things He didn't do, then they mocked Him and repeatedly struck Him with their fists.

A part of Jeremiah did not want to read any further. From his talk with Witness, he knew what was coming next.

Glancing back at his Book, he noticed there were references to passages others had written about the same events, so he quickly turned over to read their accounts of the trial before the religious leaders. In one passage, the man in charge finally asked Him directly, "Are you the Son of God?" When Jesus answered yes, the whole group cried, "Blasphemy!" Later these rulers would say that Jesus had committed a crime worthy of death because He said he was God's Son. Jeremiah now understood what the Jews of that day had understood. To be God's Son meant that He Himself was also God—God the Son. To these religious leaders the idea was blasphemy, but according to this Book, it was the Truth.

Continuing on, Jeremiah read of Jesus being taken to the Roman Governor, Pilate. This important ruler wanted out of the whole thing, but the religious leaders were determined to have Jesus crucified. Pilate finally gave in, giving the religious rulers what they always wanted.

Jeremiah read what all three of the other Gospel writers had to say about Jesus' trial before Pilate and His crucifixion. He read how badly Jesus was beaten and tortured, and how He was made to carry His cross. They drove nails into His wrists and hung Him up to die like a common criminal. Even in His last moments, Jesus said, "Father forgive them, for they know not what they are doing."

Suddenly, as if being struck by lightning, Jeremiah comprehended that Jesus had done all of this for him. Tears began to flow down Jeremiah's face. He now realized that the reason this story impacted him so profoundly was not because it was emotional, but because it was real.

He wasn't sure why, but he believed every word he had read. After flipping back in his Book to John, he read about the glorious triumph of the resurrection of Jesus Christ.

Jeremiah could feel himself rejoicing as he read. When Jesus appeared to all the disciples, Thomas declared what they all now knew, Jesus was their Lord and their God! John had written all these things so that those reading might believe that Jesus was the Son of God and receive eternal life through Him.

Lifting his eyes toward heaven, Jeremiah declared, "This Book, this wonderful Book, was written for me."

There were only about four hours of daylight left, but Jeremiah felt compelled to reach the Building of Reflection before the day was over. He could not wait for tomorrow. After returning to his room, he speedily packed everything up and started on his way.

5

A NEW CREATION

Jeremiah hurried down the road as fast as he could, saying "Lord Jesus, help me to make it to the Building of Reflection before dark." Shaking his head, he realized he had just said a prayer. So much about him was changing, but he didn't have time to stop and think about it right now.

After traveling a couple of hours, he saw a large structure set back off the road. Jeremiah paused, then approached the entrance. Reaching the top of the steps, he saw a sign, "The Building of Reflection." He had finally arrived.

From the outside, the building looked plain and simple. It was made of wood that had grayed with aging, and wasn't the kind of building one would think to enter without a good reason.

Slowly Jeremiah opened the door and stepped inside. The interior of the building was also plain and unremarkable. Just enough light seeped through the cracks so he could see where he was going. The floors were solid, but they were obviously worn and old, making a creaking sound as he walked.

He followed a long hallway to another door which he cautiously opened. Upon entering the room, he was immediately confronted by an extremely large mirror that rose nearly twenty feet into the air. But instead of showing his physical features, the reflection magnified the worst flaws in his character. He saw a person that was arrogant, prideful, manipulative, and jealous. How had he missed all of these horrible qualities for so many years? Why had he never seen such things before? He had always thought of himself as a good person, but what he saw in the mirror before him was very different.

Jeremiah closed the door behind him, and the mirror sunk into the floor. Another hallway was revealed that lead to another door. What kind of place is this, he thought? After cautiously moving down the hall, he opened the next door and peeked inside. It appeared to be empty, so he entered and looked around, trying to figure out its purpose.

After a few minutes, he glanced up to see a mirror fastened on the ceiling. Gazing into the reflection, he could see all of his sinful thoughts. Lust, anger, hatred, pride, and other corrupt imaginations filled the mirror above. Seeing these thoughts forced him to admit that not only was he sinful in what he did, but also in who he was.

All Jeremiah could say was, "Lord, forgive me."

Another door appeared, leading to another hall. Jeremiah wondered what else would be revealed in this building. He wasn't sure, but he had to keep going. Soon he reached another door, and after pausing for a moment, he entered the next room.

Jeremiah immediately noticed that the floor was nothing but one big mirror. He hesitated, but at last looked down. This time it was his good works that were being displayed. He saw the many kind and noble acts he had done for other people, such as giving to those in need and helping the sick and the elderly. He was relieved that something good about him was being revealed.

But as Jeremiah looked closer, shadows formed behind the scenes of his good deeds. He stooped down to get a better look. The dark shadows were his true motives behind each action—his selfishness, and his desire to feel good about himself based on his works. After going through these three rooms, he now understood why the Book said, "There is no one who is righteous, not even one." He also understood why Witness had said that man was not able to clean up his own mess. Man was not capable of doing anything truly good when measured against the perfection of God.

Jeremiah bowed his head. "Lord Jesus, within me there is nothing good."

Another door opened leading to another room. By now Jeremiah understood the purpose of this building, but what would be the outcome? What would happen when he reached the end? He trudged into the next room, and immediately a mirror rose up from the floor. He slowly crept up to it and discovered that it was perfectly shaped for his body. After staring into the reflection, the room became dark, and he saw glowing black sludge completely filling the mirror. It was one thing to think about being sinful, but it was quite another to see just how sinful he really was. By now he was starting to wonder if God could even accept him.

Jeremiah threw open his arms. "Lord, I have nothing to give you."

Light returned to the room, and the floor began to rumble. Toward the back wall a space opened up, that was just big enough for him to crawl through. What else could he possibly learn about himself? How much worse could it be?

After crawling through the opening, Jeremiah stood up. A sign hung directly in front of him. "Now You Must See What It Costs To Pay Your Debt." In this room, there were no mirrors at all. In fact, one of the walls was missing, enabling him to see clearly outside. Written on the other walls were verses he recognized from the third chapter of Romans, each reminding him of his sinfulness.

As Jeremiah walked toward the outside, he heard the awful sound of someone screaming in pain. The loud echo of stone pounding against metal rang out, and with each blow, another scream pierced his ears.

A telescope sat at the edge of the room and was pointed in the direction the cries were coming from. Jeremiah thought he knew what was causing the disturbing sounds, but he was afraid to look. After taking a deep breath and shaking his head, he bent down to peer through the lens.

His fears were confirmed. Jesus wailed in agony as a man pounded large metal spikes into His wrists. And when the man turned toward him, Jeremiah saw the worst thing of all. He was the one swinging the hammer.

Collapsing to the floor, Jeremiah cried out, "No Lord, no Lord! I wouldn't do that! Please know that I wouldn't do such an awful thing. I know you did all of this for me. Please let me be one of your sheep. I do not want to go back to the way things were."

A gentle breeze blew through the room. "Jeremiah."

He glanced around but saw no one. He wasn't sure if the voice calling him was on the inside or on the outside, but he listened to see if he could hear it again.

A feeling of comfort and peace surrounded him. "Jeremiah, I am the Holy Spirit. I have been with God the Father and God the Son,

Jesus Christ for all of eternity. I was sent by them to convict the world of sin and to point people to Jesus as the answer. While He was on this earth, Jesus said, 'All those who the Father gives to me, will come to me, and all the ones who come to me, I will by no means reject.' "

Jeremiah didn't know what to say. After seeing himself swing that hammer, he was so sure he was about to be rejected. But now he was hearing the most excellent thing a person could ever hear.

"Thank you!" said Jeremiah, raising his hands into the air.

The Holy Spirit continued. "All of your sinfulness, which you have seen in this building, you must take up the Hill of Calvary. There, you must repent for your sins and accept what Jesus did for you."

Jeremiah stood to his feet. He still felt the weight of his sins, but now there was hope. As terrible as it was to see all of his sinfulness, it served to amplify just how great the solution was. Jeremiah walked out of the building and up the Hill of Calvary. Along the way, he saw a sign that said, "Whoever calls upon the name of the Lord will be saved." Then Jeremiah saw the cross and knelt down in front of where Jesus had died for him.

Jeremiah lifted up his eyes and prayed, "Lord Jesus, please forgive me for not believing in you before. I was so arrogant and prideful. I thought I knew everything. I didn't think I was in need of any kind of a savior, but now I know differently. I do believe in you, and I want to receive all that you've done for me. I repent and turn away from my sins, and I ask that you forgive all of them. I want you to be my Lord and my Savior. I give my life to you. I want to serve you from this day forward."

Jeremiah felt the entire burden of his sins being lifted off. At the same time, he felt like a completely new person.

A voice boomed from heaven, "If any man be in Christ, he is a new creation. Behold, the old things have passed away, behold, all things have become new!"

Jeremiah began to rejoice and shout. What a glorious day this turned out to be. He had been completely forgiven of his sins, and was now a new creation! He walked back down the hill and saw a small clearing off to the right. In the middle of it stood another mirror which was labeled "How God sees you." After stepping in front of it, Jeremiah saw himself clothed with a beautiful robe. The words, "The Righteousness of Christ" shown in bright letters across his chest. He opened the robe just enough to reveal that although there was a new light on the inside, the black sludge of sin still existed there too. He closed the robe and stepped back.

A man by the name of Teacher arrived to talk to him about everything that had just happened. He taught Jeremiah about his new life in Christ, and how his old nature was now nailed to that cross. He let Jeremiah know that he was a completely new person, and he could live his life in service to God and not be a slave to his old nature anymore.

Jeremiah pointed at the mirror. "Can you explain to me how I can be righteous and sinful at the same time?"

Teacher stepped in front of the mirror, and then glanced at Jeremiah. "When you become a new creation you still have the flesh to contend with. What makes you acceptable to God is that you are given the righteousness that Christ earned for you through His perfect and sinless life. Even though you will still commit sins, you can approach God in full assurance that He will not reject you. Christ's record of perfection has been placed on your account, which makes you acceptable to the Father. It is a righteousness that you did not and could not earn, but was given to you freely by grace."

Jeremiah looked back toward the cross. "I am so thankful for this free grace. I know now that I could not have done anything to earn God's favor. But what happens when I sin? Will I lose God's favor?"

Teacher replied, "Oh no, your right standing with God is not based on what you do, but on what Christ has done. God's acceptance of you is not conditional. We can always come before Him, even though we will fall short of what He expects each and every day. As we continue to come into His presence, freely admitting where we've fallen short, He transforms us more and more into His image. This causes our behavior to get better, and causes us to sin less."

"I can understand God's acceptance and favor of me if I'm doing what is good," said Jeremiah, "but it's much harder to grasp that He is just as accepting and loving of me when I've done something wrong."

Nodding his head, Teacher stood next to Jeremiah. "It's hard to understand because our sinful flesh tells us that we must earn God's favor. Our old nature has been nailed to the cross, but it wants to get off that cross and live. It tells us that while we may have been put in right standing with God through grace, we must maintain this right standing through our works. A person that is truly familiar with their sinfulness knows that not only could they not have earned their salvation, but they are in no shape to maintain it afterward either. It is all of grace from beginning to end."

Jeremiah sighed. "There was a time when I thought I knew everything, and now I see there is so much I need to learn."

Teacher put his hand on Jeremiah's shoulder. "There's always more to discover. Learn what you can each day from this Book and apply it to your life. Someday I believe our paths will cross again, and I can show you much more at my house."

Teacher pointed toward a meadow surrounded by hills. "The next thing I would suggest is to go over there to that empty tomb that once held the body of Jesus before He was resurrected. While you are there reflect on what it means."

After shaking hands with Teacher and telling him goodbye, Jeremiah made his way to the empty tomb. He sat down next to the large rock and thought about what the day Jesus rose from the dead must have been like. When he read about it in the Gospel of John, he thought it must have been such a joyous day. He took out his Book and opened it to the second bookmark Witness had placed inside. The selection was toward the end of a letter which was written to a group named Corinthians.

The passage started out as a summary of the Gospel message and then went on to list the different people that saw Jesus after He arose. Jeremiah continued reading and discovered that one day he too was going to be resurrected and have a new body. What a joyous day that would be, when everyone who believed in Jesus would forevermore live together with their God and Savior. Jeremiah once again praised God for everything He had done for him on this wonderful day.

Rising to his feet, Jeremiah decided to look for Pastor George's house since it was supposed to be close by. He glanced around and spotted a sign in the distance. He hurried up to it and discovered that the sign pointed to a House of Instruction. He headed in that direction thinking the people there may know where Pastor George lived.

After a short hike, Jeremiah spotted a wooden building, unlike any house he had ever seen. A steeple sat on top with a bell on the inside. The building appeared to be almost as big as an inn and certainly large enough for several families to live in. Was this the House of Instruction the sign pointed to? Jeremiah walked up to the door and knocked. There was no answer at first. Maybe he was in the wrong place? Footsteps pounded toward the entrance, and then the door swung open. Standing in the entryway was Pastor George.

6

PASTOR GEORGE

Pastor George smiled and gave Jeremiah a big hug. When they parted, he laughed with great joy. "I knew you would come. I knew you would come."

Jeremiah stepped back. "All of this feels like a dream, but I'm here, and I'm so glad you stopped by my place that night. It's changed my life."

Pastor George waved him inside. "Come on in. I've got a big pot of stew, and I'd love to share it with you while you tell me all about your journey."

He led Jeremiah to a table, then served them both a bowl of stew. Jeremiah didn't realize how hungry he was until he started eating. In minutes he'd finished all of it. He pushed the bowl away, then shared all that happened since the night they first met. Pastor George listened intently, excited to see the working of the Holy Spirit at each stage of the journey.

After Jeremiah finished, Pastor George lifted his hands. "God is so good, and I just know He has big plans for your life. I would love for you to spend a few days with me here if you can."

Jeremiah leaned back. "That would be great. Thank you."

They continued talking for another hour, then Pastor George stood up. "I can see that you're tired. Let me show you to your room, and then we can talk more tomorrow."

Jeremiah followed him to a spacious bedroom, then said goodnight. As he stretched out on his bed, he thought about all that had happened that day and the events which led up to it. Jeremiah could see how God had been working in his life even when he didn't realize it was Him. He once again thanked God, then drifted off to a restful sleep.

When he came downstairs the next morning, Pastor George had breakfast ready. After they finished eating, Pastor George taught him about baptism. Jeremiah learned that baptism represented being buried with Christ and being resurrected with Him to newness of life. He wanted to be baptized right then, so they went outside to a small stream. As he waded into the water, Jeremiah looked toward heaven, thinking of how his Savior was watching all of this.

Pastor George instructed him to fold his arms across his chest. He then placed his right hand on the upper part of Jeremiah's back, while raising his left hand toward heaven. "Lord Jesus, we come here today to honor Your commandment to baptize those who believe in You."

Pastor George placed his left hand on top of Jeremiah's folded hands and started to lower him into the water. "Jeremiah, upon your profession of faith, in accepting Jesus Christ as your Lord and Savior, I now baptize you in the Name of the Father, in the Name of the Son, and in the Name of the Holy Spirit."

As Jeremiah was submerged underwater, he pictured his sinful nature dying on the cross with Jesus and being buried with Him in the tomb. As he came out of the water, he thought of being resurrected with Christ to newness of life. He felt energy all around him, as if lightning had just struck nearby.

Being baptized solidified the truth of what had taken place in his life. He wasn't having an emotional experience or engaging in a temporary intellectual experiment. Something miraculous and supernatural had taken place at the Hill of Calvary. He had been born again.

Jeremiah was full of joy as they walked back inside. After he changed into some dry clothes, they sat at the kitchen table, and Pastor George taught him about communion.

Jeremiah reflected on what he had read in the Gospel of John about that last night before Jesus was betrayed. Jesus took the bread and the cup and gave them to His disciples. These represented His body and His blood which He would give for them. As they partook of the Lord's Supper, Jeremiah was full of thankfulness for the sacrifice of Christ.

Afterward, Pastor George led him to a room full of books. "In here you will find some very important writings such as creeds and confessions that outline the most vital doctrines of the Christian faith."

Jeremiah scanned the shelves remembering his own private collection. "I used to think my books were so valuable, but these writings seem much more important."

Pastor George nodded. "God has gifted many men down through the ages to share their insights about His word. It's important to learn from those who have traveled this Quest before us."

At last, they headed for the door.

As they were leaving, Jeremiah turned to gaze at the shelves. "I'd like to come back here later and spend more time."

"Take as much time as you like," said Pastor George.

He then took Jeremiah all around the building, showing him the different rooms and explaining the purpose of a House of Instruction. When they were done, Pastor George suggested they walk outside so he could show him around the grounds. Everywhere they went the scenery was stunning and testified to God's glory.

When they stopped to admire a beautiful waterfall, Jeremiah said, "That night you were in the Town of Rationalism, why did you come by my eatery?"

Pastor George smiled, as he placed his hand on his stomach. "Because I was hungry."

Jeremiah laughed. "So you weren't on a mission from God."

Still grinning, Pastor George said, "Oh yes I was. I just didn't know it. I was looking for a place to get something to eat, and yours was the only one that looked open. Once we started talking though, I knew I was there for a much greater purpose."

"So what now? I mean, what happens now?" asked Jeremiah.

Pastor George motioned for him to sit down. "You've started on a journey called The Quest—a life-long journey of following the path God has for you. It won't always be easy, but God will be with you each step of the way."

Jeremiah stared into the waterfall, thinking about how each drop of water was being moved on its own journey. "I'm excited to begin this new life, but at the same time I don't know what's ahead."

"This Quest is a journey of faith. We follow our path and believe that God is working all things out for our good," said Pastor George, as he stood to his feet.

He then led them along a trail, which passed through a small wooded area.

A short way further, Jeremiah stopped and turned toward Pastor George. "How will I know if I'm following God's path for my life?"

Taking out his Book, Pastor George said, "The most important thing you can do is spend time in God's word every single day, and throughout each day meditate on what you've read. Memorize as much as you can and always be eager to talk about it with others. This Book is a light unto your path and a lamp unto your feet. As you walk along, you'll notice that the path you're to follow is raised just a little higher than the ground around it. But you'll only notice this if you've spent time in your Book."

"Will it always be that easy?"

"No, there are times when you make the best decision you can with the information you have. God will train you with experience, and at times the Holy Spirit will prompt you on the inside. As you travel, always commit your steps to the Lord, trusting that He will get you to where you need to be."

After winding along another trail and crossing an open field, Pastor George led them back to the house, where Jeremiah spent the rest of the day in the reading room. That evening they had dinner together and talked some more.

"How did your reading go?" asked Pastor George, as he cleared the table.

Standing up to help him with the remaining dishes, Jeremiah said, "It was fascinating. I didn't realize there were so many great Christian thinkers. I always thought that the truly great thinkers were philosophers and men of science, but I see that the Christian faith has produced some very remarkable men. I did feel overwhelmed though, because the more I read, the more I realized how much there is to study and learn."

Setting the dishes in the sink, Pastor George replied, "Yes, there are several lifetimes of reading that could be done, and of course we'll never exhaust all of the wisdom that is to be gained in the Book itself. As I've been praying for you today, I've felt like there's something you should consider."

"What's that?" said Jeremiah, handing him a casserole dish.

Pastor George motioned for them to go back and have a seat at the table. "I think you may enjoy starting off your Quest at a House of Knowledge."

Jeremiah sat down, thinking about the possibility of going back to school again. "I studied for four semesters at a local university in the Town of Rationalism, and I did enjoy learning new things."

"A House of Knowledge would enable you to learn the basics of the Christian faith, and it would give you the opportunity to challenge the worldview that you had before starting this Quest."

Jeremiah leaned forward. "Do you know of a House of Knowledge that I could go to?"

Pastor George nodded. "Yes I do. There's one not too far from here that I think would be great for you. I've taught there a few times myself, and I've been a guest speaker at some of their chapel services. It's only about a half a day's journey. Pray about it tonight, and we can talk more about it tomorrow."

Jeremiah thought about what it would be like to be surrounded by people wanting to learn more about God. "Thank you. I'll definitely pray about it." Suddenly realizing what he had just said, Jeremiah asked, "How do we pray?"

Always eager to teach from his Book, Pastor George said, "Let's start with what's called the Lord's Prayer. Jesus used this to teach His disciples how to pray."

He turned a few pages in his Book and began reading. "In this manner, therefore, pray: Our Father in heaven, Let Your name be honored as holy."

Pastor George pointed upward. "It's tempting to begin prayer by talking about us and what we need, but prayer should start by focusing on God. We see in this verse that we can address Him as our Father. He is our loving Heavenly Father who watches over us continuously." He noticed that Jeremiah appeared deep in thought. "What are you thinking about?"

Jeremiah took a deep breath. "I never had a father. When I picture God, I see Him as someone who's far away and who's only available for really important things."

Pastor George nodded. "It's hard to understand how the God of the universe could take a personal interest in us, but He calls us His children, and Jesus encourages us to approach God as our Father."

Pastor George glanced down at his Book. "We should pray and desire for God's name to be honored and revered as holy. The ultimate purpose in all things is to bring glory and honor to His name."

He continued reading. "Your kingdom come, Your will be done, On earth as it is in heaven."

"What's important," said Pastor George, "is that God's will be done in all circumstances. The goal of our prayers should be seeking to come into alignment with His desires for any situation. The more confident we are that we're praying according to His will, the more confident we are that our prayers will be answered."

Jeremiah sat back, his gaze roaming from place to place. "I'm realizing just how much my life has been centered on me. It makes sense that prayer would begin by focusing on God and His will rather than what I want."

"Yes," said Pastor George, "God is concerned about us and our needs, but He wants us to seek Him and His kingdom first."

Grasping his Book, Pastor George continued reading. "Give us this day our daily bread."

"This verse is a reminder that we rely on God for everything that we need. It is He that gives us our daily food, and in fact, He is the one that gives us the very breath that sustains us each moment. We are to focus on what we need for each day, taking no thought about tomorrow."

Jeremiah shifted in his seat. "So this is what you meant when you said this Quest is a life of faith. But it seems like it would be so hard to only concentrate on one day at a time."

Pastor George's expression communicated that he too struggled with this. "I wish I could tell you it's easy, but it's not. We all want certainty in our lives, but there are seasons when God calls us to walk one step at a time, trusting him for the next step. It's not comfortable, but it does build our faith."

Jeremiah folded his hands together. "I will keep that in mind."

Pastor George nodded and found his place again in the Book. "Next Jesus says, 'And forgive us our sins, as we also forgive those who have sinned against us.' Daily we are to acknowledge our sins. This keeps us in a place of humility and dependence on God. As we realize our need for God's grace and forgiveness, we give out this same grace to those who have sinned against us."

"Isn't it hard to always have an attitude of forgiveness?" asked Jeremiah.

Pastor George put his hand to his chin. "Yes it is, but when we have a hard time forgiving others, we should remember just how much we've been forgiven."

Jeremiah thought back to the Building of Reflection, and all the sin he saw in himself. He had been forgiven of so much, and it was only right that he also forgive others.

Pastor George paused for a moment, as if he too was thinking about what he had just said. A few moments later he continued. "The next thing Jesus says is, 'And do not lead us into temptation, but deliver us from the evil one.' "

Setting his book down, Pastor George said, "This part has troubled many, but I believe it means that we should ask God to watch over us in such a way that we are not led into temptation and to deliver us from the snares and traps of the devil."

Jeremiah didn't know much about who the devil was, but he gathered that he was an evil spiritual being who was opposed to all things that were good. For now, Jeremiah knew enough to ask God for help in dealing with him.

Pastor George straightened up as he prepared to read again. He lifted his hands as if he was an orchestra leader directing a grand finale. "For Yours is the kingdom, *and* the power *and* the glory forever. Amen!"

Pastor George had an elated look on his face. "We are to end our prayers, just like we start them, by praising our wonderful God, focusing on His kingdom, His power, and His glory!"

Jeremiah felt the power of God's word as he heard it read out loud. After few moments of silence, he took a deep breath. "I've read many of the great philosophers of history, but it seems their wisdom is so little in comparison to God's. It's as if these philosophers were trying to describe a room while groping about in the dark, tripping and stumbling over everything. Yet God sees all things with perfect clarity and perfect light."

"Yes," said Pastor George, as he closed his Book, "God's thoughts are truly far above the thoughts of man."

Jeremiah stood up. "It's been a wonderful day, and now I think I'll go upstairs and do some more reading before going to bed."

Pastor George stood too. "Have a good night's sleep, and I'll see you tomorrow."

The next day, Jeremiah once again started out with a nice breakfast with Pastor George. They had a good conversation, and then Jeremiah went back to the reading room. He spent many hours there until it was time for lunch.

After eating, they went outside for another walk. As they strolled along a dirt trail, Jeremiah marveled at the dazzling displays of nature that surrounded them. The majestic waterfall feeding the pool of water below, a small grove of apple trees proudly displaying their fruit, beautiful flowers growing all around, and the crystal blue sky towering above them, all a testament to the glory of God.

Jeremiah took it all in, briefly closing his eyes as the warmth of the sun washed over him. "I see nature so much differently than I did before. From what I know of science, everything has its proper place, and now I know that's because God designed it that way. Before I started this Quest, it made so much sense to think of creation as the result of random mutations. But now it makes much more sense that it was all done by Intelligent Design. It makes me wonder why I couldn't see these things before."

Pastor George stopped by the stream where Jeremiah was baptized. "This Book says that the god of this world, Satan, has blinded the minds of those who do not believe. When we are born again, a whole new world and reality opens up to us. Some think Christianity is taking a blind leap of faith into the unknown. That's not true at all. Being born again opens our eyes to the evidence that was already around us."

"I wish all my friends could experience what I have," said Jeremiah, as he stooped down to take a drink of water from the stream.

"Someday," said Pastor George, "I believe you'll go back to the Town of Rationalism, and share with your friends what you've learned. Be prepared though. They won't be able to understand what's happened to you. The concept of becoming a new creation will not make sense to them. They'll try to analyze you and attribute your change to some kind of brainwashing or emotional experience."

Jeremiah stood back up and shrugged his shoulders. "But I feel more rational than I ever have. Things are making a lot more sense to me now."

"Yes they do," said Pastor George nodding, "but this isn't something you can put in a jar and hand to someone. You can't get inside them to make them understand. We share with others what God lays on our hearts, then we leave the results to Him."

Jeremiah thought about Food for Thought, his friends, his home, and all he had left behind. He wondered when God would lead him back there. They finished their walk and then returned to their places at the table.

Pastor George noticed that Jeremiah seemed to be deep in thought. "Jeremiah, what's on your mind? Jeremiah?"

Not realizing he had been daydreaming, Jeremiah quickly glanced up. "I've been thinking about my next step on this journey. Each time I've been in the reading room, I see how much there is to learn. I think it might be good to spend at least a year at a House of Knowledge before I go further on this Quest."

Sitting back, Pastor George said, "I believe you could benefit from what you would learn there. It would also help equip you to teach others."

Jeremiah pushed his chair from the table, "I'll pray more tonight, but I believe that is where God is leading."

Standing up, Pastor George said, "When you see that your path is moving away from here, we'll know more by the direction it's heading. When that time comes, there are some things I need to give you before you leave."

Jeremiah went to the reading room and studied for the rest of the day until dinner. After eating with Pastor George, he went to his room to read in his Book. Before going to sleep, he prayed again, feeling even more excited at the prospect of enrolling in a House of Knowledge. Drifting off to sleep, he wondered what Pastor George had to give him before he left.

7

THE WISDOM OF THIS WORLD

The next morning Jeremiah went outside and discovered that his path was moving away.

Pastor George joined him. "I thought this day would come soon, and just as I expected, your path is heading straight toward the House of Knowledge I told you about."

"I'm not surprised either," said Jeremiah. "I'm excited to continue my Quest with learning even more about God and His word."

Pastor George turned to go back inside. "Let's have some breakfast, then I have something very important to show you before you leave."

After eating, He led Jeremiah into a large room which looked like a place where an army would be equipped for war.

Staring at all the battle gear which hung along the walls, Jeremiah said, "Wow! What is the purpose for all this?"

Pastor George waved his hand around. "This is for you. It is the full armor of God, which you will need to be successful on your journey."

He gave Jeremiah the different pieces of equipment and explained what each one was for. Jeremiah was excited to receive all of his armor, and he was especially amazed at how his Book turned into a Sword.

Looking into a mirror, Jeremiah was concerned about how he was going to manage everything. "This is a lot to carry around."

"Let me show you something," said Pastor George. He then took Jeremiah's Shield and placed it on the back of his Breastplate. At once it shrank to a small size. He then removed it again and showed Jeremiah how it returned to full size once it was held out. He also showed him how he could tap his chest twice to make his armor appear and reappear.

Jeremiah held out his Sword and turned it side to side. "So what types of adversaries will I be facing that I need all of this?"

Tapping on the Shield, Pastor George said, "Your warfare will not be against flesh and blood, but your struggle will be against the different kinds of enemies that the devil will place along your path. Some will be the size of a giant while others may be barely visible. Some will be subtle and crafty, and some will be angry and aggressive. Do not be afraid. God always knows what's ahead, and He'll prepare you for your battles."

Jeremiah stepped back from the mirror and scanned everything along the walls. "I can't believe all this is happening. A few days ago I didn't even know there was a spiritual dimension where battles took place and where enemies existed. Sometimes in our discussions in the Town of Rationalism, we would speculate about other dimensions. We talked about what it might be like if there were that sort of thing, but to us, it was all science fiction. It was the kind of thing you talked about, but certainly not something you lived."

Tapping his chest twice to make his armor appear, Pastor George said, "Yes there is a spiritual dimension, and it's just as real as what you can see. We're told to put on this armor so that we can stand up against all the schemes of the devil. Evil spiritual forces exist that are continuously trying to work against God's will on this earth. We are to walk on the path that God lays out for us, and if we encounter any of these enemies, then we can face them, knowing that God has given us the victory over them."

Jeremiah thanked Pastor George for the armor, then went to his room and retrieved his backpack. When he came downstairs, Pastor George gave him a satchel to carry his Book in, then accompanied him outside.

Jeremiah gave him a hug. "I'm so glad God placed you in my life. I do hope our paths cross again in the future."

Pastor George patted Jeremiah on the shoulder, as he stepped back. "I believe we'll see each other again. I can't wait to hear about all the wonderful things God is going to do in your life."

They prayed together then said goodbye.

As Jeremiah left the house, he noticed that a path formed that was just a little higher than the ground around it. He stepped onto it and started off. So many thoughts raced through his mind. What adventures lay ahead? What would it be like to attend a House of Knowledge that was dedicated to teaching principles from God's word?

Suddenly, Jeremiah felt the air around him getting heavy. Looking up, he saw a dark mist hovering above him. The mist dropped closer, and the heaviness grew stronger until it felt as if a python had wrapped itself around his head and was squeezing with all its strength. The oppressive force pushed down on his entire body, causing him to go to one knee. What was happening? Not knowing what to do, he silently prayed, asking God for help.

An angry voice yelled in his ear. "I am the Wisdom of this World. I rule over the Town of Rationalism and many towns like it. At one time I owned you. If you do not go back and get off this Quest, I will be your constant enemy. I will cause those who once admired you, to despise you and to make fun of you. I will take away all the friends you had, and you will be a constant joke in the Town of Rationalism. Don't be a fool Jeremiah, go back where you came from."

Thoughts of fear flooded over him. Could these threats really happen? Could he lose all his friends and end up being someone they ridiculed?

The possibility of being constantly harassed by this powerful force was terrifying. Nevertheless, Jeremiah was determined that no matter what happened, he was not going to quit his Quest. He felt truly alive for the first time in his life, and he was not going to abandon his Lord and Savior after all He had done for him. But what was he to do now? The pressure on his head made it difficult to concentrate.

Focusing his mind, Jeremiah prayed for God to give him wisdom. He attempted to take his Book out of his satchel, but every movement felt as if he was trying to advance while sinking in quicksand. As he reached for his Book, he could feel the rage of the dark mist growing more violent.

Exerting all his strength, he grabbed the edge of his satchel and pulled. As the growing pressure from his enemy pushed his head toward the ground, a verse he had read the day before rose up in his thoughts. Barely able to mouth the words, he whispered, "Not by might, nor by power, but by your Spirit, Oh LORD."

Despite the force from the dark mist growing stronger, a new strength radiated through Jeremiah's body and made its way up to his arms. He was able to unfasten the satchel and slowly draw out his Book. As he did, the Holy Spirit brought to his remembrance two different verses from Paul's first letter to the Corinthians.

Gradually raising his Book, Jeremiah said, "I will gladly be a fool for Christ in order that I might be wise in Him, for the wisdom of this world is foolishness to God."

Now Jeremiah could lift up his head. He fastened his eyes upon the dark mist, determined that no weapon formed against him would prosper.

Another verse popped into his mind. "Finally my brothers, continue becoming strong in the Lord, and in the power of His might."

Jeremiah shouted toward the mist, "The message of the cross is indeed foolishness to the ones perishing, but to us, the ones who are saved, it is the power of God!"

Instantly he was able to fully raise his Book until it became a Sword. As he attempted to rise to his feet, a shrill, penetrating sound emanated from the mist.

Finally able to stand upright, Jeremiah thrust his Sword toward the Wisdom of this World. "God says, 'I will destroy the wisdom of the ones who think they are wise, and I will set aside as nothing the intelligence of the ones who think they are intelligent.' "

The mist tried to exert its strength once again, but Jeremiah could feel his enemy getting weaker. Still holding out his Sword, he shouted, "Where is the philosopher? Where is the scholar? Where is the proud debater of this present age? Has God not shown that the wisdom of this world is foolishness!"

The thick mist swirled around before lifting into the air and out of sight. Jeremiah realized he'd just been in his first battle, and it was the words of his Book that enabled him to fight off his enemy. If the word of God was always going to be his main weapon, he would need to study it regularly. The more he knew, the more the Holy Spirit could bring verses to his mind when he needed them.

Jeremiah also realized that in his own strength he was no match for his enemies. He was a strong man, but he was not able to overcome the evil mist on his own. While it was a humbling experience, it was also an important lesson that he needed to learn early in his Quest.

Dusting himself off, Jeremiah continued on his path, stopping only to eat a quick lunch that Pastor George had packed for him. Within a couple of hours, he saw a sign, announcing there was a House of Knowledge just ahead. Excited to get there, he picked up his pace.

Soon he arrived, and an especially beautiful campus stretched out before him. It was filled with several buildings of all sizes. The grass was exceptionally green, and the campus grounds looked like they had been sculpted out of the earth.

Many young men and women were rushing around, carrying their textbooks and talking excitedly about the upcoming school year. He had arrived just in time, because the new semester was starting the next day.

One young man passing by was courteous enough to ask Jeremiah if he needed any help. After learning he was new to the campus, the young man directed him to the admissions office. Once there a very nice lady greeted him and asked about his academic experience and what he was interested in studying. The lady was incredibly helpful, and Jeremiah felt welcomed the moment he stepped into her office. After taking down all of his information, she sent him to the business office, where he paid for a year's tuition.

Jeremiah was then directed to go to a Professor Williams' office at the north end of the campus. Once he arrived, he saw a studious-looking man sitting behind a broad desk, busily shifting papers around. Professor Williams was much shorter than Jeremiah and slightly pudgy. He had a trimmed beard and mustache, though his head was mostly bald. He shifted in his chair and constantly pushed his glasses back in place. When the professor noticed Jeremiah, he motioned for him to come in.

Still moving things around on his desk, as he pointed to a chair, he said, "Have a seat. I'm Professor Williams."

"Thank you, I'm Jeremiah."

The professor sat down and smiled at him. "If they've sent you to me, then that must mean you're interested in learning how to teach and preach God's word."

"I'm not sure if God will use me in that capacity," said Jeremiah, as he handed him some forms, "but it was the closest to what I wanted to study."

Looking over Jeremiah's information, Professor Williams said, "Everything seems to be in order, so let's get your schedule set up, and then you can go get your room assignment."

Professor Williams searched through different sets of file folders, scribbling things down as he went, and then handed a piece of paper to Jeremiah. "There you go. The building and room numbers are listed beside each course."

"Thank you," said Jeremiah as he received the paper.

"You'll be in my Old Testament class, as well as my Biblical Greek class. I hope you're ready to work," said Professor Williams, as he peered over his glasses and smiled.

Jeremiah wasn't sure if the smile was a friendly smile or a warning.

He stood up to leave, and Professor Williams extended his hand. "It was nice meeting you Jeremiah, and I look forward to having you in my classes."

After receiving his room assignment and directions, Jeremiah headed to the place he'd be living for the next year. The building was two stories with eight rooms on the first level and six rooms on the second level. He scanned his paper, double-checking his room assignment.

A young man carrying an armful of books walked by and noticed Jeremiah looked a little lost. "Can I help you find something?"

Jeremiah looked up from his paper. "I think I'm in the right place."

Glancing over Jeremiah's shoulder, the young man said, "Yes, this is the right dorm. You're on the first floor." Pointing toward the building, he said, "That should be your room right over there. My name is Jacob by the way. Nice to have you on campus."

"Thanks," said Jeremiah.

The lady at the admissions office told him that his roommate had already checked in, so he was anxious to meet him. Hesitant at first, he slipped up to the door and knocked.

The door swung open, and a young man eating an apple appeared at the entrance. "Hello, can I help you?"

Holding out the paper with his room assignment, Jeremiah said,

"It looks like this is where they've assigned me to live."

The young man glanced at the paper then smiled. "Yes, you're at the right place. Welcome. My name is Mark. It looks like we're going to be roommates."

Mark stepped to the side. "Over there is your bed, and that space next to it is where you can put all your stuff."

Setting his backpack down on his bed, he reached out his hand. "I forgot to introduce myself. I'm Jeremiah."

"Nice to meet you," said Mark shaking his hand. "What brings you to our House of Knowledge?"

Jeremiah sat down, and starting from the beginning when Pastor George visited his eatery, he shared with Mark everything that led up to him being there.

After he finished sharing his story, Mark said, "It definitely sounds like God has brought you here, and we're excited you're going to be joining us. There's a group of us who get together through the week to talk about God's word and to pray together. Would you like to join us?"

Jeremiah was thrilled. This was exactly what he was hoping for. He wanted to learn all he could in a classroom, but he also wanted to form relationships with people he could study with and pray with.

"That would be great," said Jeremiah, as he hung up a spare set of clothes. "Just let me know what time."

"We meet right here after dinner."

Mark then looked over Jeremiah's schedule and gave him a tour of the campus, showing him where everything was and where each of his classes would meet. Next Mark took him to the bookstore where Jeremiah purchased the books he would need.

After returning to their room and putting up his textbooks, Jeremiah followed Mark over to the cafeteria. A group of guys immediately stepped forward, and Mark introduced Jeremiah to them. Once they had their food, they found an unoccupied table and sat down. Mark told the others that Jeremiah wanted to join them for their study and prayer group.

Besides Mark, there were four others. Rick was a tall, good-looking guy who was laid back and friendly, and he appeared to be well respected by the others. There were also two brothers named Aaron and Eric. Mark said they were both strong and worked well together as a team. Then there was Greg, who enjoyed telling jokes and tried to keep things from getting too serious.

When they were done eating, everyone went to Mark and Jeremiah's room.

Rick held out his hand toward Jeremiah. "Mark says you have an interesting testimony about how you began your Quest, so why don't you start things off and share it with us."

As Jeremiah shared his story, they were fascinated that he had come from the Town of Rationalism. They didn't see many people from that town become Christians.

Jeremiah then told them of his battle with the Wisdom of this World. "Is it normal to face an enemy this soon on your journey?"

Nodding his head, Rick said, "It's very common. The devil would love to try and hinder us as early as possible because he knows that the more progress we make, the stronger we become."

Looking around the circle of friends, Jeremiah asked, "Do you all see many enemies?"

Mark said, "We do see some from time to time. On the weekends we pray about where we are to go, and sometimes we are led on an adventure."

"I don't know if I'm ready," said Jeremiah, "but if it's God's will, I would like to come with you. I may not be much help, but I'll do what I can."

Rick said, "It's always great to have one more joining us on our adventures. We all started out as beginners, and we all had to learn."

They had a great time of study and discussion and then prayed for each other. After that, the others went to their rooms to get a good night's rest before the first day of school. When they left, Mark and Jeremiah got ready for bed as well.

As Jeremiah lay down, he couldn't wait for the next day to arrive. He had already completed most of the required general education courses at the university he'd attended, so he was able to jump right into his core studies. Along with Old Testament and Biblical Greek, he was also taking New Testament, Systematic Theology, and The Teachings of Paul.

The next day arrived, and Jeremiah speedily got ready, barely taking time to eat an apple before heading out the door. His first class was Biblical Greek with Professor Williams. As the professor handed out the syllabus and course outline, Jeremiah noticed that same smile he saw the day before. This Professor Williams must be a friendly fellow, he thought.

The first three weeks went great, and Jeremiah was becoming known as a brilliant student. He loved all of his teachers, soaking up everything they taught like a sponge. At first, Jeremiah felt overwhelmed with how much there was to learn, but his professors helped to reassure him that learning was a step-by-step process that was ongoing for the rest of his life.

At the end of the week Mark, Rick, Jeremiah, and the rest of the group all met together for their study and prayer time. As they discussed what they were going to be doing over the weekend, everyone sensed they were being prepared for an adventure. Not knowing exactly what it would be, they all agreed to meet together the next morning to pray and discuss it further.

THE WEAPONS OF OUR WARFARE

The next morning, the group stepped outside and saw that each of their paths led away from the campus. They gathered some supplies in case they camped for the night, then prayed together one more time, asking God to lead them where He wanted them to go.

The first place their paths took them was to the home of an elderly couple who needed some work done around their house. They all pitched in and were able to make some much-needed repairs in about two hours. The couple thanked them and offered them money, but they all said no. They told the couple that they were just doing what they had been sent to do. Jeremiah thought it was great how they were able to be used to help others.

After traveling for a few more hours, they stopped to eat a quick lunch, then continued back on their path. Just as the sun was beginning to set, they arrived at a clearing which contained four recently built homes. In the middle of the clearing was another larger building that looked as if it was still under construction. Since their paths stopped there, they set down their backpacks and scanned the area. As they walked up to the larger building, a man named Tom came out to greet them.

Extending his hand, Rick said, "We're from a local House of Knowledge, and each weekend we pray about where God wants us to go. Today we've been led here. Is there anything you need help with?"

Tom hesitated at first, but as his wife came out to join him, he said, "Well there is something we need help with. Four families, including ours, felt led to settle in this area and start a House of Instruction. We were excited at first, and we were able to swiftly clear the land. After that, we built our homes, and then started working on the House of Instruction."

Tom's wife, Susan stepped forward. "But within a few days, we came under attack by some wicked creatures, determined to keep us from finishing our task. It takes most of the day to fight them off, and then there is little daylight for construction work. We feel that if we were able to build without interruption, we could have the House of Instruction ready for meetings within a few weeks."

Rick said, "Could you describe what these creatures look like, and how they're attacking you?"

Tom pointed into the air. "These enemies are able to fly. They kind of resemble flying baboons, but ones that are violent and hateful. They throw rocks and other objects while screaming at us. They say that we'll never be able to complete the work, and even if we did, no one would ever show up anyway."

Looking around at the other guys, Rick said, "We'll spend some time discussing your situation and praying for wisdom. Let the other families know that we would like to meet with all of you after dinner, and we'll share with you what we believe God is placing on our hearts about your struggle."

Tom was thankful for their willingness to help and agreed to gather everyone together after dinner so they could talk. Rick, Jeremiah, Mark, and the others found a small brook and sat down next to it.

Rick started things off. "So now we know why we've been brought here, but what do we do?"

Mark glanced over his shoulder at the partially built structure. "Just helping them to fight off these enemies will not be enough because these creatures will be right back the next day."

"I agree," said Rick. "We have to ask God for a solution that takes care of the problem for good."

After a time of prayer, Aaron spoke up. "In my Old Testament class, my professor taught us about Nehemiah. After the children of Judah had been in captivity for many years, God sent some of them back to Jerusalem to rebuild the walls of the city. Nehemiah was sent to lead the effort, but they faced opposition from those living around them."

"Yes," said Eric, reaching for his Book, "I remember that too, but the returning captives persevered and rebuilt the walls. The story of Nehemiah shows that when God's people keep doing what He's said, while not allowing room for discouragement, they will succeed."

Jeremiah started to say something but stopped.

Holding out his hand toward him, Rick said, "What is it? If you have something to share, please do."

Hesitating for a moment, Jeremiah said, "I know I'm new to this, but it doesn't seem right that these flying enemies should be able to have repeated success. I know there's always a certain amount of pressure from the enemy, but the way things are going, these people will soon give up if something doesn't change."

"I agree," said Rick, nodding. "There's no reason the enemy should be able to have this much success against them and stop the work God has called them to. Let's continue to pray, and hopefully, we'll learn more later as we talk to them."

After dinner, everyone gathered in front of the unfinished building and introduced themselves to one another. The families expressed their gratitude that the young men had come to help, and after a few minutes of discussion, it was apparent that they were almost to the point of giving up. From the very first day of the attacks, the discouragement from the enemy had worked. One by one, they admitted wondering if this project was going to succeed and if they were just wasting their time.

Rick stepped forward. "It seems that these flying creatures were able to deposit doubt into your hearts, and then you all nurtured this doubt until it had a foothold in your thoughts. Now they keep coming back without you being able to make any progress against them."

Looking around from one family to the other, Tom said, "I believe you're right. We need to repent for allowing this doubt and unbelief into our minds, and we need to focus on what God has called us to do."

Rick said, "Tomorrow is going to be an important day. We'll spend the night and then help you fight these flying baboons when they appear tomorrow."

All the families thanked the young men, and then Rick, Jeremiah, and the rest of the group set up their camp. Once everything was completed, they all sat down to read in their Books.

After a few minutes, Mark pointed to his Book. "This is what Nehemiah said to those who were harassing them, 'The God of heaven Himself will prosper us, therefore we His servants will arise and build.' "

"Here is another verse that I believe will be helpful," said Rick, "Shall I bring to the point of birth and not cause it to be completed? says the LORD. Shall I, the one who causes the birthing to happen, shut the womb? says your God."

Aaron placed a big piece of wood on the fire so it would last through the night, and then turned toward the rest of the guys. "We need to share these verses with the families tomorrow."

Everyone agreed. As they went to their tents to get some sleep, each one was thinking about the battle to come.

The next morning they again spent some time reading in their Books, then assembled in front of the unfinished House of Instruction with the families.

Mark stepped forward and read the verse from Nehemiah. "I believe it's important to remember that it's God who is in charge of this work, and it's through His strength that this House of Instruction will be built."

Rick then read the verse from Isaiah. "God did not call you here to fail. He conceived this project, and He will bring it to completion."

They all prayed together and were encouraged, sensing this battle would be different. It wasn't long before the flying baboons began to approach, flapping their large wings, while holding rocks in their claws.

The four families nodded toward each other, tapping their chests twice to reveal their armor. Everyone took out their Books, then raised them until they became Swords.

The flying creatures hurled large rocks at them while screaming, "You will never succeed! God did not call you here. You called yourselves here, and you will fail."

Quoting the verses from Nehemiah and Isaiah, while holding their Shields above their heads, they were able to block the rocks. Seeing that the families were not giving up this time, the creatures flew lower, trying to wrestle their Shields out of their hands.

Raising his Sword, Rick said, "Now is the time to strike out at your enemies, proclaiming what God has said in His word!"

They each landed hard blows on the creatures with their Swords until the baboons couldn't take anymore and scrambled away. These enemies were not about to give up though. They flew twenty feet into the air, regrouped, and then swooped down again.

The flying creatures knew Tom was the leader of the work, so two of them descended toward him. One flew toward his head, but Tom thrust his Shield upward and knocked it away. The other one flew toward his knees, bearing its teeth, but Tom kicked the creature and sent it rolling backwards.

The first baboon flew toward him again, and Tom readied his Sword. "I believe that I shall see the goodness of the Lord in the land of the living. Therefore I will wait on Him and be encouraged. Yes, I will wait on the Lord and be strengthened."

Tom struck the creature in its left wing, wounding it so severely that it was barely able to stay in the air. The other flying baboon had recovered and flew toward his Breastplate. Tom smashed the creature in the face with his Shield. The baboon was dazed by the blow and hovered just above him. Tom quickly thrust his Shield toward it and knocked it up into the other baboon with the wounded wing. Both tumbled toward the ground, and Tom pounced on them, striking them several times with his Sword.

The other baboons saw their comrades in trouble, and two more flew toward Tom, occupying him just long enough for the two wounded ones to get away.

While Tom had been in a battle, one of the flying creatures swooped toward Susan and tried to claw her shoulders. She slammed her Shield into its head, then struck it on the side with her Sword.

She stepped back and proclaimed, "I will not fear or be discouraged, for my God is with me. He will strengthen me and help me. He will uphold me with his righteous right hand."

The angry baboon lunged toward her, but Susan swatted it out of the air with her Sword. The creature quickly took flight and disappeared.

Rick, Jeremiah, and the others had also dealt severe blows to several more of the flying creatures, and soon all the baboons flew out of sight. Everything got quiet, and all the warriors rested for a moment. Then suddenly the air was filled with the fierce flapping of large wings. The baboons who were still able to attack returned with even larger rocks.

The creatures screamed at the families. "You can't beat us. We will always return. Go back to where you came from, or never enjoy peace again."

Susan held up her Shield. "I will say of the LORD, He is my refuge and my fortress, My God, in Him I will trust."

When the creatures threw the large rocks, everyone blocked them with their Shields, but this time the rocks bounced back toward their enemies. The flying creatures dodged the rocks, then once again flew lower, desperately trying to take away their Shields.

By now though, the families had gained confidence and strength. They struck the creatures even harder, and after only a few minutes of battle, their enemies could take no more. Badly wounded and barely able to fly, the forces of Doubt and Unbelief fled.

Everyone returned their Swords to their sides thinking the battle was over. Then they heard a low growling sound from the wooded area to the north. As the growling grew, louder large black wolves emerged from the woods, showing their teeth and acting as if they were about to attack.

Rick glanced at everyone. "In Nehemiah, when discouragement didn't work against those rebuilding the walls, their enemies began to threaten them. Stay strong and of good courage. We'll defeat this enemy as well."

The wolves split up into two packs, and almost immediately six of them began growling at Rick and the guys as if they were about to pounce.

Mark glanced over and saw that Jeremiah appeared nervous. Mark motioned toward him with his Sword. "You can do this."

As one of the wolves approached, Jeremiah dug in with his Shoes. The wolf darted toward him and jumped into the air. Jeremiah crouched low and braced for impact. The creature bounced off his Shield, but it immediately recovered and lunged at him again. Jeremiah stepped to the side and struck it on the back. The wolf tried to get in behind him, but he quickly turned and struck it again.

Mark battled back one of the fiercest enemies, striking it with multiple blows with his Sword. He then darted over to help Jeremiah finish off the wolf he was fighting.

While one group of wolves had the guys occupied, the other pack rushed toward the families. Tom raised up his Sword. "Though an army encamps against me, my heart shall not fear. If war should rise up against me, even then I will still be confident."

All of the families held firm and drove their enemies back. The wolves appeared frustrated at their lack of success and started to circle around as they growled even louder.

Tom lifted his hands toward heaven. "Lord God it is you that fights our battles for us!"

Suddenly a bright light surrounded them, creating a barrier between them and the wolves. A couple of the creatures tried to penetrate the barrier, but as soon as they came close, the light blasted them back several feet. The wolves continued to circle for a few more minutes, growling and showing their teeth. At last, they slowly retreated back into the woods and left.

Everyone let out a loud shout of victory! The families hugged one another while praising God for enabling them to triumph over their enemies.

Rick stared into the woods. "Many Houses of Instruction are built with little opposition, so why have you come under such an intense attack?"

Tom nodded. "I've been wondering the same thing."

Recognizing that they were still surrounded by the barrier of light, Rick said, "I think I know how we can find out."

Tom held out his hand. "What do you suggest?"

As Rick took a step forward, the light moved with him. He then glanced back at Tom. "With this light protecting us, I say we go into those woods where the wolves came from and see what's there."

As they all moved forward together, the light continued to surround them. Once they reached the wooded area, one by one they ducked past the first trees and into the small forest. After carefully creeping along, they soon noticed that they were almost to the far edge. Stepping out into a clearing, they discovered they were near a wide road which intersected with many other roads.

Aaron stepped forward. "I've heard about this place. This is where people traveling from different towns cross paths as they go back and forth."

Joining him on the road, Rick said, "No wonder your enemies don't want you building a House of Instruction near here. This is a very strategic area, and the devil wants to maintain control over it."

The families felt instantly encouraged by this news. The battles they had been facing were evidence that the enemy considered them a threat. They trekked back through the woods, arriving at the outside of the unfinished House of Instruction.

Tom raised his hand. "Today we will gather inside this building, incomplete as it is, and we will worship God and study His word. Then tomorrow we will start to build again."

Everyone had a great time of singing praises to God and studying His word. Afterward, the families invited the young men to stay for a meal. When they finished eating, all the guys agreed that they needed to go if they were going to get back on campus before dark.

Tom shook each of their hands. "Thank you so much for being obedient and coming here. We're going to finish this work, and it's going to bring glory to God."

Rick said, "I know you'll succeed. Sometimes we just need a little bit of encouragement to remind us of what God has said, and then we can rise up and complete what He has given us to do."

After shaking hands with the rest of the families, Jeremiah, Rick, Mark, and the others started back toward campus. They planned to return and help the families with the building the next weekend.

Throughout the week, the families took turns keeping watch as the others worked on the building. Sometimes they heard a low growling noise coming from the woods, but the wolves did not appear again, and neither did the flying creatures.

Within a few weeks, the basic structure of the building was completed. It was too far for Jeremiah and the others to travel there often, but they would visit them every few months, joining them for worship. The families kept improving the building until it became known as one of the nicest in the area. The House of Instruction continued to grow, and other families settled in the area as well.

Jeremiah learned an important lesson from this battle. The primary weapon of his enemies was the thoughts they could plant in his mind that were opposite of God's word. He would later read in his Book where it said, "For though we live in the flesh, we do not wage war according to the flesh, for the weapons that we use in our warfare are not fleshly, but mighty before God to the tearing down of strongholds, casting down imaginations and every high thing that is exalted against the knowledge of God, and bringing every thought into captivity to the obedience of Christ."

When these families began meditating on doubt, fear, and discouragement, negative thoughts built up and became a fortress for the enemy. These thoughts had to be cast down and replaced with God's truth.

After returning to campus, it was time to focus on their classes once again. All the guys in Jeremiah's study group continued to meet together, and over the coming weeks, they embarked on more adventures. Sometimes they went out and encouraged those whose path they crossed, and sometimes they helped others with what seemed to be everyday sorts of tasks.

Jeremiah and the others didn't know it yet, but they would soon encounter another vicious enemy. In fact, this battle would take place near the very House of Knowledge where they lived.

9

THE ZULON

As the first semester was coming to a close, Jeremiah and the rest of the prayer group were growing concerned about what was happening on campus. On one particular evening when meeting together, they were praying for all those attending the House of Knowledge, asking God to work in their lives.

Mark had a troubled look on his face. "Something has been bothering me for some time now, but I haven't said anything. I didn't want to sound critical or judgmental, so I've kept it to myself."

"What is it?" asked Rick.

"I've felt that the atmosphere around campus has grown colder. I don't see as many students reading their Books, or talking about the things of God as I did at the beginning of the semester."

Aaron rocked forward, nodding. "I've noticed the same thing. I've had to fight some of these same feelings myself. It's as if someone took a big wet blanket and threw it over the whole campus."

"I'm still new to all of this," said Jeremiah, "but I noticed it too. I thought maybe it was just how things were supposed to be."

Staring at the floor, as if he was searching for answers, Rick said, "I've seen the same things, and I've been praying about how to bring it up. We can't just go around telling people to become more committed to God. They'll look at us as if we're self-righteous and trying to prove we're better than them."

"Well, since we're all seeing the same thing," said Eric, as he paced in front of the window, "it's evident something is going on. Maybe this change is being revealed to us because God wants us to do something about it, but what?"

Mark held up his hand. "I believe the first thing we need to do is ask God to search our own hearts to see where we may have grown complacent in our spiritual lives."

They all prayed together then agreed to meet at the same time the next evening. The following day went by quickly, and as soon as dinner was over, they all filed into Mark and Jeremiah's room.

As everyone was settling into their seats, Jeremiah opened up his Book. "I was reading this yesterday from the prophet Isaiah, 'For thus says the High and Exalted One Who inhabits eternity and whose name is Holy, I dwell in the high and holy place, with those who are thoroughly sorrowful about their sins and who are of a humble spirit, to revive the spirit of the humble, and to revive the hearts of the ones who are truly repentant for their sins.' "

"That's something I need to hear," said Mark, pointing to his Book. "It's real easy to become complacent about our sin, dismissing it like it's not that big of a deal."

After a time of prayer and confession, Aaron leaned forward. "One thing I believe we need to do is expand the number of us who are praying about this."

Rick nodded in agreement. "Yes, that sounds like a great idea. Let's spread the word, letting people know that we're praying for revival on campus. We can start using the prayer chapel."

The next day Aaron and Eric spoke with a young man named Jacob, who had a good reputation on campus. They discovered that he was part of a group that also met regularly. Jacob and some others had met a person named Disciple during the summer, and after that, they had started getting together for study and prayer.

Jacob agreed to begin praying with them and to invite others as well. Within a week, twelve people were gathering together. They would repent for their own sin and lack of enthusiasm, then pray for God to revive the fire of the students on campus.

One night while they were gathered in the prayer chapel, Jeremiah motioned toward his Book, as he moved to the center of the room. "I want to read something John wrote to the church at Ephesus. 'I know you are enduring patiently and bearing up for my name's sake, and you have not grown weary. But I have this against you, that you have abandoned your first love.' "

Jeremiah looked up from reading. "We're not just called to go through the motions of Christianity, but we're called to live out our lives with a fervent love toward God. Let's all pray that our first love would be rekindled."

Everyone said amen and confessed this had been a problem in their own lives at times.

As the days went by, there was a sense that they were making progress. They continued to meet in the chapel during the evenings while encouraging one another throughout the day. As they walked around the campus, they became more aware of small pockets of damp, cold air surrounding them. Whenever they sensed these cold places were nearby, they would quietly speak God's word: "Therefore, my beloved brethren, be steadfast, immovable, always abounding in the work of the Lord, knowing that your labor is not in vain in the Lord."

Through their time of prayer during the evenings, and their battles during the day, they could sense that things were changing. They certainly noticed a difference within themselves, but at the same time, they also noticed that the intensity of the opposition was growing stronger.

That Friday evening as they gathered in the chapel, they all noticed that their paths were leading off campus and to the north.

Rick addressed the group. "We've made a lot of progress, but it looks like we're now about to take this battle directly to our enemy. Let's meet here again tomorrow morning and follow our paths to wherever they lead."

They all met together the next morning, including Jacob and his friends, and right after a quick breakfast, they headed off to the north.

When they had hiked for nearly an hour, Mark motioned for everyone to stop. "I sense that something is close by."

"I agree," said Rick. "There's a heaviness in the air."

Everyone began to walk more slowly, and soon they noticed something strange off in the distance. At first, it looked like a tree, but it was different from any tree they had ever seen. As they got closer, small vapor-like clouds shot out of this tree-like being. These clouds were almost transparent, so that a person had to be looking right at them to see them.

Aaron held up his hand. "I've heard of these creatures. They are called the Zulon."

"So this is the source of the cold, damp clouds of complacency we've been seeing around campus," Rick said.

Two guys from Jacob's group took out their Swords and ran toward the Zulon. They didn't get very far though because the air became heavier as they drew closer, weighing them down with an overwhelming desire to go to sleep. Jacob and Stephen, one of Jacob's friends, recognized what was happening, and ran out to pull them back.

Motioning for everyone to withdraw to a small patch of grass, Rick said, "Obviously we can't just go charging at this enemy. We're going to need a strategy."

Jeremiah held out his Book. "Yes, and we're going to need more Scripture about sluggishness and complacency."

The group sat in a circle, and several verses were suggested. After discussing them for a few minutes, they felt ready to begin the attack.

Rick stood up. "Mark, I believe we'll need to start with the verse you found. The first thing we'll need to resist is this heavy slumber that comes upon a person as soon as they start to go near this thing."

Standing up, Jeremiah motioned toward the Zulon with his Sword. "I suggest that rather than all of us approaching it from the same point, we should surround it and come at it from different angles. We can close in on it at the same time, weakening its power."

Everyone agreed, and after praying together, they took up positions around the Zulon. Grasping their Swords and Shields, they inched toward the creature a few steps at a time. As they approached, they could feel the heaviness of slumber starting to take effect.

Mark held his Shield firmly while raising his Sword in the air. "We will not sleep, as others may do, but we will be watchful, alert, and clearheaded!"

Mark then began to aggressively swing his Sword out into the air in front of him, while repeating the verse. Everyone else did the same, and they could feel the oppression starting to break. Within a few minutes, the heavy feelings of apathy and slumber were broken.

Emboldened by this victory, they moved a little closer toward the creature. Suddenly the Zulon released several rounds of darts toward them. Everyone ducked behind their Shields, but Aaron didn't move fast enough and was grazed on his elbow. He dropped to one knee, barely able to hold up his Shield.

Eric quickly made his way over to him and touched the tip of his Sword to Aaron's wound. "God's words are life to those who find them and health to all their flesh."

Aaron immediately recovered, and Eric raced back to his position while avoiding the darts on the way.

Holding out his Shield, Eric shouted, "We will not be sluggish, but we will become imitators of those who through faith and patience inherit the promises."

The darts continued to fly at them, but as they quoted this verse, the projectiles disappeared as soon as they struck their Shields. After the Zulon fired a few more rounds, the darts stopped.

Rick motioned for them to pause and take a short break. When everyone signaled they were ready, the group started closing in on the creature again. But after a few steps, the ground started rumbling, then buckled upward, forcing them to climb uphill at a steep angle.

Jeremiah shouted, "I believe this is where we need to remember that it's the love of Christ that compels us. We do not just move forward when it's convenient, but we press on to the upward call of God in Christ Jesus."

Digging in with their Shoes of the Gospel, the group pushed up the steep slope, bringing them to within fifty feet of the Zulon. As they firmly planted their Shoes into the soil, the ground stopped shaking and leveled off. The group glanced around at one another as a sudden quietness draped over the whole area.

Was this the end of the battle? Had the Zulon been defeated? Suddenly a fierce wind blew from the creature, knocking them all back a few feet. They dug in their Shoes and pushed out toward the wind with their Shields.

Mark struggled to keep his balance, but he was determined to stay on his feet. "We will not be moved back! We will be steadfast, immovable, and ALWAYS abounding in the work of the Lord!"

Everyone took courage from his declaration, and they strained forward to make their way toward the creature. It took them several minutes, but they were able to press and strain until they reached the Zulon. At once the wind stopped.

Now that they were up close, they could better see what they were fighting. The Zulon resembled a tree in that it seemed to spring up from the ground and had several arm-like branches. The substance of the creature, though, was not wood, but it was made of a thick, dark sponge-like material. It soaked up death and decay from beneath the ground, and then released these small vapor-like clouds filled with sluggishness and complacency.

As the group stood around, studying the creature, they noticed that the ground beneath them felt mushy and slimy. The smell of rot and decay filled the air, as an icy chill descended on them. Suddenly a low pitched creepy sound emanated from the creature. The Zulon shook violently as if it were coming alive, then aggressively swiped at them with its arms.

Blocking one blow with his Shield, Rick shouted, "Be alert! We must defeat all of these branches and strike them down."

Each of them raised their Shields to block the assault, then used their Swords to cut off the arms little by little. The Zulon reached out with one of its branches and grabbed Rick. Jeremiah fought his way over toward him, ducking underneath one of the arms as it came toward his head while blocking another branch with his Shield. When Jeremiah reached him, Rick was dangling in the air, held in the grip of the Zulon's arm. Jeremiah swung his Sword vigorously at the branch and connected several times.

As another branch came swinging toward them, Rick yelled, "Watch out!"

Glancing over his shoulder just in time, Jeremiah ducked as the arm passed over him. The branch swept back toward them again, and Jeremiah blocked it with his Shield, then cut it off with one blow from his Sword. Focusing his attention on the branch holding Rick, Jeremiah struck it as hard as he could, until it released him.

Back on his feet, Rick was then able to finish it off. Everyone continued to battle until they had cut off all the arms of the creature.

Sensing that victory was near, Rick pointed his Sword toward the bottom of the Zulon. "We must now destroy this enemy, trusting God to uproot it completely. After I say this next verse, I want us to thrust our Swords at the base of the creature."

Rick bowed his head. "Oh Lord, will You not revive us again, that Your people may rejoice in You?"

Everyone thrust their Swords into the ground. The earth shook, and the Zulon began to sway. The creature trembled violently one more time, then tumbled over with its roots in the air. Everyone knelt down for a moment, thanking God for the victory. After resting for a few minutes, they dragged what was left of the creature away and burned it.

The group made their way back to the campus singing and rejoicing. Over that next week, they noticed that those who had been praying for revival were more passionate than ever, and those who had been struggling became more consistent. All those who fought in this battle knew there would not be an instant change in everyone, nor did they expect that everyone would be touched by the results.

What they learned from this experience was that when God began to call for revival, His foremost desire was to stir up the ones who were already following Him. Then as their fire was rekindled and burned brighter, their passion would have an effect on those around them.

10

YOU CAN'T GO HOME AGAIN

The Semester was nearly over, and only final exams remained. The schedule for that week was so demanding that Jeremiah felt he hardly had time to catch his breath. When finals were complete, the whole campus had a day of fun to celebrate the end of the term. The staff organized a variety of games and events, and they made sure there was plenty of food for everyone.

The professors took turns in a dunking booth, while their students threw balls at the lever to try and release them into the water. Each time they were successful, the rest of the students cheered! The professors enjoyed it as well, though they reminded them that there would be another semester coming soon. The students laughed and tried all the more to send them into the water.

In the midst of the festivities, Jeremiah sat down by himself, deep in thought.

Mark spotted him and sat down beside him. "What are you planning to do during our two-week break?"

Jeremiah sighed. "I've thought about it a great deal, and I believe it's time for me to go back to the Town of Rationalism. I need to let all my old friends know I'm not coming back, and I need to sell my house."

Placing his hand on Jeremiah's shoulder, Mark said, "I realize this is going to be difficult, but know that all of us will be praying for you."

"Yes, it will be tough," said Jeremiah, tightly clasping his hands. "When I first arrived, I told you about my encounter with the Wisdom of This World. This enemy promised to make things hard for me."

"There is nothing your enemies can do, that God has not already prepared you for."

Jeremiah smiled and stood up. "That's true. For the rest of today, I'm going to enjoy this celebration, and I know God will be with me as I go tomorrow."

Jeremiah and Mark went back to join in on some of the games, and everyone continued to have a great time through the evening.

When the celebration was over, Jeremiah, Mark, and the rest of the guys gathered to reflect on the past semester. Jeremiah didn't want to mention anything about his plans at that time. Everyone was laughing and joking around, and it was nice to relax and not think about anything too serious. The next morning they slept in a little later before going to pick up their grades.

Jeremiah made his way over to Professor Williams' office, excited to see how he had done in his classes. When he arrived the door was open, and as usual, the professor seemed to be in the middle of doing something important. Jeremiah stood outside, not wanting to interrupt him.

Professor Williams looked up. "Ah, Jeremiah, come on in. I assume you came for your grades. Give me a moment, and I'm sure I'll find them." He sifted through stacks of folders, sliding papers back and forth. He then stood up, holding a piece of paper out in front of him.

Handing the paper to Jeremiah, Professor Williams said, "Here you go. You did well, and it was a pleasure having you in my classes."

"Thank you. I learned a lot, and I can't wait to learn even more next semester," said Jeremiah, as he looked over his grades.

"Yes," exclaimed Professor Williams, smiling his usual smile. "Next semester will be fun indeed. I see that you are in two more of my classes, so I hope you're ready to work even harder."

Jeremiah walked back to his room, where Rick, Mark, and all the other guys were hanging out, discussing their grades. All of those in the prayer group had done well, with Jeremiah receiving four *A*'s and one *B*+. The others told him he should be proud of those grades, and that there was no shame in making a *B*+ in Biblical Greek. As everyone was about to go back to their rooms, Jeremiah let them know that he was leaving within the hour to go to his hometown during the break.

Some expressed concern, but when Jeremiah showed them that his path was heading in that direction, they all prayed for him before he left. As he was about to leave the room, he stopped at the door, quickly turning back toward his friends. Each one gave him a look of reassurance that they would be with him in spirit as he traveled.

Jeremiah's path took him back to the inn where he stayed on the first day of his journey away from home. It was only about a half a day's walk from there to the Town of Rationalism, but he wanted to stay one night and be by himself before seeing his old friends again. After checking into his room, Jeremiah looked out a window and saw the bench where he sat reading the Gospel of John when he was here before.

Thinking about that day, Jeremiah raced downstairs and outside to the bench. While sitting there, he thought about how far he had come since then. God had been truly merciful and gracious toward him. It was on this bench that he went from being a skeptic to a believer. Everything started to make sense that day, as if a whole new world was opened up to him. Jeremiah would spend another hour sitting on that bench, thinking of all that happened since the last time he'd been there.

When he returned to his room and settled in for the night, the reality of what was about to happen hit him. He wondered how his friends were going to react, and how the Wisdom of This World was going to try and carry through on its threats. He wanted to prepare himself, so he read his Book late into the night, until falling asleep.

The next morning Jeremiah set out for the Town of Rationalism. When he was close enough to see the town welcome sign, feelings of apprehension washed over him. He quickly said to himself, "When I am afraid I will trust in You." Resolving to go forward, he made his way through the entrance. Jeremiah hadn't gone too far before people started to recognize him. Many greeted him and welcomed him home. He enthusiastically shook their hands, letting them know he was glad to be back.

After engaging in a few polite conversations, Jeremiah hurried to his home and knocked on the door.

The door swung open. "Jeremiah! It's great to see you," said Jeff.

"It's great to be back."

Jeff helped him with his backpack, and they walked inside.

"You've got to tell me all about your travels."

Jeremiah hesitated at first because he didn't want to say too much until everyone was gathered at the eatery in the evening.

"It's been an amazing journey," said Jeremiah, as he looked around his home. "I can't wait to talk to everyone tonight at Food For Thought, but I'll go ahead and let you know that I'm going to continue on this journey, so I'll be selling my house."

"I'm sorry to hear you won't be around anymore, but since you want to sell this place, I'd like to buy it myself. I've enjoyed living here, and I've always wanted a place like this."

Jeremiah walked up to his bookshelf and then turned around. "That will be great. We can get all the paperwork done tomorrow."

Jeff prepared some lunch for them, as Jeremiah asked about each of his friends. Jeff gave him all the latest news, but he sensed that Jeremiah wasn't ready to give too many details about the most recent events in his own life.

After they were finished eating, Jeff said, "Everyone will be really glad to see you this evening."

"I can't wait to see everyone," said Jeremiah, taking his plate to the sink. "But what I'd like to do first is walk around the town for a little while, and then I'll meet you and the others later."

Jeff stood up to accompany him to the door. "I'll head over to Food For Thought soon to let everyone know you're back and that you'll be joining us for dinner."

"Thanks," said Jeremiah as he left.

Walking around the town, Jeremiah took notice of everything in a way he never had before. He saw the people going about their routines while not thinking of anything beyond this present life. He realized he had been no different just a little over five months ago. He couldn't reach the whole town, but he could start by talking to those with whom he already had a relationship. He walked around for another hour and then headed over to his eatery, or what used to be his eatery.

Jeremiah had purposefully avoided coming to this part of the town until now. He knew seeing his old place was going to bring back a lot of emotions, and it did. He thought of all the time he had invested in this place, and all the friendships he had cultivated over the years. He thought of all the late nights he and his friends stayed up talking for hours, and all the laughs they had shared. Could he step right back into that?

At first, Jeremiah stood back at a distance, watching people go in and out of his former establishment. His mind traveled back to that day Pastor George first showed up. Jeremiah smiled as he remembered Pastor George peering through his glass door, grinning and waving to get his attention. Little did he know, everything about his life would change after that night.

When he felt ready, Jeremiah walked into the store. A patron by the door recognized him, and soon others turned to take notice of his arrival. A chorus of greetings rang out from his customers. Scott was busy behind the counter serving people their sandwiches, and the place looked as lively as he remembered it.

When Scott looked up and saw him, he smiled and waved. "Great to see you Jeremiah! Let me finish serving these customers in line, and then I'll bring you your favorite sandwich. The whole gang is in the usual spot. Go on back, and I'll join you soon."

As Jeremiah walked into the small room off to the side, Jeff, Jane, and all the others jumped up to welcome him. They started rapidly firing questions at him, excited to find out what all he had been doing since he left. Jeremiah did his best to only give general information at first, because he wanted to wait until Scott joined them before getting into the details of his journey.

Jeremiah used the time to ask everyone else about the events in their lives, and they filled him in on all the latest happenings in the Town of Rationalism. As they were finishing up, Scott arrived with two sandwiches, one for Jeremiah and one for himself.

As soon as Scott sat down, he motioned toward Jeremiah. "I hope you haven't given too many details yet. I'm dying to hear how things have been going for you."

Smiling as he looked around at his friends, Jeremiah said, "It's been a wonderful journey. So many things have happened since I left here that day. I'm currently enrolled in a House of Knowledge, and I've got about seven more months to go. Then I plan to travel around for a year while continuing my studies."

Everyone was looking at Jeff, silently prodding him to ask the question they all wanted answered.

Getting the hint, Jeff said, "Well Jeremiah, as I'm sure you can guess, we're all really anxious to find out what happened when you went to this place Pastor George sent you to. I believe you said you were going to a Building of Reflection? What happened? Did you find what you were looking for?"

Jeremiah paused, knowing it was time to share all that had been taking place on the inside of him. He took a deep breath then began. "So much has happened since I last saw all of you. As you remember, Pastor George gave me a Book, which I started reading. I didn't know if any of it was true, but I felt I had to find some answers. When I left here that day, I went to an inn, and I read for hours in the Gospel of John. As I was reading, I felt like I was really there with Jesus as He walked this earth. I saw how He proclaimed Himself to be the eternal Son of God who came down from heaven to redeem mankind. I saw how He interacted with people with such love, and all the powerful things He did while on the earth."

The others began to tense up as they listened to him.

Jeremiah could sense the tension, but he pressed on. "I read about what Jesus did for me by dying for my sins and paying the tremendous debt that I owed. Then I read how He was victoriously raised from the dead on the third day. When I finished reading, everything was so real to me, and I was convinced it was all completely true. After this, I felt I had to get to this Building of Reflection as soon as possible, so I set off to find it. Once I was there, I saw all of my sinfulness and realized there was absolutely nothing good in me. I was then directed to the Hill of Calvary where I laid all of my sins at the foot of the cross where Jesus was crucified. It was there at the cross that I repented of my sins and accepted Jesus Christ as my Lord and Savior."

All those listening were now noticeably nervous and began to shift around in their seats.

Taking out his Book from his satchel and laying it in front of him, Jeremiah continued. "I became a new creation that day, and it was the most glorious day of my life. After that, I spent time with Pastor George, learning so many wonderful things about God and His word. When I left there, I enrolled in a House of Knowledge that is dedicated to teaching principles from this Book. When I leave here I'll be going back there, and I'll spend the rest of my life serving my Lord and Savior on the Quest He has called me to."

Everyone became quiet. Jeremiah felt a sense of joy as he was sharing all that had happened to him, but after finishing, he felt extremely vulnerable. He waited for someone to say something, anything, but there was no response.

After what seemed to be a long period of silence, Scott looked around at the others and then back at Jeremiah. "You know we respect you, and you know we're always accepting of other people's views, but what you're describing sounds like an emotional experience. Remember that one guy, Kevin I think was his name. He left here and went half-way across the world, and the next thing we hear he's living in some temple, pursuing spiritual enlightenment. That kind of thing is okay I guess if that's what you want out of life, but this kind of emotionalism is not something we expected of you."

"Oh no," said Jeremiah, shaking his head, "this is much deeper than emotions. In fact, I feel more rational than ever. Everything makes sense to me now, and all the things I couldn't put together before or just guessed at, I now have the answers for."

Jeff jerked back in his seat. "Wait a minute, you mean you're one of those people who believes there is a God, and that we are so bad off He had to send someone to get beat up and die for us?"

Jeremiah paused for a moment and silently prayed for help. As he sat there, he remembered Pastor George looking at him intently, and telling him the response he was likely to get when he went back home.

After gauging the looks on his friend's faces, Jeremiah replied, "What I've come to understand is that we are all sinful, and if God had not sent his Son to die for us, then none of us would have any hope. But because of what Jesus did, we can be forgiven of our sins as if they never happened, and we can be placed in perfect, right standing with God."

"Jeremiah," said Scott, rapidly shaking his head, "You know the conversations we've had on these subjects, and you know how we feel about them. What you're saying is contrary to everything we believe. Only those who have deep-seated emotional issues would believe that we are so bad off that someone had to be killed for us. I never took you for someone with those kinds of issues, so I'm really puzzled."

Jeremiah knew this wasn't going to be easy, but a part of him had wondered if maybe they would be excited for him. That did not appear to be happening.

Grasping his Book, and holding onto it as if it was a life-line keeping him from drowning in an open sea, Jeremiah said, "I don't know how to explain it to you other than to say that as I was reading this Book, I was convinced that it was God speaking to me through these words. It was not just a onetime emotional experience. Ever since that day, I have become more convinced that these are the very words of God, and I've seen my life changing each day as a result."

Trying to relieve some of the tension, Jeff patted him on the back. "Jeremiah, we've always been friends, and we've shared a lot together. If you're happy with your life, then all I can do is wish you well."

Jane hadn't said anything up to this point, but she looked extremely agitated. She crossed her arms and glared at Jeremiah. "I've heard about those who are on this 'Quest' you're talking about. They call themselves Christians. I also know that many of these people would condemn me because I'm in a relationship with another woman. You never judged me in the past, and you said you were accepting of who I was. So has that now changed too?"

Jeremiah could sense her anger. "You've always been my friend. I never looked at you based on who you were in a relationship with, but I saw you as just another person. I still see you as a person, and I'd still like to call you my friend, but if you're asking me if I believe it's okay for men to be with men and women to be with women, then the answer is no, I do not. I've dedicated my life to following God and His word, and I see in His word that He has created sexual relationships to only be between a man and woman within marriage."

Jane shot forward, slapping her hands down on the table. "So that's it! Now all of a sudden I'm someone who's sinful? Are you going to tell me that I will spend all of eternity in a lake that burns with fire just because of who I love? I did not choose to be this way, but I'm proud of who I am. I don't believe in a god, but if there was one, then he would have been the one who created me like this in the first place. So how could he condemn me for it? I never thought this could happen to someone like you Jeremiah. You have turned into one of those awful bigots that we all used to denounce."

Everything felt awkward now, and it appeared all the others were feeling uneasy as well. Jeremiah had prepared for things to be tough, but he had not prepared for this.

Scott put his hand on Jane's shoulder. "We all know that Jeremiah has never been a bigot. How long has he been our friend? I don't agree with what he's saying either, but are we ready to blow up years of friendship over what might be a misunderstanding?"

Jane glared at Jeremiah again. "Are we misunderstanding you? You're not saying that I'm doomed for eternal fire?"

Jeremiah stared at the table and took a deep breath. "Jane, I didn't come back here to insult or condemn anyone. I just wanted to share all the wonderful things that have happened to me, but since you've asked me a direct question, I must answer it as best as I can. This Book lists certain sins and says that if a person persists in those sins throughout their life without repentance, then this shows that they never became a new creation. Based on that, they will spend eternity in the lake that burns with fire."

Jane rocked back in her chair, shaking her head and rolling her eyes.

Lifting his Book slightly off the table, Jeremiah said, "This is not just what I'm saying, but it's what this Book is saying, and because I believe this Book to be God's word, then it's in fact what God is saying. But that's not the end of the story. We were all born sinful, and we must all repent and accept what Jesus did for us as payment for our debt of sin. The wonderful message of the Gospel is that we can turn to Him for forgiveness, and He will save us just as we are no matter what our sins happen to be."

Jane jumped out of her chair. "I don't want to hear anything else Jeremiah. You are a bigot. I don't care what we were in the past. You are the one that's changed, not me. This is all on you."

Jane turned to Scott. "If this kind of conversation is going to be welcome here, then I can assure you that I and all of my friends will never eat here again."

She stormed out of the eatery, as an unsettled silence hovered over the room.

After a few minutes, Jeremiah looked around at everyone. "You all know I didn't intend to come here and cause an argument."

Scott shook his head. "It doesn't matter. It was bound to happen at some point. You're different. I can see that you're excited about what you believe, but it's not what we believe. We're not going to be able to sit around and have conversations like we used to."

Jeremiah felt crushed. "I guess I was hoping we still could. I knew I wasn't going to be here long, but I thought things would work out a lot better than they have. I was going to stay a few days, but I feel it's best if I finalize the paperwork on my house tomorrow and then leave."

Jeff stood up. "Well, I think it's time to go. Jeremiah will stay over at his house with me tonight, and then early tomorrow morning we'll go to the bank to sign all the papers."

Jeremiah shook hands with the rest of the group and said goodbye. Walking out of Food For Thought, Jeremiah felt a profound sense of sadness and loss, not knowing if he would ever see his friends again.

11

ALL THINGS WORK TOGETHER

Jeremiah and Jeff walked back to the house, with neither of them saying anything the whole way. When they arrived, Jeremiah said he was going to see if there was anything he wanted to take with him, and whatever was left Jeff could keep or sell.

As Jeremiah looked around his home, he thought about the first day he moved in. He had moved to the Town of Rationalism right after finishing his primary education. The summer before that, he worked in a popular sandwich shop, where he enjoyed listening to all the conversations between the customers. After the summer was over, his employer, Mr. Bryant, told him that once he was done with school, he could work for him full time. So later that next year, he packed everything he owned and moved.

After Jeremiah had been working there five years, Mr. Bryant decided to retire and travel the world. Jeremiah wanted to buy the eatery, but he knew it would be tough to convince a bank to loan someone his age the large sum he would need. Mr. Bryant wanted to help him out, so he put in a good word with the bank manager, a man he'd been friends with for a long time. Mr. Bryant assured the bank manager that Jeremiah was a hard worker and would make the business even more successful.

As a result, the bank manager personally approved the loan for Jeremiah. The business did so well that within a year he was able to buy a home—the very home he was standing in now. Looking back, he could see God's hand in his life even then, before he believed in Him.

Jeremiah meandered into the living room and sat down in the same chair he had always sat in when he came home from work. He looked at his bookshelf filled with rows of books and recalled all the evenings he had spent just reading and thinking.

Jeff could tell that Jeremiah was becoming emotional, so he walked over and sat on the couch across from him. "I guess it's hard to leave a place where you have so many memories."

"Yes it is, but I know I'm doing the right thing," said Jeremiah, gazing around the room.

Jeff shook his head. "I know you feel this is what you're supposed to do with your life, but you've got to understand that everything you've told us goes against our beliefs. You can't expect us to embrace what you believe, and you can't even expect us to understand it. It's like you're from another dimension or something."

Resting a hand on his Book, Jeremiah replied, "I guess in a way I am. God's word says that when you become a new creation, you are a foreigner in this world and you're citizenship is now in heaven."

Jeff shrugged his shoulders. "I can sort of understand why you might look at the world the way you do. There's a part of me that wishes there was this one big story that could explain everything and promise an everlasting future of goodness, but it's just too much of a leap for the rational mind."

Jeremiah pointed to his Book. "The rational and natural mind is not able to understand the things of God, but these truths are only opened up to us through a supernatural experience. A change has to take place on the inside of you so you can grasp these truths. I brought an extra Book that I'd like to leave with you. I'll put it on the shelf with the others, and whether you read it or not is up to you."

Jeff thought the only polite thing to do would be to agree, so he said thanks. They talked for a little longer and then went to bed. Jeff had been staying in the guest room, so Jeremiah's room was exactly as he had left it. Jeremiah laid down on his bed for what he knew would be the last time. He looked around and thought again of all the time he had spent here, and then drifted off to sleep.

The next morning Jeremiah and Jeff went to the bank and finalized the sale of the house. Jeremiah had already packed everything for his trip, so once they were done at the bank, Jeff accompanied him to the edge of town. Sadness filled Jeremiah as they walked, but they kept the conversation light.

Not far from the town boundary, Jeff stopped and shook

Jeremiah's hand. Holding back tears, Jeremiah said goodbye and walked away. The townspeople weren't nearly as friendly as when he had arrived. Apparently, word had gotten out about his conversation with Jane, and many didn't seem happy with him.

A little ways outside the town, Jeremiah turned to take one last look at his old home, but it hit him that he had looked back enough. It was time to focus on what was ahead. He had grieved for all the things he left behind—his home, his business, and his friendships. Now he needed to move on to what God had for him next.

After traveling for an hour, suddenly, Jeremiah felt an oppressive heaviness in the air, along with the feeling that someone was angrily staring at him. A force was pushing down on him, trying to bring him to his knees. Using all the strength he had to remain standing, Jeremiah looked up.

A dark mist swirled around him, as a disorienting pressure squeezed his head. The images of his friends shaking their heads at him in disbelief flooded his mind. Their voices were magnified, as they told him how foolish his beliefs were. He saw visions of the townspeople, including many of his favorite customers, giving him looks of disdain as he left the town.

An angry voice shouted at him. "I told you I would make things hard for you if you continued on your Quest. You fool! You've lost everything."

While the heaviness was strong, Jeremiah didn't feel as weak as that day when he first met the Wisdom of This World.

Raising his Book until it became a Sword, Jeremiah shouted, "Indeed, I count all things as loss because of the surpassing worth of knowing Christ Jesus my Lord for whom I have suffered the loss of all things, and I count them as garbage, that I may gain Christ."

The dark mist shot into the sky, and the heaviness lifted. After collecting himself, Jeremiah continued his journey. He was thankful for the victory God had just given him, but at the same time, he felt as if this enemy had won the battle with his friends. He had such high hopes for his visit back to his hometown, but things went about as bad as they possibly could have gone.

Several years later though, Jeremiah would learn that his visit had more of an impact than he thought. The Book he left with Jeff would sit on that shelf for three years without being touched. But during a time of personal crisis, Jeff took the Book down and began reading.

Jeremiah had placed two bookmarks in it. The first one was in the Psalms, and the second one was in the Gospel of John. Jeff spent that whole first night reading the Psalms, feeling comforted by the words. Each night for almost two weeks, he would read several more of the Psalms. When Jeff had finished all of them, he turned to the second bookmark. It had been years since his conversation with Jeremiah, but while reading through the Gospel of John, he remembered Jeremiah talking about how significantly this portion of the Book affected him. Jeff started to feel those very same feelings.

Not long after this, Jeff set off to find the Building of Reflection Jeremiah had told him about. After going all the way through it, he then made his way up to the Hill of Calvary. That day Jeff repented of his sins, asking Jesus to come into his life and save him. Later that same day he would meet Pastor George, and then a few weeks later he would enroll in the same House of Knowledge that Jeremiah attended. While there, Jeff met a Christian young woman, and they were married after graduation.

Jeff would go on to start a House of Instruction, where he trained people how to present the Gospel to those who lived in places like the Town of Rationalism. This ministry turned out to be exceptionally effective, bringing many to the Quest. And oh, when Jeff sold the very same house that Jeremiah had sold him, he purchased another Book, leaving it on the Bookshelf with some bookmarks carefully placed inside.

It would be several years into his Quest before Jeremiah would learn any of this. However, five years later Jeremiah would meet a young man who had been trained in Jeff's House of Instruction. As he listened to the young man describing the impact that Jeff had on his life, Jeremiah cried tears of joy. He learned that even the smallest of seeds can be used for building the Kingdom of God.

Jeremiah had thought his time in the Town of Rationalism was a complete bust, and that The Wisdom of This World had won a victory, but God was working all things according to the counsel of His will. God took the small seeds Jeremiah had planted and used them for His glory.

Of course, as Jeremiah was traveling back to the House of Knowledge that day, he didn't know what the future held. During this time, he was doing his best to battle feelings of discouragement and disappointment. When he arrived back on campus, he was just in time for the usual gathering with his friends. After telling them everything that happened, he began to cry. Jeremiah wasn't one to show a lot of emotion, but when he did, it was deep and heartfelt.

"Jeremiah," said Mark, putting his arm around him, "you were obedient. You shared God's word, and you shared your heart with your friends. That's all you can do. The rest is up to the Holy Spirit."

The others also comforted him with words of encouragement, and then afterward they prayed with him. Having this time with his new friends was exactly what Jeremiah needed after all he'd been through.

Two more days would pass before he no longer felt the sense of grief and loss that he'd felt when he first came back, but he knew God would make him stronger because of the experience. On the one hand, he had no desire to go through such a trying ordeal, but on the other hand, trials like that made him lean on God and deepen his relationship with Him.

12

VALLEY OF TRIALS

Now that the new semester was about to begin, Jeremiah was excited to get started. He was taking more courses in Theology and Biblical Greek, as well as three other classes. He was extremely busy, and it seemed like every waking hour had something that needed to be done. The first semester had prepared him though, so he was able to juggle all of his responsibilities and managed to stay on top of them.

As the semester continued, Jeremiah and the rest of the guys grew in their relationships with God and with each other. The semester flew by, and before long, it was time to once again get ready for final exams. When finals were complete, they had another celebration on campus, and once again, everyone had a great time. They received their grades the next day, and Jeremiah received four *A's*, and one *B+*, and yes once again the *B+* was in Biblical Greek. Jeremiah was proud of his effort that semester, but he was even more thankful for all that he had learned.

Many students were looking forward to taking a break for the entire summer. However, Jeremiah and all those in his prayer group were going to stay for the summer term and take three courses each. There was a two-week break before summer classes began, so they all met that evening in Jeremiah and Mark's room and discussed what they could do during that time.

When the meeting ended, Jeff stepped outside. "Come here guys." As they filed out of Jeremiah and Mark's room, Rick pointed to the ground. "Look where our paths are heading."

Mark shook his head. "We've never traveled in that direction. I've heard it's basically a wilderness for miles."

Rick nodded. "Well let's start packing tonight, and we should all pack enough to last for the whole two weeks if necessary. Let's get up early and meet back here right after sunup."

All of the guys started packing and then went to bed as soon as they could. The next morning they headed out, and they traveled until it was almost dark.

As they were searching for a good place to camp, Jeremiah pointed toward an entrance to a valley. "Looks like our paths are heading in there."

They all traveled a little further, and then they came upon a sign, announcing that this was The Valley of Trials. Written below the name of the place was a verse from the Book, "Blessed is the man who is patient and steadfast under trial, for when he has passed the test, he will receive the crown of life, which the Lord has promised to those who love him."

Everyone in the group agreed to set up camp for the night and explore the valley the next morning. At dawn, they entered the Valley of Trials and descended down a sloping trail for over an hour. When they finally reached the bottom, a towering hill confronted them. They began to climb but soon discovered that ascending up the hill was going to be slow and rigorous. At several points, they had to progress on their hands and knees because of the steep incline.

After an hour, they finally reached the top, only to discover that another hill, even steeper and taller, lay in front of them. So once again, they started up the hill together.

When they reached the summit, the group was exhausted. Cuts and bruises from the climb covered most of them. They went a little further and saw another hill that was extremely steep. By now the sun was at its peak, bringing with it the hottest part of the day.

At this point, Eric sat down and tossed his backpack in the dirt. "That's it. I'm tired of climbing these hills."

Jeremiah sat down beside him. "Eric, I realize this is tough, and I'm not having a lot of fun either, but this is where our paths have taken us. When we fought the Creature of Complacency, one of the verses we quoted from our Book was that it was through faith and patience that we inherit the promises."

"I know," said Eric, shaking his head, "but there doesn't seem to be any purpose in this other than wearing ourselves out."

Mark took out his canteen and joined them. "When we face trials in our lives, we often don't see the purpose until we've gone through them."

Everyone sat down and rested for several minutes while drinking plenty of water. When they started climbing the next hill, it was so steep that they had to stay close, giving one another a hand or a boost when needed. When they reached the top, their paths descended down a slippery, winding trail. Relying on their Shoes, they made it down without falling.

After they had traveled for another hour, the earth began to rumble. Suddenly vines shot up from the ground and wrapped around their legs.

Aaron reached down and grabbed one of the vines. "These are too strong. It's like they're made out of wire."

Mark tried to step out of their grasp. "These vines have such a strong grip that I can't even raise my foot off the ground."

Jeremiah removed his Book from his satchel. "I believe these are roots of bitterness. Take out your Sword and repent of any resentment you've allowed in your heart, especially while we've been in this valley."

Everyone except Eric was able to use their Swords to cut away the vines. In fact, by the time they had all freed themselves, the vines had completely engulfed Eric to the point that he was imprisoned by them. The group gathered around him, but no one was sure what to do.

Jeremiah bowed his head in prayer and then looked up at Eric. "I'm going to take my Sword and gently plunge it into these vines until it comes to the edge of your stomach. As I do, I believe it's going to reveal to you the root of this bitterness. You had a difficult time when we were climbing those hills, and it was obvious you struggled with anger and frustration. I don't believe that's the root though, but I think it goes much deeper."

Eric struggled to talk through the vines. "I trust you Jeremiah. I wasn't able to battle this on my own, so I know I need help."

Jeremiah gently pushed his Sword through the vines. When it came to the edge of Eric's belly, Jeremiah quoted from the Book. "Let all bitterness, rage, anger, quarreling, and slander be put away from you, along with all hatred."

As the sharp tip of Jeremiah's Sword touched his stomach, Eric cried out, but not because of the Sword. He could now see his bitterness. He recognized that when things had become hard in his life, he'd developed a pattern of complaining. Bitterness toward God had built up, and the trial of climbing the hills had brought this to the surface.

Crying out in repentance for his murmuring and complaining, Eric tried to raise his Book from his side. But it was difficult for him to even move an inch, because the vines remained tightly wrapped around him.

Again, he strained to raise his arm and shouted, "I will not let a root of bitterness spring up within me, but instead of complaining during hard times, I will reach out and secure God's grace."

At last, Eric raised his Book until it became a Sword, and as soon as it made contact with the vines, it sliced through them immediately. Carefully at first, he struck the vines on all sides until he was completely free. As soon as the last vine fell to the ground, Eric felt a sense of peace and contentment. The rest of the guys rejoiced with him and thanked God for their victory over bitterness and resentment.

After hiking for a few more hours, everyone agreed it would be a good time to set up camp for the evening. As the last bit of light disappeared over the horizon, a chill filled the air that was almost painful. Rick suggested they build a fire and then gather enough wood to last through the night.

They slept in shifts, taking turns staying awake to keep the fire burning, but even with the fire, it was still extremely cold. No one had a good night's sleep. As soon as the sun began to rise the next morning, everyone crowded around the fire to get warm, then after a quick breakfast, they set off once again.

After a short time, they heard a flock of birds flapping their wings overhead. Gazing upward, they saw a large number of crows diving toward them.

As the crows descended, they began to speak. "There's danger up ahead, there's danger up ahead."

The crows would swoop down toward their heads while staying out of range of their Swords. Once they flew past them, the crows would circle around and fly back, saying the same thing over and over. After making several passes, they flew away.

The group continued moving forward, but they all wondered what the danger could be. Was it a giant? Was it a wild animal? Was it some other kind of enemy? Was it even real? Not knowing what awaited them, they began to walk more slowly. Soon they were barely making any progress at all.

Rick asked everyone to stop. "Ever since those crows told us danger was ahead, we've been slowing down to a crawl. If this keeps up, we're going to stop moving at all."

Jeremiah took out his Book. "I believe this will help, 'Blessed is the man who fears the LORD, taking great pleasure in His commandments. He will not fear bad news, or live in dread of what might happen because his heart is fixed trusting in the Lord.' "

One by one, they replaced thoughts of fear with thoughts of trust in God. At last, they were able to move forward at a steady pace, believing that if danger was up ahead, God would get them through it.

As the day progressed, the air became extremely hot once again. The heat caused them to sweat profusely, and they all became incredibly uncomfortable. Suddenly the ground started to quake ferociously. Everyone stood still, holding their arms out to their side, in order to maintain their balance.

When the severe trembling stopped, they started forward again. But they hadn't gone more than fifty feet when the ground started shaking for a second time. Once again, they had to stop and work to keep their balance. This cycle repeated over and over until all of them were growing frustrated.

When the shaking paused, Mark took out his Book and read, "My brethren, count it all joy when you fall into various trials, knowing that the testing of your faith produces patience. But let patience have its perfect work, that you may be perfect and complete, lacking nothing."

Strengthened by God's word, they all persevered until the quaking finally stopped. When they started forward again, they felt more sure-footed and steadier on their feet.

After traveling a little further, the group saw that the only way forward was through a tunnel that was about seven feet wide and twenty feet long. They could easily walk through it, but there was one problem. The ground was covered in some kind of dark mixture that smelled terrible. They knew that if they tried to trudge through it, the smell would be with them for days.

Rick and Greg studied the opening and concluded there was only one way to make it through the tunnel without touching the ground. If two people braced against each other back to back, they could slide their feet along the sides of the tunnel. They would have to keep their backs firmly against one another and take slow, small side-steps along the walls, but it could be done.

Jeremiah and Mark volunteered to go first. The others helped them get up on the wall as they braced their backs against each other. Little by little, they maneuvered across the tunnel.

Aaron and Eric were next, and then Rick and Greg went last because they were the most athletic and best able to get started without help. Along the way, each pair found themselves snapping at each other. Jeremiah would get upset because he felt Mark was going too slow, or Rick would angrily accuse Greg of moving too fast. Once everyone was on the other side, they recognized that each of them had said some things they shouldn't have.

Feeling conviction, Rick took out his Book and read, "Do not let any foul or harmful word come out of your mouth, but only what is useful for building one another up, as is fitting to the need and the occasion, that it may give grace to those who hear it."

Nodding his head, Jeremiah said, "That's something I need to be reminded of. We often quote this verse to teach that we shouldn't curse or use vulgar language, and while that's true, this verse goes even further. In addition to not allowing curses to come out of our mouth, we should only be speaking words that are helpful to one another."

Aaron glanced around. "I know I can be sarcastic at times and not even realize it."

Eric lowered his gaze to the ground. "I know I can tell a joke at someone else's expense, and while it may seem harmless to me, it's actually calling attention to something negative about that person."

Mark said, "In my Marriage and Family class we learned how married couples can get in a habit of saying some really negative things to each other, but do it in such a way that is subtle and passive aggressive."

Jeremiah opened his Book. "I think James sums it up well when he writes, 'But no man can tame the tongue. It is an unruly evil, full of deadly poison. With it, we bless our God and Father, and with it, we curse men, who have been made in the likeness of God.' "

Rick said, "I think the lesson for all of us is we need to think about what we're going to say before we say it. We need to ask ourselves, is this going to be helpful? Is this what needs to be said, or is this what we want to say?"

After a time of prayer and repentance, they started out again. Soon they discovered that the exit to the valley was only about a hundred yards away, but to reach it they had to climb a massive sand dune. The group knew this next task was going to be challenging, but within a few hours the sun was going to set, and they didn't want to spend another night battling the cold.

Examining the massive sand dune, they determined to be careful and take it slow. Rick took the lead, giving the others a hand when needed. Jeremiah was in the back since he was the strongest, and he could give his friends a push whenever they got stuck. Each time they took a step, their feet would sink into the dune, making it tough to take another step. Working together as a team, they propelled one another forward.

After some time, Rick paused and wiped the sweat from his brow. "Let's all remember what was on the sign when we first entered the valley, 'Blessed is the man who is patient and steadfast under trial, for when he has passed the test, he will receive the crown of life, which the Lord has promised to those who love him.' It's not that much further. We can do this."

Finally, they all made it to the top. After exiting the valley, they traveled for another hour, then found a suitable place to camp for the night. Once the tents were set up, and the fire was built, they sat around talking about all the different tests and hardships they had endured over the last few days. The experience of going through the Valley of Trials enabled each one to see their weaknesses and where they still needed to grow.

13

THE BLACK KNIGHTS

The summer term began, and all the guys in the prayer group, including Jeremiah, worked hard. When the last day of classes came to a close, there was a sense of relief that they were that much closer to graduation. But they were also aware of something else—they were going to have to say goodbye to Jeremiah. He had already told them that after the summer term ended, he was going to leave.

He only needed five more classes to graduate, and he had made arrangements to take those courses while traveling. The rest of the group still had another year left, but Jeremiah assured them he would finish up around the same time and be back to graduate with them.

On the one hand, Jeremiah was excited about the experiences that lay ahead, but at the same time, he felt some sadness about leaving his friends. Knowing that he would see them all again at graduation made it a little easier, but he was still going to miss them. His friends wanted him to stay, but Jeremiah felt God was leading him to some new experiences out on his own. When the last day of finals was over, they all met together to pray for him.

Jeremiah sighed. "There's a part of me that wants to stay, but I feel this is what I need to do. I know you all will continue to do well, and I can't wait to see you again."

Each of those in the group talked about their favorite memory over the past year. They all agreed it had been a great time, and they were so grateful God had caused all of their paths to cross. After reminiscing a little while longer, they went back to their rooms, leaving Mark and Jeremiah alone.

Mark was helping Jeremiah finish up his last bit of packing. "Any idea what you'll be doing once you leave?"

Jeremiah stopped for a moment. "I'm not sure."

"Aren't you just a little bit anxious about going off on your own?"

"Yes I am," said Jeremiah, as he closed up his backpack, "but I believe this is going to be a time of learning to trust in God even more."

Climbing into his bed, Mark said, "Each night, as the five of us get together, we'll always pray for you. I can't wait to hear what you're going to experience."

Jeremiah and Mark talked for a few more minutes and then went to sleep. The next morning Jeremiah had just one more thing to do before leaving. He needed to see Professor Williams to get his grades and pick up all the work for his courses. As the professor was busily moving things around his office, Jeremiah waited patiently, knowing that he would soon notice him and invite him in.

After a few minutes, Professor Williams looked up. "Ah yes, Jeremiah, come in. I've been expecting you."

Shuffling around some items on his desk before finally finding what he was looking for, he held out a paper. "Here are your grades. Great job once again."

"Thank you," said Jeremiah, looking over the sheet.

Professor Williams reached for a folder of papers, then held them out to Jeremiah. "And here is what you'll need to finish up the rest of your courses."

That peculiar smile of the professor's spread across his face once again. "I do hope you're ready to work hard. I'll be the one handling all your coursework. I expect you to continue to put forth your best effort."

Jeremiah nodded. "I've enjoyed being in your classes, and I look forward to seeing you again."

All those in the prayer group were waiting outside so they could walk with him to the edge of the campus grounds. Once there, they saw Jeremiah's path leading off the campus. They wished him well, and then he started on his way.

Jeremiah felt a surge of emotions as he left. The relationships he had formed with these guys meant so much to him. Not only had they welcomed him into their House of Knowledge, but they also welcomed him into the Christian faith. They had been there to encourage him during the tough times when he really needed it. Even before starting his Quest, Jeremiah was used to always having a core group of friends to talk to and rely on for support. Now he was going to be traveling on his own, and it would be at least nine months before he returned.

Wondering what awaited him during the coming year, Jeremiah traveled forward. When the sun began to set, he found a nice camping spot near a stream and set up his tent for the night. As he lay down to go to sleep, his mind drifted back to his friends. He thought of how they were getting ready for a new semester and all the excitement that went with it. Would Mark get a new roommate? What kind of adventures would they experience while he was gone? While thinking of his friends, Jeremiah fell asleep.

The next morning he awoke to the sound of clanging metal in the distance. Rubbing his eyes, he crawled out of his tent to see what was making such an irritating noise. At first, all he could see were dark figures coming up over a hill. As they drew closer, he saw Black Knights with flashing pictures on the front of their armor. These weren't just any pictures though; they were pictures of lustful thoughts he had allowed in his mind.

Jeremiah suddenly realized he was about to fight a battle against lust. He checked his armor, then held out his Book until it became a Sword.

The Black Knights of Lust charged him, striking out furiously with their spears. He was able to block most of the blows, but there were so many coming at him at one time that he was getting hit despite all of his efforts. The Black Knights were trying to dominate him through overwhelming force.

Jeremiah desperately shouted, "Those that belong to Christ have crucified the flesh with its sinful passions and lustful desires."

Fighting with all his might, Jeremiah swung his Sword and Shield aggressively at the Black Knights. At the same time, he battled a sense of shame for allowing these pictures into his mind in the first place. He remembered the first moments these thoughts started and how pleasant they felt. Rather than interacting with the pictures at that time, he should have turned them away immediately. The Holy Spirit brought to his remembrance, "If we confess our sins, He is faithful and just to forgive us our sins and to cleanse us from all unrighteousness."

While still defending himself, Jeremiah prayed, "Lord, I gave place to these thoughts. I'm sorry, and I wish to be cleansed from my sin. Give me your grace to fight these enemies today, and continue to give me your grace as I battle lust in my mind."

Feeling strengthened, Jeremiah fought even harder. Three knights advanced against him, but he quickly blocked the thrust of their spears with his Shield. As the knight on the left prepared to attack again, Jeremiah plunged his Sword into its chest and then swiveled around to hit another knight with a forearm to the face. The third one thrust its spear toward his helmet, but Jeremiah ducked, and when the spear flew over his head, he raised up his Shield and knocked it out of the knight's hand.

Stepping back, Jeremiah shouted, "I will set no wicked thing before my eyes!"

He then knocked out the three knights with blows from his Sword and Shield. Fighting furiously, Jeremiah eliminated all the Black Knights of Lust.

After the battle, he slowly walked back to his tent, exhausted and wounded. Before this day, Jeremiah had not been aware of the danger of letting these thoughts of lust linger in his mind. It was just thoughts, right? It wasn't like he was doing anything in real life. Today though, he saw that when these thoughts of lust were allowed to roam free, they waged war against his soul. Lust promised pleasure, but what it was really doing was sedating him as it pummeled his soul, leaving him weakened and ashamed.

He spent hours reading in his Book that evening, and each time a thought of lust would present itself to his mind, he battled it by confessing God's word and asking for grace.

Through the process of the battle, Jeremiah realized just how undisciplined his mind was, and how much work still needed to be done. He knew this struggle was too difficult for him to prevail on his own. The victory could only be won through the strength of the Holy Spirit. Jeremiah was learning that it was far easier to battle these thoughts when they first entered his mind, rather than trying to uproot them after he had dwelt on them.

The Holy Spirit reminded Jeremiah that he was to meditate on God's word day and night, and it was these words that should be consuming his thoughts. The Holy Spirit was teaching him not to wait until he was in a battle to start thinking on God's word, but to do so continuously. Lying down to go to sleep, Jeremiah had to keep fighting. It seemed that the more tired he became, the harder lust fought to enter his mind.

Jeremiah woke up suddenly the next morning, as once again the sound of clanging metal echoed all around. Peering out of his tent, he saw there were more Black Knights today than there were yesterday. These knights did not want to give up the territory they were used to occupying. Jeremiah climbed out of his tent, determined to follow through on the progress he made the day before.

Tapping his chest twice to reveal his armor, Jeremiah wanted his enemies to see what was in store for them. Lust was not going to defeat him. He steadily advanced toward the field of battle, while praying. He acknowledged his dependence on the grace of God and the strength of the Holy Spirit.

As the Black Knights charged, Jeremiah ran full speed toward them, jumped into the air, and kicked out with his spiked Shoes. As he made contact with the knights, he knocked several onto their backs. Landing from his jump, he stuck his Sword into the ground to brace his fall. Rising quickly, he swung his Sword mightily to the left and then to the right. With each strike, he knocked out three knights.

Jeremiah stepped back to catch his breath, but three more from each side rushed him. He thrust out his Shield to his left, knocking those three knights to the ground.

Turning immediately to his right, he saw three knights running toward him in a straight line. He thrust his Sword straight through them so that they were all attached to the blade. He then gathered all his strength and hoisted the three knights above his head.

Jeremiah shouted, "I have made a covenant with my eyes, how then can I look upon a woman with lust." He then brought his Sword to the ground, crushing all three.

Another wave of Black Knights rushed toward him, but he kept swinging his Sword and knocking them off balance.

Just as he felt there were too many of them to contend with, Jeremiah shouted, "How can a young man keep his way pure? By keeping watch over himself according to your word, oh God."

Jeremiah swiveled around and cut down four knights with one blow of his Sword. "With my whole heart, I will seek You, O LORD, let me not wander from Your commandments."

As a final group of powerful knights charged toward him, Jeremiah bowed to one knee. "Oh God, I have stored up Your word in my heart that I might not sin against You!"

Jumping to his feet, Jeremiah thrust his Sword toward the nearest knight, running him through. With this knight still skewered on his Sword, Jeremiah swung it to his left and took out five other knights that had charged with it. He then swung around in a circle and hurled the knight attached to his Sword into a nearby tree.

He whirled to the right, but no knights advanced against him. He stood alone on the battlefield having defeated them all.

Collapsing to both knees and raising his hands into the air, Jeremiah shouted, "Thanks be unto God who always causes me to triumph through my Lord and Savior Jesus Christ!"

Barely able to stand up, Jeremiah staggered back to his tent and collapsed. As he lay there praying for strength, he fell asleep. An hour later he awoke, but he still felt the effects of the battle. At the same time, he also felt refreshed in his spirit. After eating dinner, he read some more in his Book then lay down for the night. As he had the night before, Jeremiah fought diligently against thoughts of lust before once again falling asleep.

The next morning Jeremiah slept later. When he awoke, he realized there was no sound of clanging metal. Glancing out of his tent, he saw there were no Black Knights.

Reflecting on the battle, Jeremiah prayed, "Lord, from this point forward, let me be just as vigorous against thoughts of lust, as I have been these last two days. If I ever become lazy, please remind me of the effort it took to win back this ground in my mind."

Jeremiah packed up and prepared to leave. God had given him victory over lust, and he was determined to walk in this victory from this point forward.

14

FIELD OF TRUST

After traveling for a few hours, Jeremiah saw that his path was leading him into a field of tall grass and weeds. The further he went, the taller the vegetation and shrubbery around him became. Soon it rose well above his head. He tried to clear his path with his Sword, but before long, he had difficulty seeing exactly where his path was.

Jeremiah waded through this field for hours, keeping up with his path as best he could. The sun sunk lower across the sky, but he continued on. After traveling further, he realized there wasn't enough daylight left to try and make it back the way he came. The only thing he could do was keep going forward and hopefully reach the end of the field before it was too dark to see. But no matter how hard he worked to clear his path, he didn't seem to be making much progress. As the sun dipped below the horizon, it became clear that he wasn't getting out of this field before nightfall.

Jeremiah pushed on ahead, determined to get as far as possible while he could still see. After progressing a little further, he came to a small clearing. Glancing around, he determined this would be a good place to camp, so he set up his tent and built a fire. He hadn't eaten anything since earlier that morning, so he unpacked a sandwich. While he ate, he thought about his friends, and all the times they spent in the cafeteria together. He remembered that Mark said they would be praying for him, and he hoped they were praying for him tonight.

Gazing into the dark, Jeremiah was struck with an intense feeling of being alone. There was nothing he could see that could give him any comfort. The tall stalks of vegetation blocked everything from his view except for the sky above. There were no sounds of people moving about, and there was no way to know how much further this field went. He was out in the middle of nowhere and completely vulnerable. Thinking about the possible attack of an enemy, Jeremiah realized he wouldn't be able to see anything coming near him until it was right on top of him.

At first, he thought the best strategy would be to stay up all night and keep a fire going. Being awake would enable him to spring into action if needed, and the fire would scare off any wild animals. But was this really a good idea? What if it took another full day to get through this field? He finally concluded it would be best to try and get some sleep.

Taking out his Book, Jeremiah read, "When you lie down, you will not be afraid. Yes, you will lie down, and your sleep will be sweet." In another place, he read, "I will lie down and sleep in peace, for it is You oh LORD alone that causes me to dwell in safety." Meditating on these verses, Jeremiah understood that God had brought him into this field for a purpose. He was about to go to sleep in the middle of nowhere, with no protection, and no way to get help from anyone or anything except for God.

After making sure his fire was secure and would burn itself out on its own, Jeremiah climbed into his tent to go to sleep. Just as he closed his eyes, sharp sounds erupted all around, causing him to sit straight up. He couldn't tell if the sounds were from an animal, from the wind, or if he'd imagined them. Maybe his mind was playing tricks on him. He knew he needed to keep his thoughts on the words from his Book rather than on his fears, but he had never felt more vulnerable in his entire life.

Laying back down, Jeremiah thought on another Psalm. "Yea, though I walk through the valley of the shadow of death, I will fear no evil; For You are with me; Your rod and Your staff, they comfort me." He also recalled the verse that said, "Whoever diligently listens to Me shall dwell securely, and shall be peaceful, without fear or dread of evil."

God's word was saying it wasn't his ability to see out into the distance that kept him safe. It wasn't a fire, other people, or anything else that ultimately protected him. It was God alone that could keep him safe. This truth brought to his remembrance another Psalm. "If God does not watch the city, then those who watch it, watch in vain."

Jeremiah closed his eyes, trying to go to sleep. Several times, as he was about to drift off, a sound would snap him back awake. But each time, he would immediately think on God's word again. Finally falling asleep, he slept until rays of sunlight began to shine through his tent. After he packed everything up, Jeremiah prayed for guidance, then searched for his path. Seeing the direction he needed to go, he began clearing the stalks of weeds and trudged on.

When he had walked for what seemed to be several hours, Jeremiah heard a dog barking. His path was going straight toward the sound, so he pressed on ahead a little more rapidly, thinking the end of the field must be near. The vegetation began to decrease in size, and Jeremiah could see that he was close to the end. Just outside the field was a small cabin with a dog on the front porch. As he approached, the dog barked more loudly.

Jeremiah stopped at the end of the field.

A man appeared from inside the cabin and stood beside the dog. "Don't worry about him, he's just excited that we're having company."

Jeremiah marched forward, and the closer he got, the more excited the dog became. Once he stepped onto the porch, the playful German Shepherd began to jump on him. Jeremiah reached down to pet the dog, and the man motioned for him to have a seat in one of the chairs on the porch.

Extending his hand, the man said, "My name is Jack, and my dog there is Samson."

Jeremiah shook Jack's hand, then sat down in the rocking chair next to him. "Nice to meet you, my name is Jeremiah."

The German Shepherd sat close by, and Jeremiah reached over to pet him.

Jack leaned forward and spit off the porch. "So what brings you to these parts?"

"I was traveling," said Jeremiah, as he played with Samson, "and my path led me into that field. I had to spend the night in the middle of it, and I've been trying to get out since this morning."

Spitting again, Jack said, "That's what we call The Field of Trust. God brings travelers through there as a way to help build their faith in Him. Several years ago I felt God led me to build this cabin here, and Samson and I like to think of ourselves as guardians of that field. You may have felt like you were all alone, but I can guarantee you that if there had been any danger near, Samson would have taken care of it. When travelers make it all the way through, we welcome them for a little bit of rest before they continue their journey."

Jeremiah smiled. "I'm so glad God put you two here, but I must say that I would have loved to have known this information last night as I was going to sleep."

Leaning forward in his rocking chair, Jack spit off the porch again. "I'm sure you would have, but would you have learned the same lesson?"

Thinking about this for a moment, Jeremiah knew Jack was right. If he would have known they were so close, he wouldn't have fought as hard the night before to keep his mind centered on God's word.

Jack offered Jeremiah some lemonade and a bowl of fresh strawberries. "If you're not in a hurry, I'd enjoy hearing about what all you've experienced on your journey so far. Listening to others talk about their Quest is what I enjoy most about being out here in this cabin."

While enjoying the snack, Jack provided, Jeremiah started at the beginning and shared his story. When he finished the strawberries, he set his bowl and cup to the side and talked with Jack a little longer as he played with Samson.

After having a great time of fellowship, Jeremiah stood up, preparing to leave. "Thank you so much for your hospitality. This was exactly what I needed after going through that field, but I believe it's time I start on my way."

Reaching down to pet the playful dog one more time, Jeremiah said, "And it was nice to meet you too Samson."

As Jeremiah left the porch, Samson followed him. Jeremiah smiled at the dog, thinking he would only accompany him a little ways and then go back home. But after walking a little further, Samson continued following him. Jeremiah turned around and led him back to the porch.

After patting the dog on the head, Jeremiah departed, and again Samson followed him. Once more, he led the playful German Shepherd back, but as soon as he tried to leave, Samson followed him again.

Jeremiah called to Jack. "It looks like you're going to have to hold him while I leave."

Jack stood up and spat off the side of the porch. "I don't think that's going to be the answer. I've been here for years, and I've never seen Samson try to follow someone as they left. I think God is sending him with you."

Scratching his head, Jeremiah said, "Why would God do that? I thought you said He placed you two here to guard the Field of Trust."

"That's true," said Jack, climbing down off the porch, "but I thought this day might be coming because I've kind of felt Samson had a destiny that went far beyond this old cabin. He fathered some puppies that were born about six months ago, and we've gone over and visited them every day. The mother's owner said I could have any of them I wanted. One, in particular, seems a lot like his daddy, and I felt God might have him take Samson's place here with me someday."

Jeremiah had never owned a pet before, but from the moment he met Samson, he seemed like an old friend.

Petting him on the head, Jeremiah looked back at Jack. "Aren't you going to miss him?"

"Of course I will," said Jack, as he walked over and knelt down beside him. "You don't spend time with a dog like Samson and not develop a strong love for him. But I know that if God is sending him with you, he'll be in good hands. You said you'd be coming back this way in nine months to go to your graduation, so just promise me that you two will come by and spend some time with me when you do."

"I certainly will," said Jeremiah.

Jack took Samson's face in his hands, "I'm going to miss you old friend, but I'll see you again soon."

Jeremiah could tell Jack was emotional, and it seemed Samson understood what was happening.

Jack fought back a tear, as he stood up. "As soon as you two are out of sight, I'm going over to get Samson's son. You never know if God will bring someone through that field again tonight, so we'll need to be ready."

Jeremiah smiled at Samson. "Looks like we're now on this adventure together."

As they started off, Jack made his way back to the porch and watched them leave. When they were about fifty yards away, Samson stopped, turned around, and barked twice in Jack's direction. Jack waved at him and then Samson turned back around and trotted ahead of Jeremiah.

15

PRISON OF CONDEMNATION

Having a dog for a companion was a new thing for Jeremiah, but he got used to it quickly. He was learning more about Samson each day, and it seemed Samson was studying him as well.

After traveling for two days together, they came upon a House of Instruction. Kneeling down to reassure Samson he wouldn't be gone long, Jeremiah told him to stay on the porch while he went inside. A kind young man dressed in a suit helped him find a seat just in time for the singing. It was a great time of praising the Lord, and afterward, the leader gave a wonderful message on the grace of God.

When the service was over, several members came up to Jeremiah and invited him and Samson to a picnic. Jeremiah thanked them and accepted their invitation.

Several ladies had prepared roast chickens, and as they were separating the meat from the bones, one of them observed Samson watching them intently. As soon as she finished clearing all the meat off one of the chickens, she gave a drumstick to Samson with some of the meat still attached to it. In truth, she left a little bit more of the meat on the bone than she had to, but she thought Samson was being very patient as he watched everyone else get their food. After the lady set the chicken on the ground in front of him, Samson picked the bone up in his mouth and trotted over to where Jeremiah was sitting.

Some other young men had joined Jeremiah and were asking him about his travels and experiences. Jeremiah shared with them how he came to start on his Quest, his time at the House of Knowledge, and the adventures he had experienced since then. The young men were intrigued by the different kinds of battles Jeremiah had participated in.

One of them named Paul said, "We've been thinking about going on a mission to free people from a place called the Prison of Condemnation. There are many who once traveled freely on this Quest who are now locked up there."

Jeremiah sat his plate down. "Who put them there?"

"That's what's odd," said Paul, shrugging his shoulders. "No one did. They checked themselves into that prison as one would check himself into an inn. They voluntarily walked into their prison cell, and the door closed behind them."

"Have any of you tried to help set them free before?" asked Jeremiah.

Paul shook his head. "Oh no, the place is well guarded. The best we can do is shouting at them from a distance, but it's difficult for them to hear us."

Jeremiah ran his hand through Samson's fur. "I'd like to see this place for myself."

Paul glanced at the others. "As soon as we're all done eating, we should go together. We can't get too close, but we can at least see the structure and the layout of the grounds."

When they were ready, Paul, and three of his friends—Alan, Shem, and Adam—started out with Jeremiah and Samson to the Prison of Condemnation. They walked for an hour through beautiful terrain. The grass was dark green, with flowers growing all along their path. Large trees clustered in groves played host to a variety of songbirds chirping to one another in a beautiful melody.

At last, they arrived at the top of a small hill, which overlooked a large open area. The region was barren and dry with no grass, no flowers, and no trees. Red dirt covered the whole area, and the air felt humid and stifling.

Paul pulled a telescope out of his satchel and handed it to Jeremiah. "Take a look for yourself and see what we're up against."

Jeremiah gazed through the lens at a large complex made of ugly red clay. The structure was laid out in sections which formed a circle, and each section contained several prison cells. A huge gong hung in the middle of the complex. While he watched, a giant stepped up to the gong and struck it with a large hammer, then yelled out, *"Guilty."* The agitating reverberations coming from the gong could be heard all the way to where the guys were standing, producing an awful feeling of anxiety.

All around the compound, dark angry-looking trolls positioned themselves outside the prison cells and read from a list. After the trolls stated the accusations against the prisoners, the giant would strike the gong and yell out *"Guilty"* once again. Large vultures acted like guards over the complex, flying in circles while screaming words of condemnation.

As Jeremiah watched, a man approached from the far side of the open area below. As the man drew closer, three of the large vultures swooped down on him, stripped him of his armor, and beat him up with their beaks and clawed feet. When at last they let him up, he walked to the prison and into a cell.

Jeremiah gave the telescope back to Paul. "It would be difficult to get near that prison to help those people."

"We know," said Paul, putting the telescope back in his satchel. "We've been here often to pray for those in the prison, but that's all we've felt led to do. As we were talking to you today though, we thought you might be someone God could use to help us do more."

Jeremiah paused and patted Samson on the head. These guys were looking to him for leadership on this mission. Was he ready for that?

He knelt down next to Samson and said, "We'll spend the night, and I'll pray for guidance. Then if my path is heading toward this prison, I'll meet with all of you to discuss what we should do."

Everyone returned to the House of Instruction, still talking about the prison along the way. When they arrived, Alan invited Jeremiah to stay at his house since he had a spare room. Once there, Alan introduced Samson to his dog named Elijah. The two dogs playfully jumped on each other, then ran around the yard together. Alan had fixed a nice place for Elijah to sleep underneath the porch, and Samson joined him there for the night.

Alan then showed Jeremiah to his room. "It's not much, but it's a quiet place to read and pray. We're all grateful you're considering this, and we're hoping to have the opportunity to help those in that prison."

Jeremiah set all his things down on the bed. "This will be just fine. I appreciate you offering to let me use it for the night."

Alan left, leaving Jeremiah alone to consider what God wanted him to do. While thinking about those who were locked up in the

Prison of Condemnation, Jeremiah remembered doing a study on guilt and sin when he was at the House of Knowledge. After looking through his satchel and finding his notes, he looked up all the Scripture references in his Book.

As Jeremiah meditated on the verses, the Holy Spirit brought to his remembrance the things he learned from his professors and through his own study. Before going to sleep, he prayed for wisdom and guidance, knowing that tomorrow could be an important day. For a time on his Quest, he had looked to someone like Rick or Mark for leadership, but now others were going to be looking to him.

The next morning Jeremiah stepped outside to see that his path was heading in the direction of the prison. The reality of leading a mission began to set in, but he knew God wouldn't give him something to do that he wasn't prepared for. When Alan saw Jeremiah's path, he was excited and couldn't wait until they met the others, so after a quick breakfast, they started toward the House of Instruction.

Paul had already asked permission to use a small meeting room downstairs where he, Shem, and Adam were waiting. When Alan and Jeremiah entered the room, the others jumped to their feet to greet them, letting Jeremiah know how excited they were that he was going to be a part of this mission.

As soon as Jeremiah had walked into the room, he could sense the others were looking to him for leadership. He sat down and opened his Book. "Last night before going to sleep, I reviewed a study I did on being trapped in condemnation. I think we should start off by talking about what this Book says about it and then develop a strategy for how we're going to help those in the prison."

Nodding, Paul said, "That sounds like a good idea. We all know the verse that starts out, 'There is therefore now no condemnation to those who are in Christ Jesus.' We've gotten as close to the prison as we could and shouted that verse to the captives, but it doesn't seem to have helped anyone. And to be honest, we aren't sure they could even hear us."

"They probably know the verse," said Jeremiah, holding up his Book, "but they don't understand its meaning. I think we're going to have to do more than just shout from a distance. We're going to have to get closer, much closer in fact. I believe we need to look them in the eye and tell them the truths they need to hear."

Alan sat back and took a deep breath. "That sounds great, but the hard part, of course, is getting past the vultures. And if we can accomplish that, how do we deal with the giant?"

"I don't know yet," said Jeremiah, "but I believe as we talk about what God's word says, a plan will come together."

Paul placed his hand on his chin. "I like that strategy. Jeremiah, since you've studied this before, why don't you share with us some of the verses that stand out to you."

Glancing down at his notes, Jeremiah said, "The first verse I have is, 'For godly sorrow produces repentance leading to salvation, leaving no regret, but worldly sorrow produces death.' "

Jeremiah looked up. "We need to help them understand that it's good to be sorrowful for their sins, but right now they're in worldly sorrow which is only producing death and keeping them locked up."

"Do you have any suggestions as to how we can help them move from worldly sorrow to godly sorrow?" asked Alan.

Jeremiah turned several pages in his Book. "Seeing our sinfulness is painful. When Isaiah saw the holiness of God, he became acutely aware of his own sinfulness, crying out, 'Woe is me! I am undone and a man of unclean lips.' Worldly sorrow offers us a way to deal with this pain without having to give up the sin. We can beat ourselves up and avoid having to repent."

Adam said, "So in a way, worldly sorrow has become a coping mechanism for how people deal with their sinfulness."

"Yes," said Jeremiah, leaning forward, "but instead of just feeling bad about our sin, we have to be willing to turn away from it. We must come into the presence of God with a repentant heart."

"I've been praying about this," said Alan, turning pages in his Book, "and I agree with what Jeremiah is saying. I also think we must tell the captives that when they come into the presence of God, He is not going to relate to them on the basis of their sins, but according to their right standing in Christ."

Jeremiah scooted up his chair. "That's good Alan. Another aspect of this is something the Apostle Paul wrote, 'How shall we who died to sin live any longer in it?' I feel like God is reaching out to me in that verse and saying, 'I've set you free from the dominion of sin so why aren't you living like it?' I think that's important to communicate too."

Alan nodded. "I agree. Not only is there freedom from condemnation, but there is victory over the sin that causes the condemnation in the first place."

At this moment, the leader of the House of Instruction, Pastor John, poked his head through the entrance of the meeting room. "Hello everyone, and nice to see you again Jeremiah. It was great having you and Samson join us yesterday. I've been in my office next door studying, and I couldn't help but overhear your discussion about the Prison of Condemnation. I wanted to let you know that I think you're on the right track."

"Thanks Pastor John," said Paul.

Joining them in the meeting room, Pastor John said, "I'll be starting a series of teachings tonight that will cover Romans 6, 7, and 8, and the main focus will be on winning the victory over our sin. Some think that the solution to condemnation is figuring out a way to ignore our sin, so we don't feel bad about it, but that's not the answer. The way to overcome condemnation is through receiving grace, and we'll only go to God for the amount of grace that we think we need. If we recognize little of our sin, then we'll only approach God for a little of grace, but if we recognize much of our sin, then we'll approach Him for much grace. The grace of God is not so we can ignore our sin, but so we can overcome it."

"That sounds like it's going to be a great series of messages," said Jeremiah.

Pastor John retreated toward the door. "If you all have a moment I'd like to show you some equipment that might help you as you plan your attack."

They followed Pastor John down the hall and into a type of storage room.

Pointing to a long piece of thick rope, Pastor John said, "That rope is made of the same material as your belts, which you received with your armor. It represents the truth of God's word." He knelt down and reached into a crate. "And here are five slingshots with several smooth rocks which represent the hope of Christ. Our hope is not in ourselves or what we can attain on our own, but we are told to place our hope completely in the grace that is revealed to us when we receive Christ."

Jeremiah knelt to examine the rope, and then glanced up at Pastor

John. "Would you like to go with us? It would be great to have you leading us."

"I don't believe I'm supposed to go," said Pastor John, "but I'll pray for you all as you take on this assignment. I have to leave to visit someone, but I'll be back this evening in time to begin the teaching series." He then gave Jeremiah a nod, as if to reassure him that he was able to lead this mission.

The group gathered up the equipment and headed back to the meeting room.

Jeremiah picked up the rope. "I believe these items are going to be of great help to us."

Alan picked up one of the slingshots and began testing it. "I was wondering how we were going to deal with those large vultures, and I think these slingshots could be just what we need."

Paul pointed toward the corner of the room. "We need to take some of those Books to give to the prisoners."

After talking further about how to deal with the trolls and the giant, the entire group felt they had a good strategy for their attack. They prayed for God's guidance and then started toward the Prison of Condemnation.

When they arrived at the top of the hill looking down on the complex, Alan suggested they take some time to practice using their new weapon. He picked up some small rocks and the others did the same. They spread out, put the rocks in their slings and began swinging them over their heads. They then let the rocks go toward a tree branch they used as a target. They practiced and practiced until they were able to hit the spot they were aiming at.

Jeremiah pointed toward the open area below. "As soon as we start approaching the prison, those large vultures are going to attack, so be ready."

He hoisted the long rope over his shoulder and led the group down the hill. As soon as they were out in the open, five vultures swooped toward them. One by one, they swiftly loaded stones into their slings and whipped them over their head. When the vultures were within range, the guys released the stones. Four of the five vultures buckled from the impact but managed to stay in the air. They quickly recovered, then flew off to pick up large rocks and swung back toward the guys again.

As the flying predators approached, Jeremiah shouted, "Get your Shields ready!" He yanked his Shield off his back and held it out.

The vultures picked up speed as they came nearer. When they were within twenty feet of Jeremiah and the others, they hurled the large rocks at them. On each rock was a picture of a sin that the guys had committed earlier in the week.

Jeremiah said to the group, "God's word tells us that if we confess our sins, He is faithful and just to forgive us of our sins, and He also cleanses us from all the unrighteousness and guilt associated with them."

They each confessed their sins and held up their Shields. All but Adam successfully knocked away the rocks.

When Jeremiah checked on the group, Adam lay on the ground with his Breastplate beside him. As the vultures were flying away, Jeremiah raced over to him. "What happened?"

Adam sat up slowly. "When I looked at the rock coming toward me, I saw myself looking at a picture of a naked girl three days ago. I've felt so bad ever since. I've tried to ask forgiveness, but I haven't felt forgiven. I get so mad at myself each time I commit that sin, but it feels like I can't get victory. No matter how much I try to repent, it keeps happening."

Jeremiah scanned the sky then glanced at Adam. "Wherever those vultures went, they will return soon, so we have to get you back on your feet. It would have been better if you had told us about this before we started the battle."

Adam stared at the ground. "I know. The whole time we were talking about how to defeat sin and condemnation I wanted to say something, but I felt so guilty and didn't want you all to look down on me."

Jeremiah extended his hand and helped Adam to his feet. "What matters now is that you must deal with this before the vultures come back. If your Breastplate is not firmly in place by the time they return, you'll have to retreat to the hill. We'll then be short one man as we approach the prison."

Adam dusted himself off. "I desperately want to be free from this sin, and the condemnation that comes with it. But I'm afraid that if I confess and ask forgiveness, I'm only going to do it again."

"Adam," said Paul, looking him straight in the eye, "if you want to be free from this then we'll help you. One of us will talk to you each day to ask how you're doing, and whenever you're struggling, you can come to any of us for prayer. It will be a tough fight, but you won't have to do it alone."

Adam picked up his Breastplate and looked toward heaven. "Dear Lord, I've felt so ashamed each time I've committed this sin, but I don't think I've ever come to You willing to do whatever it takes to get free from it. I wanted You to help me with my guilt, but I wasn't willing to give up the sin. I repent, and I come to You in surrender. I receive the forgiveness and the cleansing that You've made available to me through Your shed blood."

Feeling strengthened and cleansed, Adam fixed his Breastplate of Righteousness firmly in place.

Paul pointed toward the sky. "The vultures have regrouped and are coming this way. Get ready!"

Everyone took up their positions and held out their Shields. This time the large vultures carried smooth, flat pieces of heavy stone. On the surface were pictures of a sin the guys had committed in their past which they had always regretted.

Jeremiah checked to see how the others reacted, then shouted, "Do not be discouraged by what you see on those stones. As far as the east is from the west, this is how far He has removed our transgressions from us."

The vultures circled directly overhead of the group and released the heavy stones. Holding up their Shields, while proclaiming their faith in the righteousness of Christ, Jeremiah and the other guys smashed the stones into small pieces. They then quickly took out their slingshots and loaded them with a stone. They each took aim at one of the predators and successfully struck all five of the vultures. Dazed and barely able to fly, they tried to escape."

Paul quickly reloaded his slingshot. "While they're moving slowly let's hit them again."

All of them slung another stone at the vultures, this time knocking them out of the air. One by one, they landed with a thud and lay unconscious on the ground.

Putting his slingshot away, Jeremiah shouted, "Let's storm the prison."

Everyone ran toward the middle of the complex where the giant was banging the gong.

When the massive creature saw them approaching, he raised his hammer over his head. "You are all GUILTY!"

The giant then roared loudly as he swung his hammer toward the earth and crashed it into the ground, causing a violent earthquake. From the place where his hammer had struck, cracks opened up, then spread toward Jeremiah and the others, as if the earth was trying to swallow them. They jumped back and forth to keep from falling through the fissures, then leaped over new ones that formed. The giant kept swinging his hammer, and each time it struck the earth, the ground shook ferociously. They could barely stand to their feet, and getting closer to their enemy seemed impossible.

Jeremiah took out his Sword and forcefully plunged it into the ground. "My God has brought me up out of the terrible pit, and out of the miry clay. He has set my feet upon a rock, and He has established my feet on steady ground."

He began to sing a song he had often heard in a House of Instruction.

"On Christ the Solid Rock I stand,
All other ground is sinking sand,
All other ground is sinking sand."

The others joined in, and as their praises were lifted toward heaven, the ground rumbled beneath them. The sound grew louder and louder until it was like thunder. Suddenly, at the place where Jeremiah plunged his Sword, the cracks began to close. Then the rest of the fissures closed up as well. When the closing of the earth reached the place where the giant stood, the ground around him began to shake. The giant rocked back and forth and fell to one knee.

Jeremiah held up his Sword. "Now we attack!"

As the group charged toward him, the giant clambered to his feet and swung his hammer overhead. When Jeremiah attacked, the massive creature aimed a blow at him as if to smash him into the ground. Diving to one side, Jeremiah was able to dodge the hammer. The rest of the guys surrounded the giant. Jeremiah motioned for them to start circling around so their enemy couldn't see where their attacks would be coming from.

Alan got in behind the giant and struck him on the back of his legs with his Sword. As the giant turned to swing his hammer at Alan, Paul struck him on the side. Then Shem ran up and slammed his Shield into his knees. Screaming in anger, the giant wildly swung his hammer, as he was being pummeled from all sides. The group continued to pound him until he fell face down on the earth.

Jeremiah took the rope Pastor John had given them and began wrapping it around the giant. "When we confess the truth about our sinfulness before God, we take away this giant's power to bang the gong of condemnation in our hearts."

After the rope was secure, Jeremiah said, "Let's split up and proclaim freedom to all those who are here."

As the group approached the prisoners, the dark trolls transformed into huge bees with long stingers and lifted into the air. Buzzing back and forth outside the prison cells, they were determined to prevent anyone from escaping.

Scanning the complex, Jeremiah called out, "These prisoners are going to have to be willing to fight the stinging venom of condemnation if they wish to be free."

Alan shouted to all those in their cells. "Christ is at the right hand of God, acting as an advocate on our behalf. It is His righteousness that makes us acceptable before the Father and not our own."

Paul held out his Book in his left hand and raised his right hand in the air. "Jesus took the wrath of God that we deserved, becoming a propitiation for us. Because of this, we have peace with God through our Lord Jesus Christ. God is not mad at you! Confess and turn away from your sins, knowing that He wants to cleanse you so you can enjoy fellowship with Him."

All the guys rushed different sections of the compound, and they began throwing Books to any prisoners who wanted them.

Shem shouted, "Bless the LORD, O my soul, and all that is within me, bless His holy name! He has not dealt with us according to our sins, Nor punished us according to our iniquities."

Adam pointed to his Book. "If you are in Christ, God is not keeping a record of your sins to hold against you." He then read, "If You, Lord, kept account of and treated us according to our sins, who could stand? But with You, there is forgiveness that You may be reverently feared."

As the group read from their Books, the prisoners looked up the passages and read them out loud. After hearing the word of God, more of the prisoners asked for Books too.

The huge bees flew back and forth, buzzing loudly. They stuck their stingers through the bars of the cells in an attempt to scare the prisoners. A few of the captives sidestepped them and tentatively opened their prison doors. They raised their Books until they became Swords and began quoting the verses they had just read. With each step, they thrust out their Swords toward their enemies. The bees swayed back and forth, trying to block them from getting free.

Jeremiah shouted to those who hadn't opened their doors yet. "There is no condemnation for those who are in Christ because every accusation that stood against us was nailed to the cross with Him. Stop trying to make up for something Jesus already died for."

Paul shouted, "You've been made dead to sin. It's time to start living like it. Stop trying to deal with your sinfulness through your own efforts and start surrendering to God and His grace."

The prisoners who received Books were filled with hope. One by one, they took a step out of their cells.

Jeremiah held out his Sword. "Now that they've taken the first step, we can help them fight their condemnation."

The group fanned out to assist the captives. Jeremiah joined a young man named Ronnie in his battle. One of the large bees buzzed back and forth still trying to keep him from getting free. Ronnie thrust out his Sword, trying to create some room to escape.

As Jeremiah approached, the bee turned toward him and tried to sting him in the face. Jeremiah raised up his Shield, and the stinger bounced off. Ronnie saw that his enemy was distracted and struck the bee on the back with his Sword. The bee swung around and thrust out its stinger toward his head. Ronnie ducked and then sliced upward with his Sword, cutting the stinger off. Immediately, the bee flew away.

Ronnie joined Jeremiah, and they ran to help others with their battle. With the extra support, the prisoners soon overcame the gigantic bees and cut off their stingers. At last, all the captives who received Books were free.

Jeremiah motioned for everyone to surround the giant who still lay on the ground. "Let's get our rope back and take it with us."

The giant lifted his head up and glared at the escaped prisoners. "It's only a matter of time before you're back here again."

Alan slammed his Shield into the giant's forehead, knocking him out. "Whom the Son sets free is free indeed."

The group removed the rope and then rushed out of the compound. They raced across the open area, and back up on the hill. Once everyone reached safety, they all paused to catch their breath.

Soon the vultures recovered to full strength and flew back toward the prison. The giant regained consciousness and picked up his hammer. Immediately he began to strike the gong and yell out, *"Guilty!"* Within a few minutes, all the bees flew back with new stingers, and as soon as they touched the ground, they reverted back to trolls.

It was too late for the guardians of the prison to do anything about the ones who escaped, but they would be ready for new captives that were sure to arrive.

Jeremiah gazed toward the compound and shook his head. "I wish more had come with us."

Paul nodded. "I do too, but at the same time I'm thankful for those who are free."

Ronnie stood next to Jeremiah and extended his hand. "Thank you so much for the help."

This was his first time leading a mission, and Jeremiah realized he wouldn't always be able to help everyone. He smiled at Ronnie and shook his hand. "You're welcome."

It was a pleasant walk back, and the freed prisoners were praising God the whole way. When they reached the House of Instruction, Pastor John greeted them and invited them to attend his teaching that night and for the rest of the week. They all readily agreed and said how grateful they were to be able to receive teaching again.

Jeremiah stayed on for another week and learned a lot from the teaching series too. During the day, he would spend time with Alan and the rest of the group, while Samson played with Elijah.

Spending time with these guys reminded Jeremiah of his friends at the House of Knowledge. He thought they would be proud of him when they found out that God had used him to lead a mission.

After the week was over, Jeremiah let everyone know that he would be continuing on his journey the next day. Paul, Alan, Adam, and Shem spent some time with him that evening, once again thanking him for leading them on their first big mission. They now felt more confident that God could use them on more adventures.

When Jeremiah was about to leave, Paul took out the telescope he had been using. "I want you to have this."

"Thank you," said Jeremiah, as he reached out to accept it. "But won't you need it?"

As Alan and the others gathered around, Paul said, "We want you to have something to remember us by. I'm sure we'll get another one soon. Just do us one favor. Each time you use it, remember us and pray for us."

Jeremiah nodded. "I will. I thank God that I met all of you, and I know He's going to use you to do many great things."

He shook their hands, then started on his way. Samson said goodbye to Elijah by jumping on him one more time, then trotted to Jeremiah's side.

ELDER JENKINS

A fter traveling for almost a full day, Jeremiah and Samson came upon a majestic inn located on a beautiful piece of property. They stopped for a few moments to take in the wonderful view, then Jeremiah walked up to the door and knocked.

A proper looking fellow named Giles appeared at the door. "Well hello, are you looking for a room?"

Setting his backpack down, Jeremiah said, "Yes, I'd love to stay here a few days if you have something available."

Giles stepped outside and reached down to pet Samson. "We have plenty of room, and we have a nice space in the back where your dog can stay and play with the other dogs whose owners are here."

He first led them to the area where Samson would be staying. It was a wide open space with a stream that flowed through the middle. Samson immediately went to the stream to drink some water, then waded in and splashed around. After exploring his new surroundings, he strolled back over to Jeremiah.

Reaching down to pat him on top of his head, Jeremiah said, "Go on and play. I'll be out here later to see how you're doing."

Samson barked and then ran off.

Giles gave Jeremiah a tour of the grounds, then led him back inside and showed him to his room. After getting cleaned up, he sat on his bed to read from his Book. An hour later, there was a soft knock on the door, followed by an announcement that dinner would be served in fifteen minutes. When Jeremiah came downstairs, Giles showed him to the dining room.

The place was strikingly elegant, with beautiful paintings along the walls, depicting different kinds of nature scenes. In the center of the room was a gigantic table, which looked as if it came out of a king's palace. A large antique china cabinet stood against the back wall, and old mahogany end tables, each holding a custom piece of porcelain, occupied each corner of the room.

The floors looked like they could be a hundred years old, but they were freshly stained with a deep, rich maple color. A large candle chandelier dropped down from the ceiling and hung just above the center of the table.

After Jeremiah sat down, the staff served a dinner of roast turkey cooked to a perfect golden brown, vegetables of all varieties and colors, and mashed potatoes smothered with a rich dark gravy.

An older gentleman named Elder Jenkins seated at the head of the table called down to Jeremiah. "Hello young man. I haven't seen you before, so I assume you just recently checked in."

Jeremiah smiled and wiped his mouth with a napkin. "Yes, I feel fortunate to have found this place. It's a beautiful inn with exquisite grounds."

Elder Jenkins said, "We don't want to appear nosey, but we enjoy hearing how people came to be on this Quest and what adventures they've had."

Jeremiah finished his bite of turkey and mashed potatoes. "I don't think that's being nosey at all. I'd be glad to share some of my story."

Those seated around the table gave Jeremiah their attention, as he told them how he came from the Town of Rationalism and what led him to start on his journey. The guests nodded in appreciation of God's grace as he told them about his experiences in the Building of Reflection and at the Hill of Calvary. He also told them about his attendance at a House of Knowledge and his plans to graduate in a little less than a year.

Elder Jenkins said, "That's a great testimony, and studying at a House of Knowledge is a good way to become grounded in the Christian faith."

They all finished their dinner, and then the staff brought out freshly made strawberry pies. Jeremiah hadn't had freshly baked pie in a long time, so he served himself a piece and dug in immediately. As different guests shared their stories, he discovered there was a lot to learn from the experiences of others.

When they were almost done with their pie, one of the other

guests asked Jeremiah if he had been on many adventures. Setting his plate to the side, he told them about the battle with the Black Knights and his encounter with the Zulon. He then told them of his most recent adventure with the Prison of Condemnation.

Elder Jenkins finished his last bite of pie. "I'm so glad you were able to help those people in that prison. It's been over fifty years, but there was a time when I and some others led an assault there as well. Just like your group, we had some success, but we wished more would have followed us out. We were thankful though for those who did get free, and we learned a great deal about how condemnation works through that adventure. We left some rope and some slingshots at a nearby House of Instruction in the hopes that others would be able to use them in the future."

Jeremiah was surprised those weapons had been used so long before. "I think that rope and those slingshots have come in handy many times since then. In fact, we used them when we attacked the prison. Once the mission was over, we placed the items back where we found them so they can be utilized again."

When they were all finished, the staff began clearing the tables, and Elder Jenkins invited Jeremiah out to the back porch. The scenery was spectacular, and Jeremiah could see Samson still playing out back. It appeared he had made friends with a Great Dane, and they were walking around as if they owned the place.

Elder Jenkins sat down, inviting Jeremiah to have a seat next to him. "If you came from the Town of Rationalism then you must have encountered some resistance once you left."

Jeremiah sat down in a rocking chair next to Elder Jenkins and told him about his encounter with the Wisdom of This World. He then went on to tell about his return visit to the Town of Rationalism, and how he met that enemy again when he was leaving.

Leaning forward as he rocked, Elder Jenkins said, "The Wisdom of This World is afraid of losing people, so it will fight to keep them from starting this Quest. If it does lose someone, then it tries to make sure they are regarded as foolish and ignorant. The Wisdom of This World wants all those within its grip to believe that only they are capable of intelligent thought. It wants them to think that any belief in God, and especially the God of this Book, is a belief that is completely irrational and to be looked down on with disdain."

"I used to be one of those," said Jeremiah.

"So was I," said Elder Jenkins. "You feel so prideful thinking you have everything figured out. It's humbling when God shows you just how small your perspective is. Even today I need God to remind me of just how much I still can't see."

Elder Jenkins took out his Book and began to read. "Oh LORD, You have searched me, and you have known me. You know my times of sitting down and my times of rising up. You perceive my thoughts when they are still far off. You spread out my path before me, and You prepare the place of my lying down. You are familiar with all my ways. Even before I have spoken a word, Behold, Oh LORD, You already know it. You have enclosed me from behind and in front, and have laid Your hand upon me. Such infinite knowledge is too wonderful for me. It is too high, I cannot grasp it."

"That is humbling," said Jeremiah.

Nodding as he rocked, Elder Jenkins said, "Yes, it is. This Book says the fear of the Lord is the beginning of knowledge. You cannot truly understand why you're here and what your purpose is until you know the One who created you."

Listening to Elder Jenkins reminded Jeremiah of how much more there was to learn. One of the things he observed at the House of Knowledge was that young men tended to think they had it all figured out and knew more than all those who have come before. What he was realizing was that wisdom comes through experience, and a wise man will listen and learn.

When other new guests came outside to ask Elder Jenkins some questions, Jeremiah left to play with Samson for a little while. They traipsed around, spending the rest of the day enjoying the scenery. When it was almost dark, Jeremiah walked Samson over to the place where he'd be staying for the night, then returned to his room to go to sleep.

The next day Jeremiah took Samson out again, then returned to his room and spent more time relaxing and reading. The dinner hour appeared to be the time when everyone gathered, so Jeremiah made it a point to come down as soon as the attendant made the dinner announcement. After another great meal and a time of fellowship, he joined Elder Jenkins on the back porch. Once again, Elder Jenkins sat in his rocking chair, motioning for Jeremiah to join him.

After sitting down, Jeremiah said, "I have a question for you. Most of the time, the Holy Spirit directs me by bringing Scripture to my remembrance. At other times, though, I believe the Holy Spirit is speaking things to my spirit. We used to talk about this often at the House of Knowledge, but different people had different opinions. Even our professors didn't seem to completely agree on this subject. What do you think?"

Elder Jenkins stopped rocking for a moment. "We were talking about this sort of thing over fifty years ago when I was attending a House of Knowledge. We should be cautious about going by experiences and thinking we've heard things from God. There were many times, especially when I was new to this Quest when I thought God was trying to impress something upon me, but it turned out to be my own desires and opinions."

Jeremiah nodded. "I've had that happen to me as well."

Holding out his Book, Elder Jenkins said, "As I matured, I learned how important it was to stay centered on God's word. This Book alone is what we should be meditating on day and night. At the same time though, I'm not closed to God communicating things to me in other ways. There are occasions when the Holy Spirit will speak a specific word to your spirit that will be just what you need in that moment."

Jeremiah said, "I often heard some of those on campus say that they wanted a 'Fresh Word' from God. This sounded appealing, but at the same time it seems to imply that the words we already have from God are somehow inadequate and stale."

"That's true," said Elder Jenkins, rocking a little more rapidly. "We have sixty-six different books within this Book, all filled with fresh words from God."

Jeremiah sighed. "It seems there are those on both sides who focus on one thing to the exclusion of the other."

Elder Jenkins sat up, putting his hand on his cane. "There are some on this Quest who live too much by their subjective experiences. They are constantly trying to figure out what God is telling them while spending too little time in this Book finding out what He's already told them. At the same time, there are those on the other side who are relegating their relationship with God to a purely intellectual level. They act as if God is an absentee teacher who only relates to them as a textbook."

Leaning back, Jeremiah said, "I wish we could have both. I wish there was more focus on learning and studying this Book, and on the other side I wish there was more openness to the moving of the Holy Spirit."

Elder Jenkins slowly stood up and walked to the porch railing. "Many times man will stop where he feels comfortable, and then he will build a doctrine to support his feelings. You will find that this happens on many issues."

Jeremiah joined him at the railing and gazed out over the grounds. "I will keep that in mind as I travel my Quest."

After listening to Elder Jenkins share more of his experiences, Jeremiah went to spend time with Samson. Roaming around the grounds, he continued to be struck by how everything, from the landscaping to the architectural design, gave glory to God.

Jeremiah learned that the place was called the Inn of Experience. Over the course of the next four days, he met numerous people who had spent a long time on their Quest, and he learned even more by listening to their stories.

On his last evening at the inn, Jeremiah and Elder Jenkins again sat talking together on the back porch.

As Jeremiah adjusted his rocking chair, he asked, "Is there anything that you feel isn't being emphasized enough today?"

Elder Jenkins leaned forward, pausing to take a deep breath. "One thing I believe we need to stress is the hard work and discipline it takes to make progress on this Quest. I don't feel we're doing that right now."

"What do you mean?" said Jeremiah.

"In our preaching…It's like we're telling a farmer to go out and sprinkle some seed on top of the ground, and then instruct him to talk to it and proclaim some blessings over it, giving the impression that's all there is to it. And then when there's no crop, we teach people to blame the devil. When it comes to spiritual things, we're not instructing people on how to do the hard work of plowing, fertilizing, and getting out the weeds."

"I do recall," said Jeremiah, "that when things got hard for some at the House of Knowledge, they would blame the devil."

This appeared to get Elder Jenkins attention because he stopped rocking and firmly grasped the arms of his chair. "Our main problem is not the devil. What we all have to learn is that our biggest problem is our own sinful flesh. If we can find a devil to blame, then we don't have to do the hard work of crucifying our flesh."

Elder Jenkins opened up his Book. "The Apostle Paul writes, 'But I discipline my body and bring it into subjection, lest, when I have preached to others, I myself should become disqualified.' Then he says in another place, 'But those who belong to Christ have crucified the flesh with its passions and lusts.' These are strong words he's using. We should constantly be striking blows against the sin in our members. If we aren't killing sin, then sin is killing us."

Jeremiah could see that Elder Jenkins was fired up, so he sat back and enjoyed the sermon.

"There's an important battle going on, and some don't realize they are keeping themselves from the battlefield. They cannot be used to fight their enemies until they've first learned to fight their own sinful desires. Leaders of Houses of Instruction are not helping, for they're telling people what they want to hear rather than what they need to hear. The Prophet Jeremiah spoke this word against the prophets and priests of his day, 'For they have healed the hurt of the daughter of My people slightly, saying, peace, peace! When there is no peace.' We're so afraid of offending people that we're not giving them the counsel and instruction they need to overcome their sin."

"Why do you think it's this way?" asked Jeremiah.

Elder Jenkins stood up, signaling he was coming to a conclusion. "This Quest is about taking up our cross daily and following Christ. Many people want the abundant life, but few are willing to live the crucified life."

Jeremiah stood too, and just then, Samson ran up to the porch and greeted them. Elder Jenkins bent over to pat Samson on the head, and talked about some of the dogs that accompanied him at different times on his Quest. When they went back inside, Jeremiah thanked Elder Jenkins for all he had shared with him. He then thanked the others for sharing their experiences as well.

The next day Jeremiah said goodbye to all those at the Inn of Experience, and then he and Samson continued their journey.

17

QUEEN JEZEBEL

Walking along his path, Jeremiah traveled until noon. As he came around a corner, he saw a group of people huddling together about a hundred yards ahead. From a distance, it looked as if they were upset about something.

When he reached the spot where they were assembled, he stopped to listen for a few minutes. From what he could gather, an enemy was blocking their path up ahead, and they were discussing what to do about it.

Jeremiah cleared his throat. "May I ask what kind of enemy is blocking you from going forward on your journey?"

One man named Thomas said, "An evil queen, calling herself Queen Jezebel, has established a stronghold to block anyone from crossing the river. We've tried to get past her soldiers and their defenses, but so far we haven't made any progress."

Jeremiah studied those who were gathered. None of them seemed weak or inexperienced. What kind of enemy could put up such strong opposition?

Jeremiah said, "Could you take me to a place where I can get a closer look?"

"Sure," said Thomas.

He led Jeremiah, with Samson trotting along, to a ridge of trees that would hide them but allow them to see their enemies.

Thomas pointed toward the river. "It looks like they've been building an even larger structure to protect their position, and they've added additional obstacles to make it more difficult for us to attack them. The longer this queen is allowed to stay here, the harder it's going to be to defeat her and her forces."

Jeremiah said, "This might sound like a dumb question, but have you tried finding another way around?"

"Our paths have led us here, and this is the only place where it's safe to cross the river. This queen has picked a very strategic spot to set up her defenses. She knows we must go through this point in order to make progress on our Quest."

Jeremiah took out his telescope and studied the different barriers the queen's forces had built. "One thing I know is that if God leads a person in a certain direction, then He always intends for them to go forward no matter what enemies they are faced with."

"I agree," Thomas said, reaching down to pet Samson. "We've been praying for days asking what to do, but the longer we wait, the stronger this enemy becomes."

Jeremiah stepped back and glanced down to see that his path was leading to the river as well. "I believe I've been brought here to fight with you all."

Thomas straightened up and held out his hand. "We'll take all the help we can get."

Jeremiah firmly shook Thomas's hand to let him know they were going to be in this together.

When they returned to the group, Thomas asked everyone to gather around. "Our enemy has been busy building up more of its strongholds to keep us from going forward. A few hundred feet from the river the Queen's forces were digging large holes, pits really, and covering them up so that as we try to get near, we'll stumble into them."

Jeremiah stepped forward. "Beyond those pits, they've spread out several hundred feet of metal wire that's been twisted around to make sharp edges. I also saw rows of soldiers, and then behind them I saw a large wooden wall that was thirty feet high."

"And," said Thomas, "once we're over the wall, we must face the Queen's strongest soldiers before we get to Queen Jezebel herself."

Many in the group began to hang their heads, because it seemed their enemies were too strong.

Jeremiah could sense their discouragement. "Don't be disheartened. God did not bring us this far to fail. What looks to be an impossible obstacle is an opportunity to trust in God. No matter how big our enemy appears, God is always bigger."

A young man from the group said, "Right now we can't see

God, but we can certainly see our enemy."

Jeremiah replied, "Unless God is as real to us as our adversaries we won't have any hope of winning this battle."

Thomas shifted his gaze from person to person. "Tonight, after the sun sets, we'll meet again. In the meantime, be praying and reading in your Book. God has brought all of us here to this point, so that means He wants to use all of us in this battle."

Everyone went back to their campsites to spend time reading in their Books.

Thomas walked over to where Jeremiah was setting up his tent. "I'm so glad you've been brought here. We need those who believe this is possible."

Jeremiah drove in a tent spike and stood up. "Our enemies want us to think we are defeated before we can even get started. A person who gives into discouragement will never put up a fight."

"Do you have any initial direction?"

Jeremiah reached into his satchel. "The Queen Jezebel in this Book was a fearsome adversary, and it took a strong and determined warrior to defeat her. I believe there is much to learn by reading her story and her eventual demise."

"That sounds like a good idea," said Thomas, as he turned to leave. "When we all gather tonight please share with us anything you've learned."

Jeremiah finished setting up his tent, then settled in to read in his Book. As the sun was setting, everyone assembled to discuss how to defeat Queen Jezebel and her forces.

Thomas addressed the group first. "Jeremiah has been studying to come up with a strategy, and I believe it would be best if we started out by listening to what he's discovered."

Jeremiah stepped forward. "I learned a lot as I read in my Book this afternoon. The first thing I saw was that Jezebel's primary weapons were intimidation and fear. She used these to bring about self-doubt and discouragement. She employed this strategy against the prophet Elijah, but God delivered him from his fears by showing him that His power was infinitely greater than any other power."

Those listening seemed encouraged and sat up a little straighter.

"The next thing I saw was that to defeat Jezebel a person must be bold and determined. God sent a prophet to anoint Jehu as the next king and to tell him to carry out His vengeance against Jezebel.

Immediately Jehu rose up and drove his chariot furiously toward his enemy."

Thomas said, "Did you see any strategies for defeating Queen Jezebel?"

Jeremiah nodded. "When Jehu had successfully killed Jezebel's son, King Joram, Jezebel painted her face, fixed her hair, and looked out a window. She had been successful in the past with seduction, and she tried the same strategy with Jehu. When I went with Thomas to see the enemy at the river, I recognized her front-line soldiers — the Black Knights of Lust. If you haven't faced them before, then you must prepare to face them now."

Some of those in the group shifted around uncomfortably, knowing this was something they needed to deal with before starting the attack.

Jeremiah continued. "When Jezebel saw that lust was not going to work against Jehu, she used her best weapons which were fear and intimidation. She said something very crafty to Jehu as he approached. 'Is it peace, you Zimri, murderer of your master?' "

"Why would she say something like that?" asked Thomas.

Jeremiah held up his Book. "Several years before this, during the reign of King Elah, Zimri was a commander in the army of Israel. He rose up and killed King Elah in an attempt to set himself up as king, but God had not anointed him to be a ruler over Israel. Within seven days, the people rose up and killed Zimri. Jezebel was trying to intimidate Jehu by suggesting that he would also be killed by the people in a short amount of time if he didn't stop and spare her."

Thomas said, "That was very cunning. If Jezebel could have planted doubt in Jehu's mind about what would happen afterward, then she could have kept him from defeating her. I and others have felt that same kind of intimidation since we arrived here."

Jeremiah said, "Jehu was not fazed by this tactic because unlike Zimri, he had been commissioned by God to bring about this judgment. Once Jezebel's power of intimidation and fear was gone, then even the weakest in the kingdom were no longer afraid of her, for it was the eunuchs who threw her down to her death."

"It would appear," said Thomas, glancing around at the others, "that we must defeat this enemy's power in our thoughts before we try to face it on the field of battle. We should do that tonight because tomorrow will be a day of fierce fighting."

Everyone went to their own tent and asked God to show them any areas of lust, self-doubt, fear, or intimidation in their lives. Jeremiah spent time as well, intently searching his own heart. He knew that God wanted to use him as a leader in this attack, and for that reason, he should be even more diligent in his preparation.

The next morning they all prayed together before starting off toward the river. After arriving at the ridge of trees, Jeremiah told Samson to stay there. He knelt down to reassure him everything would be okay. The group quietly moved out together, then stopped about a hundred feet from the river, still being cloaked by a cluster of trees.

Jeremiah motioned for them to crowd around, then pointed out the places where the soldiers had been digging holes. "While the sand covering these pits may look like the rest, if you look carefully you should see some subtle differences in the ground above them."

Two brothers named James and John stepped forward.

James held up his Book. "We volunteer to lead the way. For it is written, 'The steps of a man are directed by the Lord, and He delights in his way.'"

James and John crept forward until they were past the pits. The rest of the group watched so they could avoid falling into any of the holes and then successfully followed. Next, they had to figure out how to deal with the twisted metal wire that blocked their way.

Jeremiah studied the fence carefully. "I believe this wire could be associated with one of the roots of lust which is selfishness. Lust is the desire to use someone else to fulfill our own selfish needs."

Jeremiah took out his Sword. "We should not take advantage of one another in the area of sexual immorality. For God has not called us to impurity but to holiness."

As he quoted this verse, he struck the wired fence with his Sword, slicing through it instantly.

Holding his Sword above his head, Thomas shouted, "Let each of you look out not only for his own interests but also for the interests of others."

As Thomas's Sword made contact with the fence, it sliced through the metal wire as if it was thread. All the others began to quote these verses while striking at the fence with their Swords, and they completely destroyed the barrier.

As soon as the fence was down the Black Knights charged.

Pictures intended to induce lust flashed on the front of their armor.

Jeremiah yelled out, "Keep your thoughts on things that are above where Christ is seated at the right hand of God! Do not allow any space in your thoughts for lust so that you do not fulfill these sinful desires in your mind."

There were at least five Black Knights that each one had to face, and everyone was in a battle. Five of the knights had one young man named Jared surrounded. They knocked him to the ground and pounded on him. Thomas finished off the knights he was fighting and then ran over to help. First, he instructed James nearby to occupy the Black Knights while he helped Jared.

Thomas held out his hand toward him. "We don't have a lot of time for ministry, and I'm going to need you back in this battle quickly. Whatever you've allowed to dominate your thoughts you must repent of right now and receive grace and cleansing."

Jared sat up but stared at the ground.

Thomas gave him a stern look. "We're in a battle. This is no time to give into shame. What matters is what you do from this point forward. Leave your sin behind on this battlefield and determine to make a new beginning right here, right now."

Taking Thomas's hand, Jared pulled himself to his feet, fixed his armor, and readied his Sword. As Thomas and Jared joined back in the fight, they defeated the last of the Black Knights.

Next, the group had to find a way over the thirty-foot wall which had been coated in oil to make it even harder to climb.

After they all prayed, a woman named Martha stepped forward. "I know how we can get over this wall. Our Shoes of the Gospel will provide traction no matter how slick the surface is, and we can drive our Swords into the wall and use them to pull us up little by little."

Thomas instructed everyone to spread out, and they each began to climb the wall as Martha suggested. The oil didn't make it easy, but as they firmly planted their spiked Shoes into the wood and used their Swords as leverage, they were able to make progress.

When everyone reached the top, Thomas said, "The soldiers on the other side of this wall are the most fierce yet. I believe they are Soldiers of Intimidation, and they will not be easy to defeat. Be ready to start fighting as soon as you hit the ground."

As Jeremiah was about to jump down from the wall, he raised up his Sword. "Do not in any way be intimidated by your enemies. Our refusal to be intimidated will be a sign to them of their destruction, but to us it will be a sign of salvation, and that from God."

Thrusting their Swords into the air, they all jumped down together. When they hit the ground, they immediately engaged the enemy soldiers in battle. These soldiers were six feet tall and weighed close to 300 pounds. Their heads looked like those of a wild boar, and their bodies were covered with sharp spikes. The Soldiers of Intimidation carried long chains, with a spiked metal sphere attached at the end. Whenever the metal sphere flew through the air, it made a frightening whistling sound.

The group had to be extra alert because the spiked spheres seemed to be coming from all directions. Since they had diligently prepared for the battle, every piece of their armor was holding up.

Out of nowhere, a spiked sphere whistled toward Thomas's head. Busy fighting another soldier, he didn't see it coming, but before it crushed his skull, a Shield appeared at the side of his head, blocking the metal ball.

Hearing the sphere crash into the Shield, Thomas spun toward the sound and saw Jared.

"Thanks for having my back," said Thomas.

Jared smiled and returned to the fighting. Next to him, Jeremiah was engaged in a ferocious battle with one of the soldiers who kept swinging his chain at his head and then at his legs. Jeremiah blocked, ducked, and jumped to keep from getting hit. He was able to strike the soldier with a glancing blow of his Sword, but it seemed to bounce off without doing any harm.

Suddenly a fireball flew through the air and landed in a hidden trench of oil. Flames shot up, trapping everyone between the large wall and the fiery barricade. Queen Jezebel was sending a clear message to her soldiers: win or be killed, but there would be no retreat.

Seeing the flames behind them, the Soldiers of Intimidation became even more ferocious in their attacks. The spiked spheres filled the air, as the soldiers desperately swung their chains in an attempt to end the battle. But Jeremiah, Thomas, and the other warriors were also determined to win the victory.

One of the largest soldiers whirled his chain above his head, sending it roaring toward Martha.

She charged at the soldier and shouted, "I've not been given a spirit of fear, but of power and of love and of a sound mind."

As the metal sphere zoomed toward her, she knocked it out of the way with her Shield, then ran up to the soldier and pierced him straight through the chest with her Sword. Instantly the enemy vaporized.

They now knew how to defeat the Soldiers of Intimidation.

One soldier kept slinging his chain in a straight line toward Jeremiah. More than once the spiked sphere whizzed past his head, barely missing each time.

After a few more near misses, Jeremiah shook his head. "I'm about tired of this."

The next time the soldier released the metal sphere toward him, Jeremiah ducked to one side, and swung his Sword against the chain, cutting it in half. Severed from its source, the metal ball rolled along the ground and came to a stop. Jeremiah sprinted toward the soldier, blocking what was left of the chain with his Shield as he went. Once he reached the soldier, Jeremiah rammed his Sword into the center of his chest, and immediately, the enemy disappeared.

As the group advanced toward them, the Soldiers of Intimidation began to fight more defensively, but to no avail. One at a time, Swords plunged into their chest, and they vaporized.

When the last one was gone, everyone gazed at the trench of fire, wondering how they would get across.

A voice thundered from heaven. "When you walk through the fire you will not be burned, for I will be with you."

At once, an opening appeared in the trench, allowing everyone to cross over.

All that was left was Queen Jezebel who stood atop a wooden tower that rose forty feet in the air. The Queen had long gray hair, gray skin, and eyes that were blood red with fire. She wore a long black dress that covered everything but her face, feet, and hands. She had long fingernails that were painted black, and on the fingers of both hands were three rings, each containing a black pearl.

As the group approached, Queen Jezebel yelled down in a hideous, screeching voice, "Do you really want to challenge me? Do you know what I can do to you?"

She then raised her arms, and fire flashed from her hands. Twin fireballs raced toward the group where they were standing.

Jeremiah shouted, "Raise up your Shields of Faith, and you'll block all the fiery attacks of your enemy."

More fireballs flew through the air, as they ducked in behind their Shields. Jeremiah started to his left, but a fireball immediately greeted him as he moved. He then darted to his right only to see another fireball coming straight toward him.

Jeremiah yelled over to Thomas, "Our Shields are keeping us safe, but we aren't able to move forward."

Blocking another fireball, Thomas yelled back, "I know. No matter which way I move, I have to stop and raise my Shield."

Everyone was pinned down, but Jeremiah had an idea. "Let's all get in a straight line across, putting our Shields side by side, then we can make our way toward Queen Jezebel's tower.

Thomas passed the word to all those on his right, and Jeremiah did the same with those on the left. Slowly everyone maneuvered into position and formed a line. Jeremiah gave a signal with his Sword to move forward. As one unit, they crept toward the tower. Queen Jezebel saw their advance and hurled even more fireballs toward them, but all harmlessly bounced off their Shields.

Frustrated that her attacks weren't halting the group's approach, Queen Jezebel clinched her fists and pointed her rings with the black pearls toward them. Waves of black smoke emanated from the rings and rolled toward Jeremiah and the others.

Jared yelled out, "I can't see anything."

Everyone came to a stop behind their Shields.

Barely able to see a few inches in either direction, Thomas said, "Jeremiah, are you there? Any idea what we do now? Without being able to see each other we can't keep our Shields together, and we'll be vulnerable to her fireballs."

In his strongest baritone voice, Jeremiah shouted, "Arise, shine; For your light has come! And the glory of the LORD is risen upon you."

Martha began to sing the words of that verse, and everyone else joined in as well, raising their voices to the heavens. As they sang praises to God, light began to disperse the darkness, until the darkness was completely obliterated. With a clear view of one another and the tower once again, they started moving forward. Queen Jezebel desperately pelted them with fireballs, but nothing slowed their progress.

When they were within twenty feet of the tower, Martha lifted her Shield and ran straight toward the tall wooden beams, dodging fireballs as she went. Once she was at the base of the structure, she pulled on one of the beams until the whole framework started to sway back and forth.

Pulling with all her strength, she shouted. "We will not fear or be in dread of our enemies, for the LORD our God, the great and awesome God, is in our midst!"

Jeremiah yelled out, "Let's help her!"

Everyone rushed toward the base of the structure while dodging and blocking fireballs, and once they reached it, they pulled on the support beams until the whole tower came crashing down. Queen Jezebel let out a terrible scream and then flew off.

The victorious warriors cheered and celebrated.

Thomas said, "Let's see what's so special about this river that this enemy would try and keep us from it."

When everyone waded in, they immediately felt a sense of cleansing and purifying.

Jeremiah splashed some water on his face. "I believe this is a River of Cleansing."

Taking out his Book, Jeremiah read, "Let us draw near with pure, honest, and sincere hearts in full assurance of faith, having our hearts sprinkled from a guilty conscience and our bodies cleansed with pure water."

Thomas said, "I'm also reminded of the verse which says, 'If we confess our sins, He is faithful and just to forgive us our sins and to cleanse us from all unrighteousness.'"

Martha read, "Therefore, having these promises, beloved, let us cleanse ourselves from all filthiness of the flesh and spirit, perfecting holiness in the fear of God."

Jeremiah said to all, "Our enemy did not want us to make it to this river. If God has brought you to this point on your Quest, then it must mean you've been working to defeat sin in your life, and this river is providing cleansing from the effects of that sin."

Everyone stayed in the river for a while, enjoying the cleansing relief it provided.

Thomas pointed toward where the battles had taken place. "Look over there."

When Queen Jezebel's tower had collapsed, it fell on top of the thirty foot Wall of Self Doubt and Discouragement and broke it completely apart.

Martha waded out of the river. "Before we continue on, let's clean up this mess and fill in those pits."

When all the debris had been cleared, the group went back to their campsites to pack up. Once everyone was ready to go, they started back toward the River of Cleansing, taking a few minutes to enjoy it again before crossing to the other side. After emerging from the river, they saw that all of their paths were continuing together, all except Jeremiah's. His path was going in a different direction.

Thomas turned toward him. "I wish you and Samson could go with us."

"I've enjoyed this time we've all had together," said Jeremiah, looking around at the others, "and I'll remember you in prayer as I travel. May God bless you in all that you do in service to Him."

They all wished each other well, and then Jeremiah and Samson departed.

Soon afterward, Thomas and Martha would marry, and the whole group became a powerful collection of warriors who would go on to do great exploits for the Kingdom of God.

TEACHER'S HOUSE OF WISDOM

Jeremiah spent several months traveling with Samson, meeting many interesting people, and attending several Houses of Instruction along the way. Each time he attended a service, he always felt welcomed and right at home. Samson seemed to enjoy the picnics that would often follow because he had many other animals and children to run and play with.

On one particular day, Jeremiah's path took them to a large two-story house. Someone around the back was whistling, so Jeremiah started in the direction of the sound. He had just rounded the first corner when an older man with a bounce in his step appeared from behind some shrubbery. Jeremiah smiled, instantly recognizing it was Teacher, the man he met just after going up the Hill of Calvary.

"Jeremiah!" said Teacher, putting down his hedge trimmers. "It's good to see you, and I see that you have a new friend."

Kneeling down, Jeremiah said, "Yes, this is Samson. He's been accompanying me ever since I left the Field of Trust."

Teacher bent to pet Samson. "I do hope you have time to stay for a little while. I've just brewed some tea, and I'd love to hear all about your journey since the time I last saw you. There's a stream nearby for Samson to get some water, and I'll bring out some food for him. He can roam around and enjoy the countryside as we talk."

Jeremiah motioned for Samson to go play, and immediately he took off running all over the property. It didn't take him long to find the stream where he lapped up some of the water. When Teacher brought him some food, he ate a few bites, then took off and ran some more.

Teacher led Jeremiah inside, where he was awed by the enormity of the home. Along the walls were paintings of different scenes from the Book. The main floor was covered in a beautiful carpet, embroidered with the picture of Jesus coming up out of the water as He was baptized by John the Baptist.

The ceiling was covered with a beautiful mural depicting a multitude of people in heaven kneeling before two thrones, one occupied by God the Father and the other by God the Son, Jesus Christ, while the Holy Spirit swirled around like a mighty wind.

After Teacher gave Jeremiah a tour of the home, he invited him to the dining room to enjoy some fresh tea and walnuts. As they enjoyed the snack, Jeremiah shared with him all that had happened since the day they had met.

When Jeremiah finished, Teacher held up his hands. "I am so encouraged by all that God has been doing in your life. If you have some time, you're welcome to stay with me for a few days. I enjoy showing people the many wonderful things in my house."

Jeremiah stood up to look out a window, catching a glimpse of Samson running around. "I'd love to stay for a few days, and I'm sure Samson would enjoy it too."

"That's wonderful!" said Teacher. "You go check on him, and then later we'll have some dinner."

Jeremiah went outside and saw that Samson was having a great time exploring the property. There were many different animals for him to get to know. There were goats grazing in the grass, cows mooing as they whipped their tails back and forth, horses galloping as if they were racing each other, and some ducks waddling near the stream.

There was one gray cat prancing around, which Samson didn't seem too sure about, but he enjoyed the rest of the animals. After spending some time with Samson, Jeremiah went back inside to get washed up for dinner. Teacher had prepared a delightful meal of baked chicken, fresh corn, green beans, and a colorful salad made from the vegetables grown in his garden.

Anytime Jeremiah was around someone with experience in God's word, he tried to gain as much knowledge as possible. So after enjoying a sampling of everything on his plate, he motioned to Teacher that he had a question. "What do you think is the most important thing we need to be learning on this Quest?"

Teacher finished a bite of salad and then reached for his cup of cider. "After we finish our dinner, I'll show you some things that I believe are very important for those who want to make progress on their Quest."

When the meal was over, Teacher led Jeremiah into a room where a man was writing things in a book. Jeremiah discovered that what the man was writing was all of his sins. Jeremiah saw an image of himself on the day he knelt at the Hill of Calvary with the book of his sins sitting next to him. He marveled as all those sins lifted up and out of the book and were placed on Jesus. He also saw how words were coming from Jesus, replacing the sins, and filling the book with all the perfect works Jesus had done while on the earth.

Teacher picked up the book and handed it to Jeremiah. "Keep this on the inside of your Breastplate and always remember it is Christ's righteousness that has been applied to you."

After placing the book inside his Breastplate, Jeremiah said, "I have studied justification by faith alone, but it's different when you see it in pictures like that. It makes it all the more plain that our righteousness is because of Christ and has nothing to do with us."

"Yes that's correct," said Teacher, as they walked back to the table.

Jeremiah sat down and placed his finger to the side of his face. "But we still want to feel like our works matter in some way."

"Our works do matter," said Teacher, "but what's important is the motivation for doing those works."

"What do you mean?"

Teacher removed his glasses and wiped them off. "God does not want what we can do for Him, but He wants us. When we give ourselves completely to Him, then it is He that works through us."

"How do we do that?" asked Jeremiah.

Teacher opened his Book. "Here is what Paul says in Romans, 'Therefore I call on you brothers, by the compassions of God, that you present your bodies as a living sacrifice, holy, acceptable to God, which is an act of your spiritual worship.' "

Teacher put his hand over his heart. "God wants us to give ourselves to Him as a continuous living sacrifice. We don't just give Him part of our day or a certain day of the week, but we are to serve Him continuously in our thoughts and attitudes. We are always aware of His presence as we seek to be pleasing to Him at all times."

"When I was at the House of Knowledge," said Jeremiah, "I overheard many talking about all the spiritual things they needed to do. It seemed more like they were working for an employer rather than living for God."

Teacher nodded. "That's a good observation. Spiritual disciplines such as reading in our Books, prayer, fellowship, etc. are vitally important, but we shouldn't do these things just so we can check them off a list. We may feel as if we've done our duty, but it will produce a false confidence in ourselves rather than a true confidence in God."

"I can see that," said Jeremiah.

Teacher flipped over a few pages in his Book and read, "Work out your own salvation with fear and trembling, for it is God who gives you both the desire and the ability to bring about His good pleasure."

Tapping on his Book, Teacher said, "We are to work out our salvation, but this must be done with fear and trembling, knowing that it is God that gives us both the desire to do the work and the ability to perform it. It will still not be a perfect work, but it will be a surrendered work, and God will take pleasure in it because it brings Him glory."

Teacher stood up. "I believe this is a good time to stop and get some rest. There's much more to see tomorrow. Let me show you to your room, and then you can go check on Samson and take him to the place where he can sleep for the night."

After moving into his room, Jeremiah brought Samson some leftovers from the dinner earlier. As they walked by the stream, Samson jumped in, drank some water and then splashed around.

A few moments later the prissy grey cat walked by. Samson gave a quick shake of his fur, splashing the cat and sending it running away. Samson then gave Jeremiah an "It was just an accident" look. Jeremiah laughed and then led him to a place underneath the porch that was perfect for him to sleep for the night.

When Jeremiah went back into the house, he settled into his room for the night and fell asleep almost as soon as his head hit the pillow.

The next morning he came downstairs to enjoy a delightful breakfast with Teacher.

When they were done, Teacher stood up. "There are some more

things I'd like to show you." Teacher led him outside to watch the shepherd attending his sheep and the lion that was trying to snatch one.

Next Teacher led him to the roof and showed him the same soldiers everyone saw when they came to his house. Jeremiah observed how the first soldier was being aggressive in his fight against sin, while the others were not. He was able to observe the progress of the first soldier while learning from the failures of the others.

As they were heading back downstairs, Jeremiah said, "We often hear that we are to crucify our flesh, but it's difficult to explain exactly how to do that."

Teacher headed for the door. "Let's go for a walk, and we can talk some more while enjoying the scenery."

They strolled around the property and enjoyed the smell of the fresh grass, then Teacher stopped underneath a towering elm tree. "You asked me about putting to death the sin that still lurks in our bodies. The way to do that is to deprive it of its power source. Jesus taught that sinful thoughts are what defile a man, and I believe it's sinful thoughts that nourish our old nature and keep it alive. We cannot allow sin to have free reign in our minds and expect to win the battle against it. When we deny our sinful flesh the nourishment it desires, it will then die for lack of sustenance. That is how we put it to death."

They left the shade and walked to the stream where Jeremiah knelt to get a drink of water. When he finished, he said, "The terms *crucify* and *put to death* are graphic and violent terms."

Teacher nodded. "Yes, they are. What I believe this Book is trying to make clear is that we cannot be casual in our fight against sin. We have to see it as an enemy that is seeking to end our life. Think for a moment how you would respond when faced with that kind of danger."

Jeremiah took a deep breath. "I would fight with every ounce of strength I had, knowing that failure meant death."

Raising his index finger, Teacher said, "That's right. You would fight as if your life depended on it. That's how we're to confront our sinful flesh. We cannot play around, letting a few stray thoughts in here or there. Every thought of sin seeks to do the utmost damage.

Every contemplation of lust would press us into fornication or adultery if it could. Every notion of pride seeks to convince us that we don't need God, and every deliberation of jealousy desires to destroy another person's life."

Jeremiah placed his hand to his chin. "I don't think I've thought about it quite like that, but it's what I need to hear, and it's what I need to remember."

"We all do," said Teacher. "Sin is constantly at work in our members, prodding us to do what is wrong, or hindering us from doing what is right. We read about someone like the Apostle Paul and wish we could be used for God as much as he was, but there's a price to be paid for that kind of power."

Teacher turned toward the house. "This is a good time to take a break and get something to eat. Let's go back inside and fix some lunch, and then I have some more things to show you."

THE LAW

After a refreshing lunch, Teacher showed Jeremiah the three rooms where each person was chained to their sin, and each was facing a door that said "This Way To The Throne of Grace." Jeremiah saw one man remaining in shame and guilt while holding on to his sin, another man dancing around while ignoring his sin, and another man who took his sin into the Throne Room of Grace where he could be cleansed and set free from it.

As they came out of the third room, Jeremiah said, "I don't understand why the one who felt shame and guilt didn't go into the Throne Room and receive grace. He realized he had a problem so why didn't he do something about it."

Teacher motioned for them to go back to the table and sit down. "Have you ever been thinking about something completely innocent, and then all of a sudden your thoughts turn into something perverse? You say to yourself, how could I think such a thing!"

"Yes, and I feel so ashamed when that happens," said Jeremiah, as he sat down.

"And what do you do about it?"

Jeremiah scooted his chair up to the table. "I must confess that often I'm thinking about what I can do to make up for my sin, so I don't have to feel the guilt."

Teacher held up his hand. "And that's exactly what keeps a person from the Throne Room of Grace. When we sin, our first instinct is to do something about it in our own strength. It's painful to admit we are sinful, but it's even more painful to admit we're powerless to do anything about it. Coming to that realization is what it means to die to ourselves. Paul wrote, 'For he who has died has been freed from sin.' "

Jeremiah said, "There are many who would think all of this talk about dealing with our sin is gloomy and depressing, but if they could only know the joy of receiving God's fullness of grace. For when we freely admit who we are, He can then make us who He wants us to be."

"Amen," said Teacher, raising his hands.

Jeremiah set his Book in front of him. "We've talked about taking away the nourishment from our flesh, but I also know that God's word supplies nourishment to our new nature."

Teacher leaned forward and read from his Book, "For the word of God is living and powerful, and sharper than any two-edged sword, piercing even to the division of soul and spirit, and of joints and marrow, and is a discerner of the thoughts and intents of the heart."

Teacher pointed toward his chest. "When the words of this Book penetrate deep into our souls it's like a surgeon's knife exposing what is not right. As God's word is allowed to sift, cut, and judge, it brings about the needed changes in our lives. Listen to the words of our Savior, 'Then Jesus said to those Jews who believed in Him, If ye continue in My word, then you are truly My disciples, and you shall know the truth, and the truth shall set you free.' Continuing and abiding in God's word is what brings about freedom in our lives."

Jeremiah said, "I've known some who said they spent time reading in their Books, but it didn't help them in their battle with sin."

Teacher held up his Book. "We must do more than just read God's word. We must submit to it. James writes, 'Therefore get rid of all uncleanness and rampant wickedness and receive with humility the implanted word, which is able to save your souls.' Sometimes when we learn something of God's word we immediately start thinking of everyone we can apply it to but ourselves. When we read this Book, we must do so with humility, allowing the words to go from our heads down into our hearts."

Jeremiah nodded. "Amen." He glanced around and reflected on the lessons he'd learned over the past two days. "Thank you for showing me all the things in your house."

Teacher stood up. "I'm so glad you stopped by. I enjoy sharing all the truths the Holy Spirit has taught me over the years. Let's go outside for some more fresh air."

As they walked around back, Jeremiah saw that his path was moving away.

Teacher saw it as well. "If you don't mind, I'd like to walk with you a little ways as you continue your journey. I'm sure your path is going to take you to Mount Sinai, and I usually accompany my guests there when they leave."

They went back inside, then Jeremiah gathered up all his things. When they left the house, Samson was waiting for them out front.

As they drew near to Mount Sinai, Jeremiah heard a faint rumbling.

Teacher stopped. "I'm going to let you travel on from here, and I'll go back to my house. I believe you're ready to face what you're about to see, and I believe you're ready to make the right choice."

Jeremiah extended his hand to Teacher. "Thanks again for all that you've taught me."

Teacher shook Jeremiah's hand and then knelt down to pet Samson. Once on his feet again, he turned for home.

Jeremiah traveled until he reached Mount Sinai. He watched as several people tried to climb it, and then were knocked back down to the bottom. He realized that the mountain represented the Law, which demanded that something be done about sin. When it commanded, "Thou shalt not," his sinful flesh responded, "Okay, I'll try harder," but the only honest answer to, "Thou Shalt Not" was, "But I already have, and I know I will again."

After sitting down, Jeremiah began to read Paul's letter to the Romans in the seventh chapter. When he finished, he looked up at Mount Sinai and all those who were trying to climb it. They would start up the mountain with much fanfare and celebration only to be knocked back down after progressing a few feet. Some repeated this process over and over.

Because they were convinced of their ability to climb that mountain, sin was able to keep them within its clutches and continue dominating them. Trying to deal with their sins through their own efforts only ensured that they would stay trapped in their sin.

Jeremiah remembered reading in the previous chapter that sin would no longer have dominion over him because he was not under law but under grace.

Toward the end of the seventh chapter, Jeremiah saw a

tremendous honesty in the Apostle Paul. He was able to admit that within his flesh there was nothing good. He went even further and confessed that his sinful flesh was continuously trying to sin, while at the same time he was unable to do anything good through his own efforts. Paul cried out, "What a wretched man I am! Who will deliver me from this sinful body of death?"

Jeremiah bowed his head. "Lord, give me the humility to be just as honest as the Apostle Paul about my sinfulness."

Continuing to read into the eighth chapter, Jeremiah saw that there was no condemnation to those who were in Christ. In Christ, he had died to the Law and all its demands so that he might be free to live to God. In Christ, the Law had lost its power to condemn him.

Jeremiah saw that he was under a new law. The Law of the Spirit, of life in Christ Jesus, had set him free from the law of sin and death. He now served in newness of the Spirit and not in the oldness of the letter.

He understood why Paul's critics would say to him, "Why not then continue in sin that grace should abound?" But they did not understand this wonderful teaching of grace. He had not been made free from the Law so he could live in sin. No, he had been made free from the Law so he could bear fruit for God. Trying to climb that mountain would keep him trapped in sin, but surrendering to God would set him free from it.

As Jeremiah stood up, he concluded that the Law kept sin alive because it kept his old nature alive. The true purpose of the Law was to drive him to the cross where something could be done about his sin. His desire was to die daily at the cross, so that the resurrection life of Christ could work through him. It was this process of surrender that would give him victory over sin and empower him to keep God's wonderful commandments out of love rather than out of duty.

Jeremiah turned from Mount Sinai and entered the Valley of Humility. He knelt to read each paper that was lying on the ground, eating each one and allowing the words to go deep into his soul. He would not plead his own goodness, but he would only boast in the cross of Christ.

20

GRADUATION

When Jeremiah and Samson emerged from the Valley of Humility, they traveled until arriving at a House of Instruction. Discovering they had made it just in time for the service, Jeremiah stepped inside to enjoy the preaching of God's word. Afterward Jeremiah spoke with the leader, Pastor Mike, and handed in the last of his schoolwork.

Pastor Mike informed him that graduation at the House of Knowledge would be in one week. He then asked Jeremiah to stay for an hour so he could grade the assignments for him to take with him. He had handed in other assignments while visiting other Houses of Instruction over the past year, and they had been mailing them back to the House of Knowledge. But in order for this last one to make it on time, he would need to carry it there himself.

Jeremiah went outside and talked with many of those who had attended the service, while Samson ran around playing with the children who were there.

Once the hour was up Pastor Mike came out and handed him a sealed envelope. "Here you go. From the looks of these assignments, I don't think you're going to have any problems graduating. And if you see Professor Williams, tell him I said hello."

"Thanks," said Jeremiah as he placed the envelope in his satchel, "and I'll certainly give your regards to Professor Williams."

Jeremiah said goodbye to many of the parishioners, and then he and Samson started on their way. As they were traveling, he remembered promising Jack that he would bring Samson by to see him on his way to graduation. Five days later, Jeremiah spotted Jack's cabin in the distance. As soon as Samson recognized where they were, he took off running toward the cabin. When he got closer, another dog jumped off the porch and began barking.

Samson came right up to the other dog, and they both stopped. After a few moments of walking around each other, they both began to playfully jump around.

Jeremiah caught up and approached the cabin. Jack came out onto the porch, smiling as he watched Samson and Gideon play together.

Spitting off the side of the porch, Jack called out, "I see that you made it back."

Jeremiah climbed onto the porch. "Yes I did. It's been quite a year."

Jack spit off the porch again and motioned for Jeremiah to have a seat. "I bet you and Samson have had all kinds of adventures."

"We certainly have."

Jeremiah sat down and watched Samson play with his son as he told Jack all about the different adventures of the past year.

Jack shook his head in amazement. "God has certainly been using you. Where will you go after graduation?"

"I'm not sure. This entire journey has been a walk of faith, so we'll see what God has planned."

Jack set out some food and water for Samson and Gideon, and then brought out some freshly cooked pinto beans and cornbread for himself and Jeremiah.

As they were eating, Jeremiah pointed at Samson. "You know Jack, that day I left here I wasn't too sure about having a dog travel with me, but over these past nine months, I've grown almost as close to Samson as to anyone I've known. We've become great friends, and sometimes it's as if we understand each other even though neither of us knows what the other is saying."

Jack finished a big bite of cornbread, then washed it down with a drink of apple cider. "I know how you feel. Samson is a special dog, and his son Gideon is like him in so many ways."

When they were finished eating, Jeremiah let Jack know they would have to go so they could make it to graduation in time.

Jack stood up, reaching out his hand. "Thank you for bringing Samson by. I'm glad I got to see the both of you. I don't know if you'll ever be by this way again, but if you are, know that you're both always welcome."

Jeremiah nodded as he shook his hand. After picking up his backpack, he walked off the porch.

Jack followed and called Samson over, then knelt down to give him a hug. "I've missed you old boy. I'm glad I got to see you again."

Jeremiah wanted to give them some space to say goodbye, so he walked off about ten yards from the cabin.

Jack gave Samson a final embrace. "Goodbye, my friend."

Jeremiah adjusted his backpack, preparing to leave. Samson glanced back at Jack and then trotted over to Jeremiah.

He knelt down and rubbed Samson on his back. "It's time to go."

As they headed off, Gideon ran up and barked. Samson barked back, and then Gideon went back up on the porch with Jack.

Turning to wave one more time, Jeremiah set out for the House of Knowledge. He couldn't wait to see all of his old friends as well as his instructors.

After another day of traveling, he finally arrived. As he stepped on campus, a flood of memories poured through his mind. Owen Hall stood immediately before him, the place where he had taken most of his classes. Soon he passed the chapel where a few students were gathered. They appeared to be engaged in fervent prayer, but he wasn't sure if they were praying for revival or for their grades.

Jeremiah's next stop was the main office building where he handed the staff the sealed envelope with his final coursework.

Ms. Simpson, the Dean of Academics, who always had a cheerful demeanor, stepped out of her office to greet him. "Welcome back, Jeremiah! We've received all your other assignments, and we just need to check over this last one that you've brought us."

"Thank you," said Jeremiah as he took a seat in the hall. "I'll wait right here."

Within thirty minutes, Ms. Simpson came out smiling. "Congratulations! You are qualified to graduate tomorrow."

Standing up with a wide grin on his face, Jeremiah said, "Thank you Ms. Simpson. You and the other staff members have been so helpful to me while I was here."

Ms. Simpson gave him a quick hug, and then Jeremiah started toward his old dorm room in Edwards Hall. He was both excited and nervous, as he walked the familiar path across campus. What had everyone been doing this past year? What kind of adventures did they have? Did Mark have a new roommate?

When he arrived outside his old room, he took a deep breath and knocked.

The door swung open, and there stood Mark eating an apple. Jeremiah grinned as he flashed back to the first time he had knocked on this door.

Mark looked surprised at first, but then immediately gave him a hug. "It's so great to see you again Jeremiah!"

"It's great to be back!" He stepped inside where all his old friends Rick, Aaron, Eric, and Greg were gathered.

They all stood up immediately and crowded around him.

Mark heard barking. "I didn't know there was a dog around here."

"Oh, that's my new friend," said Jeremiah, walking back to the door. "Let me introduce all of you to Samson."

Everyone followed Jeremiah outside where Samson jumped and barked at a squirrel staring down at him high up on a tree branch. Jeremiah's friends each petted him on his head, back, neck, and behind the ears all at the same time. Samson loved the attention, and they continued to play with him while they got caught up on everything that had been happening over the past nine months.

After exchanging stories, Mark took Jeremiah to go pick up his cap and gown for the graduation ceremony the next day. When he received his commencement attire, Jeremiah held up the black and red gown, then examined the black cap. All year long he'd looked forward to graduation day when he could proudly wear these colors. The next stop was the cafeteria, a familiar place to any student.

Along the way, Mark said, "As you saw, I don't have a roommate, so you're welcome to stay with me tonight."

"I'd like that. It'll be just like old times."

After arriving at the cafeteria and finding a seat, Jeremiah and Mark shared more stories from the events of the past year. Mark was amazed at all the adventures Jeremiah had experienced. When they were done, they walked around campus and greeted many of the other students. After heading back to their dorm, Jeremiah found Samson a comfortable spot outside to rest for the night.

Though it was time to go to sleep, Mark and Jeremiah sat up in their beds talking, just like they had so many nights before.

"So Jeremiah, what's next?"

"I'm not sure. I've known for the last year that this step in my life was coming, but I haven't really thought about what happens next. What about you guys, have you talked about what you're going to do?"

"Yes, we all want to travel together for a little while, and then we want to start a House of Instruction together. Why don't you come with us?"

"I'd like to," said Jeremiah, "but I don't know if that's where my path will lead. I feel there's something important coming up for me soon, but I'm not sure what it is."

Mark adjusted his pillow. "After the graduation festivities tomorrow, we're all going to stay one more night, and of course we want you to stay with us. We're planning to meet here in this room for one last evening together, then we're going to leave the next day."

"I feel certain Samson and I will be able to stay another day," Jeremiah said, as he settled into his bed to go to sleep.

Mark reached over to turn off the oil lamp. "That'll be great. All the other guys will be glad to hear you're staying."

The next morning everyone woke up early to prepare for graduation. There was a quick practice after breakfast, so they knew how to walk in during the processional, and then all the graduates went to a nearby building to wait as the guests arrived and were seated. When it was almost time for the commencement to begin, Ms. Simpson led all the graduates to the edge of the field where the ceremony would take place.

From their vantage point, the graduates could see all their friends and family waiting for them to march in. Jeremiah wished he could have invited some of his friends from the Town of Rationalism, but he wasn't sure any of them would have come. He wasn't sad though because God had given him so many new friends, and he was thankful for each one.

The music began to play, and the line of students inched forward. As Jeremiah marched to his place, his mind flashed back to his arrival on campus. Many questions filled his thoughts that day. How would he be received? Would he make new friends? What would his classes be like? Would he succeed? Approaching his designated seat, Jeremiah realized everything had gone better than he could have imagined. He would always be grateful for the time spent here.

When all the students were in their positions facing the platform, the music came to a stop. The Dean of Christian Studies stepped forward to pray and then asked everyone to be seated. There were many different speakers, and then the president of the House of Knowledge stood up to address the students. He was short and plump with the gray hair of a man in his sixties, but the youthful exuberance of a teenager.

Taking his place at the podium, the President looked out over the graduates with the delighted smile of a parent. "I want you students to know how proud we are of all of you. We know it hasn't been easy, but you've shown that through hard work and perseverance you can accomplish your goals. While you've been here, we've given you what we know, but our ultimate goal was to give you who we are.

"I, our instructors, and all of our staff seek to live a life that is pleasing to our Lord Jesus Christ. We live each day knowing that without Him we can do nothing. We desired to be an example for you to follow in your own daily walk with our Lord and Savior. As you're about to leave us and continue on your Quest, we know that a part of us will go with you.

"As you travel forward from this day, I cannot tell you that life will be easy or without challenges. We must all endure hardships as good soldiers of Jesus Christ. What I can tell you is that as you place your faith and trust in Him, all things will be worked out for your good. So in those moments when it feels like God is not there, and all hope has faded, know that God will never leave you or forsake you. He will always be an ever-present help in time of trouble.

"I hope to see many of you again as we all continue on this Quest, but what I know for sure, is one day there will be another graduation ceremony at the Judgment Seat of Christ. If I do not see you again before that time, I know I'll see you there. May God bless you in all your ways."

The President motioned for one of his staff to bring him the diplomas, then he turned toward the graduates. "Students will you please rise."

All the graduates stood with their shoulders back, heads held high, and a smile of accomplishment on their faces. After forming a line at the bottom of the steps going up to the stage, they climbed the stairs one by one when the President called their names. He handed them their diploma and then gave each a hug.

As Jeremiah drew closer, he felt a sense of excitement.

At last, the President called his name.

Beaming with a cheerful smile so big it looked as if he'd filled his cheeks full of air—Jeremiah reached the stage. The President held out his right hand while holding out the diploma in his left hand. Jeremiah quickly wiped his palm on his gown to remove the nervous perspiration, then proudly shook the President's hand and accepted his diploma.

At that moment, Samson barked three times. The students and guests chuckled. Jeremiah did too, and he realized God had sent someone to clap for him after all.

After each student received their diploma, they walked back to their original positions while remaining standing. Finally, the last graduate crossed the stage, waving his diploma, and then took his place at the end of the row.

The President held out his hand, motioning toward the graduates. "To our staff, our faculty, and all of our honored guests, I present to you our graduating class."

Loud applause rose up from the guests, and several students threw their caps into the air. Jeremiah threw his cap up in the air as well, but before it could land, Samson came flying out of nowhere and caught it before it hit the ground. Samson then walked over to Jeremiah and presented his cap to him. Kneeling down, Jeremiah hugged him, then took the cap from his mouth.

All the guests and families of the students gathered around to congratulate them. Ms. Simpson appeared on the stage to announce that the staff had prepared a reception. She then directed everyone to proceed to the dining room. As he mingled, Jeremiah spoke with all his instructors and all the other staff members. He thanked them for what they had done to welcome him and for treating him as if he was a part of their family.

The last person to come up to him was Professor Williams, smiling that peculiar smile. "Congratulations, Jeremiah!"

"Thank you Professor Williams. I learned many things in your classes that I'll take with me everywhere I go."

The intense smile from Professor Williams changed just a little, becoming more of a relaxed smile. "I want you to know that I saw tremendous potential in you from the first day we met. I felt it was my duty to challenge you to realize every ounce of that potential while you were here."

Jeremiah laughed. "I certainly felt challenged."

Professor Williams laughed as well but swiftly looked around to make sure no one else saw it. He then placed his hand on Jeremiah's shoulder. "God has called us professors to prepare students such as yourselves, knowing that what we deposit in you, you'll deposit into the lives of many others."

"I thank God for all the time you and the other professors poured into our lives."

Professor Williams patted Jeremiah on the back, as he turned to leave.

Jeremiah called out, "Oh, Pastor Mike says hello."

Professor Williams looked back. "Ah yes, I remember him." He then went to speak with some of his other students.

While standing in line to get some punch, Jeremiah talked with many of the other graduates. He eventually made his way over to his five best friends. Rick and Greg were not alone though. Two young women stood next to them, whom they had met just after Jeremiah left.

Rick stepped forward holding one of the young women by the hand. "Jeremiah, I'm not sure if you remember Lisa, but she and I have been spending a lot of time together this past year."

Jeremiah nodded toward her. "It's nice to meet you, Lisa."

Greg also stepped forward with a young woman on his arm. "And Jeremiah, I would like to introduce you to Anna. She and I have been spending a lot of time together as well."

Jeremiah nodded again. "It's nice to meet you too, Anna."

Suddenly, Rick and Greg, each reached into their pockets and pulled out small boxes. They then dropped to one knee. Lisa placed her hands over her mouth, while Anna grasped Greg's shoulder.

Both Rick and Greg opened the boxes to reveal rings and then took turns speaking.

Rick took Lisa's hand. "I've been waiting to do this almost since the day I met you. I'm completely in love with you. I've been so blessed since you came into my life, and I want to spend the rest of my days with you. Will you marry me?"

Taking Anna's hand, Greg said, "Each passing day that I've known you, I've felt an ever-increasing love for you. You make me feel more alive than I've ever been. I want to be with you for all of my life, showing you each day just how special you are. Will you marry me?"

Both girls smiled at each other, then at the guys holding the rings. The girl's parents gathered around as did more friends.

Lisa's father put his arm around her. "I want you to know that Rick wrote to us a few weeks ago, asking to meet us in order to discuss his future with you. We wrote back to let him know we would arrive a day early for the graduation and stay at a nearby inn. Yesterday we met with Rick for several hours, and he asked for my permission to propose. Your mother and I talked it over and gave him our blessing."

Anna's father told his daughter the same thing about Greg.

Both girls began to smile even more.

Anna's father said, "Well are you going to give these boys an answer or not?"

Both girls almost simultaneously said, "Yes!"

Rick and Greg hugged the girls, and their friends began congratulating them. What Rick and Greg didn't know was that both girls had also written to their families and told them that they felt these were the men they were supposed to marry. They planned to introduce them to their parents at graduation.

The reception continued for another hour, with everyone thoroughly enjoying themselves, but eventually, the guests began to leave. Most of the graduates had made plans to depart right after the reception, so there weren't many left on campus by the time evening came. Just as planned, the close friends gathered together in Mark and Jeremiah's room.

Jeremiah spoke first. "Wow guys, I didn't see that coming. Congratulations again!"

Rick glanced over at Greg. "Thank you. We've been talking about the possibility of doing this for a little over a month, and we both decided to write to the girl's parents and see what they thought. When they both agreed to meet us yesterday, everything came together."

Greg said, "We wanted to say something to you guys, but we needed to keep this a secret so it would be a surprise. Anna and Lisa are best friends, and Rick and I thought it would be a great idea for them to be engaged on the same day."

"So does this change any of the plans you've made?" asked Jeremiah.

Mark, Aaron, and Eric had been wondering the same thing.

Rick responded, "No, Greg and I talked to the girls about what might happen after graduation, and how great it would be if we were all involved in starting a House of Instruction together. We've known that Lisa and Anna's parents live near each other, and yesterday we found out that there isn't a House of Instruction within an hour of their place."

Greg put his hand on Rick's shoulder. "So, yesterday after we had talked to the parents individually, we joined both sets of parents together for dinner and talked about starting a House of Instruction near them. I know this is kind of sudden for the rest of you guys, but this is our surprise to you as well. We've all known we wanted to do this together, but we weren't sure where we would end up. If the rest of you are in agreement, we'd like to start this House of Instruction in Cedar Grove. The girl's parents have promised to help in any way they can, including furnishing many of the supplies we'll need."

Mark said, "Well, I can't speak for everyone, but this sounds like a great idea to me."

Aaron and Eric agreed.

Rick turned to Jeremiah. "We still want you to consider being a part of this with us. Lisa and Anna are going back with their parents tomorrow, and we're supposed to meet them in a week to get started."

"It all sounds great," said Jeremiah as he glanced at his friends, "and I'll certainly pray about it, but I'm feeling that my path will probably go in a different direction."

Mark motioned for everyone to come together in a circle for prayer. "Well, we have at least one more night together, and I say we pray about what comes next."

"Wouldn't it be nice to have one more adventure together?" said Aaron before bowing his head.

After prayer, the rest of the guys left, and Jeremiah and Mark prepared to go to sleep. When they woke the next morning, they headed to the dining hall for breakfast. On the way, they saw that all their paths were heading in the same direction including Jeremiah's.

Jeremiah stooped down and placed his hand under Samson's chin. "Well old boy, it looks like you're going on an adventure with me and my friends."

Samson barked as if he was excited about the idea.

21

MOVING FORWARD

While the others packed for their upcoming adventure, Rick and Greg met with their fiancées and their families. After saying goodbye to the girls and assuring them they would see them in a week, they went back to their dorms to pack.

Jeremiah and Mark started cleaning up their room for the last time.

"Seems like yesterday," said Jeremiah, "when I just moved in here. I still remember that first night. I was nervous, but you really helped me feel at ease. That was the moment I felt like everything was going to be okay."

Mark swept some trash into a dustpan and emptied it into the trashcan. "I was nervous too. You probably didn't realize it at the time, but although you were new to the Quest, you appeared to have it together. I was just hoping I could be a good example for you."

Jeremiah placed the bed frames back in their place. "That's surprising to hear, because I felt challenged being around you. You were always pressing toward that next level in your relationship with Christ, and I wanted to be right there with you."

Mark tied up the trash bag and set it down near the window. "I guess it just proves the principle in Scripture that even as iron sharpens iron, so do good friends in Christ."

As Mark and Jeremiah set their backpacks next to the door, Rick, Greg, Aaron, and Eric arrived. Standing there in the room where they had spent so much time together, they silently acknowledged what this moment meant. This room represented their friendship, and the bond they would carry with them forever.

Rick set his backpack down and sighed. "I have so many

memories of the times we shared here."

"I know," said Greg. "We studied together, laughed together, prayed together, and shared God's word together."

Jeremiah nodded. "Each time we met here, I felt encouraged and motivated."

Mark put his hand on Jeremiah's shoulder. "After you left, there were occasions when we had some intense times of prayer for you. We didn't know what was going on, but we felt we were right there with you, battling whatever it was that you were dealing with."

"Thanks," said Jeremiah, "there were many times in the past year when I needed that kind of support."

Aaron prowled from one corner of the room to the other as if he was examining every square inch. "I wonder about the next group of guys that will live here. I hope they take advantage of their time to build a solid foundation for the rest of their Quest."

Rick said, "Meeting together certainly helped all of us."

They all fell silent. It was one of those moments that was ripe with emotion. At last, Rick gave Mark a slap on the back, signaling it was time to go.

When they reached the edge of the campus grounds, they looked back as if to take one more mental picture of the place where they had spent so much time and learned so much.

"I'm going to miss this place," said Eric, setting down his backpack for a moment.

"Me too," said Greg.

Jeremiah sighed. "I know I was only here for a year, but it was the first year of my Quest, and it was everything I needed after coming out of the Town of Rationalism."

Mark looked back toward the campus. "I think what we'll miss more than anything is the people. We'll miss the instructors, the staff, and all the students we spent time with."

Rick looked at each of the guys. "That's true, but we're so blessed to be able to begin this next phase of our Quest together. We're going to meet so many new and wonderful people that God is going to bring into our lives."

"Amen," said everyone, then they started on their journey.

Their path took them to the place where they helped the families to fight off the flying baboons and the wolves. Tom and Susan came out to welcome them and invited them to stay for lunch. When the other families learned they were there, it turned into a picnic with everyone joining in. Rick and Greg told the families of their plans to build a House of Instruction soon, and the community insisted on giving them some money to put toward the building.

Tom gave the guys an update on their House of Instruction, which had tripled in attendance since the last time they were there. When they finished eating, the recent graduates thanked their friends for their hospitality and their gift. Tom and Susan gave them a tour of the finished House of Instruction, and then they departed.

From there, their path took them to the homes of other families they had helped on various weekend adventures while at the House of Knowledge. Everywhere they stopped, the people expressed their gratitude and wished them well in whatever God had in store for them next.

After traveling for an hour, their path led them toward a thick forest. As they stood outside the entrance, a soft melody greeted them from within. Even though there was no wind, the trees appeared to sway back and forth to the music. Inching forward, the guys entered the forest, while keeping their guard up for the first sign of danger.

As they traveled further, the music sounded as if it was coming from all around them. Soon they heard the faint echo of singing from multiple voices—a soft, melodic, and hypnotic tune. As the melody grew louder, colorful strands of lights swirled around the tops of the swaying trees, seemingly dancing with them. Slowly the lights descended through the branches. When the colorful beams were within ten feet of the guys, they realized the lights were images of beautiful young women clothed in multi-colored dresses.

"What is this?" said Mark, looking up at the beautiful figures.

Jeremiah put his hand on his Book, ready to raise it if necessary. "I'm not sure."

Now the figures began to whirl around the guys, singing an even more hypnotic tune, and looking even more beautiful.

"Are these the heavenly beings we've heard about?" asked Greg, admiring the shapes of the figures.

The beautiful creatures whirled around them once more then rose into the trees. Moments later, they descended again and came even closer. Each of the guys felt drawn to the movement and the shape of the forms dancing around them. When they left, the guys longed for them to return and come closer. Soon the figures descended right next to them and touched them ever so slightly, then rose up out of sight.

All of the guys stared into the trees, hoping the beautiful figures would return soon. The slight touch of those beings injected pleasure throughout their bodies.

Samson started to bark, but the guys patted him on the head and told him to be quiet.

To the delight of the guys, the figures returned but stayed just out of reach as they sang the words, "Sit down. Sit down. Sit down."

At once as if in a trance, the guys reclined in the grass. One by one the figures touched them on the shoulder, then flew up into the trees.

"They're so beautiful," said Aaron.

After a few minutes, the enchanted beings swirled down again, singing the words, "Lie down. Lie down. Lie down."

The young men, now responding almost robotically, stretched out on the ground. The alluring images touched them on the shoulder before whirling back up into the trees again. The next time the beautiful figures flew down, they hovered over the young men but just out of reach.

"Follow us. Follow us. Follow us," sang the exotic figures in unison.

The young men knew they would not experience the touch of these dazzling creatures unless they followed them. As the guys sat up, they saw the beautiful figures going toward a dark and winding trail. Longing for another touch of pleasure, the guys stood.

Suddenly, Jeremiah shook his head in an effort to shake off the trance. "What are we doing?"

The figures quickly flew back toward the young men and swirled around their heads. In a hurried tone of voice, they sang, "Come with us. Come with us. Come with us."

Rick looked around at the others. "I'm with Jeremiah. What are we doing? This isn't right."

Each of them took out their Books, raising them until they

became Swords. The figures began to swirl furiously among the trees, and when they approached the group again, they didn't look the same. They were now dressed in black and had wrinkled gray faces. Their eyes were blood-red, and their ears were pointed and hairy. Protruding out of their hands were long, sharp needles.

Each time these figures had touched the guys, they injected them with a potion that made them feel pleasant but also numbed them to all other sensation. The needles served another purpose as well—they extracted spiritual energy every time the guys surrendered to their touch. Seeing these hideous beings as they really were, showed the group what had been happening to them.

The voices of the figures now sounded deep and menacing. "If you will not come with us, then you will not leave this forest!"

Jeremiah raised his Sword. "I will flee youthful lusts, but I will pursue righteousness, faith, love, and peace, as I call on the Lord with a pure heart."

All of the guys repeated the same verse as they prepared for battle. The hideous creatures hissed as they buzzed around them, looking for an opening where they could inject their needles. Each of the guys thrust out their Shield in different directions, blocking the needles before they made contact.

Rick shouted, "We need to do what that verse says and get out of here quickly."

As the guys headed for the exit, the figures moved to block their way.

One spoke in a screeching and condemning voice. "Why do you want to leave all of a sudden? It was you that wanted us, remember?"

The ugly hags laughed a wicked laugh, showing their black teeth, as they stretched out their hands to reveal their needles.

Jeremiah lunged at the figures with his Sword. "As a young man, I will keep my life pure by keeping a guard over it according to the word of God."

The figures dashed out of the way, then regrouped a little further ahead where they could still block them from leaving.

Striking out with his Sword, Mark said, "I will not give anyone a reason to look down upon me because of my youth, but I will be an example to all believers in my speech, my love, my faith, and in my purity."

Swirling away to avoid Mark's Sword, the creatures then flew back, once again positioning themselves further down the path, still trying to block them from exiting the forest.

As the guys drew closer, the ugly hags hissed, then sang in a hideous tone, "You're filthy, you're dirty, you're just like us!"

Rick ran toward the figures, holding out his Sword. "Whatever is true, whatever is honorable, whatever is just, whatever is pure, whatever is motivated by love, whatever is commendable, virtuous, and worthy of praise, these are the things I will think on."

Following Rick's lead, everyone rushed toward the creatures with their Swords, sending them flying up into the air.

Jeremiah pointed toward the exit. "Let's make a run for it."

As the guys started to sprint, they realized they had less energy because of being drained by the figures earlier. Samson jumped out in front of them, barking as if to encourage them to continue on. They pushed on as fast as they could and were now able to see the end of the forest. Before they could escape, the dark figures dashed toward them in one last desperate attempt to keep them from leaving.

The guys kept running while blocking the needles with their Shields and striking out with their Swords. Finally, they reached the end, and the hideous creatures disappeared deep into the forest. Exhausted, the guys collapsed on the grass and lay flat on their backs.

Mark raised his head. "What was that?"

"I don't know, but I'm glad we got out of there," said Eric.

Jeremiah sat all the way up, looking back over his shoulder. "I believe that was the Forest of Seduction."

Aaron said, "I guess we should be thankful we made it out with as little damage as we did, but that's not what I'm thinking about right now."

Mark stared at the ground. "I know exactly what you mean. Why didn't we see the dangers of those figures earlier? Why did we give into seduction to the degree that we did?"

"I feel the same way," Rick said, shaking his head.

Jeremiah held out his hand. "Here is what I know about dealing with sin. The first thing we have to do is be honest. We were seduced by those figures because we wanted to be. There was something of our fleshly nature that was drawn to this seduction, something that we have not crucified."

Rick sighed as he shook his head. "I feel even worse because I'm about to be married in a few months. What does this say about me?"

Jeremiah put his hand on Rick's shoulder. "It says you're a fallen human who's prone to sin. What matters for you, and for the rest of us, is what we do now. Do we repent and surrender these areas to God, or do we beat ourselves up and look for a different way to deal with our guilt?"

Greg said, "I want to deal with this now. I'm about to be married soon as well, and I don't want this to be an issue."

Mark looked at Rick and Greg. "Whether we're married or single, we all need to be aware of our weaknesses in this area. Can we all admit that maybe we were a little over-confident, and we just got humbled?"

Rick nodded in agreement. "Yes, we just graduated from a House of Knowledge, and I think we believed we were somehow above this kind of temptation."

Scratching his head, Eric said, "Something is bothering me though. Our path led straight into that forest. Why would God take us to a place where he knew temptation awaited?"

Jeremiah took out his Book and read. "Let no man say, when he is tempted, I am being tempted by God, for God is not able to be tempted by evil, and He Himself does not tempt anyone. But each one of us is tempted and seduced by our own lusts. When lust has conceived, it gives birth to sin, and when sin becomes full-grown, it brings forth death."

Jeremiah closed his Book. "Jesus was led into the wilderness to be tempted by Satan as a time of testing. God brought us through a place where He knew temptation would confront us, but it was our own lust that caused us to fall for that temptation. I believe God brought us through that forest to show us where we are weak, so that we might deal with it before it becomes a bigger problem."

Mark said, "That's a good point. Today we were seduced, and we did sin in our thoughts, but it could have been worse. What if we had followed those figures? What if we are faced with seduction in the future, and we haven't dealt with these areas in our flesh? How much damage could be done to our personal ministry and to our House of Instruction?"

"Where do you think those figures would have taken us if we had followed?" asked Eric.

Jeremiah said, "I think we all know they were going to lead us to the Camp of Sin. I haven't been there, but I've heard many things. It is not a place I wish to go."

Mark crossed his arms. "Let's all be honest. We know there was a part of us that wanted to go with them. God woke us up out of our slumber and gave us an opportunity to resist. There's no guarantee we would get that kind of preventive grace again if we persisted in giving in to seduction."

"I agree," said Jeremiah, "God rescued us from ourselves. We need to be thankful for His goodness and loving-kindness toward us today."

Rick took out his Book and read, "Let him who thinks he stands, watch out lest he fall." He paused for a moment. "I think we need to set up camp for the evening. Let's spend the rest of the day asking God to search our hearts, and show us what is in us that was drawn to this seduction today. Let's talk later before we go to sleep."

Everyone agreed and spent the rest of the afternoon in their tent reading and praying. That night they gathered around the fire and confessed what they had discovered about themselves. They were honest about what happened to them in the forest, and what caused them to fall so easily.

As they went to sleep that night, they knew they were forgiven, but they still felt a grief and sorrow for what had happened. They did not try to make these feelings go away, but trusted that God would do a complete work in them to root up the places in their heart that needed to be plowed by His word.

The next morning they each felt cleansed and at peace. Even though the sun was shining, there was a light misting of rain. It infused them with strength, as they felt grace showering their souls. They stood outside their tents, allowing the mist to wash over them. After breakfast, they packed everything up and continued on their path.

22

ONE MORE BATTLE TOGETHER

As Jeremiah, Mark, and the others traveled for the next two days, they spent a lot of time talking about the future. They wondered about the challenges that lay ahead. Rick and Greg talked about their upcoming weddings and how life was going to change once they were married.

After going through the Forest of Seduction and experiencing their weaknesses, they did not speak as self-assured as they had before. God was slowly decreasing their dependence upon themselves so that they might lean more on Him.

Off in the distance, they could see a large hill, and as they drew closer, they saw that at the base of the hill was a ferocious looking beast. Jeremiah peered through his telescope and reported that the creature was about ten feet tall, with long shaggy hair, and dirty brown skin. It had huge feet with long toenails, hands that looked like claws, and wore a large bearskin for clothing. It carried a long wooden beam that was seven feet in length and twelve inches around.

Jeremiah passed the telescope to each of the guys. "Do any of you know what this creature is?"

"I've never seen anything like it," said Mark.

"Neither have I," said Greg, peering through the telescope.

They began to pray, asking God for wisdom and insight concerning this enemy.

When they finished, Jeremiah said, "This creature has a look that is primitive and raw. It seems ready to pounce any second. I believe this enemy has something to do with anger."

"I agree," said Mark, motioning for Jeremiah to hand him the telescope so he could look at the beast one more time.

Rick said, "Let's remember verses about anger, and charge this creature together."

Everyone pulled out their Swords and charged the Beast of Anger while shouting verses. But as they drew closer, the creature began to spin around in a violent circle, creating a mighty wind which blew all of them back by a hundred feet. They got up and charged again, but once they came nearer the beast spun around, and again they were blown back.

Jeremiah stood up and dusted himself off. "Obviously this isn't working. Let's go back and talk about it some more."

Everyone retreated to where they had been before and sat down in a circle.

Rick leaned forward. "Let's think about what this Book says about anger."

Jeremiah opened his Book. "I believe this may be important, 'Therefore, my beloved brethren, let every man be quick to hear, slow to speak, and slow to wrath.' We went charging at this creature, but it may be that running straight toward it actually gives it power."

Aaron took out his Book and read, "The one who is slow to anger has great understanding, but he who has a quick temper shows his foolishness."

"I see other places as well which emphasize being slow to anger," said Mark.

Jeremiah said, "So we need to move toward this creature slowly instead of charging it."

This new strategy seemed like a good plan, so they approached the beast again, but this time more slowly. They were able to come within fifteen feet, but once again, the creature spun around, creating a wind that knocked them back.

Rick picked himself up off the ground. "Well, we were able to get closer, and it didn't knock us back as far, but we still aren't able to get close enough to defeat it."

After returning to their planning area, Jeremiah examined their supplies. "How long do you think our rope is?"

"I'd say it was, at the most, maybe twenty-two feet. Why, what are you thinking?" asked Mark.

Jeremiah picked up the rope. "I'm thinking we have to keep this creature from spinning around, or we'll never get close enough to defeat it. God's word teaches that an angry and hot-tempered man stirs up strife, and that strife must be stopped before it gets going. If a few of us can distract it while someone else comes around from the side, maybe they can throw this rope around it and keep it still long enough for us to attack."

Mark knelt down to check out the rope. "We need at least seven feet to make a circle big enough to go around that beast, and that barely leaves enough to get close to it before it can spin again."

Jeremiah laid out the rope in a straight line. "We're going to have to make it work. We'll get as close as we can, and then someone is going to have to launch this rope around the creature and pull it tight so he can't spin. Then we have to attack before it has time to get free."

Rick looked over his shoulder. "It could work, but we're only going to get one shot at this, and then the creature is going to know what we're doing. I think we need to pull back a little further, so our enemy doesn't see what we're planning. Then let's practice before trying it for real."

As soon as they were out of sight of the beast, everyone dropped their backpacks and discussed their plan of attack. Since Jeremiah was the biggest, he was going to play the role of the creature, and they decided Greg would be the one to throw the rope. Rick led the others as they simulated approaching the creature from one direction while Greg tried to sneak up from the other direction.

Greg put the rope on his back to keep it out of sight until he was ready to launch it. As soon as he thought he was close enough, he swiftly yanked the rope from his back and hurled it toward Jeremiah. It was close, but it missed to the left. After practicing numerous times, Greg finally landed three perfect throws in a row.

Jeremiah removed the rope from around his shoulders. "I think we're ready."

After everyone gathered to pray, they started back toward the Beast of Anger. Greg was nervous because he was only going to get one chance to get this right.

Jeremiah patted him on the back. "I know you can do this. Once you've landed the rope and pulled it tight, wait for us to attack, then let go and join us."

Greg nodded.

As everyone marched over the next hill, the creature saw them approaching. Raising its long wooden beam over its head, the Beast of Anger roared at them. All but Greg took out their Swords and waved them over their heads while shouting. The creature appeared to be waiting for them to get just close enough so it could start spinning. Greg was a few steps behind, trying to look frightened so the creature would pay more attention to the others.

The plan was working. The beast focused on the ones shouting and waving their Swords. They were now as close as they could get before the creature would start spinning. Making sure they kept the creature's attention, they jumped up and down while shouting. Once they thought the beast might look in Greg's direction, they acted as if they were going to take another step toward it, and the beast shifted positions to start to spin.

Greg successfully slipped in behind the creature. He yanked the rope from behind his back, swung it over his head, and then let it go. The rope sailed through the air, and although it was just seconds, it seemed like hours as they watched where it would land.

The beast glanced up as the rope descended toward it, but the creature could not react quickly enough to get out of the way. The rope landed around its shoulders, and Greg quickly pulled it tight. Jeremiah signaled for everyone to charge.

Within seconds, the beast broke free from the rope, but before it could start to spin, Jeremiah arrived with his Sword to land a blow on the beast's right arm. Greg joined the others, and they surrounded the creature.

Determined to fight them off, the beast swung its wooden beam toward them with tremendous force. They held up their Shields, but each time the wooden beam made contact, the impact knocked them back. After blocking one of the blows from the wooden beam, Aaron fell. Seeing him on the ground, the beast swung its beam down as if to crush him. Mark quickly knelt in front of Aaron, blocking the strike with his Shield.

While the creature was off balance, Rick rushed in from the left and Jeremiah from the right. Together they struck the creature on each side. The beast growled in anger as it thrust the beam toward Rick first and then quickly toward Jeremiah. They blocked the blows, but as before the force knocked them back.

Jeremiah quickly looked around at the others. "We are instructed to put all anger and wrath away from us, and yet at the same time we are told to be angry and not sin."

The creature forcefully swung its beam toward Jeremiah's head, but he ducked just in time.

Jeremiah said, "If there is any anger that you have been holding in, be honest about it and give it to God. We can't defeat this creature until we take away any power it might have in us."

The Beast of Anger sensed it was in trouble and swung its beam from left to right trying to wipe them out. They all hit the ground and lay flat as the beam passed over them. They knew they couldn't hold out much longer like this. As they stood up, they confessed their anger and released it to God.

Rick pierced the creature in the thigh with his Sword. "I will cease from anger and forsake wrath, for it only leads to harm."

Jeremiah thrust his Shield into the beast's shoulder. "I will be swift to hear, slow to speak, and slow to wrath. For the wrath of man does not produce the righteousness of God."

The creature thrust its beam toward them as it had before, but this time they stopped the assault with their Shields without being knocked back.

Mark jumped up on a nearby rock and gashed the creature in the forehead with his Sword. "A person who is slow to anger is better than the mighty, and the one who controls his emotions is stronger than a person who captures a city."

Greg swung at the creature's chest. "The anger of a fool is quickly known, but a wise man will overlook an insult."

The beast roared in fury and cocked back its beam, preparing to knock them all out with one blow.

Jeremiah quickly motioned for all of them to hold up their Shields, then shouted, "We give our anger and wrath to God for He alone is the righteous Judge who is worthy to execute vengeance."

The creature swung down at them with brutal force, but as the wooden beam crashed against their Shields, it splintered into a thousand pieces. The creature was now desperate and swiped at them with its clawed hands.

The guys easily dodged the blows, then struck the beast even harder with their Swords. Aaron and Eric pounded the creature on its legs, as Greg got in a strike on its knees. Seeing that it was being overpowered, the Beast of Anger sprinted away and then spun out of sight.

Everyone cheered while Samson ran around barking. It was a hard-fought victory that brought a sense of accomplishment. With the beast now defeated, they wanted to find out why it had fought so hard to keep them from climbing this hill.

They hiked to the top and saw a beautiful valley spread out below. As they descended to the valley floor, they felt relaxed and peaceful as if anxiety and tension were being lifted off their shoulders.

When they reached the middle of the valley, the group stopped, absorbing all the peace that surrounded them.

After a few minutes Aaron said, "When I asked God to show me areas where I was angry, I discovered that some of what I felt was justified and some was not."

Jeremiah nodded. "But even if there's a good reason to be angry, we are to express it in a way that doesn't do harm to others."

Pointing to his Book, Rick said, "The anger of man does not accomplish the righteousness of God. Anger should be expressed properly, but it should never be used against people."

Soon they left the Valley of Peace and traveled onward. They hiked for another hour, then set up camp for the evening.

The next day they continued, and after traveling for two more days, they saw what appeared to be yellow rocks off to one side that glimmered in the sunlight.

Aaron stepped off their path and picked up one of the stones. "This looks like gold!"

Eric rushed over. "Hey, this does look like gold."

There were more of the rocks a little further off the path.

Jeremiah glanced over at Rick and Mark, and they nodded as if they knew what he was thinking.

"Aaron and Eric, come back over here and bring what you found," said Rick.

When their friends returned, Rick took the nuggets and studied them. "Just as I suspected, this is fool's gold, and we would have been fools for getting off our path to chase after it."

Jeremiah took one of the nuggets, turning it over in his hand. "This is a good lesson to learn."

Opening his Book, he read, "But the ones who desire to be rich fall into temptation, and into a snare, and into many foolish and harmful lusts which plunge people into ruin and destruction. For the love of money is a root of all kinds of evil. It is through this craving that some have departed from the faith and have pierced themselves with many sorrows."

Mark turned in his Book and read, "Conduct your life in a way that is free from the love of money, and be content with the things you have, for He has said, I will never leave you nor forsake you."

Rick threw the nuggets on the ground. "Those are good verses. There's nothing wrong with having money, but when we start to long for it in a way that consumes us, then it's going to take us off our path."

Jeremiah said, "We need to learn to be like the Apostle Paul and be content in all situations. I've found that if a person is not content when they have very little, then they'll still not be content even when they have more."

Rick started thumbing through his Book, reading and then turning over to read some more. After a few minutes, he looked up at the guys. "Do you know what's been happening? I just scanned the passages where Paul instructed Titus and Timothy regarding the qualifications for leaders. One requirement is to be the faithful husband of one wife, another one is not to be greedy, and another one is not to be quick-tempered."

Greg turned over in his Book and read the same passages. "I see what you're saying Rick. As we've been traveling, God has been dealing with us in three areas that cause leaders a lot of problems."

Jeremiah said, "Professor Williams taught us that many leaders fall into disgrace because of not dealing with these areas of their lives before they start their ministries, and then later these things come back to ruin them."

The group began to thank God for bringing them on this adventure and showing them where they were weak. After praying together, they traveled for the rest of the day and then camped that evening.

The next morning they set off early, but after an hour, Rick stopped all of a sudden.

Pointing to a lake in the distance, Rick said, "When I met with Lisa's parents they described that lake and said that once we passed it, we would only be a day's journey from their home."

The group traveled a little further and then Jeremiah saw that his path was veering off in a different direction. The others saw it too, and they came to a stop.

Mark put his hand on Jeremiah's shoulder. "I guess I knew this day was coming, but I hoped it wouldn't. You've been a great friend and roommate. I learned a lot from you, and I'm grateful that God caused your path to come in contact with mine."

Jeremiah gave Mark a hug, then stepped back. "I'm thankful to have had you as a friend as well." He glanced around. "And that goes for all of you, Rick, Greg, Aaron, and Eric. You don't know how much it has meant to me to have good friends like you. There's a part of me that wishes I could go with you, but I know you're going to do great things for God."

Jeremiah reached into his bag. "I want you all to have some of the money I received from selling my home. I want you to take it and use it for your House of Instruction."

"Are you sure? This is a lot of money," said Rick.

"I still have more left over, and God will take care of me. I've known that I was to give it to you since the day you all told me what you were going to do after graduation."

Mark put his arm around Jeremiah. "I know what we should do. When our first building is completed, we'll name a classroom for you. We'll call it The Jeremiah Room. You'll always be a part of the work that God does with us."

After a few more hugs, all the guys said goodbye to him and then to Samson as well. As he walked away, Jeremiah was sad to leave his friends, but what he didn't know was that soon his life was about to change in a way he could never have imagined.

23

JEREMIAH MEETS ZEAL

After Jeremiah and Samson had traveled for a couple of hours, they stopped to rest near a small brook. Samson instantly lapped up some water and a little further upstream Jeremiah filled his canteen. They sat by the brook and rested, enjoying the calming effects of the trickling water. Within a few minutes, a young lady approached from the distance. She was walking with her head bowed as if she was upset about something.

As she drew closer, Jeremiah felt attracted to her in a way he had never felt toward a young woman before. She was of African heritage just like himself. She had a pretty face, kind brown eyes, and neatly styled hair that came down to her shoulders. And while he found her physically appealing, what grabbed his attention more than anything was her determined walk. It was as if she was in a hurry to get somewhere, but at the same time didn't know where she was going.

Jeremiah wanted to get her attention, but he wondered if she would even notice him.

When she was a few feet away, Jeremiah stood up. "Hello, how are you doing today?"

The young woman stopped. "Well… hmm… hello, I'm doing fine I guess."

Taking a step closer, he said, "My name is Jeremiah, and this is Samson."

Samson trotted over to the young lady and looked up at her. She almost smiled, then knelt down and started petting him.

"My name is Zeal."

"That's a lovely name," said Jeremiah, trying to make eye contact with her.

Zeal continued to pet Samson. "Thank you. It was my grandmother's idea. She said when I was born that I was full of zeal."

Still trying to make eye contact, Jeremiah said, "Zeal is a great thing to have."

"I suppose it is, but I don't feel like I have a lot of zeal right now." After giving Samson one more pat on the head, she stood up.

Jeremiah clasped his hands. "I don't wish to intrude, but I couldn't help but notice that you were walking as if something was bothering you."

"Yes," said Zeal, as she stared at the ground, "I was not able to advance on my path, so now I'm going back in the direction I came from, hoping to find some other way forward."

"Why is that?"

"My path led me to a place where there is a terrible giant in the way, and I don't believe I can defeat him."

Jeremiah studied his path. "It appears I will be heading in the direction you came from, so I suppose I'll be meeting this giant soon."

Zeal glanced over her shoulder. "Yes you will."

Jeremiah spoke in a soft and reassuring tone. "I don't want to seem as though I'm trying to give you advice after only knowing you for a few minutes, but if this is the way your path has taken you, then won't God cause you to be victorious over this enemy?"

Looking away, Zeal said, "Others told me the same thing, but this giant speaks terrible insults to people who try to fight him, and I cannot bear to hear such things. Not only do I not think I can defeat him, but I would probably just break down and cry. That would be humiliating."

Jeremiah did not want their time together to end right here, but he also sensed that Zeal was capable of more than she thought. "I don't want to trouble you or cause you to go through any more anguish than you already have, but if you could accompany me and Samson to see this giant, I would greatly appreciate it. Maybe along the way you can tell me a little more about him and what strategy he uses."

Zeal appeared hesitant, but Samson nudged her hand and barked twice.

She reached down to rub Samson's cheeks. "Well, I guess I can walk with you for a little ways."

They started off, and Zeal told Jeremiah about how this enemy ridiculed people and then laughed at them as he beat them up.

Within fifteen minutes, they came upon a sign. "All those on this Quest must defeat the Giant of Shame and enter the River of Healing. Once you bring him to his knees, the giant must let you come back and forth as you wish."

Jeremiah turned around. "So this is the Giant of Shame."

"Yes," said Zeal, "just saying the name makes me feel afraid."

"Why?"

"Nobody likes criticism of any kind, but this giant gets extremely personal. It's as if he knows your entire past, and he picks out the most hurtful things you could possibly say to someone. I've seen others try to fight him and be brought to tears many times. I don't want that to be me."

"Let's go see this Giant of Shame," said Jeremiah with a determined voice.

"I don't know. I said when I left I was never going to look at him or listen to him speak again."

Samson strolled over to Zeal and barked.

Jeremiah smiled. "It looks as if my friend believes you should come too."

Zeal took a deep breath. "Okay, but I may not stay very long."

Jeremiah walked forward to discover a massive rock wall, which appeared to rise up out of the ground a thousand feet into the air. The wall stretched out for miles on either side, with a small opening carved out in the middle. The Giant of Shame stood in front of the opening, blocking the entrance to a beautiful river which flowed with crystal-clear water.

The ground leading up to the giant was packed down from all the battles that had taken place there. Those waiting to face this enemy set up camp on either side of the narrow path leading to the battle area.

As Jeremiah arrived, the Giant of Shame was hurling insults at a young man who was angrily charging him. After a few minutes of toying with the youth, the giant swatted him with his club, sending him flying through the air and flat on his back. The giant taunted him, as well as all those standing on the side watching.

The Giant of Shame was about nine and a half feet tall. He had large, broad shoulders; strong, muscular arms; legs that were the size of a tree trunk; and a thick, scruffy beard that looked as if it hadn't been cleaned in months. His armor was made out of thick black leather, and he carried a large club which he could swing so fast that it created a gust of wind when it passed by.

After knocking his last victim on his back, the giant continued to laugh and sneer at all those who were watching. "So who's next?"

Hearing the arrogant laughter, Jeremiah wanted to charge at him immediately, but he knew now was not the time. Jeremiah, Zeal, and Samson walked over to where the others were gathered.

Immediately a young woman ran over and embraced Zeal. "I'm so glad you're back!

Zeal glanced at Jeremiah. "This is my friend Elizabeth. She has already defeated the Giant of Shame, but she has remained to help others in their battle."

Reaching out his hand, he said, "Nice to meet you Elizabeth. I'm Jeremiah."

Elizabeth shook his hand. "It's nice to meet you too." She then turned back toward Zeal. "I've been praying for you since you left. I know you can defeat this enemy."

"Thank you for your confidence in me," said Zeal, "but I didn't come back to fight the giant. I ran into Jeremiah as I was leaving, and he asked me to walk with him and give him some information about this enemy. I don't think I'll be around much longer though."

Elizabeth knelt to pet Samson but kept her gaze on Zeal. "Please think about it. Going through the River of Healing is a tremendous experience, and it's just what you need to make great progress on this Quest."

Zeal remained silent.

Jeremiah turned to Elizabeth. "So why did you decide to stay around after you defeated the giant?"

"When I arrived here there was a young woman named Overcomer who was teaching people how to defeat the Giant of Shame. I learned a lot from her, and it helped me to win my battle. Her path moved on, but mine remained here, so I took over what she started."

"What can you tell me about this enemy?" asked Jeremiah.

Elizabeth looked over at the giant. "He knows everything about you. Everything he says isn't true, but he wouldn't say it unless he thought you believed it."

Jeremiah said, "That does sound challenging."

"It is," said Elizabeth, "and if there's anything that you haven't received grace for, he's going to know it."

As they were talking, two others tried to fight the giant, and both were soundly defeated.

Jeremiah said, "I think I should camp overnight and spend some time with God before I try to defeat this enemy. I don't believe this will be easy, and I want to be prepared."

Elizabeth gently took Zeal's hand. "Will you please stay another night? I'd love to spend a little more time with you."

"I suppose I can stay one more night," said Zeal. "It will give me a chance to say goodbye to some of the others."

Jeremiah turned toward Zeal, giving her his best smile. "Thank you for accompanying me and Samson. Maybe we'll see you again before you go."

"It was no problem," said Zeal. "I guess it was best to come back here and say goodbye to people rather than just walking off like I did."

Elizabeth and Zeal left.

Jeremiah knelt down and held Samson's face in his hands. "I like that young woman a whole lot, but I don't know if our paths will be going in the same direction after tomorrow."

He found a nice camping spot and started setting up his tent for the night. Samson walked toward the River of Healing to get some water. As he trotted past the opening, the giant gave him a mean look, but Samson just growled at him and strolled on by. When he had finished drinking, he came back and sat beside the tent.

As Jeremiah was reading in his Book, a man walked by and stopped. "Well hello. You must be new here."

Jeremiah stood to his feet and held out his hand. "Hi there. Yes, we just arrived today. My name is Jeremiah, and this here is Samson."

Shaking Jeremiah's hand, the man said, "Well it's nice to meet you. My name is Graham. I've been here a few days."

"Have you faced the giant yet?"

"Me?" said Graham. "No. I don't think I'm ready."

Jeremiah said, "I'm going to be taking the rest of the day and at least some of tomorrow to prepare before I think about trying."

"That's a good idea. I've seen a lot of men and women fail."

"Have you seen any succeed?"

"A few," said Graham, rubbing the hair on his chin, "but it was a very tough battle for them. They faced things about themselves that they probably never faced before."

Jeremiah motioned for him to sit down. "This is what I've been led to read, and it's what I'm going to meditate on: 'Fixing our eyes on Jesus, the author, and perfecter of our faith, who for the joy that was set before Him, endured the cross, disregarding the shame, and has sat down at the right hand of the throne of God.' "

"That's a great verse," said Graham.

Jeremiah pointed to his Book. "When the sins of the world were laid upon Jesus, so was the shame and guilt of those sins. Yet He disregarded that shame, choosing instead to focus on the joy that was set before Him. God wants us to be aware of our sinfulness and the guilt that goes with it, but He wants us to look beyond our shame and toward Him as the answer."

Graham said, "Great point, but I'm sure you know accomplishing that is a lot harder than it might sound."

Jeremiah nodded. "It's difficult to let go of our shame because it means admitting we're powerless to do anything about it. I've had many battles with my own shame, and I'm sure I'll have an even bigger battle when I face this giant. What I do know, though, is there is nothing shameful about me that Jesus has not already paid for, and that God has not already provided grace for."

"Thank you," said Graham, "I needed to hear that encouragement. I think I've gotten caught up in seeing so many fail that I've lost sight of the fact that God has provided victory. I'm going to meditate on that for the rest of the day."

Graham went back to his campsite, and Jeremiah continued to read. A part of him wanted to walk around and see if Zeal was still there and possibly talk to her some more. However he knew the next day was going to present a significant challenge, so he focused on his Book for the rest of the evening. When the sun began to set,

Jeremiah looked around to see if he could spot Zeal, but she was nowhere in sight.

As he prepared for bed, he wondered if she had already left. After climbing into his tent and lying down, he remembered back to the first moments he saw her. Why couldn't he have met her under better circumstances? What if he never saw her again? Jeremiah could feel the tug on his emotions, but he quickly snapped himself back into focus, realizing the importance of what was waiting for him the next day.

GIANT OF SHAME

The next morning Jeremiah woke up early, still wondering if Zeal had left, but he was determined to focus on the battle that lay ahead. After setting out some food for Samson and eating a light breakfast of bananas and nuts, he began reading in his Book.

After an hour of study, Jeremiah lifted his eyes toward heaven. "Dear Lord, give me the strength to confront whatever challenge is set before me today. I know that You would not have brought me here without making a way for me to prevail."

He stood up and made his way to where everyone was waiting for the day's battles to begin. No one had challenged the giant so far, and it appeared he was even cockier than usual. Slowly, Jeremiah made his way through the crowd and out to the beaten down dirt path. Samson walked over and sat where he could see what was happening.

The Giant of Shame saw him approaching and smirked at him, then spoke in a condescending tone. "Well, who do we have here? Is that you Jeremiah? I'm afraid I'm going to have to destroy you and your little dog too." He let out a hearty laugh.

Taking a deep breath, Jeremiah looked the giant straight in the eyes. "I'm sure you have many degrading things to say to me, but I want you to know that my standing before God is not determined by anything you can say here today. My righteousness is in Jesus Christ. I stand before God as completely accepted based on the perfect record of Christ's obedience."

The Giant of Shame smiled a wicked smile. "Oh, you have me all wrong. I don't care what God thinks about you. I only care what you think about yourself, and rarely are those the same."

Jeremiah raised his Book until it became a Sword. "God made

Jesus to be sin, Who knew no sin, so that I might become the righteousness of God in Him! That's the great exchange giant. Jesus was counted as sinful even though He never sinned, so that I could be counted as righteous even though I am only sinful."

Swinging his Sword with authority, Jeremiah landed a vicious strike to the giant's left leg, causing him to grimace in pain. The giant swatted at him with his club, but Jeremiah swiftly dodged out of the way. Dashing toward the giant's right side, Jeremiah slashed him on his arm.

The giant let out a yell and swung toward Jeremiah's head. But no matter how fast he swung his club, Jeremiah was able to block or dodge every blow. The giant was becoming concerned. Very few had gotten by him over the last couple of months, and he could see those who were watching, becoming emboldened as this new challenger was having success.

Deciding it was time to turn the tide of the battle, the Giant of Shame gave Jeremiah an evil look and raised his club high above his head. He then slammed his club into the ground, and yelled, "Jeremiah! You no good *nigger!*"

Startled, Jeremiah stepped back.

"Oh No He Didn't!" exclaimed Zeal, attempting to rise to her feet. She had arrived to watch with the others just as Jeremiah first walked out to the battlefield.

Jeremiah motioned toward Zeal with his hand to let her know that he had this.

Silence settled over everyone who was watching, as they wondered what Jeremiah would do next.

He hadn't heard that degrading word, that awful, terrible word in a long time. He remembered back when he was a little boy and his mom, who was sick at the time, sent him to the store to get the things she needed. A few men stood outside, and as he walked by, they called him that awful name. As Jeremiah got older, he understood that those who used this word despised him because of the color of his skin.

After his mom died when he was sixteen, he lived with different friends until finishing his primary education. Determined to show everyone that he was worthy of respect, Jeremiah graduated near the top of his class. Anytime he took a job, he made sure to do it better than anyone had before. It was this kind of work ethic that enabled him to have his own business at such an early age.

When he enrolled in the House of Knowledge, he wanted to show people that he belonged and could excel. He achieved that, earning the respect of his instructors and of the other students as well. For as long as he could remember, he had this need to prove himself worthy of the acceptance of others.

As all of these thoughts and memories flashed through his head, the Holy Spirit brought to Jeremiah's attention that there was a small part deep within him that was always trying to prove that he was not what the Giant of Shame had called him.

As Jeremiah knelt to pray, the Holy Spirit ministered healing and acceptance to his soul. Jeremiah looked toward heaven and tears began to flow down his cheeks. Seeing this, Zeal jumped to her feet, but once again, Jeremiah motioned to her that it was all right.

The giant sneered at him. "Ahhhh, what's the matter Jeremiah. Would you like me to get you a tissue?"

As the giant was laughing, Samson barked and growled at him.

Jeremiah stood to his feet. "I'm not crying because I'm sad. I'm crying because God is setting me free. What you meant for harm, God meant for my good."

Pointing his club at him, the Giant of Shame said, "That's a nice bluff, but I know weakness when I see it."

"Oh," said Jeremiah taking a step forward, "you do see weakness, but it's a different kind of weakness than what you think. For all these years, I've allowed the words of others to affect me, and it was one particular word that affected me greatly. But I say to you Giant of Shame that God has much more powerful words for me than the one you've called me! For God calls me Redeemed, Righteous, Holy, Forgiven, and He calls me His son!"

Raising his Sword, Jeremiah said, "And you know what else giant, Jesus is not ashamed to call me His brother. That's right. The Lord of the Universe is not ashamed of me because of the color of my skin, for He loves me and welcomes me into the family of God."

Jeremiah began swinging his Sword in front of him in a circular motion until it made a loud whooshing sound. He then stepped forward with a bold and determined look on his face.

As soon as Jeremiah was within range, the giant swung his club at him with tremendous force. While looking the giant straight in the eyes, Jeremiah quickly raised his Shield, blocking the club and stopping it cold. No one had ever seen such a thing. As soon as the club made contact with the Shield, it was as if it was frozen in mid-air.

Jeremiah shouted, "The Lord God alone is my rock and my salvation. He is my strong defense. I shall not be moved."

With a loud roar, Jeremiah thrust out his Shield against the club. The giant's arm flew back toward his head, his own club striking him in the face. As he stumbled backwards, Jeremiah rushed in and slammed his Shield into his stomach. The giant doubled over, and Jeremiah struck him on the head with his Sword.

Angry and embarrassed that Jeremiah was doing so well, the giant let out a thunderous yell, swinging his club even faster than normal. The gust of wind it created blew the ones watching back a step.

Jeremiah braced himself behind his Shield once again. "But thou, O LORD, art a shield for me. You're my glory, and the lifter of my head."

When the club made contact with the Shield, it bounced off with such force that the giant's arm swung back and turned him around backward.

Seeing that his enemy was vulnerable, Jeremiah drove his Sword into the back of his legs. The giant tried to quickly turn around, but this last strike from Jeremiah's Sword slowed him down considerably. Now desperate, the Giant of Shame swung his club wildly, but all he accomplished was to make himself even more vulnerable.

Jeremiah easily blocked all the attacks, then took a step back. "God has made all mankind from one blood, and by the blood of One, Jesus Christ, we have all been redeemed!"

Jeremiah struck the giant with his Sword on his shoulders and arms, then slammed his Shield into his face. "God does not favor one people group over another, for He is calling all men everywhere to repentance. It is not the color of one's skin that matters, but the condition of one's heart."

The giant was now wobbling, and Jeremiah was determined to defeat this enemy and all that he represented.

Jeremiah pointed his Sword at the Giant of Shame. "In Christ, there is neither black or white, male or female, nobleman or peasant, for we are all one in Him!"

Jeremiah took three steps back, then ran toward his enemy and leaped into the air. As he reached the top of his jump, he swung his Sword at the giant's head and knocked him out cold. As Jeremiah landed on one knee, the giant collapsed to the ground with a thud.

Zeal jumped up immediately and yelled, "Praise God!"

Samson started barking and jumping around. Jeremiah called for him, and they went into the River of Healing together. Jeremiah stood in the river and gazed toward heaven. The water felt so refreshing, and he could sense shame and guilt being washed away. He no longer felt the need to prove himself to others or to God.

Breathing deeply as he closed his eyes, Jeremiah stood there for several minutes letting the water flow over him. When he opened his eyes, he looked back to see that the Giant of Shame had risen to his feet. He then glanced over at Zeal who was seated on the ground next to Elizabeth with her head in her hands.

There was a lot more going on with Zeal than what Jeremiah could know at that time. When she had seen him kneeling down and praying after being called that awful name, she felt something she had never felt for another human being. It was not pity as one might suppose. No, it was much more powerful than that. And afterward, when Jeremiah rose to his feet to confront the giant, she felt so proud of him, but her emotions ran deeper still. And as he defeated this enemy, Zeal heard herself say something that shocked her. Within her heart, she said, "I love that man!"

Once she saw Jeremiah wade into the River of Healing, Zeal came back to reality. She had not defeated the giant, and this man who had just come into her life was about to leave.

Jeremiah nodded toward Samson. "I don't feel our mission here is complete."

Together they walked back, making their way over to Zeal and Elizabeth. Jeremiah sat down beside Zeal, and Samson sat behind her with his head on her shoulder.

After a few moments, Jeremiah said, "I know you can do this."

"I wish I could. I really wish I could," said Zeal, staring at the ground.

"But you can, there is no difference between you and me. It's God working through us that gives us the strength we need to overcome anything."

Still not lifting up her head, Zeal said, "I want to believe that, but—"

Not wanting her to spend any more time on the problem, Jeremiah interrupted, "But what? You've been in battles before haven't you?"

"Yes," said Zeal, "but it's always been with other people and with someone else leading. I had no trouble believing God would be with the group and with the one leading, but now I have to stand in front of this enemy by myself, and there will be no one to help me."

Jeremiah placed his hand on top of Zeal's. "I'll be here."

Zeal looked up, and though she tried to hide it, she couldn't help but smile as her heart raced.

Samson nudged her on the arm.

"We'll not leave until you defeat this giant," said Jeremiah, gently squeezing her hand.

Elizabeth leaned over and put her arm around Zeal. "I know you'll be successful. We spent all yesterday evening and most of this morning preparing for this. You're ready."

Zeal closed her eyes and prayed, clinching her fist and nodding her head. She then stood up and marched toward her enemy.

The giant knew he couldn't afford to lose two battles in a row. Those watching from the sidelines had already gained some confidence, and if this woman, who had already walked away once, was able to defeat him, then it might embolden many of those there.

The Giant of Shame glared at Zeal and began smacking the palm of his hand with his club. "Well, if it isn't the coward who ran away. I'm sure you know the way out of here, so why don't you save us both some time and just leave."

Zeal stood her ground.

The Giant of Shame pointed at her with his club. "I like your outfit. Who threw that away so you could have something to wear?"

The giant then let out a loud, obnoxious laugh.

As a little girl Zeal wore mostly clothes that someone had donated. She hadn't thought about those days in a long while.

The giant leaned over and gave her a hateful look. "I see your new boyfriend has given you some confidence. But we both know that having a boyfriend isn't something you know too much about."

Zeal felt fear and embarrassment rise up inside and threaten to choke off the little bit of conviction she had gained.

The giant sensed his words were having an effect, and he slammed his club against the ground. "And don't even try to act like little miss perfect. What would your new boyfriend think if he knew how sinful your thoughts were?"

Jeremiah called out, "What has God said?"

Zeal shifted her gaze to Jeremiah. His belief in her shone in his eyes. Bowing her head, she prayed that God would remind her of what was really true. The Holy Spirit immediately called forth a verse that had been a favorite of hers as a child, "If God is for us, then who can be against us."

Gripping her Shield, Zeal took a step toward the giant. "It doesn't matter how much money I have, or what type of home I grew up in, or what the color of my skin is. For while man looks on the outward things, God looks upon the heart."

Zeal dashed toward the giant, swinging her Sword toward his left side. He blocked the attack, but she swiftly brought her Sword back across her body and swung it toward his right side. The giant tried to block this blow as well but was too late. Her Sword sliced into his side. Not giving him time to recover, Zeal spun around and hit him on his left leg.

Stepping back and pointing at the giant with her Sword, Zeal proclaimed, "I have a High Priest who is able to sympathize with all my weaknesses, for He went through all the things that I do and yet did not sin."

Barely able to move his left leg, the Giant of Shame swung his club at Zeal's feet trying to knock her off balance, but she jumped over it.

"Therefore," declared Zeal, "I will come boldly before the Throne of Grace to receive mercy and obtain the help I need for all my sins and weaknesses."

She rushed straight up to the giant, piercing him in the gut. He grabbed his stomach and doubled over, groaning in pain.

Zeal shouted, "All those who look to God for their confidence, shall be radiant, and their faces will never be covered in shame." She then brought her Sword down on top of his head.

The giant rocked back and forth, then fell to one knee. He tried to recover and get back on both feet, but Zeal was determined to finish him off.

She shouted, "I give praise to God who accepts me as I am, for it is by His hand that I am fearfully and wonderfully made."

Zeal ran toward the giant, jumped on his leg and sprang into the air. As she rose upward, she plunged her Sword into the side of his neck.

The Giant of Shame wobbled back and forth for a moment, then fell face down in the dirt.

Jeremiah jumped up pumping his fist in the air. "Yes! Yes!"

Samson barked loudly, Elizabeth cried, and all the others who had been watching began to cheer. Elizabeth gave Zeal a hug and walked with her into the River of Healing. When Zeal entered the water, she felt shame being washed away along with all the fear and insecurity that came with it.

Jeremiah called to Samson. "Let's go join them."

Samson barked, and they waded into the River of Healing.

Zeal was enjoying the refreshing, cleansing nature of the water. When Jeremiah drew close, she said, "Thank you."

"You're welcome. I knew you could do it."

Zeal splashed a little water on Samson. "Thank you too."

When she looked up, she was immediately drawn to Jeremiah's eyes. There was a strength and a softness in his gaze that was captivating.

Jeremiah was mesmerized by Zeal's beauty, both inward and outward.

As they stood there in the water, enthralled with one another as if no one else in the world existed, Elizabeth cleared her voice. "I think I'm going to go back and encourage some more people. You both have given much-needed hope to those who still need to face this giant."

"Yes, that would be a good thing," said Jeremiah, his gaze still locked into Zeal's eyes.

"Yes," said Zeal, her face all aglow, "that would be a very good thing."

Elizabeth just grinned and walked back toward the others.

"So...," said Zeal.

"So, where will you go now?" asked Jeremiah.

"My father is a leader of a House of Instruction that's about two hours from here. I can make it there by dark since it appears that's where my path is leading."

At last looking from Jeremiah, Zeal checked to see where his path was heading. When she spotted it going in the same direction, excitement surged inside, but she fought to keep it down.

Jeremiah said, "It appears that's the direction my path is going too."

Zeal smiled. "So I guess we'll be traveling together."

"It looks like we will," said Jeremiah, wearing a big grin.

Zeal glanced back across the river. "I first want to say goodbye to Elizabeth and the others, and then I'll be ready to go."

"Samson and I will wait here."

Zeal hurried to the other side and thanked Elizabeth for all her encouragement and support. She then motivated many of the others who were about to face the Giant of Shame. Several would defeat him that day, one of his worst ever.

Zeal returned to Jeremiah. "I'm ready."

25

ZEAL'S FAMILY

Jeremiah and Zeal strolled leisurely along their paths, wanting to squeeze every minute they could out of the journey. They each talked about their childhoods, and how they began their Quest. Zeal had been brought up in a loving Christian home. When she was a little girl, her father started a House of Instruction, and not long afterward, she asked her parents if they would walk with her to the Building of Reflection.

On that same day, Zeal went up the Hill of Calvary and accepted Jesus Christ as her Lord and Savior. Soon afterward, she received her armor from her father and had worn it ever since. She had not been perfect, but she remained faithful throughout her time on the Quest.

Zeal spent two years at a House of Knowledge before going back to help her father, where she taught classes for all the girls from ages five to seventeen. Just a week ago she had set out on what she thought would be a routine journey, but her path took her to the Giant of Shame. She hoped her parents weren't worried because she'd been gone so long, but more than anything, she was enjoying this time walking and talking with Jeremiah.

The more she came to know him the more she realized how genuine her feelings were toward him. With each minute that passed, she felt more respect for the man he was.

For his part, Jeremiah had known there was something special about Zeal the moment he saw her. He just hoped she would see something in him. Although neither could say it out loud at the time, they both hoped they would always be together from that day forward.

When they were near Zeal's home, she saw her father sitting on the front porch as if he was waiting for her. As soon as he saw her cresting over the hill, he immediately stood up and left the porch. Zeal ran toward him, and when she reached him, he embraced her and lifted her off the ground.

After he set her down, he said, "I'm so glad you're home! We were starting to get a little concerned."

"God has been with me," she said, giving him another hug.

Zeal's father was a stout and husky man who stood a few inches taller than Jeremiah.

Her mother heard all the commotion and came outside. When she saw Zeal, she rushed over and hugged her as well. Her mother had a kind and gracious demeanor, and Zeal favored her in both her looks and mannerisms.

While they celebrated her safe return home, an older lady came outside, and Zeal immediately hugged her neck and gave her a kiss on the cheek.

After stepping back, Zeal noticed her father was staring at something behind her. Turning around, she realized it was Jeremiah. "I have someone I want all of you to meet."

Hurrying over to him, Zeal took Jeremiah's arm and escorted him to her family. Her father stared at her hand on Jeremiah's arm and cleared his throat.

Zeal pulled her hand down to her side but still beamed from ear to ear. "This is Jeremiah, and that's his dog, Samson."

Motioning toward her dad, she said, "This is my father. His name is Sanford."

Her dad once again cleared his throat.

"You can call him Pastor Sanford," said Zeal.

Her father held out his hand. "It's nice to meet you Jeremiah."

"It's nice to meet you too, sir," he said, firmly shaking his hand.

Zeal slipped next to her mom and rested her hand on her arm. "This is my mother, Beatrice."

"It's nice to meet you Jeremiah. You may call me what everyone else does, Mama Beatrice."

Jeremiah nodded while looking toward Pastor Sanford to make sure it was okay. "Thank you, Mama Beatrice."

The older lady stepped forward. "Let me get out here and have a gander at this fine-looking young man."

Zeal smiled and hugged her neck. "This is my grandmother—Grandma Pearl."

Jeremiah could see that Pastor Sanford was a little annoyed at the brashness of Grandma Pearl, but he could also tell that she kind of enjoyed the fact that he was annoyed. Grandma Pearl was a feisty but good-natured woman. She was around five feet two inches tall, slender, and full of energy. When her husband died eight years earlier, she came to live with her daughter, Beatrice and her son-in-law, Sanford. Zeal had always been close to her grandmother, but after she came to live with them, the two became even closer.

"Well now," said Grandma Pearl, "how did you meet this nice young man?"

"That's a long story," said Zeal glancing at Jeremiah with a grin.

Pastor Sanford said, "Well, you two come on in and tell us all about it."

Zeal's father led them into their house located next door to the House of Instruction. Their home was quaint and welcoming, made in the style of a log cabin with two levels. The first level contained a living room area with chairs and couches situated around a cozy fireplace. Toward the back was a small kitchen, and to the left was a dining room with an antique table and chairs. The upstairs area appeared to be reserved for bedrooms.

Everyone sat down in the living room, Zeal leading Jeremiah to a couch where they sat side by side. She then began telling her family what had happened from the time she left.

When she started to describe all the nasty things the Giant of Shame had said, Grandma Pearl interrupted. "I remember that giant. I faced him when I was twenty-five years old. He tried to make me feel ashamed, but I whacked him on the head."

"Now Grandma Pearl," said Pastor Sanford, "I'm sure there was more to it than that."

"There might have been, but that's what I remember," said Grandma Pearl, looking a little irritated that she didn't get to tell more of her story.

"Go on Zeal," said Mama Beatrice.

Zeal told how she became discouraged and left but then ran into Jeremiah.

"So," said Pastor Sanford, glancing over at Zeal, "He just wanted you to accompany him back to the giant so you could give him information?"

Zeal gave her father a clenched-teeth smile and then continued. She told her parents that after she came back, she spent extra time with Elizabeth preparing for the possibility of battling the giant. They spent the next morning together studying and praying, and then as they were finishing up, people were rushing out to see who was going to step out onto the battlefield first. As she and Elizabeth made their way toward the crowd, she saw Jeremiah step forward.

Zeal described what the giant said to him, particularly the name he called him, and then reported how Jeremiah handled it. Pastor Sanford sat up a little, giving Jeremiah a nod of respect. Zeal then explained that after he had defeated the giant, he came back and encouraged her. Zeal's mother gave Jeremiah an especially bright smile, showing how much she respected his support of her daughter.

Grandma Pearl had already shown how much she respected Jeremiah by giving him a fist pump when she heard how he whacked the giant on the head and knocked him out cold.

When Zeal finished, Grandma Pearl leaned forward and began swinging her arms as if she was holding her Sword. "I could still take that giant today."

"I'm sure you could, Grandma Pearl," said Pastor Sanford.

"You better believe I could," she said, muttering under her breath.

Pastor Sanford turned to Jeremiah. "Why don't you tell us a little about yourself."

Jeremiah gave them a summary of his life and how he came to start his Quest. He then shared with them how he had graduated from a House of Knowledge before starting out on his own just under a week ago.

"That is a fine House of Knowledge you attended," said Pastor Sanford. "Beatrice and I both graduated from there. I'm impressed with all that God has brought you through in your life, and it sounds like you've already had a lot of adventure in a short amount of time."

"Yes," said Jeremiah, "it's been an exciting journey so far."

Mama Beatrice said, "What do you plan to do now?"

Zeal tried to catch her mom's eye, but Mama Beatrice kept her focus on Jeremiah.

"Well, it appears my path has led me here. If it's okay with all of you, I'd like to spend some time speaking with Zeal's father."

Pastor Sanford stood up. "Sure, we can go out on the porch where we can sit and talk."

As soon as they left, Zeal shot a look at her mom. "Why are you putting him on the spot like that?"

Her mother smiled. "I'm not putting him on the spot. It's obvious why he came here, and the next step is for him to talk to your father."

Smiling and pointing toward the porch, Zeal said, "So what do you think about him?"

Grandma Pearl leaned forward and nodded. "I tell you what I think. I think he's a fine young man. You did good Zeal."

Mama Beatrice glanced over at Grandma Pearl and then back to Zeal. "He seems like a nice young man, and it's clear that he thinks a lot of you."

"Do you think so?" said Zeal in a giddy high pitched voice. "I mean do you really think he does?"

Her mother replied, "Yes, I do. And it doesn't take a lot of discernment to figure out you like him as well."

"Mom, I really believe he could be the one," said Zeal, gazing starry-eyed toward the ceiling.

"Hold on now," said her mother, "you've only known him for two days."

Grandma Pearl said, "Now Beatrice, you and I both know that the very day you met Sanford you came home all excited saying he was going to be your husband."

Mama Beatrice gave Grandma Pearl a forced smile. "That may be true, but a lifetime relationship is something you don't want to rush into. I may have felt he was going to be my husband, but I gave it time to make sure."

Zeal said, "But if his path led him here, then we'll have that time."

Mama Beatrice peered through the window. "I'm sure that's what he and your father are talking about now."

After he and Jeremiah stepped out on the porch and sat down, Pastor Sanford leaned back in his chair. "So what did you want to talk about?"

Grabbing the collar of his shirt as he began to talk, Jeremiah said, "Well sir, I've come to realize…I mean I believe…What I'm trying to say is, I know that I've only known your daughter for two days, but I have feelings for her, and I believe God has led me here to meet you and to spend more time with her."

Tapping his thumbs together, Pastor Sanford said, "God could have led you here for many reasons. How do you know it has to do with my daughter?"

Zeal's father was the kind of man who didn't waste any words. He said what he meant and expected others to do the same. A young man who wanted to get to know his daughter, better be honest and up front about his motives from the beginning.

Jeremiah twisted around in his chair, trying to find the right words to express his feelings. "Sir, I don't know how to say this since I've only known your daughter for a short amount of time, but I've never felt about anyone like I do about her. I want to spend more time getting to know her, with your permission of course."

"Do you love my daughter?"

Love? That was a strong word. Yes he had thought about it, and he certainly felt it, but could he say something like that after only two days? Pastor Sanford knew he had put Jeremiah on the spot, but he wanted to see what he would do.

"Sir, I feel toward your daughter something that is only second to the way I feel about God Himself. From the moment I saw her, I was drawn to her, and yes, I asked her to accompany me back to the giant because I didn't want to see her leave. The next day I thought she had gone, and when I realized she was still there, I felt a sense of relief and excitement all at the same time. After I had defeated the Giant of Shame, I looked back at Zeal and knew I didn't want to leave without her."

Pastor Sanford sat forward. "That's what I wanted to know. You may stay here for a little while to get to know my daughter. There will be certain rules of course."

"Of course," said Jeremiah.

"First, there's the matter of where you'll stay. We have a small room on the second floor of the House of Instruction that we use for visiting pastors. You can stay there. There are repairs that need to be done around the building which you can do during the day, and during the evening you and Zeal may spend time out here on the porch or out in the front yard."

"Thank you sir, thank you so much. I'm grateful for your hospitality."

"You're welcome."

Samson came up beside them, and Pastor Sanford leaned over to pat his head. "Samson can stay here on the porch at night. There's a stream just behind the House of Instruction, so you can take him there to get some water. I'll go in and see what we have left over from dinner for him to eat."

Pastor Sanford stood up to go back inside. "You can stay on the porch for just a few more minutes before heading over to your room. I suspect someone is going to want to come out here and speak with you."

Zeal jumped up when she heard the door. As soon as she saw her father, she darted toward him. "What did you talk about? Where's Jeremiah?"

Her father smiled, as he put his hands on her shoulders. "Everything is okay. He's out on the porch, and he'll be staying around for a little while. He's going to sleep in the guest room above the House of Instruction."

Zeal gave her father a tight hug. "Thank you! May I go out to tell him goodnight?"

"Yes, you may."

Zeal hurried out to the porch.

After she left, Mama Beatrice went to her husband and took his hand. "You know, a man who can support our daughter through a battle with the Giant of Shame, is a man who will stand beside her during anything."

Putting both arms around her and pulling her toward him, Pastor Sanford said, "That's true, but you and I both know there's more to marriage than that. We're going to have a chance to get to know Jeremiah, and he and Zeal will have a chance to get to know each other."

Grandma Pearl stood up from her chair. "Here's what I know. There's about to be some romance around here, and we could use a little excitement."

Pastor Sanford and Mama Beatrice grinned and shook their heads as Grandma Pearl headed upstairs to her room.

Zeal stepped out onto the porch where Jeremiah was kneeling down playing with Samson. At the sound of her footsteps, he glanced up.

Smiling, she said, "My father tells me you're going to be staying for a little while."

"Yes, I am. He has things for me to do during the day, but I'll have time during the evenings for myself."

"What will you be doing with that time?" asked Zeal.

After giving Samson a quick pat on the head, Jeremiah stood up. "Well, of course, I'll be spending time with God, and Samson here will want to have some time with me too."

That wasn't exactly the answer she expected, and he could tell she was a little aggravated.

Jeremiah smiled and took a step toward her. "And of course I'll want to spend time with you."

Zeal held out her hand. "How much time?"

"As much as I can," said Jeremiah, grasping her hand.

They both stood there for a moment gazing into each other's eyes.

Tap. Tap. Tap.

Zeal turned to see that it was her mother tapping on the window and knew it was her cue to come back inside.

She put her hand on the doorknob. "I'll see you tomorrow then."

"Yes, you will."

Zeal walked back into the house, and Jeremiah led Samson over to the stream to get some water. Pastor Sanford came outside and joined them, then led Jeremiah to his room. Feeling as if he was in a dream, Jeremiah unpacked and went to bed.

26

YOUNG LOVE

The next morning Jeremiah awoke to the sound of a rooster. When he came downstairs, he passed a room to his left, where Pastor Sanford was reading in his Book and taking notes. Jeremiah was unsure if he should knock or if he could go in uninvited, so he stood outside the door for a few moments.

Before long Pastor Sanford looked up from his Book. "Good morning, Jeremiah."

"Good morning, sir."

"Beatrice fixed you some breakfast, and I put it in the room down the hall, on the right. We use it for small classes, but you're welcome to use it to eat your meals. You certainly won't go hungry around here. My wife always cooks extra food."

Jeremiah nodded. "Thank you, and I'll be sure and thank her the next time I see her."

He turned down the hall to go to the classroom. When he finished eating, he returned to Pastor Sanford's office, again waiting until he looked up.

When Pastor Sanford nodded to him, Jeremiah said, "Sir, what would you like for me to do today?"

"There are loose boards all around this building. You'll find a ladder, hammer, and nails in the shed out back."

"Yes sir."

He found the shed with everything he needed and went to work. At lunchtime, he heard Zeal calling his name.

"I'm back here on the ladder," Jeremiah hollered as he finished nailing in a board.

Zeal popped her head around the corner. "I put your lunch in the classroom."

"Thank you."

"I can't stay, but I'll see you later. My father says you can eat your dinners with us each night."

"That'll be great," said Jeremiah, climbing up a step to reach another loose board. "I'll see you then."

After nailing three more boards, Jeremiah went inside to eat his lunch. After a short rest, he went back to work. Fixing the loose boards wasn't hard, and before long his mind drifted to Zeal. He couldn't wait until dinner when he would be able to see her and talk to her again.

The rest of the day went by quickly, and after washing up, he went straight to Zeal's house for dinner.

Mama Beatrice had prepared another fine meal, but what Jeremiah was most interested in was spending time with Zeal. After dinner, the two of them went out on the porch. This pattern would become their routine during the coming weeks. Jeremiah would work during the day, join the family for dinner, and then he and Zeal would spend the rest of the evening talking.

The next two weeks went by quickly, and with the passing of each day, Jeremiah and Zeal fell more in love. They talked about everything and soon felt as if they had known each other for their entire lives. When they sat out on the porch, talking and laughing, they seemed to be the only two people in the world. That was, of course, until the familiar tapping on the window which signaled that another day was coming to an end.

Four weeks passed, and Jeremiah and Zeal sat out on the porch as usual. For the first time, they began to talk about what comes next. They had enjoyed this time of getting to know one another, but they now started to think about the future.

"How much longer do you think you'll be staying?" asked Zeal.

Jeremiah had asked himself the same question. "I don't know."

Zeal reached out and touched his arm. "How much longer do you want to stay?"

Jeremiah knew what he wanted to say, but was it time? Taking a deep breath, he said, "I don't know how much longer I'm supposed to stay, but what I do know is that I don't want to leave you."

Zeal felt as if she could float away, and she gave Jeremiah the kind of look that every man wished to experience. Passion filled her voice. "I don't want you to leave at all." She longed for Jeremiah to take her into his arms and just hold her—

Tap. Tap. Tap.

Turning toward the sound, they saw the smiling face of Mama Beatrice.

Walking backwards toward the door, Zeal said, "Goodnight Jeremiah."

"Goodnight Zeal."

As Jeremiah trudged back to his room, he knew that he never wanted to be away from Zeal, but he also knew he wasn't ready to propose marriage. They had become very close, but he sensed there was still more that God needed to do with them. Soon it would be time to speak with Zeal's father on a much more serious level.

After finishing his breakfast the next morning, Jeremiah stopped by Pastor Sanford's office.

Zeal's father peered up at him. "Hello Jeremiah, is there something that you need?"

"Yes, I need to speak with you."

He gave Jeremiah a smile and a nod as if he could tell the young man wanted to talk about something serious. "Come on in and have a seat."

Jeremiah sat down and fiddled with his hands while surveying the room.

Pastor Sanford put down his pen and sat back in his chair. "What is it you'd like to talk about?"

Clearing his throat a few times, Jeremiah rubbed his hands together. "Well sir, you know that I felt I was led here to spend time with your daughter."

"Yes," said Pastor Sanford, rocking back in his chair.

"And," said Jeremiah, "you know we've been spending a lot of time together."

"Yes, I've seen that."

"Well, the more time we have together, the more I want to be around her."

Zeal's father leaned forward and rested his hands on top of his desk. "Jeremiah, that first night you were here, I asked you a question that you sort of answered. I want to ask you that question again. Do you love my daughter?"

Jeremiah squirmed in his chair. He lowered his gaze a moment then made eye contact with Pastor Sanford. "Yes I do. I love your daughter with all of my heart."

"I see. Have you told her?"

"Not yet. I've been waiting for the right time."

"I sense there's something more you'd like to discuss with me," said Pastor Sanford.

"Yes, there is." Jeremiah glanced around the room. "I don't know how much longer my path will stay here, but I can't imagine leaving Zeal."

Pastor Sanford picked up his pen and tapped it on his desk. "What is it you're trying to tell me?"

Looking out the window, Jeremiah said, "I guess what I'm really concerned about is God sending me away to continue my journey. I don't want to leave your daughter."

Pastor Sanford folded his hands and sighed. "I'm sure she wouldn't want you to leave either, but both of you have to be willing to surrender everything into God's hands."

"That's going to be hard," said Jeremiah, shaking his head. "I've never felt like this before, and the thought of giving up Zeal is painful."

"God is only able to bless the things we give to Him. If we keep something under our own control, we'll eventually lose it, but if we lose something for His sake, then He can give it back to us with His full blessing."

"But," said Jeremiah, "what if we give it away and God doesn't give it back?"

Pastor Sanford nodded. "That's the risk everyone must take. If God intends for you and Zeal to be together, then you'll be together. It's possible He could send you away for awhile and then bring you back. The important thing is that you must be willing to be obedient to whatever He says."

Jeremiah sighed. "I know what you're saying is true, but it really scares me."

"Is that why you haven't told her that you love her? Are you afraid you're going to tell her and then have to leave?"

Jeremiah paused then glanced up. "That's part of the reason. I guess I'm just nervous in general, but yes, I'm concerned that if I express how I feel and then have to leave, it will hurt even more."

Pastor Sanford sat back and nodded. "And how would you feel if you left without telling her at all?"

He hadn't thought about that before. "I guess I would feel even worse."

Sitting forward, Pastor Sanford said, "Pray about it, and don't be afraid to follow your feelings."

"Thank you, I'll do that." Jeremiah stood up to leave. "By the way, I'm ready to begin something new."

"Very good, you've done a great job with fixing all the loose boards, and the landscaping around the building has never looked better. The next thing would be to give this House of Instruction a good paint job. You'll find everything you need in the shed."

After leaving the office, Jeremiah got to work on the painting. He continued his same routine, working during the day and spending his evenings with Zeal.

A week later when they were sitting out on the porch, Zeal noticed that Jeremiah appeared to be in a daze. "Is something wrong?"

He didn't answer.

She placed her hand on his arm. "Are you ok?"

Jeremiah jerked his head up as if he had just awoken. "Oh yes, everything is fine."

"What are you thinking about that has you so distracted today?"

Jeremiah took a deep breath. "Zeal, since the day I saw you I've felt something that I've never felt before. Each day that I've been with you that feeling has grown stronger. It's more than just a human feeling. I feel as if God Himself placed it inside me—"

"What is it you feel?" Zeal said, her eyes widening.

Jeremiah paused for a moment. When he felt ready, he gazed into her dark brown eyes with a longing from deep within his soul. "I love you Zeal. I love you."

"I love you, too!" exclaimed Zeal as she almost jumped out of her chair.

Jeremiah felt a surge of excitement and relief all at the same time. She loved him too. He inched closer and took her hands in his. "I've wanted to tell you for weeks, and it feels so good to be able to tell you now. Ever since I met you, I've not been able to imagine my life without you."

"Me either," said Zeal as her fingers tightened around his. "I imagined the day I would hear those words, but nothing compares to hearing them from you."

Exhilaration flooded Jeremiah's heart, but he felt something else, too, something he had not felt before with another human being. He felt vulnerable.

"I'm so glad I told you how I feel," said Jeremiah, "but what's even better is hearing that you feel the same way."

"Oh yes," said Zeal, "I feel it too." She leaned back. Her face was glowing, and her head moved side to side as if in time with a tune only she could hear.

Tap. Tap. Tap.

She sighed and stood to go inside, but her body swayed ever so slightly.

Jeremiah stood too and took a step toward her. "Before you go I want to tell you one more time. I love you."

"I love you too," said Zeal.

When at last, she went inside, Zeal danced around the room as if she was in a ballroom.

Her mother said, "What is all this excitement about?"

Zeal just smiled, as she continued to dance.

Grandma Pearl said, "Well, come on girl, don't be keeping all this good stuff to yourself."

Zeal stopped and threw her hands out wide. "He loves me!"

Mama Beatrice nudged her husband's arm. "Did you hear that?"

"Yes, I did."

She stared at him with a quizzical look. "You don't seem surprised."

Patting her hand, he said, "I'll talk to you about it later."

Zeal had gone back to dancing, but stopped for just a moment to say, "I love you too." She continued her dance, circling the sofa.

Grandma Pearl sat up in her chair. "Well girl, all I can say is it's about time. You two been looking at each other with them goo-goo eyes every evening. It's about time we got this thing moving along."

Zeal danced up to her room.

Grandma Pearl stood up to go to bed. "It looks like we may have a wedding around here. That's good, because I've got the perfect dress and the perfect hat. I'm going to be looking mighty fine."

After Grandma Pearl headed up the stairs and into her room, Mama Beatrice turned to face Pastor Sanford. "So tell me what you know."

He took her hand and led her to the couch. Starting at the beginning, he told her all about his conversation with Jeremiah the previous week. As they talked, she made sure to get every ounce of detail she could.

After he finished, she could tell something was bothering him. "What is it you're thinking about?"

Pastor Sanford sighed. "I guess I'm starting to think about the possibility of our daughter getting married and the possibility that she may not be living here anymore."

Mama Beatrice grabbed his hand. "I know you've always wanted Zeal to marry a young man who could help you with the House of Instruction."

He nodded. "That's been my dream. There's a nice piece of land not too far from here that would be perfect to build a house. She could come by every day, and it would almost be like she was still here."

She squeezed his hand. "But what if that isn't what God has planned?"

"I don't know. It's not something I want to think about."

She gently touched his cheek. "It would seem that you may need to listen to the same advice you gave Jeremiah and be willing to surrender all things into God's hands. We both have known for some time now that they were destined to be together."

"I know," said Pastor Sanford, placing his hand over hers. "I just wish we had more time."

They sat together in silence for another few minutes before turning off the oil lamps and going to bed.

27

A CHANGE OF PLANS

Another week passed, and Jeremiah finally completed painting the House of Instruction. Everyone who stopped by complimented him on how nice it looked. After getting all the paint off his hands, he washed up to get ready for dinner. Ever since he told Zeal that he loved her, it seemed their time together was even more enjoyable.

That evening they went outside as usual. It was such a clear, beautiful night with the stars and the moon painting a romantic scene in the sky that seemed to be meant just for them.

Zeal faced him and squeezed his hands. "Do you think about what it would be like to be married and have a family?"

Jeremiah grinned, "I certainly do, but something tells me your dreams are much more detailed than mine."

Zeal eased her hands out of his and glided backwards a few steps. "I see a little home with a flower bed underneath the front window, and a nicely manicured lawn enclosed by a brown picket fence. The house has a natural wood stained finish and is just big enough for us and two children."

"Only two?" said Jeremiah as he smiled.

She held up her finger. "Two to start with." She gazed upward as if she was refocusing on a vivid picture in her head. "I see our children playing out front, and as soon as you step into the yard, they run up and give you a hug."

"I like that, tell me more."

Zeal tilted her head to the side. "I come out on the front porch, and you march up with one child in your right arm and the other one holding your left hand. Just as you reach me, you lean forward and give me a kiss."

"This is getting interesting," said Jeremiah. "What happens next?"

Still looking as if she was in a daydream, Zeal continued. "We go inside, and oh Jeremiah, it's the cutest thing. The most perfect little blue curtains hang on the windows. There's a wide open space for a living room where a brown couch sits in the middle with a beautiful rug spread out in front. There's a fireplace to the left, and in the floor is two coloring books that the children have been coloring in."

Jeremiah eased up beside her and placed his arm around her. "Sounds like the kind of place I'd like to live."

"Me too." She continued to stare out into the distance. "I call you and the children over to the kitchen table, where I've prepared a meal of chicken and dumplings."

Jeremiah rubbed his stomach. "This just keeps getting better."

Zeal smiled and relaxed into his grasp. "The meal-time together is pleasant, and after we clear the dishes away, we sit in the living room near the fire and read stories to the children. Then we take them to bed and tuck them in."

Jeremiah squeezed her shoulder. "Then what?"

Tap. Tap. Tap.

Zeal turned to see her mother smiling and motioning for her to come inside.

Zeal held up one finger to let her mom know she'd be there in just a minute. Resting her head on his shoulder, she said, "I can't wait for the future to begin."

Jeremiah pulled her in closer. "I can't either." Reluctantly, he released her.

Zeal started back toward her house, but then quickly turned around. "I love you."

Nodding, Jeremiah said, "I love you too."

The next morning Jeremiah stopped by to see what Pastor Sanford had for him to do next, but he wasn't in his office. Excited to start another day, he stepped outside.

Surveying the yard, Jeremiah saw something he had not seen in months. His path had changed, and it was now leading away. This was the day he had feared since arriving with Zeal. Jeremiah studied the ground and then lifted his eyes toward heaven. A tear started to roll down his face. He knew he had to trust God, but right now all he could think about was leaving the woman he loved.

All of a sudden, he heard Zeal squealing excitedly for her family to come out onto the porch. As her mom and dad rushed outside to see what was wrong, she was jumping up and down while pointing at her path. To everyone's surprise, her path had changed too, and it was now leading away with Jeremiah's. Excited and a little confused, Jeremiah wiped away his tear and headed toward the house.

As soon as Zeal saw him, she jumped into the air and came running toward him. "Jeremiah, do you see it? Do you see it? Do you see where our paths are going?"

"Yes, I see," he said, smiling as Zeal jumped up and down.

He glanced at her father who didn't seem to share his daughter's enthusiasm.

Pastor Sanford's eyes narrowed just a little as he took a deep breath. "I'm going to spend the day praying, and I suggest you two do the same. We'll talk more about this at dinner tonight."

Her parents walked back inside, but Zeal, as hyper as a little girl, couldn't stand still.

Grabbing Jeremiah's elbow, she said, "Isn't this exciting?"

"Yes, it is," said Jeremiah, studying their paths to make sure they were seeing what they thought they were seeing.

He wasn't sure what to make of all this. He'd thought that either God would send him away by himself, or he would stay until they were married, but he was definitely not expecting this.

Zeal looked back toward her house. "Don't worry about my father. He'll follow whatever God says, and it's obvious that God is leading us to be together."

Jeremiah nodded. "I'm going to do what he has asked and go spend some time reading and praying until dinner tonight."

"I will too," said Zeal, "and I can't wait to see you at dinner."

Jeremiah went back to his room to read and pray. He felt certain they could travel together and maintain proper boundaries, but going out alone did not seem like the ideal next step for them as a couple.

When it was time for dinner, he went over to their home. Zeal immediately greeted him at the door and stepped outside. It was obvious that her excitement had not diminished, and in fact, it may have increased. As they stood talking, her parents came out onto the porch.

Zeal grabbed her father's arm. "Look, there's Jeremiah's path, and there's my path. Isn't this exciting?"

"Yes it is," said Pastor Sanford, "and you know what else is exciting?"

"What's that," said Zeal, speaking in an excited high pitch tone.

"Your mother and I have been praying, and we've discovered that Grandma Pearl's path is going in the exact same direction!"

Zeal stepped back, looking at her father as if she didn't quite hear him correctly.

Grandma Pearl tromped out onto the porch. "When are we leaving? Let's get this show on the road."

Pastor Sanford had a huge smile on his face. "Now Grandma Pearl, there's no need to be in a hurry. We can have a good dinner this evening, and then you three can start packing. Tomorrow will be a good time to leave."

Zeal had a forced smile on her face and she clenched her teeth as she spoke. "But father, she can't walk all that distance."

Grandma Pearl held up her hands. "Who said anything about walking? That farmer down the road always told us that if we ever needed to borrow his donkey to just ask him. I'm going to be riding in style."

"But father," said Zeal, still looking at him with a forced smile, "we may not be able to stay in an inn every night. What if we have to camp?"

Grandma Pearl rolled her eyes and shook her head. "Girl, what are you trying to say? I've been camping longer than you've been alive. You don't worry about me. You just take care of yourself."

Zeal could see that her father was still smiling as big as she had ever seen him smile, and she could tell he was enjoying every moment of this situation. She could also see that it had already been decided.

Jeremiah had a relieved look on his face. He didn't want to say anything, but he was glad that God was sending someone else along.

Grandma Pearl turned to walk back in the house. "Well, if we aren't leaving then let's eat."

They all went back inside and sat down for dinner. There was a lot of talk about what might lie ahead and what kind of adventures they might experience.

Jeremiah motioned toward Pastor Sanford. "What do you think God is doing by sending us out like this?"

Pastor Sanford finished his bite of food and put down his fork. "So far, you and Zeal have been getting to know one another in a safe and predictable environment. Now I believe God wants to place you in situations that are not always going to be easy or predictable."

Zeal smiled at Jeremiah. "I'm sure we'll be able to handle anything that comes along."

Her parents looked at each other with a slight grin, knowing the challenges they were going to encounter. They also knew, though, that they couldn't tell them about these challenges ahead of time, but they would have to experience them together.

"Here's what I know," said Grandma Pearl, "there's going to be some rules, so let's go ahead and get them out of the way. First of all, when we stay at an inn, Zeal and I will have a room together. When we camp, my tent will be next to Zeal's, and Jeremiah, your tent will be further down. And something I want you both to know is that I'm a very light sleeper."

Everyone covered their mouth to hide their laughter, but Grandma Pearl gave them a slight frown to let them know she meant business. After they were done with dinner, Jeremiah and Zeal went out onto the porch as they always had.

Zeal had accepted that Grandma Pearl was coming along, and now she was more focused on the fact that God was sending them out together. "Jeremiah, I can't wait until we start on our journey tomorrow. I'm ready to get out and experience life."

"I'm excited, too," said Jeremiah, staring in the direction where their path was leading. "I know God has great things for us."

They didn't talk as long that night because they both had a lot to do to get ready to leave. Zeal returned home, and Jeremiah went back to his room to start packing.

On the way, Jeremiah saw Samson and bent down to pet him. "It looks like we're about to start another adventure."

Jeremiah wasn't sure if Samson understood, but he certainly jumped around as if he did.

When morning came, there was a lot of nervous excitement in the air. The farmer had already brought the donkey up and tied it to the railing. Grandma Pearl and Zeal were busy setting their bags out on the front porch, and Pastor Sanford was fixing an old cart to carry everything. Jeremiah brought his things over and then helped load up the cart.

Once everything was ready, Jeremiah asked Pastor Sanford if he could speak with him before they left.

"Sure," he said, "let's walk over to my office."

As they entered the room, he motioned for Jeremiah to have a seat. "What would you like to talk about?"

"Sir, all of this was kind of sudden for me. I didn't think I'd be leaving here with your daughter unless we were married."

"I see," said Pastor Sanford, "and I must admit it was a little surprising to me at first, but then I could see the benefit of you two spending some time together away from here."

"I guess what I want to ask you is, if I feel it's time to propose to your daughter while we're on this journey, may I have your permission?"

Pastor Sanford knew this question was eventually coming, so he wasn't unprepared, but it still wasn't easy. He looked down at a picture of Zeal when she was a little girl and remembered the times she would be playing in the front yard, then run up to hug him the moment she saw him. A part of him wished he could always keep her as his little girl, but he knew that answering Jeremiah's question would be one of the final acts of letting that go.

"Jeremiah, I've gotten to know you over these past months, and I've been impressed with your love for God, and your love for my daughter. You're a man of character, and I would be honored to have you as a part of our family. You most definitely have my permission to propose to my daughter."

Pastor Sanford stood up and extended his hand.

Jeremiah also rose and firmly grasped his hand. "Thank you, that means a lot coming from you."

"You're welcome. I do want you to know that I don't believe this journey is going to be easy. At the same time though, if a relationship does not have to go through any adversity, it cannot grow stronger."

"I'll try and remember that."

As they walked out of the office, Pastor Sanford put his hand on Jeremiah's back. "Take care of my daughter."

"I will," said Jeremiah.

When they reached the house, Pastor Sanford hooked up the cart then stepped back.

Grandma Pearl hopped on the donkey. "I'm tired of all this standing around. Let's get going."

Zeal hugged her parents, and then Mama Beatrice gave Jeremiah a hug. Samson strolled over toward Pastor Sanford and Mama Beatrice wagging his tail. They reached down to pet him and told him goodbye. After Samson circled around them, rubbing up against their legs, he trotted over to Jeremiah.

Grandma Pearl gave a gentle kick to the side of the donkey. "Giddy up."

28

THE ADVENTURES OF JEREMIAH & ZEAL

Jeremiah and Zeal were excited to start their adventure together. For the first week of their travels they spent most of the day walking along and talking, and then toward evening they looked for an inn and spent the evening there. Grandma Pearl always enjoyed meeting new people, and it seemed like at every stop she met other women close to her age. They would enjoy a nice cup of coffee together and discuss the many adventures they had experienced in life.

One day as they were traveling, the sound of rushing water echoed in the distance. After going a little further, they could see a wide river with a fast-moving current. A bridge had been built across the river, but Jeremiah thought he saw something in front of it. Motioning for everyone to stop, he took out his telescope and pointed it toward the bridge. Guarding the entrance were ten small but fierce looking creatures, wearing black pointed helmets and carrying long whips.

Jeremiah put down his telescope. "It looks like we have to defeat those enemies before we can cross the bridge."

"This is exciting!" said Zeal. "We're about to have our first battle together."

Grandma Pearl dismounted from her donkey. "Samson and I will stay here. This looks like a battle for you two, but you'll need to work together to defeat them."

Jeremiah quickly raised his Book until it became a Sword and charged toward the bridge. "Let's go."

"Wait for me," said Zeal as she hurried behind him.

As they drew closer, the creatures cracked their whips in front of them.

Quickly glancing over his shoulder, Jeremiah said, "We'll have to stay behind our Shields until we can get close enough to attack."

Jeremiah took another step but didn't realize he was already within range of the whips. One of the creatures quickly snapped their whip toward Jeremiah's legs. As the leather strand wrapped around his ankle, the creature jerked the handle. Jeremiah's feet flew out from under him, and he flipped onto his back. Three of the other creatures dashed toward him and began to crack their whips at his legs.

"Zeal! I need you to block their attacks so I can get untangled and get back on my feet."

But Zeal was in her own battle because as soon as the creatures had Jeremiah on the ground, they began cracking their whips at her. She blocked most of the strikes, but some got through and raised welts on her arms.

"I can't Jeremiah!" shouted Zeal, as another whip struck her on the wrist. "It's all I can do to keep from getting hit myself."

After enduring numerous stinging blows, Jeremiah finally unwound the whip from his ankle and jumped back to his feet.

He darted out of range, then said, "Let's rush them."

As Jeremiah stormed the creatures, he immediately found himself surrounded. Five of them sent their lashes toward his head while another one tried to wrap its whip around his ankles again. He swung around with his Shield to block as many as possible while jumping to avoid the lash that came toward his legs. He glanced back expecting to see Zeal charging up behind him, but she had not moved forward.

"Zeal, I need help! I'm surrounded!"

Engaged in her own battle, Zeal ducked and blocked the whips as best she could. "I can't Jeremiah. If I go any further, I'm going to get hit even more."

Jeremiah decided to retreat. He tried to block as many blows as possible, holding his Shield in front of him and backing away. "This isn't working! We need to get out of here."

"I don't want to give up, Jeremiah!"

"We have to, at least for now."

Shaking her head, Zeal followed him and backed out of range of the whips.

When they were safe, she put down her Sword and Shield, then placed her hands on her hips. "Why did you quit? We could have defeated them if we kept fighting."

"No," said Jeremiah pointing toward the creatures, "we would only have taken a worse beating."

He could tell by her tone that Zeal was disappointed in him, and this was far worse than the defeat he had just suffered. Silently they returned to Grandma Pearl and Samson.

Grandma Pearl saw the welts and cuts on their arms and went to get some ointment out of her bags.

Zeal turned to Jeremiah. "Let's talk about what just happened."

Jeremiah started off toward a wooded area. "I'm going for a walk."

Holding out her hands, Zeal said, "What do you mean you're going for a walk? We need to talk about this."

Jeremiah kept walking.

Grandma Pearl returned with some ointment and rubbed it on Zeal's cuts. The damage was not too severe—more than anything, the wounds just stung.

"Hurry up," said Zeal, looking anxious to get away. "I need to follow him and talk to him."

"Oh no," said Grandma Pearl, "now is not the time to do that."

"What do you mean? I feel like if I don't get all this out, I'm going to explode."

Grandma Pearl rubbed a little more ointment on Zeal's arms. "If you go talk to him right now there's going to be an explosion all right."

"I don't understand," said Zeal. "Why doesn't he want to talk? How can we solve a problem if we don't discuss it?"

Grandma Pearl finished putting a bandage on Zeal's left arm and stepped back. "Child, there's a lot you're going to have to learn about men, but here is the first thing. Sometimes when a man needs to solve a problem, he wants to be alone. I know that runs counter to everything you're feeling right now, but that's the way most men are. Jeremiah probably feels like a failure. This was the first battle you two fought together, and he was not able to lead you to a victory. If you go to him right now offering all kinds of suggestions, then that's just going to make him feel even more like a failure."

Shaking her head, Zeal said, "I just want to help him understand what went wrong so we can fix it."

Putting up the ointment and bandages, Grandma Pearl said, "I kind of think what you really mean is, you want to help him understand what he did wrong so you can fix him. But whether that is what you mean or not, if you go to him right now like this, that's what he's going to think."

Zeal lowered her head as her arms drooped at her sides. "What do I do then? I feel as if he's left me. I feel abandoned. How do I know he's coming back? Is it over already?"

Grandma Pearl put her arms around Zeal. "You listen to me child, nothing is over. You two are just beginning. You're going to get through this just like you're going to get through a thousand other things. I know it looks and feels really big right now, but it's going to be okay."

Resting her head on Grandma Pearl's shoulders, Zeal asked, "But how is it going to be okay if we don't talk about it?"

Grandma Pearl patted her on the arm. "You'll be able to talk about it. You just won't be able to talk about it as soon as you wish. Here's what we're going to do. Let's walk back just a little ways to that nice spot we passed and set up camp. We'll put up all the tents, and if Jeremiah isn't back by then, you and Samson can go look for him. I'm sure he didn't go too far."

As they started setting up all the tents, Zeal felt like each second was an eternity. Over and over she scanned the area to see if Jeremiah was back. She tried to hurriedly set up the tents, but Grandma Pearl kept slowing her down to make sure everything was done right. After an hour had passed, they finally had everything set up, but Jeremiah was still not back.

Grandma Pearl could tell Zeal was anxious. "Okay, now you and Samson go on, but when you find him don't let your first words be about the battle. This will let him know you aren't there to attack him or blame him. Speak to him in a way that lets him know you're on his side, and you want to figure this out with him."

Zeal quickly called Samson over, and they began walking in the direction that Jeremiah had headed off to. They didn't walk too far before they saw him sitting under a tree, shaking his head and mumbling as he drew in the dirt with a stick. Samson trotted over and began rubbing his head against his side.

Jeremiah petted Samson. He knew Zeal was there too, but he still hadn't figured out what he was going to say. While he had been alone, he kept thinking about how badly the battle had gone. Was this the type of leader he was going to be? If he couldn't lead them to victory in this battle, how would he be able to do it in the future?

Zeal walked over and sat down beside him, then started to pet Samson. "We've already set up the tents. It'll be dark in a few hours, and we wanted to go ahead and get that done."

"Thank you," said Jeremiah, as he briefly looked into her eyes.

They sat in silence for another five minutes as they rubbed Samson's fur.

After praying for wisdom, Zeal asked, "What do you think went wrong?"

Jeremiah shook his head. "I don't know. I've been sitting here thinking about it. Obviously, we didn't go in with a very good plan."

"We didn't go in with any plan," said Zeal.

"I guess that's true," said Jeremiah, "but I wanted to show you that I could do this, that I had the answers, that I could lead us to a victory."

Zeal sat up as she slightly shook her head. "I don't want someone with all the answers Jeremiah. I just want someone who's willing to search for the answers, and more importantly, someone who wants to search for those answers with me."

Jeremiah stared at Samson. He knew she was right. In his desire to prove his manhood, he went rushing out toward an enemy with no plan and no strategy, as if his own abilities were going to be enough.

"You're right. I didn't stop and ask for your input, and I also didn't stop and ask God for His input."

Zeal put her hand on Jeremiah's shoulder. "I know I made mistakes, too. In my stubbornness, I didn't want to admit that you were right and that we just needed to get out of there. I know that you must have been feeling terrible, and I made it worse when I questioned why you didn't keep fighting. Sometimes I can be stubborn, and I'll want to keep doing something even though it isn't working."

Jeremiah smiled and nodded. "It looks like we both have a lot to learn."

Zeal smiled back. She felt so much better. What had seemed impossible earlier now felt manageable. "What do we do next?"

Jeremiah stood up and held out his hand. "We must find a way to defeat these enemies."

Taking his hand, she rose to her feet. "We'll figure it out together."

Grandma Pearl had walked up to within shouting distance. "You two need to come on back. It will be dark soon, and we need to get a fire built."

As they returned to the campsite, Jeremiah put his arm around Zeal and gave her a quick hug. "Thank you for giving me some time. I felt like I had let you down."

When they arrived, Jeremiah went to gather wood for the fire.

Zeal stood next to Grandma Pearl and whispered, "You were right."

Grandma Pearl grinned. "Of course I was right. You don't live with a man like your grandpa for all those years without learning something."

"How long did it take you to learn these things?"

Sitting down on a stool while motioning for Zeal to do the same, Grandma Pearl said, "Oh, it took me a long time. We were both young and inexperienced, and we made a lot of mistakes. Anytime something went wrong, I wanted to immediately tell him how I thought things should have been done differently. I didn't understand why each time I did this, he would shut down. I was angry and frustrated, and I felt like he didn't care. Over time, I discovered that it made all the difference as to how and when I approached him. When a man thinks you're out to fix him, blame him, or attack him, then his defenses go up, and you're not getting through that wall."

"But," said Zeal, "don't we eventually need to talk about things, so they don't get worse? What if it doesn't go like today and he stays shut down for awhile?"

Grandma Pearl said, "It's going to be different each time. But, if you both put in the hard work of building a relationship, then you're not going to let things come in and defeat all that hard work. What you have to remember is that you must let him know you're on his side. No matter what you two may face, you have to face it together. If a man feels his wife is with him, then this gives him a tremendous boost of confidence, but if he feels she is against him, then it creates a whole lot of self-doubt. Always let him know that you want to solve the problem *with* him, and not solve the problem *for* him."

Zeal squirmed on her stool and rubbed her hands together. "This all sounds good, but what about his part?"

Grandma Pearl smiled as she patted Zeal on the knee. "Well, right now, he's not the one asking for my advice. You must always focus on what it is you can do to change. You can share your feelings about the changes you want to see in others, but you only have control over what you will do. We all have to learn to work on ourselves, and let God work on everybody else."

"That sounds so hard," said Zeal, pursing her lips and putting her hands on the side of her face. "It's such a risk. You can put all of yourself out there, and there's no guarantee what the other person will do."

Grandma Pearl clapped her hands together. "Zeal girl, that is exactly what it means to be in a relationship. All that time you two spent together back at your house, that was just the beginning. Now is when the real part begins. I promise you this, if you two learn how to work through problems together now, then it's going to pay off later."

Zeal ducked into her tent for a minute. While she was gone, Jeremiah walked up with an armful of twigs and fallen branches.

Grandma Pearl waited for him to set the wood down, then she whispered, "I know there will be occasions when you need to take time to yourself, but when you do, it would really help Zeal if you'd just tell her that you'll be back."

"Thank you Grandma Pearl," said Jeremiah. "I'll remember that."

Zeal came back out as Jeremiah was arranging the wood in position to start the fire.

After putting the last piece in place, Jeremiah stood up. "As soon as we get this fire going we can talk about what happened today. The first thing we need to figure out is exactly what it is we're fighting."

Grandma Pearl said, "Oh, that's the easy part. I can tell you what they are."

Jeremiah and Zeal looked at each other and then back to Grandma Pearl.

"Well," said Grandma Pearl, shrugging her shoulders, "I would have told you if you would have asked me, but you two rushed on out there all in a hurry, so I figured you knew what you were doing."

Zeal said, "So what are they?"

Grandma Pearl struck a match and lit the fire. "Those enemies you're facing are the Goblins of Contention and Strife. Your grandpa and I fought them several times, and we had to learn to battle them together."

29

CONTENTION AND STRIFE

Grandma Pearl motioned for Jeremiah and Zeal to pull up a stool next to the fire. "This enemy has a way of turning you against each other. Before you know it you're battling each other instead of concentrating on the real problem."

"What is the real problem?" asked Zeal.

Raising her index finger, Grandma Pearl said, "The real problem is selfishness and pride. We want something someone else has, or we're trying to protect something we already have so someone else doesn't get it. The object could be possessions or money, but most of the time it has to do with position, status, or territory."

Grandma Pearl took out her Book. "Let me read a couple of things in James. 'For wherever there is envy and selfish ambition, there will also be instability, confusion, and every evil work.' A little further down he wrote, 'What leads to strife and discord, and how do conflicts and quarrels arise among you? Do they not come from your selfish desires that are always at work in your flesh?' "

Zeal said, "So then what is the answer?"

Grandma Pearl turned in her Book to another section. "Fulfill my joy by being of the same mind, having the same love, being in unity together. Do nothing out of strife or selfish ambition, but in humility consider others as more important than yourselves. Not just being concerned about your own things, but also about the things of others."

Jeremiah sat up. "So to defeat Strife and Contention, we must battle for each other and not against each other."

"That's right Jeremiah," said Grandma Pearl. "You must put the needs of the other ahead of your own, fighting for their best interests instead of seeking your own."

Jeremiah took Zeal's hand in his. "What is it you need during this battle?"

Zeal relaxed and put her other hand on top of his. "I need you to view me as a partner. I don't want you to go out to battle and just expect me to follow. I want you to involve me in the planning."

Jeremiah nodded. "I can do that."

Zeal said, "What is it you need?"

Jeremiah put his hand to his chin. "Once we've agreed on what to do, and it's time to act, I need for you to trust me as a leader. If the plan isn't working, then we'll figure it out together and try something different."

Grandma Pearl nodded then stood up. "It's getting late so let's all get some sleep, and you two can talk more about this tomorrow."

After getting a good night's rest, Jeremiah and Zeal woke to the smell of Grandma Pearl cooking breakfast.

When they came out of their tent and sat down, she put some freshly cooked eggs on their plates. "Now you need to think about how you're going to work together and get us by these creatures. I want to get moving."

Jeremiah turned to Zeal. "What do you think we need to do differently?"

Zeal grinned at him then said, "In our first battle you split off from me and attacked on your own. I think we need to stay closer this next time."

"I agree," said Jeremiah, "and if we keep our Shields close together, we can block their whips more easily."

Zeal said, "I also think we should keep reminding ourselves that we are not each other's enemy. As soon as we felt the sting of those whips, I think we started to take it out on each other."

"That's a good point," said Jeremiah.

Grandma Pearl picked up the plates. "All right, I expect you two to have those enemies cleared away by the time I've cleaned up and taken these tents down. You can help me finish packing when you get back."

Before heading out, Jeremiah bowed his head and prayed, "Dear Lord, give us wisdom as we fight this enemy together. Forgive me for not coming to you the first time we battled Strife and Contention.

Help me to view Zeal as a partner, and let me not be concerned with proving myself or my manhood."

Smiling at each other, Jeremiah and Zeal stood up. They held out their Books until they became Swords, then marched toward the bridge together. The goblins spotted their approach and once again began to crack their whips. With each snap of the long leather straps, Jeremiah and Zeal remembered just how much it stung to get hit by them. Drawing closer, they crept much more cautiously this time, holding their Shields side by side.

Advancing a little further, Jeremiah could see they were almost to the same place where he'd been pulled off his feet the day before. Motioning for Zeal to stop, he put out his foot like he was going to take another step. One of the goblins flung their whip toward Jeremiah's ankle, but he quickly drew it back and thrust his Sword into the ground where his foot would have been.

The lash sailed through the air, then wrapped around his Sword. Jeremiah jerked his Sword toward him, pulling the creature through the air until it landed a few feet in front of him. The goblin tried to stand up, but Jeremiah immediately struck it with his Sword on both shoulders, knocking it to its knees. Taking two steps back so he could get a running start, Jeremiah rushed toward the creature and punted it into the river.

Watching the goblin float helplessly with the current, Jeremiah and Zeal now had confidence that they could defeat Strife and Contention.

Jeremiah glanced at Zeal and whispered, "Let's rush toward the middle. I don't think they'll be expecting that, and we should be able to land several blows before they can react."

Zeal nodded. "I'm ready."

Jeremiah pointed his Sword. "Now!"

Rushing toward the very center, Jeremiah and Zeal surprised them with their quickness and were able to strike the three middle goblins on their head and neck, knocking them to the ground. Just as the other ones on the ends tried to come in and help, Jeremiah and Zeal held up their Shields, blocking all of the blows from the whips. As the three goblins on the ground got to their feet, Jeremiah and Zeal hit them with their Shields, sending them backwards into the river. They then quickly retreated before the others could surround them.

At the beginning of the fight, Jeremiah and Zeal had faced ten goblins, and now there were only six. Those remaining arranged themselves in a tight formation to make sure the entrance to the bridge was securely blocked. Cracking their whips furiously, first in the air, then on the ground, the creatures attempted to scare Jeremiah and Zeal so they wouldn't come closer.

Zeal pointed toward the goblins. "I have an idea. If we time it just right, we can cut those whips with our Swords while they're still mid-air. I've got the perfect verse to quote when we're ready."

Jeremiah nodded. "That's a good plan. Let's move to one side and minimize the number that can strike at us."

Holding their Shields close together, Jeremiah and Zeal advanced toward the creatures on the left.

When they were close enough for the whips to make contact with their Shield, Zeal shouted, "In the name of our Lord Jesus Christ, we will walk in unity so that there will be no divisions among us, and we will be perfectly united in the same mind and in the same purpose."

Feeling the cracks of the whips against their Shields, Jeremiah and Zeal quickly lowered them and prepared to strike. As soon as the whips snapped toward them again, they stepped to the side and sliced down with their Swords, cutting off a length of each whip. Working together they cut off another length and then another until they were within striking distance of the two goblins on the left.

As their enemies reared back to hit them with what was left of their whips, Jeremiah and Zeal rushed them, then stabbed them in their mid-sections. The goblins doubled over, and Jeremiah and Zeal brought their Swords down on the back of their necks, knocking them to the ground. The other creatures tried to save them, but Jeremiah held his Shield up and blocked the blows coming from the right. The two goblins that had been knocked down raised their heads in an effort to get back up, but Jeremiah and Zeal kicked them into the river.

Now there were only four Goblins of Strife and Contention left. These four stopped cracking their whips and crowded together in front of the bridge. As Jeremiah and Zeal marched slowly toward them, the goblins lowered their heads and aimed their spiked helmets straight at them.

Jeremiah crouched down. "Get low and hold your Shield as firm as possible."

Peeking over their Shields, Jeremiah and Zeal waited until the four goblins charged them. With all their strength and determination, Jeremiah and Zeal kept their Shields together. The goblins rammed them with their helmets but bounced off. The creatures backed up and tried again, but still, they couldn't separate their Shields.

Jeremiah nodded toward Zeal. "It's time to finish them."

They stood up, and moving as one, they charged at their enemies.

The two goblins Zeal was targeting saw her coming and tried to defend themselves with their whips, but she was on top of them before they could uncoil their weapons. She backhanded one with her Shield then swung around and slashed the other with her Sword. Both rocked side to side then crashed to the ground.

The last two goblins tried to ram into Jeremiah, but as they came at him, he swung his Sword so hard that he instantly knocked them off their feet. The two goblins Zeal had laid out on their backs were struggling to stand. Jeremiah quickly joined Zeal, and they swatted the two creatures into the water.

The two goblins that Jeremiah had knocked down got to their feet and came wobbling toward them. Jeremiah and Zeal smiled at each other, then wound up with their Swords, and swung upward. The force of their Swords sent the creatures flying up in the air and into the river.

Zeal let out a shout of joy. "We did it Jeremiah! We did it!"

With a sigh of relief, Jeremiah looked toward heaven and thanked God for the victory. This battle had been successful, but even more importantly he and Zeal had succeeded together. He took her hands and pulled her closer. They gazed into each other's eyes—

"Come on you two," shouted Grandma Pearl, "we'll celebrate later. Samson and I are ready to go."

After packing everything up and loading it into the cart, they started toward the bridge. When they were halfway across, they saw a sign: This is the Bridge of Unity. All those who cross have learned to work together."

When they reached the other side, they saw another sign announcing the river's name: "The River of Peace."

Written just below the name was this verse: "Therefore let us pursue the things which make for peace and the things by which we may build up one another."

Jeremiah and Zeal learned that day that peace didn't just happen, but it must be pursued, and when peace was pursued, it would wash away Contention and Strife.

30

PREPARATION FOR BATTLE

Jeremiah, Zeal, Grandma Pearl, and the faithful dog Samson continued to travel together for the next week. They did not face any enemies during this time, and it was an opportunity for Jeremiah and Zeal to spend lots of time talking.

Since their battle with Strife and Contention, they spent more time communicating about serious issues such as their differences and how to deal with those differences. Jeremiah and Zeal were coming to understand that falling in love was the easy part of a relationship, but what followed required a lot of hard work.

After a week of spending their evenings in inns, their path led them into a deep canyon. Large rock walls lined each side, and the canyon floor was covered in rusty, tan colored soil. No plants or trees grew in the hard ground, and in fact, there were no signs of life at all.

When the group had traveled for another hour, a loud crash reverberated against the walls. Everyone stopped and looked around, trying to identify the sound. Jeremiah took out his telescope and scanned the area.

Two huge Cyclops stood in front of a large wall toward the rear of the canyon. Each one was picking up boulders and smashing them on the ground. As the rocks broke into tiny pieces, another crash echoed through the canyon, and brown puffs of dust rose into the air.

Behind the Cyclops, toward the bottom of the towering wall, was a small opening that appeared to go through to the other side. That opening, Jeremiah thought, must be the exit and those Cyclops were smashing the boulders right in front of it.

Zeal motioned to Jeremiah to let her have a look. After studying the creatures, she handed the telescope to Grandma Pearl.

Zeal said, "There's no way we're getting out of here unless we do something about those Cyclops. Anyone who tries to go through that exit would be instantly ground to powder by those boulders."

Grandma Pearl peered through the telescope. "Oh my, I didn't think we'd be seeing these two this soon."

Zeal gave her a curious look. "You mean you know what they are?"

Giving the telescope back to Jeremiah, Grandma Pearl said, "Oh yes, these are the Twin Cyclops of Control and Domination. They represent the greatest weaknesses in both men and women, which all goes back to the fall of man."

"What do you mean?" asked Zeal.

Grandma Pearl dismounted her donkey. "As a result of sin entering the world, God told Adam and Eve that they would each seek to gain an advantage over the other. Rather than living in a loving and mutually supportive relationship, they would now become locked in a power struggle to see who could get their way at the expense of the other."

Jeremiah took another look through his telescope. "What can you tell us about defeating these enemies?"

"Here's what my husband and I learned," said Grandma Pearl. "Those boulders represent the fear of loss. Men and women seek to get their way through sinful means because they're afraid they will lose something. Before long, their efforts turn into a game, with one trying to gain mastery over the other. But what's important to understand is that fear is the driving force behind their struggle."

Zeal said, "Can you give us the strategy you used?"

Shaking her head, Grandma Pearl said, "There's no one formula that works for everyone. These sinful tendencies don't always manifest in the same way, and you have to discover your own weaknesses in these areas and fight to overcome them. A good place to start is to read the letter that the Apostle Paul wrote to the Ephesians. There God teaches what a relationship should look like, and it's the complete opposite of the sinful tendencies that came with the fall. You two sit down and study while I make us a nice lunch."

Jeremiah and Zeal pulled their stools from the cart and began reading through the letter to the Ephesians. When they came to the part where Paul was talking about marriage, the first thing they saw was that the wife was to follow the leadership of the husband, with an attitude of doing so as unto the Lord. After this, they read that the husband should love his wife and cherish her even as he would his own body.

When Grandma Pearl finished making lunch, she served up the food. As she sat down with them, she could tell that Jeremiah and Zeal had a lot on their mind, but since they were also hungry, they ate their lunch without saying much.

When everyone finished eating, Grandma Pearl said, "So what did you discover as you were reading?"

Zeal sighed. "We discovered this isn't going to be easy."

Grandma Pearl chuckled. "No, it isn't."

Jeremiah put his hand on his chin. "You said earlier that these sinful tendencies in both men and women are powered by fear. What else can you tell us about that?"

Grandma Pearl set her plate down. "Fear works in a husband so that he's afraid if he doesn't dominate and take things into his own hands, he won't get what he wants. He can try to dominate in different ways. Some men will use intimidation, while some will go as far as physical violence. Others become loud and threatening, whereas others use more subtle manipulation through being passive aggressive. But the goal is the same. Each wants to get his way."

"And how does this fear work in women?" asked Zeal.

"Well," said Grandma Pearl, "this fear tells a woman that if she's not in control, she can be taken advantage of and abused. Rather than trusting the leadership of her husband it causes her to pull away to preserve her safety."

"But," said Zeal, "aren't there some women who are abused by their husbands? Aren't these fears legitimate?"

"Oh yes," said Grandma Pearl, "there are definitely some women who are abused, but that has nothing to do with what Paul is teaching in Ephesians. If a woman is being abused, she needs to seek help and get out of that relationship. No one should remain in a situation where they're being hurt."

Zeal again read through the portion of her Book about wives. "It seems like God gave women the really tough part."

Grandma Pearl nodded. "It might look like that at first glance, but if a man truly follows the teaching in Ephesians, he has a lot of responsibility."

Turning to Jeremiah, Grandma Pearl said, "After reading those verses did you feel like you had the easy part?"

"No, I didn't," said Jeremiah, shaking his head. "Reading through those commands made me feel the weight of responsibility that comes with being a husband."

"That's right," said Grandma Pearl. "Leadership is hard because it involves being responsible and accountable. That's why a strong leader takes all the help he can get and seeks to have his wife as a partner alongside him."

"I can see that," said Jeremiah. "If I lead us in a wrong direction, I'll feel terrible. The easy thing to do would be to let the wife make the decision, then I don't have to feel responsible if things don't work out."

Nodding Grandma Pearl said, "That is indeed the easy thing, and it's exactly what the first man, Adam, did in the Garden of Eden. He was right there the whole time as the serpent tempted Eve, and he just stood there letting her make the decision on her own. A wife might think this is a good thing at first, but just as soon as something goes wrong, the husband is right there to remind her that it was her choice and therefore her fault. That's exactly what Adam did."

Zeal shrugged her shoulders. "So what if we talk about a decision we must make and can't come to an agreement?"

Grandma Pearl smiled. "That's where you learn the most important thing of all. You learn how to compromise. Rarely will you talk through a problem and come to a solution that's exactly in line with what one person sees. It's almost always going to be a blend of what both of you see as a solution."

Jeremiah said, "When I've been around other men, we're usually able to compromise rather easily, but I suppose it isn't quite as easy between men and women."

"No, it isn't," said Grandma Pearl, "because men and women are different, and they are going to see things differently. But this is also the beauty of a relationship, because if you both listen to one another, you'll be able to see the problem from each other's point of view. This will enable you to arrive at a solution that is far better."

Zeal put her hand to her forehead as she studied her Book. "All of this sounds good, and it seems like how a really good husband and wife team should work together. But if what we really need is good teamwork and communication, then why is there a need for someone to be in charge? Why can't we just be equal?"

Grandma Pearl smiled again. "You are equal. As far as God is concerned, there is no male and female in His presence, but for any team to function properly there needs to be one person who is accountable and responsible. Sometimes a decision just has to be made, and the husband is designated as the person to make that decision. You can be equal in a relationship even though you have a different role."

"I don't understand that," said Zeal.

Grandma Pearl took out her Book and read, "But I want you to know that the head of every man is Christ, the head of the woman is the man, and the head of Christ is God."

Grandma Pearl looked up from her Book. "You see, in heaven God the Father and God the Son are equal because they both have all the qualities of Deity. They both have existed throughout all of eternity, but at the same time, they have always existed as God the Father and God the Son. Just from the titles alone, we see there is a difference in their roles. The Father sent the Son. The Father created all things through the Son. So while they are equal, they have different roles."

Zeal said, "I think I see what you're saying. Just because the wife has a different role that does not mean she is any less important."

"Correct. And any man who is honest will tell you that there is no way he could be a successful leader in his marriage without the full help and participation of his wife."

Zeal looked over at Jeremiah who had been very quiet. "What do you think of all of this?"

Jeremiah pressed his lips together as he leaned forward. "I think there's a lot of responsibility to being a husband."

Zeal put her hand on his shoulder. "I know you're going to be a great leader."

Jeremiah sat up and smiled.

Grandma Pearl said, "Well right now you two need to figure out how to take all of this counsel from God's word and turn it into a strategy to get past those two Cyclops."

THE CYCLOPS

Jeremiah and Zeal huddled together to plan how they were going to battle this new enemy. The Cyclops were enormous, standing about fourteen feet tall and weighing at least eight hundred pounds. Their hands were huge, enabling them to pick up massive boulders easily. They only had one eye in the middle of their forehead, but when they turned it on someone, they seemed to see right through a person, enabling them to detect any fear or weakness.

Jeremiah again studied them through the telescope. "Their main weapons appear to be those boulders. If we can do something about them, we can get close enough to the Cyclops to attack."

He handed the telescope to Zeal. After surveying the situation, she said, "I agree. It appears that these sinful tendencies of domination and control are driven by fear, so if we deal with the fear that those boulders represent, then it will be much easier to defeat our enemy."

After praying together they each began to look through their Books.

Soon Jeremiah turned to Zeal. "This verse really speaks to me, 'The LORD is my light and my salvation; Whom shall I fear? The LORD is the strength of my life; Of whom shall I be afraid?' The Lord is the one who provides all that I need, and He is a strong refuge that I can run to when I fear things are not going my way. I don't have to dominate others in order to feel safe. I can go into the fortress of God's presence and feel secure."

Zeal nodded, "That's good Jeremiah. I found this verse also, 'Do not worry or have any anxiety about anything, but in every situation pray and make your requests known to God with thanksgiving. And

God's peace, which surpasses all understanding, will surround your hearts and minds in Christ Jesus.' "

Setting her Book down in front of her, Zeal said, "Whenever I get anxious about things, I sometimes feel I have to take control of my surroundings. Rather than giving into that, I want to learn to trust God instead."

Jeremiah stood up and extended his hand. "I think we both know what we need to do, so let's go do it."

"I'm ready," said Zeal, taking his hand and standing to her feet.

As they marched toward the Cyclops, they raised their Books until they became Swords. Grasping their Shields tightly in their left hands, they tapped their chest twice to reveal their armor. They both made sure their Helmets and Breastplates were properly adjusted, then dug their feet into the ground to test that their Shoes were providing proper traction.

When they were almost to the Cyclops, Jeremiah swerved to the right. "We're going to have to defeat these two enemies at the same time. I'll take the one that represents domination."

"And I'll take the one that represents control," said Zeal as she veered to the left.

As they drew closer, they could see a seemingly endless supply of boulders that each Cyclops had at their disposal. As soon as they smashed one, another rolled right up to them. The boulders appeared to be fed to them from behind a large hill on each side."

Jeremiah shouted over at Zeal and pointed toward the boulders with his Sword. "We have to stop the supply of these weapons if we're going to be able to get close."

With her Sword directed at the top of the hill on her side, Zeal shouted back, "We're going to have to go up those hills to find the source. I'll take the one on this side."

As Zeal started to make her way up the hill, the Cyclops of Control threw boulders in her direction. Bobbing and weaving, she made it to the top. Peeking over the ledge, she saw a small cave that was being guarded by a giant lizard the size of a horse. It had a large head, powerful jaws, and a mouth filled with sharp, jagged teeth. It had a long scaly tail, and as boulders popped out of the cave, the lizard would swat them with its tail, sending them down the hill to the Cyclops.

Jeremiah reached the top of the hill on his side and saw a second giant lizard delivering boulders below. As each prayed for wisdom, they both felt the caves represented unbelief which causes doubt in God's promises. The Holy Spirit reminded them of the verse, "Watch out, brothers, lest any of you have an evil heart of unbelief causing you to withdraw from the living God." They each recognized that a lack of trust in God would cause them to withdraw from Him and take matters into their own hands.

After praying some more, Jeremiah and Zeal came to the conclusion that the lizards represented rivalry. The Holy Spirit reminded them both of the verse in James that said, "But if you have bitter jealousy and rivalry toward one another in your heart, stop boasting and lying against the truth." In relationships, rivalry gave power to fears by convincing each person that the other was out to take something from them. Watching those lizards, they both wondered how many couples saw themselves as rivals rather than as partners.

Even though Jeremiah and Zeal couldn't see each other, they trusted that God was guiding the other, and He was. Zeal leaped into action first. As she approached, the lizard turned toward her and whipped its tail toward her legs. Zeal jumped over the tail, then darted up to the lizard and pierced it with her Sword.

Wounded, the lizard swung its tail at her again, but she easily jumped over the feeble effort and struck it on the head. Angry and desperate, the lizard lunged at her with its teeth, but she quickly raised her Shield and slammed it into the lizard's mouth. As the creature attempted to swing its tail again, Zeal repeatedly struck the lizard on the side of its head until she knocked it completely out.

As Jeremiah crested the hill on his side, the lizard pulled back its tail, preparing to strike one of the boulders, but once the creature saw him, it redirected its aim and swatted the boulder toward his head. Jeremiah ducked as the large rock passed over him, then quickly advanced toward the lizard as it snapped its tail back and forth.

Keeping an eye on the tail, Jeremiah counted the seconds between each change in direction. Suddenly he swung his Sword downward and cut the tail off completely. The lizard staggered toward him reaching at him with its short claws. Sidestepping the danger, Jeremiah slammed his Shield into the head of the lizard and then pierced it through the heart with his Sword.

With their lizards dispatched, both Jeremiah and Zeal peeked into the caves. The boulders were still forming, as if hatched by the rocky canyon.

Zeal repeatedly struck the cave on her side with her Sword and shouted, "I will not give into my fears, but I will trust in the Lord. He is my refuge and my fortress; My God, in Him I will trust."

Jeremiah bludgeoned the cave on his side while shouting, "I will not give in to unbelief, but I will put my trust in the Lord. He is my refuge and my strength, a very present help in times of trouble."

The earth rumbled beneath each cave, and then they collapsed. No more boulders would reach the Cyclops.

Rapidly descending the hills while dodging the remaining boulders being thrown at them, Jeremiah and Zeal made it back to the canyon floor.

Jeremiah looked over at Zeal. "How'd it go?"

She pointed toward the hill. "I killed the lizard sending the boulders down and destroyed the cave where they were coming from."

"Great job!"

"Thanks," said Zeal smiling. "What about you?"

"Same thing. There won't be any more boulders coming from up there!"

"I'm so proud of you Jeremiah."

He smiled and stood a little straighter. Now that they'd stopped the flow of boulders from above, they had to deal with the few the Cyclops still had on hand.

Jeremiah and Zeal rushed toward the Cyclops while dodging the large rocks being thrown at them. Finally, each Cyclops was down to only one boulder, and it was twice the size of all the others.

Zeal shouted to Jeremiah, "For this last one, we'll need our Shields!"

She rushed toward the Cyclops of Control. When she came within range, the creature threw its massive boulder at her as hard as it could.

Holding up her Shield, Zeal proclaimed, "The Lord is a shield to all those who trust in Him!"

When the boulder made contact with her Shield, it broke up into powder. Jeremiah then rushed the Cyclops of Domination, and his Shield also blocked the last boulder and caused it to disintegrate. Having lost their best weapons, the Cyclops roared in anger. They began to swing their arms wildly to keep Jeremiah and Zeal from getting close to them.

Zeal blocked the attacks with her Shield. "Lord whoever You give me to be my husband," she whispered under her breath, "Please Lord let it be Jeremiah," then continued, "I will follow his leadership, and I will support him as the helper You have created me to be."

The Cyclops reached down to grab her, but Zeal raised her Sword high above her head then quickly swung it toward the brute's arms. The Cyclops yelled in pain, then slammed its fists into the dirt, determined to pound her into the ground. Zeal rolled out of the way, then leaped to her feet.

The Cyclops flailed at Zeal with its left hand, trying to take her head off. As the giant paw hurtled toward her, she ducked just in time, then forcefully slammed her Shield into the Cyclops' hand. The creature screamed in pain and yanked its hand back.

Zeal advanced, swinging her Sword. "I will not allow my fears to terrify me, but I will be a true daughter of Sarah, submitting to my husband."

As her Sword crashed into the left arm of the Cyclops, she heard a loud snap. The limb dangled uselessly at the creature's side. The Cyclops of Control howled with pain then reached toward her with its right hand. Zeal swung her Sword at the right arm and broke it as well.

Moaning, the Cyclops tried to kick at Zeal, but she struck its legs. The Cyclops trembled, then fell to its knees. Zeal reared back with her Sword, then thrust it straight into the single eye in the middle of the forehead. The creature let out one last groan, then collapsed and died.

In the meantime, Jeremiah had also been fighting the Cyclops of Domination who was trying to step on him and crush him into the ground, but Jeremiah was quick on his feet and repeatedly darted out of the way.

Finally, he stared into the Cyclops' eye and said, "I will be a servant leader, loving and cherishing my wife as my own body. I will not seek to dominate or manipulate, but I will treat her as an equal partner, knowing that we are heirs together of the grace of life."

Still, the Cyclops tried to stomp him again, but Jeremiah sidestepped the blow and ran through its legs. As soon as he was behind the Cyclops, he struck it on the back of its legs. Slightly off balance, the brute whirled around trying to hit him, but Jeremiah was too fast. He easily blocked the blows with his Shield and then struck the creature on its ankles.

Nearly crippled, the Cyclops clasped its hands together and swung forcefully down toward his head. Jeremiah dodged to the right, and the Cyclops lost its balance. Taking advantage of the opportunity, Jeremiah jumped and struck the creature in the back. The brute stumbled forward then fell to its knees.

Jeremiah lifted his Sword. "I will dwell with my wife according to a right understanding of what she needs, and I will not allow bitterness or resentment in my heart toward her."

Jeremiah pierced the Cyclops through the chest, then pulled his Sword back and struck it on the side of the neck. The Cyclops of Domination roared in pain, then collapsed and rolled on its back. Jeremiah thrust his Sword into the single eye of the creature. The Cyclops' whole body trembled, then the last gasps of life left its body.

Zeal had watched Jeremiah as he delivered the final blow to the Cyclops of Domination.

Running over to him, Zeal said. "We did it! We defeated these Cyclops and all they represent!"

Jeremiah and Zeal threw their arms around each other and jumped around in a circle.

"Okay, you two," said Grandma Pearl, as she walked up with Samson, "that's enough celebration. There are more battles ahead."

Glancing over at her, Jeremiah and Zeal laughed together.

Grandma Pearl smiled. "You two are starting to get the hang of this."

Walking side-by-side, Jeremiah and Zeal passed through the narrow opening that had been blocked by the Cyclops. Grandma Pearl and Samson followed close behind. After coming out the other side, they saw a beautiful waterfall. Zeal immediately grabbed Jeremiah's hand and pulled him toward it. As the stream tumbled over the sharp, gray rocks into the pool of water below, it created a cool refreshing mist.

Jeremiah and Zeal could feel the spray as it floated in the air around them. It was invigorating and reminded them of God's love. Just like the flow from the waterfall, there would always be a new supply of His love pouring out and renewing all those who received it. Instead of giving into fears, they could rely on God's love, and as this love was perfected in their hearts, it would drive away their fears.

32

GRANDMA PEARL

The group spent the next seven days traveling and camping. Toward the end of that week, their paths took them through a rich fertile area that was teeming with fruit trees and wild berries. As they came around a bend, they spotted a large two-story home out in the distance. Even from afar, the house appeared to be of a grand design.

Jeremiah took out his telescope and studied it in some detail. The style of the home suggested it had been built a long time ago, but everything had been wonderfully preserved. He saw crystal clear windows with black shutters evenly spaced out over the first and second stories. A wide balcony on the second level overlooked a spacious porch on the first level. Joining the balcony and porch were eight sturdy columns, which rose from the ground to the roof.

In the center of the first level was a tall double-sided glass door with brightly polished brass doorknobs. Leading up to the porch were perfectly placed brick steps. Out front was a courtyard, which featured a beautiful fountain encircled by an elegant brick pathway. Water shot up from the center of the fountain in three streams, one to the left, one to the right, and one straight up.

The house was surrounded by land that seemed as if it went on forever. The property was divided into different fields, and within each section stood old wooden shacks.

Jeremiah placed his telescope in his satchel, and they set off toward the house. As they drew closer, Grandma Pearl became uncharacteristically quiet. Finally, she brought her donkey to a complete stop. She stared intently at the home while remaining silent.

Zeal left Jeremiah's side and went back to join her. "What's wrong? Do you know who lives there?"

At first, Grandma Pearl continued to stare at the house without answering. After a few minutes, she said, "I know who used to live there."

Seeing the intensity in Grandma Pearl's expression, Zeal wasn't sure how many questions she should ask. By now Jeremiah had walked over and joined them. Samson even seemed to understand the somberness of the moment because he sat quietly, wagging his tail and looking up at Grandma Pearl.

Dismounting from her donkey, she said, "Let's take a break and rest here for a little bit."

Jeremiah and Zeal helped her spread out a blanket, and then they prepared lunch. Everyone sat without talking, and Jeremiah and Zeal quietly prayed as they ate. When they finished eating, everyone cleaned up, then they sat back down on the blanket.

After sitting in silence for another few minutes, Grandma Pearl turned and looked toward the home. "The last time I saw that house, I was a little girl traveling with my grandfather and grandmother. My grandfather traveled around speaking at different Houses of Instruction. Back at that time, people like us weren't allowed to stay at most inns, so we traveled and camped between stops. One day we were traveling by this way, and as we passed this house, my grandmother began to cry. I was only eleven, and I had never seen my grandmother that upset. I went over to her and asked what was wrong."

"What was it?" asked Zeal.

"My grandmother cried for a little longer as my grandfather held her. Finally, she began to share that she used to live in one of those small wooden shacks across that field. She further explained that this was during a time when people of our color were owned by others."

Zeal said, "I've heard my father and mother talk about this before, but I guess it always seemed like far-off history. I can't imagine living in those circumstances."

Letting out a sigh, Grandma Pearl continued. "I could tell it was hard for my grandmother to talk about those times. She didn't tell me very much that day, but I learned later that this house was the source of a lot of terrible memories. When she was only a little girl, she saw her father whipped to the point that he almost died. Her mother had not wanted her to see it, but their owner insisted that the whole family be there to witness the whipping so they would learn something from it. My grandmother later told me that her mother held her as tight as she could and whispered to close her eyes. That didn't help much though because she could hear each of the blows as they landed on her father's back, and she heard him screaming in pain with each lash."

Jeremiah put his hand on Grandma Pearl's shoulder. "That's a horrible thing for a child to have to witness."

Grandma Pearl nodded. "Ten years after that there was no more people owning people, and they were all set free. My grandmother said her father did all he could to provide for them. He worked hard and managed to save enough to buy some scrap lumber to build them a little house. Her mother planted a garden and sold vegetables to help too."

Grandma Pearl stopped for a minute to take a deep breath, then continued. "My grandmother told me that her parents made sure she learned how to read, and the very first thing she read was the Book. My grandmother was a strong woman of God, and she needed every bit of that strength too. It wasn't too long after they were free that her father became ill and died. All those hours out in the field along with all the beatings just wore him down."

"That's terrible," said Zeal. "So it was just your grandmother and her mother that were left. How did they make it during those times?"

"It was hard," said Grandma Pearl. "My grandmother was around fifteen when her dad died, and she tried to help by doing any job she could find. She didn't care how small or large the task was or how much it paid. She did any job someone would give her to earn even a little bit of money."

"She sounds like a hard worker," said Zeal.

"Yes, she was. A year later she met my grandfather while cleaning a House of Instruction. This particular congregation had been started just for people of our color. My grandfather worked around the building during the day and then studied with the leader through the evening. He wanted to learn to preach out of this Book more than anything."

"Was it your grandparents that taught you so much about God's word?" asked Zeal.

"Yes it was. Of course, my parents were great Christians too, and they taught me a lot, but I probably learned the most whenever I'd travel with my grandmother and grandfather."

Jeremiah said, "I guess life was not easy for your grandparents starting out newly married during that time."

"No, it wasn't. My grandfather had been making just enough to barely scrape by himself, but when they were married, he took on not only the support of my grandmother but of her mother as well. They all lived together until her mother died about five years later. After that, my grandfather felt God had called him to travel around and preach. He and my grandmother would set out on their path believing that God would guide them to where they were supposed to go. People back then didn't have much money, but they would give my grandfather some food and whatever clothing or supplies they could spare in appreciation for him ministering God's word to them."

"We don't really understand just how much we are blessed today do we?" said Jeremiah.

Grandma Pearl replied, "No, we don't."

"What was it like traveling with your grandfather and grandmother when you were a little girl?" asked Zeal.

"By the time I started going with them, my grandfather was well known among many Houses of Instruction. At that time he was receiving enough in offerings so that he and my grandmother had more than they needed. Each time before we'd leave one House of Instruction to go to another, I always saw my grandfather give to someone in need. He remembered what it was like to have very little, and he believed that God had blessed him so he could be a giver."

"He sounds like a generous man," said Jeremiah.

"Oh, he was, and in more ways than just money. He would minister to people every chance he got. He loved God's word, and he believed that knowing the teachings and doctrines in this Book was the key to living life to its fullest potential."

After sitting for a few more minutes, Grandma Pearl stood up signaling that she was ready to continue on. Once they started moving, they discovered that their path was taking them right by the home.

As they got closer Zeal asked, "Who do you suppose lives there now?"

Shaking her head, Grandma Pearl said, "I don't know. It's been a long time since I was by this way, and the last time I was here this house was not in good condition. It appeared as if no one had lived in it for many years, but now it looks like someone has recently fixed it up. I think it's the kind of house though that should have been destroyed."

Grandma Pearl rode her donkey slowly as if she was trying to delay getting there as long as possible. Jeremiah and Zeal didn't rush either because they felt this was something Grandma Pearl needed to do at her own pace. As they got closer, they could all see what Jeremiah had witnessed earlier through the telescope. They marveled at the craftsmanship it took to restore this home to its present condition, and it appeared it had been recently painted a bright white color.

When they arrived in front of the house, the sound of joyful singing filled the air. Zeal, Jeremiah, and Grandma Pearl stopped and stared at each other in surprise. While they listened to the singing, an elderly gentleman stepped outside.

Getting the man's attention, Jeremiah said, "Is this a House of Instruction?"

The gentleman said, "No sir, we just be praising God. We all live here, and we gather together downstairs each day so we can talk about the Book and praise the Lord. Y'all are welcome to come inside and join us if you like."

Grandma Pearl was curious as to why people were living here, but she was even more curious because the elderly man who spoke to them was a man of color the same as them. Why would they be living in a house like this, she thought? Did they not know its history?

Zeal placed her hand on her shoulder. "Do you want to go in?"

Grandma Pearl was silent for a moment, and then she hopped down from her donkey. "I always wondered what it looked like on the inside. My grandmother said she'd never seen the inside of that house, and she never wanted to, but I believe I'd like to see it."

Jeremiah, Zeal, and Grandma Pearl walked up to the door while Samson stayed with the donkey. They knocked and were immediately greeted by a dark-skinned elderly woman with a joyful look on her face.

She swayed back and forth to the music and held out her hand. "Y'all come on in. We just started singing, and we always love having visitors."

They followed her inside and immediately noticed that all the people gathered were of African heritage. The singing was uplifting, and Grandma Pearl seemed to thoroughly enjoy herself. It was the first time she had heard some of those songs since she was a little girl traveling with her grandparents.

After the singing, different people shared a short teaching from God's word. Jeremiah was struck by the fact that all those who spoke had a depth of wisdom that he wished to have one day. After the time of sharing was over, everyone was invited into a dining area where the ladies had prepared different cakes and pies. Fresh coffee and tea was served, and everyone sat around having a great time of fellowship.

Grandma Pearl surveyed the room, noticing just how big everything was. The space they had been singing in was so big that she thought you could have probably fit two houses in just that one area. The dining area was also huge. Several smaller dining tables that would seat six to eight people filled the space. A large fireplace sat against the back wall, with candles lining the hearth. Small end tables were set all around the room, decorated with lace doilies and vases of fresh flowers. The wall that faced outside was made up of several tall glass windows, giving everyone an incredible view of the property.

After a little while, a well-dressed man everyone called Mr. Clyde stood up to speak. "Whenever we have visitors, we like to have them share a little bit about their journey. I spoke briefly with Pearl, and I've asked her to share with us whatever is on her heart."

Grandma Pearl looked around the room as everyone got quiet. She then proceeded to tell them about the time she had been by this way with her grandparents, and what her grandmother had told her about the home. Some of the people had tears in their eyes because they recalled similar stories they had heard from their own grandparents.

When Grandma Pearl finished speaking, Zeal decided to ask the question that she knew Grandma Pearl wanted to ask. "I'm wondering as to how all of you came to live here."

The elderly woman who greeted them, whose name was Julia,

spoke up. "I think what you're asking is why would we want to live in a home that has the history this one does. That's a good question. About fifteen years ago, some of us were coming by this way, and we noticed this old house. The outside needed a lot of work, but the inside wasn't too bad. We learned about all the things that happened here, and our first instinct was to leave it alone. But we all prayed, and within a few days, we felt God wanted us to restore this place and use it for something good. So we fixed it up so it could be a place for people to go when they got older. We could be a help to one another when we needed it, and we could keep each other company."

Jeremiah said, "It's just like God to take something that had been used for evil and use it for His good."

Mr. Clyde smiled and nodded, "Yes, it is. We serve a great God."

Zeal said, "Do people come by and visit you?"

Mr. Clyde said, "Sometimes our families come by to see us, but most of the time its strangers like you. We get to tell people a little bit about the history of this home, and we also share with them some of the experiences we've had on this Quest. Most of the time its young people such as yourselves that God brings by here."

"Why is that?" said Jeremiah.

"Well," said Mr. Clyde, "I think it's for different reasons, but for one, young people of color such as yourselves need to know a little bit of your history, and all the men and women of God that came before you who helped pave the way for the progress you are able to experience today."

"What is it you feel is most important for us to learn?" asked Jeremiah.

Leaning forward, Mr. Clyde said, "Probably the first thing is to understand that the day we were declared free was the beginning of our struggle and not the end. When people have viewed you as property for so long, those views don't change easily. You might be free according to the law, but in men's hearts you are still just property, no different than that donkey you have outside."

Grandma Pearl said, "I often heard my grandfather speak of the long struggle it was. It took men and women of courage to make it through those days."

Mr. Clyde nodded. "And Pearl you know we had our own struggles coming up as children as well. Our parents and grandparents made things better for us, but there were still things we had to go through."

Zeal said, "Grandma, I've never heard you talk much about those days."

Grandma Pearl seemed uncomfortable, but she looked around at all those who were gathered in this home, and she felt a peace coming from them. "Yes, Mr. Clyde, it wasn't always easy. You could see it in people's eyes. You wanted to be respected just like any other human being, but the looks they gave you let you know that wasn't always going to be."

Mr. Clyde shifted his gaze as if he was remembering something painful. "I know those feelings. You knew that people were making judgments about you based solely on the color of your skin, and you never got a chance to prove the kind of person you were on the inside."

Zeal said, "How did you handle that?"

Mr. Clyde shook his head. "To be perfectly honest, not always as good as I would have liked. You'd hear someone calling you names as they laughed, and you'd want to go over and knock them upside the head. But during those days you didn't even dare look them in the eye, or something bad could happen. You had to handle it just like you do any kind of adversity. You had to rely on God's grace."

Jeremiah remembered his battle with the Giant of Shame. "When I was a boy, and through my teenage years, I had to deal with being called a degrading name, and that alone brought in shame. I can't imagine what it was like during the time you grew up."

Mr. Clyde said, "It was by God's grace. The early Christians had to go through a lot of suffering, and God was with them as they went through it. All of us here, including Pearl, can tell you that God was with us as well."

Zeal sat up in her seat. "So how should we handle it when we feel we are being treated differently because of our color? I see those looks sometimes, and I just try to ignore them as if they weren't there."

Mr. Clyde said, "You can't just ignore it. Those looks affect you whether you want to admit it or not. You should feel all the feelings that come with such a look, and then give those feelings to God so you don't become bitter or resentful. You also should remind yourself that God sees you as in Christ and clothed with His righteousness. You can't get any better than that. Regardless of how people look at you, you are always accepted and loved before the Throne of God."

Mr. Clyde paused, smiling as if he was experiencing some of the grace he had talked about. He then glanced back at Zeal. "Whenever you get one of those looks from someone, there's something else you must do that is extremely important."

"What's that?" asked Zeal.

"You must forgive the person that gave you that look, knowing it is due to sin in their heart. We have been forgiven of all of our sins, and we too must forgive others of their sins."

Grandma Pearl said, "I remember hearing my grandmother talk about how she had to forgive those who beat her father. It took the love of God in her heart to forgive, but over time she was able to do it."

"Yes," said Mr. Clyde, "the love of God is the answer. It's really hard, but Jesus commands us to be loving our enemies, to be blessing the ones who curse us, to be doing good to the ones who hate us, and to be praying for those who mistreat and persecute us."

Jeremiah said, "I knew many young men my age and race who were angry and resentful about a lot of things."

Mr. Clyde took a deep breath. "I've seen that too, and it's something that disturbs me. During the time that I, and Pearl, were coming up, we knew there was injustice on every side. We worked to make changes where we could, but we were taught not to allow the injustice that was around us to become bitterness and resentment within us."

Grandma Pearl nodded in agreement. "Nowadays we have young people who want to blame everyone and everything around them for their own sin. Sin is ultimately against God, and it's rebellion toward His rule in their life. There are no excuses before God. He is completely just and fair."

Mr. Clyde nodded. "That's right, Pearl. Personal responsibility has almost become a dirty word, but taking full responsibility for our sinful thoughts and behaviors is the only thing that matters. All else is excuses, and excuses don't cut it with God."

Jeremiah said, "My mom is no longer with us, but before she died she taught me that I couldn't wait around for the world to be just right. She told me that if I wanted to find an excuse to fail there would always be one available, but if I wanted to succeed there would always be an opportunity. She said I might have to work twice as hard for half the recognition, but to realize I was not only doing it for myself, but also for all those who would come after me."

Mr. Clyde put his hand on top of Jeremiah's. "Your mom was a wise woman. We need to be teaching our young people what your mom taught you. Don't wait for the world to be as you wish it to be, but go out and do what you can to help make it what it ought to be."

Grandma Pearl leaned forward. "That's a good word Mr. Clyde."

He turned to Jeremiah. "I overheard you say earlier that you had studied at a House of Knowledge."

Nodding, Jeremiah said, "Yes, I graduated this past summer."

"Do you think you might lead a House of Instruction one day?"

"I'm not sure, but I do want to teach others the doctrines of this Book."

Mr. Clyde took Jeremiah's hand. "When you do, preach the gospel of Jesus Christ. People need to know that they are sinful and in need of a Savior. It's important to talk about the problems in our society and work for change, but it's far more important to talk about the condition of men's hearts and the answer to their sinful condition. It is my belief that the change that takes place on the inside of a person as a result of their relationship with Jesus Christ is what will transform society and bring about true social justice."

"Amen," said Grandma Pearl.

Mr. Clyde, Julia, and the others talked for hours about the challenges they faced growing up, as well as the challenges of their parents and grandparents. When they were finished talking, Mr. Clyde and Julia took all of them on a tour of the house and the grounds. What started out as a very tense day for Grandma Pearl ended up being a very peaceful day.

Julia informed them that there were some extra rooms, and they were all welcome to stay overnight. The next morning they said goodbye to everyone, and the people of the house prayed with them before they left.

As they traveled along, Jeremiah and Zeal realized they had learned more about their history in these two days than their entire life up to this point. They both thanked God for the men and women of color who fought for freedom and justice with such great courage.

33

TRUE LOVE

The next few days of travel were peaceful and relaxing. Grandma Pearl was back to her old self, and in fact, she seemed to be doing better than ever. One day as they traveled, Jeremiah spotted a House of Instruction up ahead. When they arrived out front, a kind young lady let them know that it would be an hour before the service started, but they were welcome to come in and have a seat.

Grandma Pearl asked if she could use one of the rooms downstairs to change, and after getting permission, she unpacked one of her favorite dresses and a special hat she had been waiting for an opportunity to wear.

Jeremiah and Zeal went in and sat down, using the time to read in their Books. When Grandma Pearl came upstairs, she was walking with a spring in her step, appearing quite happy to be able to look her best. Soon, the service began with singing, and everyone lifted up their voices in praise, magnifying their Lord and Savior Jesus Christ. Next, the leader, Pastor James, stepped forward and asked everyone to open up in their Books to the first letter to the Corinthians, the thirteenth chapter.

Pastor James then began to teach on love—not a storybook romantic kind of love, but a true love. Pastor James taught from the Book that love was patient and kind. It was not envious or jealous. True love was not boastful, arrogant, or prideful, and was not rude or disrespectful. Love did not seek its own way but looked to build up others. Love was not touchy or looking for reasons to be offended. Love did not keep a list of all the wrongs it suffered. Love did not rejoice in unrighteousness, but it rejoiced in the truth. Love was willing to put up with people and circumstances even when they weren't perfect, and true love was ready and willing to believe the best of every person. Love continuously hoped for the best and endured through all hardships.

Jeremiah and Zeal sat through the teaching, both wondering how the love they had for each other measured up against this standard. When Pastor James was concluding his message, he reminded the congregation that they would often fall short of these verses in their love for God and one another. He then encouraged everyone to daily confess where they fell short, and ask God to help them make the necessary changes in their lives.

When it was time for the closing prayer, Jeremiah and Zeal prayed earnestly before God to forgive them for their selfishness and pride and to work His love in them and through them. Pastor James then asked the congregation to rise and sing one more song in joyful praise to the Lord.

When the service was over, everyone stopped by to greet them. Grandma Pearl received many compliments on her dress and hat, and she enjoyed each one. As they were leaving, Pastor James stood by the door and greeted everyone. When they reached the walkway, one of the ushers let them know that there was going to be a picnic and invited them to stay.

Grandma Pearl loved picnics and no sooner had she gotten some food then she was whisked away by two older women who were widows just like her. As Jeremiah and Zeal waited in line to get their food, they could see Grandma Pearl chatting away and laughing with her new friends. They could also see Samson sitting in front of the food table, wagging his tail and looking up at the women who were serving the food. It didn't take long before Samson was served a turkey drumstick. He happily gripped it with his teeth and plopped down under a tree.

When Jeremiah and Zeal had their food, they sat down at a table by themselves. Within a few minutes, a young couple named Joe and Paula walked up and asked if they could join them.

Jeremiah said, "Of course, please do."

After they each introduced themselves, Joe said, "It was so good to have you all here today. Wasn't that a great message on love?"

Jeremiah took a drink of water. "Yes, it was. It really made you think too."

Paula looked over at Zeal. "Are you two—"

Zeal knew what she was about to ask, and in order to avoid the awkward answer she interrupted by saying, "We're praying for God's will in our lives."

Paula got the message quickly. She too had to wait awhile before Joe proposed to her.

Jeremiah said, "How long have you been together?"

Joe wiped his mouth with a napkin. "We've known each other since childhood, but we've been married just a little over a year."

Zeal touched Paula's hand. "That's great."

"It hasn't always been easy," said Paula, "but we've learned a lot."

Jeremiah sensed this was a good opportunity to learn from a couple that was newly married. "I don't want to put you two on the spot, but what is it you feel you've learned?"

Zeal put down her fork, anxiously waiting to hear what they would say, because she too was curious.

The couple could sense how much Jeremiah and Zeal wanted to know what marriage was really like.

Joe smiled at Paula. "I love this woman more today than when I married her. What I learned though, is that love is more of an action then it is a feeling. Just as we learned in the message today, you have to constantly be aware of your own selfishness. Our sinful flesh always wants to take instead of give. Love wants to give, and it delights in giving."

Paula smiled back at Joe as she put her hand on his shoulder. "Yes. When you first go into marriage, you're thinking about what it's going to do for you, and how the other person is going to meet all of your needs. You soon learn that the other person is coming into the marriage thinking the exact same thing. If both spouses are looking at marriage in terms of what it can do for them, then very soon both are going to be frustrated and discouraged."

Jeremiah and Zeal exchanged a knowing look as if they both just learned something important.

Zeal gestured toward Paula. "So how did you handle this?"

Paula said, "It was challenging. It was just three months into the marriage when we both realized we were unhappy. We had gone from the bliss of the honeymoon to feelings of hopelessness and despair within a short amount of time. At first, we were afraid to admit this even to one another. We came to services and put on a good face for everyone else, but on the inside, we were hurting."

Joe nodded. "Pastor James was able to detect that something was wrong. One day after a service, he asked us if we would meet with him just to see how things were going. At first, we tried to convince him everything was okay, but his questions made it clear that he knew something wasn't right. Then Paula just started crying."

Paula took a deep breath. "All of the emotions I had pressed down seemed to come rushing up at the same time. I felt like a failure as a wife and as a person."

"And I think I felt like even more of a failure," said Joe pointing to himself, "because I was supposed to be the leader of this home, and things weren't going well at all."

"What happened after that?" asked Jeremiah.

"At first," said Paula, "I think Joe was surprised by how emotional I was, but soon he put his arm around me."

Taking her hand, Joe said, "It was difficult in the beginning, because everything I heard Paula say sounded like she was blaming me for why things were wrong. Pastor James had to help me understand that she needed to say everything she felt, and I just needed to listen and not try to defend myself. The more I listened, the more secure Paula felt, and then it became clear that more than anything she was blaming herself."

"That's true," said Paula nodding. "I felt like I must have done something to cause Joe not to love me."

Zeal saw how loving and affectionate the couple were toward one another. "You seem like you're doing great now. How did you get from there to here?"

Joe smiled as he rubbed Paula's hand. "It was a process. That day was a new beginning for us, and over time we learned to listen to one another rather than blame one another."

"And," said Paula, "we had to learn to work on ourselves instead of trying to change the other person."

Jeremiah put his hand to his chin. "What do you think new couples need to know more than anything?"

Joe sat up straighter. "Pastor James helped us understand that marriage is joining two sinful people together, and when that happens, there's bound to be conflict. You're going to discover things about yourself that you might never see if you stayed single. Marriage has a way of pulling out all of our selfish tendencies."

Paula looked at Joe. "Yes, couples should know going into marriage that there will be these kinds of challenges. What's important is learning to work together to resolve problems rather than trying to avoid them. Having problems does not mean you have a bad marriage. In fact the more you work on these problems, the better your marriage becomes, and the better person you become."

Jeremiah saw that Grandma Pearl had finished talking with her new friends and was saying goodbye to Pastor James.

"Thank you so much," said Jeremiah, "for all that you've shared with us."

"Yes, thank you for joining us today and being so willing to share your experiences," said Zeal.

Paula said, "You're very welcome. It was so good to meet the both of you."

Joe stood up and held out his hand to Jeremiah. "If you're ever near here again please do stop by."

"Thank you. We certainly will," said Jeremiah as he shook Joe's hand.

Jeremiah and Zeal said goodbye to the couple and then joined Grandma Pearl who stood near the donkey ready to leave. Jeremiah called out to Samson, and he trotted up beside them.

34

THE HARVEST

As they departed from the House of Instruction, Grandma Pearl suggested they stay at a nearby inn she was familiar with. After arriving and checking into their rooms, the three relaxed for the evening.

When morning came, they all started back on their journey. It was a peaceful time of travel as their paths took them through a beautiful meadow. The fresh fragrance of the many different flowers rose up together to form a multitude of pleasant smells. Grandma Pearl rode on her donkey humming a gospel song, while Jeremiah and Zeal talked and laughed with one another.

After a peaceful and pleasant afternoon of travel, suddenly a heavy darkness descended all around them. It was the kind of darkness a person could feel, as if one could reach out and touch it. Not only did it block most of the light from the sun, but it hovered about them as if it was watching them.

Zeal stepped closer to Jeremiah. "What is this? It's the middle of the day, and the sky has been clear until just a few minutes ago?"

Jeremiah placed his hand on his Book, ready to raise it if necessary. "I'm not sure. There hasn't been a cloud in the sky all day, and more than that, this feels like a different kind of darkness."

All of a sudden, there was an awful screeching sound from above. They stared at the sky and saw two giant bats circling overhead. Jeremiah began to raise his Book, and Zeal pulled hers from her satchel. Both transformed into Swords, but the giant bats didn't appear to be interested in attacking, at least not yet. The bats would release an ear-piercing scream as they soared through the darkness, and then just as the sound began to fade, they let out another jarring shriek. Jeremiah and Zeal remained cautious, waiting to see if there would be an attack. The bats continued to circle but retreated to an area that was further ahead.

"What's going on?" said Zeal, staring into the sky. "First the heavy darkness and now these bats show up."

Satisfied that an attack wasn't imminent, Jeremiah lowered his Sword until it became a Book. "Those bats don't seem to be coming any closer, so we're probably safe for now. Let's get a tent set up for Grandma Pearl, and then you and I can go a little further to check things out."

Grandma Pearl felt like they were being overprotective of her, but she agreed to stay.

Zeal helped her set up her tent. "Remain here until we come back. Samson will be here with you to keep watch as well."

"You don't worry about me," said Grandma Pearl as she turned to go into her tent. "I'll be just fine. You and Jeremiah should worry about what's up ahead. Those giant bats aren't circling just to get some exercise."

After Grandma Pearl was inside, Zeal closed up the flap.

Jeremiah knelt beside Samson. "You stay here and take care of her. We'll be back soon."

Samson barked as he lay down in front of the tent door.

Jeremiah and Zeal stalked through a wide-open field for about ten minutes. Suddenly the wind started to blow, and the sky grew even darker.

Zeal pointed toward shadowy shapes coming toward them. "What is that?"

Jeremiah took out his telescope and spotted a big, ugly ogre rapidly marching toward them, carrying a thick club covered with spikes. On either side of the ogre was a giant pig the size of a cow. Each had sharp teeth and a horn protruding from its forehead. The ogre itself was ten feet tall with the face of a hog and large brown warts all over its body.

When the ogre was within fifty yards, he called out in a loud, hateful voice. "Jeremiah and Zeal, I know who you are. You will go no further. My master has sent me to give you a warning. Turn back, and you may live, but if you go forward, you will be destroyed. As you can see, I brought two friends with me who are each hungry, and if there's anything left, my other two friends in the sky will fight for the leftovers."

Jeremiah glanced at Zeal as he nervously tried to unlatch his satchel to retrieve his Book. "This looks dangerous."

Zeal stared at the ogre and then back at Jeremiah. "We have to also think about Grandma Pearl. What will happen to her if these creatures destroy us?"

Jeremiah took Zeal's hand and bowed his head. "Dear Lord, we do not wish to test you. We only wish to follow you. Guide us according to your wisdom."

They looked up to see that their paths were heading straight toward the ogre. In fact, this was the clearest they had ever seen their paths, for they were lighted with a bright white light. The Holy Spirit reminded Jeremiah of the time when Elisha was surrounded by an enemy army, and how Elisha reassured his servant by showing him that an even greater army of God's warriors watched over them.

Jeremiah studied the ogre, the enormous pigs, and the giant bats circling overhead. He then gently squeezed Zeal's hand. "There are more with us than with them."

Zeal was still afraid, as was Jeremiah, but they were going to trust God.

When the ogre saw that Jeremiah and Zeal were not leaving, he pointed at them with his spiked club. "You are a foolish man Jeremiah. You're going to get people killed today."

The ogre then swatted both giant pigs with his club, sending them running toward Jeremiah and Zeal.

Jeremiah shouted, "Bend your knees and hold your Shield as tight as you can!"

Crouching down, they placed their shoulders against their Shields, bracing for impact. The pigs rammed into them, hitting them with such force that it pushed them backwards ten feet. As they recovered from the collision, the pigs circled them. Jeremiah and Zeal stood back, preparing for the next assault. Suddenly the pigs charged from opposite directions, one taking aim at Jeremiah and the other at Zeal.

Once again, they held out their Shields, and by bracing up against one another's backs, they were able to hold off the charge.

After letting out an angry snort, the pigs started circling again as if they were stalking their prey.

Jeremiah whispered to Zeal, "When I give the signal, quickly dart out to your right."

The pigs circled a few more times and then once again launched at them from opposite directions.

As they were getting close, Jeremiah shouted, "Now!"

They both darted out of the way, causing the pigs to crash into each other.

Jeremiah struck one of the pigs with his Sword. "Now we attack!"

The large swine were still stunned from colliding into one another, giving Jeremiah and Zeal the opportunity to repeatedly strike them with their Swords. The pigs staggered backwards then regrouped. They then lowered their heads and charged again, this time trying to maneuver their horns underneath the Shields. Seeing what the pigs were attempting to do, Jeremiah and Zeal slammed their Shields straight down on the pigs' horns. The collision made a thunderous noise, and the horns broke from the pigs' foreheads.

The creatures staggered around for a minute, but then recovered and began digging their front hoofs into the ground. Suddenly one of the pigs tried to jump up on Jeremiah's Shield, but he yanked the Shield back and hit the pig on the head with it. He then took his Sword and pierced the pig in the throat. The giant pig grunted and squealed as it floundered around, then collapsed in a lifeless heap on the ground.

Now even angrier, the other pig rushed straight toward Zeal, knocking her on her back. But before the enemy could take advantage, she jumped to her feet and struck the pig in the mouth with her Sword. The giant pig backed up, then charged her again. As the swine was about to crash into her, she thrust out her Shield, hitting it between the eyes. Zeal then slid to the right and plunged her Sword deep into the side of the creature. The pig stumbled around, then fell over dead.

Jeremiah and Zeal tried to catch their breath, but they temporarily forgot that the pigs were not the only enemies ready to attack. All of a sudden, the ground rumbled beneath their feet. They looked up and saw the ogre charging toward them in a full sprint—each stride sending concussions through the earth.

"You will pay for killing my pets Jeremiah!"

When the ogre came within range, he swung his long club at

Jeremiah's neck. He ducked just in time, but the ogre quickly drew his club back over his head, then slammed it straight down. Jeremiah darted out of the way just as the spikes plunged past him into the ground.

Zeal had now moved into position to help Jeremiah.

The ogre smirked at her. "Isn't it sweet that you would help out your boyfriend. Oh well, you know what they say, the couple that fights together, DIES TOGETHER!"

The ogre angrily swung his club toward Zeal, and she barely rolled out of the way. Reacting swiftly, Jeremiah thrust his Sword toward the ogre, and Zeal jumped to her feet. Jeremiah then motioned for her to split out wide. They started circling around the ogre, making it difficult for their foe to see them both at the same time.

Suddenly Jeremiah charged his enemy. The ogre swung at him with his spiked club, but he blocked the blow with his Shield and then lashed out with his Sword. The ogre easily avoided the attack, but he didn't notice that Zeal had worked her way in behind him. She then struck the back of the ogre's legs so hard that he went down to one knee. Jeremiah then pounced and struck the right arm of the ogre with his Sword, knocking the spiked club out of his hand.

The ogre quickly jumped to his feet and reached to retrieve his club. Zeal struck again, slashing him on the legs. Angry and shouting, the massive creature swung around and flailed at Zeal. She raised her Shield in time to block the assault, but the force of the ogre's club knocked her backward. Jeremiah lunged at the ogre and struck him in the thigh with his Sword.

The creature staggered and fought to stay on his feet. Jeremiah followed up with a blow to the side of the ogre's legs, bringing him to his knees. Back on her feet, Zeal ran toward the ogre, jumped into the air, and landed on his back. She then plunged her Sword into his neck. The ogre fell face down in the dirt and lay still.

Zeal smiled at Jeremiah, preparing to celebrate, but the creature suddenly jumped to his feet, lifting Zeal off the ground as she clung to her Sword, which was still stuck in the back of the ogre's neck.

"Help!" screamed Zeal as she dangled in the air, desperately trying to hang onto her Sword.

The ogre reached back and tried to pull her Sword out of his neck. Jeremiah quickly slammed his Shield into the ogre's stomach. Again, their enemy went down to his knees, and Zeal pulled out her Sword and struck him on the head. Jeremiah followed up by driving his Sword straight into the creature's heart. The ogre grasped at his chest and fell forward.

Taking his last breath, the ogre glared at Jeremiah. "This isn't over."

Jeremiah suddenly heard the thunderous flapping of wings, and he turned just in time to see Zeal's feet lifting off the ground. One of the giant bats had swooped down and was trying to carry her off. He ran toward the flying creature as it was attempting to take her away, and jumped just high enough to swing his Sword at its claws. As soon as his Sword made contact, the bat dropped Zeal.

As she hit the ground, she shouted, "Watch out!"

Jeremiah turned to see the other giant bat coming straight toward him. Barely ducking in time, he felt sharp claws glancing against his shoulders. Standing to their feet, Jeremiah and Zeal stared into the dark sky and soon caught a glimpse of their enemies circling overhead, preparing to strike again.

Suddenly the giant bats swooped in and knocked them off their feet. As soon as they stood up, the bats flew toward them again.

"Duck!" shouted Zeal.

The bats, with their claws extended, barely missed them as they flew over.

Jeremiah scanned the sky trying to figure out where they went, but there was no sign of them.

Then a sharp, piercing scream emanated above their head, and Zeal turned just in time to see the creatures approaching from behind. "Turn around!" she shouted.

They turned just in time, and the large bats crashed into their Shields and caromed backwards onto the ground. Jeremiah and Zeal stood shoulder to shoulder, watching as their enemies rose up on their clawed feet and waddled toward them. The bats made a hissing sound as they came near, flapping their wings and flashing their spiked teeth.

Jeremiah whispered to Zeal. "When I give the signal, strike out and up with your Sword."

The bats closed in, and Jeremiah yelled, "Now!"

Jeremiah and Zeal lurched forward and thrust their Swords out and up, catching each of the bats under their chin. Angry and wounded, the bats flew into the air and then dove straight toward them. One of the bats knocked Jeremiah on his back and then landed on top of him. Zeal couldn't help him because she was attacked by the other bat at the same time.

The one on top of Jeremiah was digging into his legs with its claws. Jeremiah thrashed about as he groaned in pain. Looking toward heaven, he raised his Sword as far as he could and then thrust it into the side of the bat. The creature toppled off him and tried to fly, but this last blow had pierced its wing.

Jeremiah struggled to his feet and darted toward his enemy. He pounded it with his Sword. The bat attempted to get away, but Jeremiah kept up the pressure, not giving the creature any opportunity to recover. The bat desperately swiped at Jeremiah with its claws, but Jeremiah blocked the attack, then swung his Sword and connected with a fatal blow to the bat's head. It fell backwards, with its claws pointing straight in the air.

Jeremiah had swung with so much force that he lost his balance and stumbled forward. Falling to the ground, he spotted Zeal being knocked backwards by the giant bat she had been battling. It was about to plunge its teeth into her, and he knew he couldn't reach her in time.

Jeremiah cried out, "Zeal!"

Out of nowhere, a Sword struck the bat on the head. It was Grandma Pearl! She swung her Sword again and hit the creature on the neck until it jumped off Zeal. The bat flapped its wings and showed its teeth. Grandma Pearl waved her Sword above her head and showed her teeth.

The bat lifted off the ground and lunged at Grandma Pearl with its claws, but she quickly stepped to the right and slammed her Shield into the side of its head. Jeremiah sprinted toward her, but before he could arrive, Grandma Pearl pierced the giant bat straight through its chest. The creature stumbled backwards and fell flat on its back. When Jeremiah reached her side, the bat was dead.

Grandma Pearl's eyes darted back and forth between Jeremiah and Zeal. "Don't look at me all surprised. I can still use my Sword."

Zeal jumped up and gave her a hug, and Jeremiah wrapped his

arms around both of them.

Lowering her Sword until it became a Book, Grandma Pearl said, "It looks like we're done here. Let's go."

As Grandma Pearl walked off, they thought they heard her muttering under her breath, "Tell me to stay in my tent, will they. Next time I'll tell them to stay in their tent."

Zeal turned toward Jeremiah. "Do you think we'll be that feisty when we're that age?"

Jeremiah gazed into her eyes. "I hope so."

In that moment, his mind flashed to him and Zeal sitting on a porch in their old age, watching their grandchildren play in the front yard.

Reaching out to her with one hand, Jeremiah dug into his pocket with the other, then got down on one knee. He pulled out the ring his mother had given him just before she died. She had been given this ring by her mother, but she never got the opportunity to wear it since she never married.

As Jeremiah's mom lay dying, she called him over and handed him the ring. She told him that even though she would not be around to see it, she hoped he would find someone special to give it to one day. Jeremiah knew this was the day.

Zeal's hand trembled, and tears welled up in her eyes.

"I love you so much," said Jeremiah squeezing her hand. "I still remember the first day I saw you. You were walking with such purpose, and even though you thought you were walking away from something, it was that day that God caused you to walk into my life. From the moment I met you, I wished that you would be mine. Each day that I've gotten to know you, that feeling has grown even stronger. I want to spend the rest of my life with you. Zeal, will you make me the happiest man alive and marry me?"

The tears that had welled up in her eyes now spilled over. Zeal gazed at the ring and then at Jeremiah. She dabbed at her eyes and tried to catch her breath.

All of the love she had felt for him from the very beginning came bursting out. "Yes, Yes, Yes!"

Jeremiah beamed with joy as he slid the ring on her finger. Standing up, he immediately embraced her, then swung her in a circle. Samson came running up, barking.

Grandma Pearl had stopped and turned around just in time to see the proposal. Smiling, she said, "Well it's about time. I'm ready to go home and annoy Zeal's father some more."

When they were all back at the tent, Jeremiah knelt beside Samson. "Grandma Pearl, I'm curious about something. We're extremely grateful for your help in that battle, but didn't Samson try to prevent you from coming out of your tent?"

"Prevent me?" said Grandma Pearl, putting her hands on her hips. "Who do you think came and got me? Samson must have gone looking for you and saw that you were in trouble, because he came running up to the tent, barking. He then put my Book in his mouth and handed it to me. I barely got to my feet then he started pulling me in your direction. I knew then that something was wrong, so we started out looking for you. Good thing too."

Samson was sitting quietly, breathing casually, his tongue hanging out and wagging his tail.

Jeremiah rubbed him behind the ears. "Thank you."

Samson sat up and barked.

Zeal looked back toward the battlefield. "I wonder what that was all about. Why were such fierce enemies placed here to stop us?"

Jeremiah looked back as well. "I've been thinking the same thing. I believe we'll have to go a little further to find out."

Jeremiah and Zeal helped Grandma Pearl get loaded up, and then they made their way back to the place where the attacks began. Everything looked different now because the darkness had lifted, and the sun was shining brightly once again.

They continued a little further and came to a small hill. Once they reached the top, they stared down to see a large field where thousands of people were digging in the dirt, each wearing chains on their hands and feet.

Zeal grabbed Jeremiah's arm. "What's going on here?"

"I don't know," he said, looking out over the field. "Let's go talk to them."

Jeremiah approached an older man in tattered clothes. "Why are you digging in this field, and why are you chained. Is there a reason you left your Quest?"

The old man nervously glanced around. "As long as I can

remember I've always had these chains. A terrible ogre watches over us and threatens us with giant pigs if we don't work hard enough. There are giant bats that watch everyone from the air, so no one tries to escape. I have no idea what a Quest is. I've been a slave to this ogre for as long as I can remember."

Jeremiah returned to Grandma Pearl and Zeal. "These people are not on the Quest. They've been kept under darkness and in chains since the day they were born."

Zeal pointed past the field. "Look! It's a Building of Reflection, and there's the Hill of Calvary right behind it."

Grandma Pearl said, "Yes, God places them in different locations throughout this earth."

Jeremiah took out his telescope and aimed it beyond the Building of Reflection. "Just as I thought. A House of Instruction is being built not too far from there. This is why the ogre was sent out to stop us. His master saw that God was working to bring deliverance to these people, and the devil knew God had brought us here to do our part."

"What is our part?" asked Zeal.

Pointing toward all those who were in chains, Jeremiah said, "Look out unto the fields, for they are white and ready for harvest. For truly the harvest is plentiful, but the laborers are few. Pray to the Lord of the Harvest that He would send laborers out into the fields to gather in his crops."

Grandma Pearl nodded. "For whoever calls upon the name of the Lord will be saved, but how shall they call upon Him Whom they have not believed, and how shall they believe on Him Whom they have not heard, and how shall they hear without a preacher?"

Jeremiah, Zeal, and Grandma Pearl took out their Books and began walking toward the field. They stood in different sections and began to proclaim the gospel message to all. They let the captives know that they didn't have to remain in slavery and that their enemy had been defeated. Most just kept on digging, but some raised their hands toward heaven, crying out to God.

The trio began leading all those who wished to be free out of the field. They then led them to the Building of Reflection, and as each one went up the Hill of Calvary, all of their chains fell off.

Everyone then walked toward the location for the new House of

Instruction. Jeremiah, Zeal, and Grandma Pearl spent the next two weeks ministering to all those who started their Quest that day and helped the owners of the House of Instruction to finish the building. When the two weeks were done, they loaded up to leave.

Jeremiah and Zeal surveyed what they had accomplished. The first two weeks of their engagement had been spent in service to others, and they realized this is how their marriage would be used as well.

Everyone said goodbye, then Grandma Pearl mounted her donkey. "Let's go you two. We've got a wedding to plan."

35

A WEDDING

Grandma Pearl recognized where their path was leading. "It won't be too long before we're back home. I'd say it will take us a week if we make good time."

The trio traveled a little more swiftly than they had before, wanting to get back as soon as possible. The first chance he got, Jeremiah sent off two letters hoping they would reach their destinations in time. During the next week of travel, they stayed at inns all along the way and started each new day feeling rested and refreshed.

Over those seven days, Zeal turned her attention toward wedding plans. She must have gone over every detail at least three times, as she and Jeremiah walked together. She chatted away while waving her hands in the air, and Jeremiah enjoyed seeing how excited she was.

As Zeal talked about how she was going to decorate the main sanctuary, Jeremiah realized that she couldn't wait to be married in the House of Instruction she grew up in. He thought about all the improvements Pastor Sanford had asked him to make on the building. Did he know something all along?

The week seemed to fly by, and then the day came when they arrived back at Zeal's home. It was close to sunset, and her father was sitting out on the porch. As soon as he saw them coming, he jumped up and hurried toward them.

Zeal ran toward him and jumped into his arms like she was a little girl again. She then stepped back and held out her hand to show him the ring. "Look father! I'm engaged!"

"Congratulations!" said Pastor Sanford.

Her mother came out onto the porch, and Zeal hugged her and

showed her the ring as well.

"Congratulations! I love that ring," said Mama Beatrice.

Taking her sweet time, Grandma Pearl came riding up on her donkey. She then dismounted and looked up at Pastor Sanford. "Well, are you just going to stand there, or are you going to help me get this donkey unloaded."

Pastor Sanford smiled. "It's good to see you too."

Grandma Pearl smiled back. She was glad to be home.

Samson seemed happy to be back as well, and he went straight for the stream.

Everyone went inside, and Jeremiah, Zeal, and Grandma Pearl took turns telling of all the exciting things that happened on their journey. Of course, Grandma Pearl made it a point of special emphasis to talk about her role in the last battle.

She grinned at Pastor Sanford, a twinkle in her eye. "I told you I could still take that giant."

Everyone laughed, and yes, even Pastor Sanford laughed too.

Zeal grasped her mom's hand. "I know this is short notice, but I'd like to have the wedding in two weeks."

Mama Beatrice took a deep breath. "That doesn't give us a lot of time, but I'll talk to the other ladies who attend our House of Instruction and enlist their help. If we all pitch in, we might just be able to pull it off."

Zeal gave her mom a hug, then turned to Jeremiah. "I've got a short list of some tasks that I just know you'd be great at."

Pastor Sanford glanced over at him and smiled, knowing there were many more lists in Jeremiah's future.

The next day everyone started to work. Grandma Pearl was in charge of flowers and the reception, while Zeal and her mother focused on decorating the sanctuary. Part of Jeremiah's duties was to repair many of the pews so all the guests would have comfortable places to sit. After twelve days had passed, they were almost ready.

Celebrating the end of a long day's work, everyone sat down for a nice dinner together. Just as they were finishing up, they heard someone knocking.

Pastor Sanford went to the door and opened it. At first he stood at the entrance without saying anything, then a moment later he said,

"You better not have come empty-handed."

A man's voice replied, "Ah yes, I have what I need, but what makes you think this time will be different?"

Jeremiah thought he recognized the voice.

Pastor Sanford and the other man laughed and gave each other a hug. It was Pastor George! Jeremiah had written to him in hopes that he would be able to come to the wedding.

When Pastor George stepped into the house, Zeal jumped up and ran over to him. "Uncle George!"

Jeremiah stood up as Zeal hugged Pastor George's neck. "You already know everyone?"

"Well, sure I do, Jeremiah," said Pastor George as he stepped back to admire how much Zeal had grown since he last saw her. "I went to the same House of Knowledge as Sanford and Beatrice, and right after graduation, I was Sanford's best man at his wedding. After they were married, I traveled around with them for a while. The last time I saw Zeal she was just a little girl."

Jeremiah gestured toward Zeal. "Are you her uncle?"

Pastor George laughed. "Oh no, that's just what she calls me."

Pastor Sanford led Pastor George into the living room.

Jeremiah gave them a curious look. "I couldn't help but overhear the exchange between you two at the beginning. I thought you were mad at each other."

Pastor Sanford smiled. "Oh that, yes, you see George and I would often play a game of chess, and I once told him that anytime he visited he had to bring his chess board and chess pieces."

Pastor George pointed toward his bag. "And I brought them too."

For the rest of the evening, Jeremiah and Zeal caught Pastor George up on everything that had happened since they first met.

Pastor George grinned as he spotted them holding hands. "Jeremiah, when I got your letter I was so thrilled to hear that God had placed a special young woman in your life. And then when I saw that her name was Zeal, I couldn't help but wonder if it was the same Zeal I had known all those years ago who just happened to be the daughter of one of my best friends."

Jeremiah said, "I'm so glad you could make it." He turned to Pastor Sanford. "Of course I wanted Pastor George to be here for my wedding, but I also asked him in the letter if he would do the wedding ceremony. I hope that's okay?"

Pastor Sanford nodded toward Pastor George. "It's more than okay. I'd say it's about perfect."

They talked through the evening, and then Pastor Sanford showed Pastor George to the guest room.

The next day was the final day of preparations, and just after lunch, everyone finished their tasks. Jeremiah was making his way from the House of Instruction to Zeal's house when he thought he heard someone calling his name.

"Jeremiah!"

Turning around, he saw all his old friends from the House of Knowledge—Rick, Mark, Greg, Eric, and Aaron. Rick and Greg had brought their wives, Lisa and Anna. The second letter Jeremiah had sent was to Mark to let all his friends know he was getting married.

Jeremiah ran up to them. "I can't believe you made it!"

"Of course we made it," said Mark, giving Jeremiah a hug. "We wouldn't have missed this for anything."

Rick looked over Jeremiah's shoulder. "We can't wait to meet the woman who captured your heart."

Hearing all the laughter, Zeal walked outside and stood next to Jeremiah. "Are these your friends you've told me so much about?"

"Yes," he said. "And I'm so glad they could make it to the wedding."

Jeremiah introduced Zeal to each of them, sharing something about each one's personality and some of their exploits on their different adventures.

All the women patiently nodded and smiled as Jeremiah and the guys talked about all the great times they had together.

As soon as the guys started on another story, Zeal caught Lisa and Anna's eye. "Why don't I show you the House of Instruction and all of the decorations?"

Lisa and Anna exchanged a grin, and they both quickly nodded. "Yes, that would be great," said Lisa.

When Zeal learned that they had recently had their own weddings, she was anxious to hear every detail. They spent the next hour talking about every moment of their ceremonies. While they were sitting on one of the pews talking together, another young woman walked in.

Zeal jumped up. "Sheila! I'm so glad you could make it."

Zeal walked Sheila over to where Lisa and Anna were sitting. "This is my best friend Sheila who is going to be my maid of honor. We've been friends since we were five years old. She's been away at a House of Knowledge, and I wrote to her letting her know that I was getting married."

Sheila shook hands with Lisa and Anna and then put her arm around Zeal. "I came as soon as I got your letter. While I was traveling here, I thought about all those times as little girls when we used to dress up and pretend we were getting married. I'm so excited to be able to be here with you."

Putting her finger to her chin Zeal said, "You know what I just realized? I'm positive Jeremiah is going to ask all his friends to be in the wedding, and that means we'll have two more guys than we have bridesmaids. Lisa and Anna, would you like to be in the wedding and walk down the aisle with your husbands?"

Lisa's eyes lit up as Anna looked over and smiled. "We'd love to!"

Zeal stood up and motioned for them to follow her. "When the ladies were making the bridesmaid dresses, they made one that was too small." Pointing toward Anna, she said, "But I believe it will be a perfect fit for you." Gesturing toward Lisa, she said, "And I'm sure there's enough material to make one more. I'll talk to the ladies who did the sewing and see if they can make just one more before tomorrow."

Zeal led everyone into a side room to see where they were keeping the dresses. Each was light pink with lace sleeves and pink ribbons around the waist.

Lisa ran her hand down the fabric. "These are so pretty."

Sheila took a dress off the hanger and held it in front of her. "This is beautiful. I can't wait to wear it tomorrow."

As soon as the girls had headed for the sanctuary, Jeremiah and the rest of the guys went back to telling stories and caught each other up on everything that had been happening since they last saw each other.

Rick shook his head and smiled. "With all of us standing here talking, it's just like we were back in Jeremiah and Mark's room sharing about our lives."

Mark nodded. "I was thinking the same thing." Turning to Jeremiah, he said, "I can't believe how much God has done with you and Zeal in such a short amount of time."

"I know," said Jeremiah. "We've faced so many challenges, but each one has brought us even closer together."

Pastor Sanford and Mama Beatrice came out to greet Jeremiah's friends, and Pastor Sanford came up with the idea to have a picnic. Mama Beatrice returned to the kitchen, and she and Grandma Pearl busily prepared the food.

When everything was ready, they all sat down to a great meal and a great time of fellowship together. Jeremiah's friends took advantage of the opportunity to talk to Pastor Sanford and Pastor George. They wanted to learn as much as they could from these seasoned warriors and leaders. Lisa and Anna had a great time getting to know Grandma Pearl, and yes, she told them about the time she whacked the Giant of Shame over the head.

When the picnic was over, Jeremiah told Zeal that he was going to walk with his friends to the inn where they were staying and then come right back. Along the way, he asked Mark to be his best man, and the other guys to stand beside him as well.

When Jeremiah and his friends left, Mama Beatrice and Grandma Pearl walked over to Zeal with a grin on their faces.

Her mother put her hand on Zeal's shoulder. "We've been waiting to reveal a surprise. You told us the day you arrived back home that you wanted to wear the same wedding dress that Grandma Pearl and I wore at our weddings. Well, after we measured you in it that day, we invited some of the ladies who were good at sewing to help us make it a little more unique for your wedding. We can't wait for you to see it."

Zeal clapped her hands together. "Where is it?"

Grandma Pearl pointed to the sewing room next to the kitchen. "Come on girl, let's go see it."

They led Zeal into the room where the dress was proudly displayed on a standing rack where it could be seen at full length. It had been fully cleaned and looked just as white as the first day it had been made. The ladies added some extra lace to the hem of the dress and around the shoulders. Zeal thought it was beautiful.

She hugged them both. "Thank you!"

****

The next day arrived, and all the bridesmaids were helping Zeal to get ready. They made sure everything from her hair down to her shoes was just right.

At last, everyone except her mother and Grandma Pearl left for the House of Instruction.

Zeal stood before the mirror. "I can't believe this is really happening."

Grandma Pearl kissed her cheek. "Child, you look absolutely gorgeous."

Her mother put her arm around her waist. "Yes you do. I'm so happy for you."

"Thank you," said Zeal. She gave them each a hug.

She turned back to the mirror. "Do you think I'm ready? Am I ready to be a wife?"

Grandma Pearl adjusted her veil. "You're ready, and you're going to be a great wife."

Her mother gave her a squeeze. "There's nothing to worry about. God has been preparing you for this moment since the day you were born."

There was a knock at the door. "It's me," said Pastor Sanford, "May I come in?"

Grandma Pearl opened the door. "Come on in. She's just about ready."

"There's my beautiful baby girl," said her father as he walked into the room.

Mama Beatrice gave him a quick kiss. "Grandma Pearl, let's get over to the House of Instruction. It's almost time."

Grandma Pearl and Mama Beatrice left, and Aaron and Eric were waiting outside to escort them into the sanctuary. Grandma Pearl had worn her best dress and her best hat, and everyone agreed she was looking mighty fine.

Aaron and Eric showed them to their seats, then joined Jeremiah and the other guys in a small classroom.

Pastor George walked into the room. "Jeremiah, I can't believe all that's happened. It seems like just yesterday I was outside your eatery, hoping to get a sandwich, and now here we are."

"I know," said Jeremiah, shaking his head. "I can hardly believe it myself."

Pastor George greeted all of Jeremiah's friends and then glanced back toward the front of the sanctuary. "It's time."

Rick, Aaron, Eric, and Greg went toward the back and escorted the bridesmaids to the front of the altar. The maid of honor, Sheila, walked in next. After that, Pastor George, Jeremiah, and Mark walked in from the side. The wedding party was now in position, and everyone eagerly anticipated the arrival of the bride.

Back at the house, Pastor Sanford stood beside Zeal. "I can't believe this day is here. It's a day that every father dreads, but rejoices when it arrives."

"I love you dad. Thank you so much for all you've done for me."

Wiping a tear from under his eye, her father said, "I know you're going to be happy, and I know God is going to bless you two. It's hard to let you go, but I know Jeremiah is a good man."

"Yes, he is, and I pray he will be just as loving a husband and father as you've been," said Zeal. She then kissed him on the cheek.

Her father hugged her and then wiped his eyes. "I think a young man is waiting on you, so we better head over there and join him." He walked Zeal over to the House of Instruction.

The sanctuary was beautifully decorated with fresh daisies and sunflowers all around the front of the altar. A silver candelabra sat in the center. Pink and white ribbons draped the pews, and fresh yellow rose petals lined the center of the aisle.

Pastor Sanford and Zeal waited outside until they were given the cue. Then the music for the bride started, and her father walked her down the aisle. Everyone stood, and there were whispers all around, declaring how beautiful Zeal looked.

As Jeremiah saw her approaching, he put his hand over his heart, thinking of just how much he loved her. Pastor Sanford escorted her to Jeremiah's side, then sat in the front row next to his wife and Grandma Pearl.

Pastor George asked everyone to be seated. "We are gathered here today before God and all of you witnesses to join this man and this woman together in marriage. Marriage was created by God to unite one man with one woman, representing the relationship between Christ and the church."

Pastor George read from his Book, "For this reason, a man shall leave his father and his mother and be joined to his wife, and the two shall be one flesh."

Pastor George held out his hand toward Jeremiah and Zeal. "As you are about to exchange vows, remember that you will always need God's grace to carry them out."

Jeremiah took a deep breath as he held Zeal's hands in his and gazed into her eyes. "I Jeremiah, take you Zeal, to be my wife. I pledge to you my love for as long as we both shall live. I promise to be there for you when you are weak as well as when you are strong. I commit to being the husband that God has called me to be and to love you as Christ loves the church."

Zeal smiled as she looked into Jeremiah's eyes. "Jeremiah, I take you this day to be my husband. I will love you with all of my heart for as long as we both shall live. I pledge to support you as the leader of our home, and I will be there by your side in times of strength as well as in times of weakness. I love you with all of my heart."

Pastor George turned to Jeremiah. "Do you take Zeal to be your wife?"

"I do."

Jeremiah placed the ring on her finger.

Pastor George turned to Zeal. "Do you take Jeremiah to be your husband?"

"Yes, I do."

Zeal put the ring on his finger.

Pastor George motioned toward Jeremiah. "You may kiss the bride."

Zeal shot a quick look at Grandma Pearl, and Grandma Pearl gave her a wink and nod. As Jeremiah leaned in to kiss her, Zeal threw her arms around his neck, pulled him close, and passionately kissed him.

Pastor Sanford wrinkled his forehead just a little.

Mama Beatrice smiled and blushed.

Grandma Pearl raised her hand in the air. "That's my girl!"

Pastor George surveyed the guests. "Jeremiah and Zeal, would you turn and face all those who are gathered."

Pastor George motioned for everyone to stand up. "I now present to you for the first time as husband and wife, Jeremiah and Zeal."

Music began to play, and they walked down the aisle arm and arm. All the guests cheered and clapped.

The door in the back had been left open per Jeremiah's request so Samson could stand out on the steps and watch the whole thing. As Jeremiah and Zeal were walking down the aisle, he began to jump up and down and bark.

Once the bride and groom left the sanctuary, Jeremiah's friends escorted the bridesmaids and maid of honor out as well. Then Pastor George, Pastor Sanford, Mama Beatrice, and Grandma Pearl followed. All of the rest of the guests then proceeded outside and waited in line for an opportunity to congratulate the newlyweds.

With the help of the other ladies from the House of Instruction, Grandma Pearl planned a great outdoor reception. There was plenty of punch, finger sandwiches, and of course, a special two-tiered cake that Grandma Pearl had made herself. Everyone thoroughly enjoyed the food, music, and fellowship.

After a few hours of great fun and laughter, Zeal gathered all the single women together, because it was time to throw the bouquet.

Once they were all lined up, Zeal turned her back and threw the bouquet of pink and white roses over her shoulders. It sailed through the air, then all of a sudden a hand shot up from out of nowhere to grab it. It was Grandma Pearl! She had jumped up to catch the bouquet mid-air.

Grandma Pearl's eyes darted back and forth. "Y'all don't look at me like that. There's still some fire in this furnace."

Everyone couldn't help but smile and laugh.

After this, the guests began to leave. Jeremiah's friends came up and wished him well as they, too, were preparing to head back to Cedar Grove. Jeremiah embraced all of them and told them how thankful he was that they were able to come.

At last, all the guests had left except for Pastor George. He said goodbye to Zeal's father and mother, then approached the newly married couple. "God bless both of you. I can't wait to hear about all the things you're going to accomplish for the Kingdom of God."

Jeremiah and Zeal gave Pastor George a hug, and then he left.

Zeal's parents had arranged for them to spend a week at an inn for their honeymoon. Some of the men fixed up a horse and wagon to transport them, and the bridesmaids had decorated it with flowers.

The driver of the wagon pulled up next to the newlyweds.

Zeal smiled at her parents and grandmother. "Thank you so much for making this day so special. Everything was perfect. We'll see you again at the end of the week."

They all gave Jeremiah and Zeal one last hug.

As Jeremiah was thanking Pastor Sanford for everything he had done, Zeal leaned over and quickly whispered to Grandma Pearl. "Do you have any advice as we're about to go to the inn."

Grandma Pearl smiled and then leaned over to give Zeal another hug. She whispered, "Girl, the way I saw you kiss Jeremiah, I don't think you need any advice. You're going to be just fine."

Zeal blushed and smiled.

Samson stood by watching. He seemed to be worn out from all of the excitement of the day. Pastor Sanford offered to keep him with them during the week, and Samson seemed to be okay with that.

Jeremiah helped Zeal into the wagon, and then he climbed onboard. They waved to everyone as the wagon drove off toward the sunset. When they checked into the inn, they walked up to their room, and then Jeremiah insisted on carrying Zeal through the door. Once inside, they discovered that the ladies from the House of Instruction had made up a beautiful gift basket of fresh fruits and had it delivered to their room.

After setting down their things in front of a closet, Jeremiah put his hands on the side of Zeal's shoulders. "For so long I've been waiting for this day when I could finally call you my wife. Tomorrow we will wake up together, and I look forward to waking up with you every day for the rest of my life."

Jeremiah pulled Zeal close, and she relaxed into his arms.

It was a wonderful honeymoon week. When they were not in their room, they were taking long walks and talking about their future. They met another couple who was also on their honeymoon, and they spent time getting to know them and eating some of their meals together. As the week was ending, Jeremiah and Zeal felt they had grown together so much in just a short amount of time.

On the last day, as they were packing up and preparing to leave, Zeal knew it was soon going to be time to say goodbye to her family. She and Jeremiah had both felt for a while that God was calling them to go out on their own. Zeal hadn't said anything to her father and mother, but she knew her parents realized it was coming. After checking out of the inn, they rode the same wagon back to the house.

When they arrived, Pastor Sanford, Mama Beatrice, and Grandma Pearl came out to greet them. As soon as Samson saw them get off the wagon, he jumped on Jeremiah with such enthusiasm that he almost knocked him down. Laughing at how excited Samson was, Jeremiah knelt down and grabbed his face in his hands. Standing back up, he picked up their bags and took them inside. He and Zeal then joined everyone in the living room for a wonderful evening together.

As the evening drew to a close, Zeal told her family that their paths were leading away, and they were going to be leaving the next morning. Her parents made it easy for them because God had already prepared their hearts for what was to come.

After a time of prayer with the family, Jeremiah and Zeal stepped out onto the porch.

Jeremiah gazed up at the stars. "Can you believe it wasn't that long ago that we stood out here for the first time?"

Zeal stared at the moon. "We've been through so much together already."

Jeremiah pulled Zeal into his arms and held her tight. "And I can't wait for all that is to come."

Tap. Tap. Tap.

After hearing the all too familiar tapping on the window, they turned around to see Grandma Pearl and Mama Beatrice smiling.

Grandma Pearl stepped out onto the porch. "I'm going on to bed, but I thought you two might want to hear that tapping sound just one more time. I'll see you tomorrow before you leave."

Mama Beatrice held open the door, and Jeremiah and Zeal stepped back inside.

Pastor Sanford joined them. "Your mother and I prepared one of the guest rooms upstairs for you two."

Zeal gave her parents a good night kiss, and they went off to bed. She then turned to Jeremiah. "You go on up. I'll be there soon."

Jeremiah went on into the guest room while Zeal stayed behind. Standing there in the living room, she looked around thinking of all the memories this house held for her. Staring at the fireplace, she remembered those cold nights when they would all huddle around the fire to stay warm. She then walked into the dining room, sliding her hand across the table, as she thought of all the stories and laughter that were shared there.

Next, she went into the sewing room, remembering the time when Grandma Pearl and Mama Beatrice taught her to make her first dress. She smiled as she saw herself at five years old holding up a finished dress with one arm twice as long as the other.

Zeal then sauntered back into the living room and sat on the sofa. She remembered back to when she was a little girl, and how her father used to sit in this very seat. Each night she would jump into his lap so he could read to her from his Book. Her father read the Book with such passion that she felt a part of the stories. Sitting there on that sofa, she rode in the ark with Noah, she crossed the Red Sea with Moses, she stood nearby as David slew Goliath, and she walked in the fiery furnace with Shadrach, Meshach, and Abednego. It was here that she also huddled with Daniel while he was in the lion's den, and she traveled with Jesus as He went about teaching and doing good.

Taking note of her surroundings for a few more minutes, Zeal then rose to her feet and went upstairs. After reaching the top of the steps, she walked into her old room. This room had been a special place for her. As a little girl, she imagined it was a fortress that was protected by a great king where no enemy could do her harm. It was the place she came for comfort, and it was the place she came to dream.

Zeal glanced over in the corner to see her old doll, Lacey, that had kept her company on so many occasions. She picked the doll up and smiled, reflecting back to the Christmas she received it as a gift from Grandma Pearl. She fixed Lacey's hair, then set her back down.

Zeal turned to leave, but just as she reached the door, she looked back one more time. Taking a deep breath, she closed the door behind her, then joined Jeremiah in their room.

36

NEW BEGINNINGS

The next morning Jeremiah and Zeal packed their belongings. The farmer, who had loaned the donkey to Grandma Pearl, gave it to them as a wedding present. Pastor Sanford helped load everything up then stepped back and joined his wife.

Jeremiah said goodbye to Pastor Sanford, Mama Beatrice, and Grandma Pearl, and then he and Samson walked over to the donkey, leaving Zeal to have a few minutes alone with her family.

Zeal didn't try to hide her tears. She was excited to start her new life with Jeremiah, but she wasn't going to try and deny the sadness of leaving her family.

Her father gave her a hug and a kiss. "Write to us, and we expect you two to come by when you can."

Her mother gave her a hug and a kiss. "Be safe and know that we're always praying for you."

Grandma Pearl gave her a hug and a kiss. "Girl, you're going to be just fine."

Zeal smiled and then turned around to join Jeremiah. When she stepped up beside him, he gave her a quick kiss, and they started out on their path together. Grandma Pearl went inside not long afterward and then her mother, but her father stood outside and watched until he couldn't see them anymore.

Jeremiah and Zeal traveled for weeks discovering that their path was taking them in a new direction. They spent most of their evenings in inns at first, but then their path led further out into the country where they had to camp. One day as they were traveling, they saw that their path was heading straight toward two tents. Two men came out, and Samson started to bark.

One of the men walked toward them. "Hello, my name is Disciple."

The other man came forward as well. "And I'm Peter."

Jeremiah and Zeal introduced themselves, and they all sat down to talk. It didn't take long before they recognized that they had all been brought together by God. Disciple and Peter led them to a spot where they could look out over a valley.

Disciple motioned toward the wide open space below. "Toward the far end is a large camp of ogres and giants. Whatever God has planned is not going to be easy."

Jeremiah took out his telescope. "I see what you're saying. This is going to be a difficult mission."

Receiving the telescope from Jeremiah, Zeal scanned the enemy's camp as well. "I wonder what will happen next."

After returning to the campsite, Jeremiah studied the ground, then shifted his gaze to Disciple. "Our path has stopped at the same place as yours. We'll set up our tent to spend the night, and then tomorrow we'll see if our paths have moved."

Disciple nodded. "Since we got here, we've felt that God was not going to lead us any further until others arrived. Let's see what happens tomorrow."

The next morning Jeremiah and Zeal joined Disciple and Peter outside their tents, but none of their paths had moved.

Jeremiah took Zeal's hand in his. "It looks like we're waiting for more to arrive."

****

Jeremiah is right. More are on the way.

****

DON'T STOP READING!
Disciples Quest 3: Esther & Overcomer, Women of God IS NOW AVAILABLE!

Disciples Quest: The Adventure Begins

Disciples Quest 4: Warriors of God

Join me on Facebook:
https://www.facebook.com/DisciplesQuestBooks

SCRIPTURE REFERENCES

Some of these quotes are only partial quotations from Scripture, and some are loose paraphrases designed to fit the dialogue.

Chapter 1

Pastor George said, "This Book is special because it is the very words of God Himself." (2 Timothy 3:16)

Pastor George said, "Oh there is much more to it than just competing intellectual theories. You see, when I look around at nature I see the handiwork of God. I see everything operating in an ordered way with a purpose, and I believe behind all of this is a cause." (Romans 1:18-20) (Psalms 19:1)

Pastor George said, "I don't try and convince anyone of anything. In this Book it says that everyone already has the knowledge that God exists on the inside of them. The question is, what are they going to do about it." (Romans 1:18-21)

Chapter 2

The Scriptures that Jeremiah read when he arrived at his home: (Romans 1:18-25) (Hebrews 11:3) (Genesis 1) (Acts 17:18-34)
The Scripture that Jeremiah read the next day at his home: (Romans 3)

Chapter 3

Witness said, "Yes, God knew from the beginning that man was going to rebel, and He had a plan to provide a solution even before creating man." (Revelation 13:8) (1 Peter 1:20)

"You are right," said Witness, nodding, "man deserves to be punished, and God was in no way obligated to provide an answer. But even while we were sinful, God showed His love toward us, by sending His Son to die for us.

(Romans 5:8) The Son of God took all the punishment that we deserved because of how much He loved us." (Ephesians 2:4-7)

Jeremiah said, "I read in this Book that there is no one that does good, there is none that seeks after God, and in fact, there is nothing in man to love." (Romans 3:10-12)

Witness said, "God is very logical. He is the source of all wisdom and knowledge. His thoughts are far above our thoughts, and His ways are far above our ways." (Isaiah 55:8, 9)

Chapter 4

Jeremiah read that Jesus was with the Father from the beginning and in fact was Himself God. (John 1:1-14)

Jeremiah remembered that God referred to Himself in the plural when He said, "Let Us make man..." (Genesis 1:29)

Jeremiah read about the birth of Jesus. (Luke 2:1-20)

Jeremiah read about Nicodemus coming to visit Jesus by night. (John 3:1-21)

Jeremiah read about the crippled man being healed by the pool. (John 5:1-18)

Jeremiah read that the religious leaders became angry and jealous because

Jesus made Himself to be equal with God. (John 5:18)

Jeremiah read that Jesus said that the same honor that they would give the

Father should also be given to Him. (John 5:22-23)
Jesus said to them, "Most assuredly I say to you, before Abraham was, I AM." (John 8:58 NKJV)

Jeremiah read about Moses and the burning bush. (Exodus 3:1-14)
God refers to Himself with the name of I AM that I AM. (Exodus 3:14)
Jesus said that the reason they did not believe was because they were not of His sheep. (John 10:26)

Jesus declared, "I and My Father are one." (John 10:30 NKJV)

Jeremiah read of the prophecy in Isaiah about Jesus. (John 12:37-40)

Jeremiah read that Isaiah saw Jesus in His glory. (John 12:41) (Isaiah 6:1-10)

Jeremiah read that Jesus was accused of blasphemy for saying He was God's son. (John 19:7)

Jeremiah read about the trial and crucifixion of Jesus. (John 18, 19)

Jesus said, "Father forgive them, for they know not what they are doing." (Luke 23:34)

When Jesus appeared to all the disciples, Thomas declared what they all now knew; Jesus was their Lord and their God! (John 20:28)

John had written all these things so that all those reading might believe that

Jesus is the Son of God and receive eternal life through Him. (John 20:31)

Chapter 5

Jeremiah now understood why this Book said, there is no one who is righteous, not even one. (Romans 3:10)

Jesus said, "All those who the Father gives to me, will come to me, and all the ones who come to me, I will by no means reject." (John 6:37)

Jeremiah saw a sign that said, "Whoever calls upon the name of the Lord will be saved." (Romans 10:13)

Jeremiah heard a voice booming from heaven, "If any man be in Christ, he is a new creation. Behold, the old things have passed away, behold, all things have become new!" (2 Corinthians 5:17 NKJV)

At the tomb Jeremiah reads: (1 Corinthians 15)

Chapter 6

During his baptism Jeremiah thought of being resurrected with Christ to newness of life. (Romans 6:4)

Taking out his Book, Pastor George said, "The most important thing you can do is spend time in this Book every single day, and throughout your day meditate on what you've read. Memorize as much as you can and always be eager to talk about it with others. (Deuteronomy 6:6-9) This Book is a light unto your path and a lamp unto your feet." (Psalms 119:105)

Pastor George said, "As you travel, always commit your steps to the Lord, trusting that He will get you to where you need to be." (Psalms 37:5, 6)

Pastor George teaches Jeremiah the Lord's Prayer. (Matthew 6:9-13 NKJV)
*Verse 12 is my own wording

Pastor George said, "When we are born again, a whole new world and reality is opened up to us." (2 Corinthians 4:3, 4)

Chapter 7

Pastor George said, "Your warfare will not be against flesh and blood, but your struggle will be against the different kinds of enemies that the devil will place along your path." (Ephesians 6:12)

Pastor George said, "Yes there is a spiritual dimension, and it's just as real as what you can see. We are told to put on this armor so that we can stand up against all the schemes of the devil. (Ephesians 6:11)

Jeremiah said, "Not by might, nor by power, but by your Spirit, Oh LORD." (Zechariah 4:6 NKJV)
Jeremiah said, "I will gladly be a fool for Christ in order that I might be wise in Him, for the wisdom of this world is foolishness to God." (1 Cor. 3:19)

Jeremiah was now able to lift up his head, fastening his eyes upon the dark mist, determined that no weapon formed against him was going to prosper. (Isaiah 54:17)

A verse suddenly appeared before Jeremiah's thoughts, "Finally my brothers, continue becoming strong in the Lord, and in the power of His might." (Ephesians 6:10)

Jeremiah shouted toward the mist, "The message of the cross is indeed foolishness to the ones perishing, but to us, the ones who are saved, it is the power of God!" (1 Cor. 1:18)

Jeremiah thrust his Sword toward the Wisdom of this World. "God says, I will destroy the wisdom of the ones who think they are wise, and I will set aside as nothing the intelligence of the ones who think they are intelligent." (1 Cor. 1:19)

Jeremiah shouted, "Where is the philosopher? Where is the scholar? Where is the proud debater of this present age? Has God not shown that the wisdom of this world is foolishness!" (1 Cor. 1:20)

Chapter 8

Jeremiah and his friends discuss Nehemiah and the rebuilding of the walls in Jerusalem. (Nehemiah 1-6)

Mark pointed to his Book. "This is what Nehemiah said to those who were harassing the ones rebuilding the walls of Jerusalem, 'The God of heaven Himself will prosper us, therefore we His servants will arise and build.' " (Nehemiah 2:20 NKJV)

Rick said, "Shall I bring to the point of birth and not cause it to be completed? says the LORD. Shall I, the one who causes the birthing to happen, shut the womb? says your God." (Isaiah 66:9)

Susan proclaimed, "I will not fear or be discouraged, for my God is with me. He will strengthen me and help me. He will uphold me with his righteous right hand." (Isaiah 41:10)

Susan held up her Shield. "I will say of the LORD, He is my refuge and my fortress, My God, in Him I will trust." (Psalms 91:2 NKJV)

Tom declared, "I believe that I shall see the goodness of the Lord in the land of the living. Therefore I will wait on Him and be encouraged. Yes, I will wait on the Lord and be strengthened." (Psalms 27: 13, 14)

Tom raised up his Sword. "Though an army encamps against me, my heart shall not fear. If war should rise up against me, even then I will still be confident." (Psalms 27:3)

Tom lifted up his hands toward heaven. "Lord God it is you that fights our battles for us!" (2 Chronicles 32:8)

Jeremiah would later read in his Book where it said, "For though we live in the flesh, we do not wage war according to the flesh, for the weapons that we use in our warfare are not fleshly, but mighty before God to the tearing down of strongholds, casting down imaginations and every high thing that is exalted against the knowledge of God, and bringing every thought into captivity to the obedience of Christ." (2 Corinthians 10:3-5)

Chapter 9

Jeremiah opened up his Book. "I was reading this yesterday from the prophet Isaiah, 'For thus says the High and Exalted One Who inhabits eternity and whose name is Holy, I dwell in the high and holy place, with those who are thoroughly sorrowful about their sins and who are of a humble spirit, to revive the spirit of the humble, and to revive the hearts of the ones who are truly repentant for their sins.' " (Isaiah 57:15)

Jeremiah read, "I know you are enduring patiently and bearing up for my name's sake, and you have not grown weary. But I have this against you, that you have abandoned your first love." (Rev. 2:3, 4)

When Jeremiah and his friends sensed the cold damp air of complacency they quoted this: "Therefore, my beloved brethren, be steadfast, immovable, always abounding in the work of the Lord, knowing that your labor is not in vain in the Lord." (1 Cor. 15:58 NKJV)

Mark held his Shield firmly, while raising his Sword in the air. "We will not sleep, as others may do, but we will be watchful, alert, and clearheaded!" (1 Thessalonians 5:6)

Eric touched the tip of his Sword to Aaron's wound. "God's words are life to those who find them and health to all their flesh." (Proverbs 4:22 NKJV)

Holding out his Shield, Eric shouted, "We will not be sluggish, but we will become imitators of those who through faith and patience inherit the promises." (Hebrews 6:12 NKJV)

Jeremiah shouted, "I believe this is where we need to remember that it's the Love of Christ that compels us. (2 Corinthians 5:14) We do not just move forward when it's convenient, but we press on to the upward call of God in Christ Jesus." (Philippians 3:14)

Mark struggled against the wind, but was determined to stay on his feet. "We will not be moved back! We will be steadfast, immovable, and ALWAYS abounding in the work of the Lord!" (1 Cor. 15:58)

Rick lifted up his Sword. "Oh Lord, Will You not revive us again, That Your people may rejoice in You?" (Psalms 85:6 NKJV)

Chapter 10

Jeremiah said, "When I am afraid I will trust in you." (Psalms 56:3)

Jeremiah said, "This Book lists certain sins where it says that if a person persists in those sins through their life without repentance, then it shows that they never accepted what Jesus did for them and never became a new creation. Based on that, they will spend eternity in the lake that burns with fire." (1 Corinthians 6:9)

Chapter 11

Jeremiah replied, "This Book says that when you become a new creation you are now a foreigner in this world and you're citizenship is in heaven." (Philippians 3:20) (Heb. 11:13)

Jeremiah said, "This Book says that the rational and natural mind is not able to understand the things of God." (1 Cor. 2:14)

Raising his Book, until it became a Sword, Jeremiah shouted, "Indeed, I count all things as loss because of the surpassing worth of knowing Christ

Jesus my Lord for whom I have suffered the loss of all things, and I count them as garbage, that I may gain Christ." (Philippians 3:8)

Jeremiah had thought his time in the Town of Rationalism was a complete bust, and that The Wisdom of This World had won a victory, but God was working all things according to the counsel of his will. God took the small seeds Jeremiah had planted and used them for His glory. (Ephesians 1:11)

Chapter 12

Below the name of the valley was written a verse from the Book, Blessed is the man who is patient and steadfast under trial, for when he has passed the test he will receive the crown of life, which the Lord has promised to those who love him. (James 1:12)

Jeremiah said, "When we fought the Creature of Complacency, one of the verses we quoted from our Book was that it was through faith and patience that we inherit the promises." (Hebrews 6:12)

Jeremiah said, "I believe these are roots of bitterness. Take out your Sword and repent of any bitterness you've allowed in your heart and especially while we have been in this valley." (Heb. 12:15)

Jeremiah thrust his Sword toward Eric's belly believing that it would reveal his thoughts. (Hebrews 4:12)

Jeremiah quoted from the Book. "Let all bitterness, rage, anger, quarreling, and slander be put away from you, along with all hatred." (Ephesians 4:31) Eric shouted, "I will not let a root of bitterness spring up within me, but instead of complaining during hard times, I will reach out and secure God's grace." (Heb. 12:15)

Jeremiah took out his Book. "I believe this will help, Blessed is the man who fears the LORD, taking great pleasure in His commandments. He will not fear bad news, or live in dread of what might happen because his heart is fixed trusting in the Lord." (Psalms 112:1, 7)

Mark read, "My brethren, count it all joy when you fall into various trials, knowing that the testing of your faith produces patience. But let patience have its perfect work, that you may be perfect and complete, lacking nothing." (James 1:2-4 NKJV)

Rick took out his Book and read, "Do not let any foul or harmful word come out of your mouth, but only what is useful for building one another up, as is fitting to the need and the occasion, that it may give grace to those who hear it." (Eph. 4:29)

Jeremiah opened his Book. "I think James sums it up well when he writes, 'But no man can tame the tongue. It is an unruly evil, full of deadly poison. With it we bless our God and Father, and with it we curse men, who have been made in the likeness of God.' " (James 3:8, 9 NKJV)

Rick paused and looked back. "Let's all remember what was on the sign when we first entered the valley, 'Blessed is the man who is patient and steadfast under trial, for when he has passed the test he will receive the crown of life, which the Lord has promised to those who love him.' " (James 1:12)

Chapter 13

Jeremiah desperately shouted, "Those that belong to Christ have crucified the flesh with its sinful passions and lustful desires." (Galatians 5:24)
The Holy Spirit brought to Jeremiah's remembrance, "If we confess our sins, He is faithful and just to forgive us our sins and to cleanse us from all unrighteousness." (1 John 1:9 NKJV)

Jeremiah shouted, "I will set no wicked thing before my eyes!" (Psalms 101:3)

Jeremiah saw that when thoughts of lust are allowed to roam free, they wage war against the soul. (1 Peter 2:11)
The Holy Spirit reminded Jeremiah that he was to meditate on God's word day and night, and this was what should be consuming his thoughts. (Psalms 1:1-3)

Jeremiah said, "I have made a covenant with my eyes, how then can I look upon a woman with lust." (Job 31:1)

Jeremiah shouted, "How can a young man keep his way pure? By keeping watch over himself according to your word, oh God." (Psalms 119:9)

Jeremiah swiveled around and cut down four knights with one blow. "With my whole heart, I will seek You OH LORD, let me not wander from Your commandments." (Psalms 119:10 NKJV)

Jeremiah bowed to one knee. "Oh God, I have stored up Your word in my heart that I might not sin against You!" (Psalms 119:11 ESV)

Jeremiah shouted, "Thanks be unto you God who always causes me to triumph through my Lord and Savior Jesus Christ!" (2 Corinthians 2:14)

Chapter 14

Taking out his Book, Jeremiah read, "When you lie down, you will not be afraid. Yes, you will lie down, and your sleep will be sweet." (Proverbs 3:24 NKJV)

In another place he read, "I will lie down and sleep in peace, for it is You oh LORD alone that causes me to dwell in safety." (Psalms 4:8)

Jeremiah thought on another Psalm. "Yea, though I walk through the valley of the shadow of death, I will fear no evil; For You are with me; Your rod and Your staff, they comfort me." (Psalms 23:4 NKJV)

Jeremiah also recalled the verse, "Whoever diligently listens to me shall dwell securely, and shall be peaceful, without fear or dread of evil." (Proverbs 1:33)

Jeremiah remembered another Psalm. "If God does not watch the city, then those who watch it, watch in vain." (Psalms 127:1)

Chapter 15

"There is therefore now no condemnation to those who are in Christ Jesus..." (Romans 8:1a NKJV)

Jeremiah said, "The first verse I have is, 'For godly sorrow produces repentance leading to salvation, leaving no regret, but worldly sorrow produces death.' " (2 Cor. 7:10)

Jeremiah said, "The Apostle Paul wrote, 'How shall we who died to sin live any longer in it?' " (Romans 6:2 NKJV)

Pastor John said, "Our hope is not in ourselves or what we can attain on our own, but we are told to place our hope completely in the grace that is revealed to us when we receive Christ." (1 Peter 1:13) *Note: You will notice that I take a different approach to the translation of this verse than most English Versions. The word translated "revealed" is a continuous participle, which does not have tense. An actual word for word literal translation of the entire verse would read as follows: "For this reason, having tied up at the waist the clothes of your mind, being sober, place your hope completely upon the grace being brought to you in the revelation of Jesus Christ." Martin Luther and others through Church History believed this verse was referring to placing our hope in the grace that is revealed to us in the Gospel.*

Jeremiah said to the group, "This Book tells us that if we confess our sins, He is faithful and just to forgive us of our sins and cleanses us from all the unrighteousness associated with it. This means that we can also be cleansed from the guilt that comes with our sin." (1 John 1:9)

Jeremiah shouted, "As far as the east is from the west, this is how far He has removed our transgressions from us." (Psalms 103:12 NKJV)

Jeremiah took out his Sword, and forcefully plunged it into the ground. "My God has brought me up out of the terrible pit, and out of the miry clay. He has set my feet upon a rock, and He has established my feet on steady ground." (Psalms 40:2)

Alan shouted to all those in their cells. "Christ is at the right hand of God, acting as an advocate on our behalf. It is His righteousness that makes us acceptable before the Father and not our own." (1 John 2:1)

Paul held out his Book in his left hand, as he raised his right hand into the air. "Jesus took the wrath of God that we deserved, becoming a propitiation for us. (Romans 3:25, 1 John 2:2) Because of this, we have peace with God through our Lord Jesus Christ. (Romans 5:1) God is not mad at you! Confess and turn away from your sins, knowing that He wants to cleanse you so you can enjoy fellowship with Him."

Shem shouted, "Bless the LORD, O my soul, and all that is within me, bless His holy name! He has not dealt with us according to our sins, Nor punished us according to our iniquities." (Psalms 103:1, 10 NKJV)

Adam said, "If you are in Christ, God is not keeping a record of your sins to hold against you." He then read, "If You, Lord, kept account of and treated us according to our sins, who could stand? But with You there is forgiveness that You may be reverently feared." (Psalms 130:3, 4)

Jeremiah shouted. "There is no condemnation for those who are in Christ because every accusation that stood against us was nailed to the cross with Him." (Colossians 2:14)

Paul shouted, "You've been made dead to sin. It's time to start living like it. Stop trying to deal with your sinfulness through your own efforts and start surrendering to God and His grace." (Romans 6:1-13)

Alan slammed his Shield into the forehead of the giant, knocking him out. "Whom the Son sets free is free indeed." (John 8:36)

Chapter 16

Elder Jenkins took out his Book and began to read. "Oh LORD, You have searched me, and you have known me. You know my times of sitting down and my times of rising up. You perceive my thoughts when they are still far off. You spread out my path before me, and you prepare the place of my lying down. You are familiar with all my ways. Even before I have spoken a word, Behold, Oh LORD, You already know it. You have enclosed me from behind and in front, and have laid Your hand upon me. Such infinite knowledge is too wonderful for me. It is too high, I cannot grasp it." (Psalms 139:1-6)

Elder Jenkins said, "Yes it is. This Book says the fear of the Lord is the beginning of knowledge." (Proverbs 1:7 NKJV)

Jeremiah realized that wisdom comes through experience, and a wise man will listen and learn. (Proverbs 1:5, 19:20)

Elder Jenkins opened up his Book. "The Apostle Paul writes, 'But I discipline my body and bring it into subjection, lest, when I have preached to others, I myself should become disqualified.' (1 Cor. 9:27 NKJV) Then he says in another place, 'But those who belong to Christ have crucified the flesh with its passions and lusts.' " (Galatians 5:24)

Elder Jenkins said, "The Prophet Jeremiah spoke this concerning the prophets and priests of his day, 'For they have healed the hurt of the daughter of My people slightly, Saying, 'Peace, peace!' When there is no peace.' " (Jeremiah 8:11 NKJV)

Elder Jenkins stood up, signaling he was coming to the conclusion. "This Quest is about taking up our cross daily and following Christ. Many people want the abundant life, but few are willing to live the crucified life." (Luke 9:23)

Chapter 17

The story of Jehu conquering Jezebel. (2 Kings 9:1-37)

The story of Jezebel intimidating Elijah and how God showed Elijah His power. (1 Kings 19)

Jeremiah continued. "When Jezebel saw that lust was not going to work against Jehu, she used her best weapons which were fear and intimidation.

She said something very crafty to Jehu. She said to him, Is it peace, you

Zimri, murderer of your master? (2 Kings 9:31)

The story of Zimri. (1 Kings 16:8-20)

James held up his Book. "We will lead the way. For it is written, 'The steps of a man are directed by the Lord, and He delights in his way.' " (Psalms 37:23)

Jeremiah took out his Sword. "We should not take advantage of one another in the area of sexual immorality. For God has not called us to impurity but to holiness." (I Thessalonians 4:6, 7)

Thomas shouted, "Let each of you look out not only for his own interests, but also for the interests of others." (Philippians 2:4 NKJV)

Jeremiah yelled out, "Keep your thoughts on things that are above where Christ is seated at the right hand of God! (Colossians 3:1) Do not allow any space in your thoughts for lust so that you do not fulfill these sinful desires in your mind." (Romans 13:14)

Jeremiah instructed everyone to push the Knights toward the pits they had dug, trapping all of them in their own holes. (Proverbs 26:27)

Jeremiah pointed his Sword toward the wall. "Do not lose your confidence, because it will bring you great reward. What you need is endurance, so that after you have done the will of God, you may receive what you've been promised." (Hebrews 10:35, 36)

Jeremiah said, "Do not in any way be intimidated by your enemies. Our refusal to be intimidated will be a sign to them of their destruction, but to us it will be a sign of salvation, and that from God." (Philippians 1:28)

Martha shouted, "I've not been given a spirit of fear, but of power and of love and of a sound mind." (II Timothy 1:7 NKJV)

A voice thundered from heaven. "When you walk through the fire you will not be burned, for I will be with you." (Isaiah 43:2)

When the voice finished speaking, an opening was made in the trench, allowing everyone to cross over. (Psalms 29:7)

Jeremiah shouted, "Arise, shine; For your light has come! And the glory of the LORD is risen upon you." (Isaiah 60:1 NKJV)

Martha shouted. "We will not fear or be in dread of our enemies, for the LORD our God, the great and awesome God, is in our midst!" (Deuteronomy 7:21)

Jeremiah read, "Let us draw near with pure, honest, and sincere hearts in full assurance of faith, having our hearts sprinkled from a guilty conscience and our bodies cleansed with pure water." (Heb. 10:22)

Thomas said, "I'm also reminded of the verse which says, 'If we confess our sins, He is faithful and just to forgive us our sins and to cleanse us from all unrighteousness.' " (I John 1:9)

Martha read, "Therefore, having these promises, beloved, let us cleanse ourselves from all filthiness of the flesh and spirit, perfecting holiness in the fear of God." (2 Cor. 7:1 NKJV)

Chapter 18

Teacher read, "Work out your own salvation with fear and trembling, for it is God who gives you both the desire and the ability to bring about His good pleasure." (Philippians 2:12, 13)

Teacher read, "Therefore I call on you brothers, by the compassions of God, that you present your bodies as a living sacrifice, holy, acceptable to God, which is an act of your spiritual worship." (Romans 12:1)
Teacher said, "You asked me about putting our sinful nature to death. The way to do that is to deprive it of its power source. Jesus taught that sinful thoughts are what defile a man, and I believe it is sinful thoughts that nourish our old nature and keep it alive." (Matthew 15:17, 18)

Chapter 19

Teacher said, "For he who has died has been freed from sin." (Romans 6:7 NKJV)

Teacher nodded and read from his Book, "For the word of God is living and powerful, and sharper than any two-edged sword, piercing even to the division of soul and spirit, and of joints and marrow, and is a discerner of the thoughts and intents of the heart." (Hebrews 4:12 NKJV)

Teacher said, "Then Jesus said to those Jews who believed in him, If ye continue in my word, then you are truly my disciples, and you shall know the truth, and the truth shall set you free." (John 8:31, 32)

Teacher said, "Therefore get rid of all uncleanness and rampant wickedness and receive with humility the implanted word, which is able to save your souls." (James 1:21)

Jeremiah remembered reading just a few pages before this, that sin will no longer have dominion over us because we are not under law but under grace. (Romans 6:14)

God knew that because of the weakness of our flesh we could never do what the law demands, so He sent His Son to fulfill all the righteous requirements of the Law for us. (Romans 8:3, 4)

Toward the end of the seventh chapter, Jeremiah saw a tremendous honesty in the Apostle Paul. Paul was able to admit that within his flesh there was nothing good. He went even further and confessed that his sinful flesh was continuously putting forth sin, while he was unable to do anything good through his own efforts. Paul cried out, "What a wretched man I am! Who will deliver me from this sinful body of death?" (Romans 7:24)

Continuing to read, Jeremiah saw that there is no condemnation to those who are in Christ. (Romans 8:1) In Christ we have died to the law (Romans 7:4) and all its demands so that we might be free to live to God. (Galatians 2:19) In Christ, the Law has lost its power to condemn us. The demands of the law were nailed to the cross with Christ and have been canceled. (Colossians 2:14)

Jeremiah saw that we are under a new Law. The Law of the Spirit, of life in Christ Jesus, has set us free from the law of sin and death. (Romans 8:2 NKJV) We now serve in newness of the Spirit and not in the oldness of the letter. (Romans 7:6 NKJV) He understood why Paul's critics would say to him, why not then continue in sin that grace should abound? (Romans 6:1) But they did not understand this wonderful teaching of grace. We have not been made free from the Law so we can sin. No, we have been made free from the Law so we can bear fruit for God. (Romans 7:4)

As Jeremiah stood up, he concluded that The Law keeps sin alive because it keeps us alive. In contrast, his desire was to die daily at the cross, where the resurrection life of Christ could work through him. (Romans 6:4, 5) It was this process of surrender that would give him victory over sin, empowering him to keep God's wonderful commandments out of love rather than out of duty. (Romans 6:6)

Jeremiah would only boast in the cross of Christ. (Galatians 6:14)

Chapter 20

In the graduation address the president said, "We must all endure hardships as good soldiers of Jesus Christ." (2 Timothy 2:3)

Chapter 21

Mark said, "I guess it just proves the principle in Scripture that even as iron sharpens iron, so does good friends in Christ." (Proverbs 27:17)

Jeremiah raised his Sword. "I will flee youthful lusts, but I will pursue righteousness, faith, love, and peace, as I call on the Lord with a pure heart." (2 Timothy 2:22 NKJV)

Jeremiah lunged at the figures with his Sword. "As a young man, I will keep my life pure by keeping a guard over it according to the word of God." (Psalms 119:9)

Mark said, "I will not give anyone a reason to look down upon me because of my youth, but I will be an example to all believers in my speech, my love, my faith, and in my purity." (1 Timothy 4:12)

Rick ran toward the figures, holding out his Sword. "Whatever is true, whatever is honorable, whatever is just, whatever is pure, whatever is motivated by love, whatever is commendable, virtuous, and worthy of praise, these are the things I will think on." (Philippians 4:8)

Jeremiah took out his Book and read. "Let no man say, when he is tempted, I am being tempted by God, for God is not able to be tempted by evil, and He Himself does not tempt anyone. But each one of us is tempted by his own lusts, being seduced. Then when lust has conceived, it gives birth to sin, and when sin becomes full-grown, it brings forth death. (James 1:13-15)

Rick took out his Book and read, "Let him who thinks he stands, watch out lest he fall." (1 Corinthians 10:12)

Chapter 22

Jeremiah read, "Therefore, my beloved brethren, let every man be quick to hear, slow to speak, and slow to wrath." (James 1:19)

Aaron took out his Book and read, "The one who is slow to anger has great understanding, but he who has a quick temper shows his foolishness." (Proverbs 14:29)

Jeremiah said, "God's word teaches that an angry and hot-tempered man stirs up strife, and that strife must be stopped before it gets going." (Proverbs 15:18, 17:14)

Jeremiah quickly looked around at the others. "We are instructed to put all anger and wrath away from us. (Ephesians 4:31) And yet at the same time we are told to be angry and not to sin." (Ephesians 4:26)

Rick pierced the creature in the thigh with his Sword. "I will cease from anger and forsake wrath, for it only leads to harm." (Psalms 37:8 NKJV)

Jeremiah thrust his Shield into the beast's shoulder. "I will be swift to hear, slow to speak, and slow to wrath. For the wrath of man does not produce the righteousness of God." (James 1:19, 20 NKJV)

Mark said, "A person who is slow to anger is better than the mighty, and the one who controls his emotions is stronger than a person who captures a city." (Proverbs 16:32)

Greg swung at the creature's chest. "The anger of a fool is quickly known, but a wise man will overlook an insult." (Proverbs 12:16)

Rick nodded in agreement. "We are told that the anger of man does not accomplish the righteousness of God." (James 1:20)

Jeremiah read, "But the ones who desire to be rich fall into temptation, and into a snare, and into many foolish and harmful lusts which plunge people into ruin and destruction. For the love of money is a root of all kinds of evils. It is through this craving that some have departed from the faith and have pierced themselves with many sorrows." (1 Timothy 6:9, 10)

Mark opened up his Book and read, "Conduct your life in a way that is free from the love of money, and be content with the things you have, for He has said, I will never leave you nor forsake you." (Hebrews 13:5)

Jeremiah said, "We need to learn to be like the Apostle Paul and be content in all situations. (Philippians 4:11) I have found that if a person is not content when they have very little, they'll still not be content even when they have more."

Qualifications for elders: (Titus 1:6-9) (1 Timothy 3:2-7)

Chapter 23

Jeremiah said, "This is what I've been led to read, and it's what I'm going to meditate on: 'Fixing our eyes on Jesus, the author and perfecter of our faith, who for the joy that was set before Him, endured the cross, disregarding the shame, and has sat down at the right hand of the throne of God.' " (Hebrews 12:2)

Chapter 24

Jeremiah determined to seek first the kingdom of God and His righteousness, while trusting Him for all other things. (Matthew 6:33)

Jeremiah raised his Book until it became a Sword. "God made Jesus to be sin, Who knew no sin so that I might become the righteousness of God in Him! That is the great exchange giant. Jesus was counted as being sinful even though He never sinned, so that I could be counted as righteous even though I am only sinful." (II Cor. 5:21)

Jeremiah shouted, "The Lord God alone is my rock and my salvation. He is my strong defense. I shall not be moved." (Psalms 62:6)

Jeremiah shouted, "But thou, O LORD, art a shield for me; my glory, and the lifter of my head." (Psalms 3:3)

Jeremiah said, "God has made all mankind from one blood, and by the blood of One, Jesus Christ, we have all been redeemed!" (Acts 17:26) (1 Peter 1:18, 19)

The Holy Spirit immediately called forth one of Zeal's favorite verses as a child, "If God is for us, then who can be against us." (Romans 8:31 NKJV) Zeal said "For while man looks on the outward things, God looks upon the heart." (1 Samuel 16:7)

Zeal proclaimed, "I have a High Priest who is able to sympathize with all my weaknesses, for He went through all the things that I do, and yet did not sin. (Hebrews 4:15)

"Therefore," declared Zeal, "I will come boldly before the Throne of Grace to receive mercy and the help I need for all my sins and weaknesses." (Hebrews 4:16)

Zeal shouted, "All those who look to God for their confidence, shall be radiant, and their faces will never be covered in shame." (Psalms 34:5)
Zeal shouted, "I give praise to God who accepts me as I am, for it is by His hand that I am fearfully and wonderfully made." (Psalms 139:14 NKJV)

Chapter 29

Grandma Pearl said, "Let me read a couple of things in James. 'For wherever there is envy and selfish ambition, there will also be instability, confusion, and every evil work.' (James 3:16) 'What leads to strife and discord, and how do conflicts and quarrels arise among you? Do they not come from your selfish desires that are always at work in your flesh?' " (James 4:1)

Grandma Pearl read, "Fulfill my joy by being of the same mind, having the same love, being in unity together. Do nothing out of strife or selfish ambition, but in humility consider others as more important than yourselves. Not just being concerned about your own things, but also about the things of others." (Philippians 2:2-4)

Zeal shouted, "In the name of our Lord Jesus Christ, we will walk in unity so that there will be no divisions among us, and we will be perfectly united in the same mind and in the same purpose." (1 Corinthians 1:10)

Written below the sign for the River of Peace was this verse: "Therefore let us pursue the things which make for peace and the things by which we may build up one another." (Romans 14:19)

Chapter 30

Grandma Pearl said, "As a result of sin entering the world, God told Adam and Eve that they would each seek to gain an advantage over the other. Rather than living in a loving and mutually supportive relationship, they would now become locked in a power struggle to see who could get their way at the expense of the other."

The above is in reference to Genesis 3:16. There has been much discussion surrounding this verse, and there are different schools of thought on how to interpret it. It is the opinion of this author that Grandma Pearl's statement is the correct way of understanding the passage. Also like Grandma Pearl, this author believes Ephesians 5: 22-33 outlines what God's original intention for marriage was and lays out for the husband and wife the very opposite tendencies that God said would be the result of the Fall.

The reference to Ephesians talking about marriage: (Ephesians 5:22-33)

Reference to Adam blaming Eve after he sat back and let her make the decision. (Genesis 3:12)

In Christ there is no difference between male and female. (Galatians 3:28)

Grandma Pearl took out her Book and read, "But I want you to know that the head of every man is Christ, the head of woman is man, and the head of Christ is God." (1 Corinthians 11:3 NKJV)

The Father sent the Son. (John 17:18) (John 20:21) (1 John 4:14)

The Father created all things through the Son. (John 1:3) *Note: Colossians 1:16 says that Jesus created all things, and that all things were created through Him. There is no contradiction. The Father and Son together created all things, but it was the Father that initiated the action.*

Chapter 31

Jeremiah quoted, "The LORD is my light and my salvation; Whom shall I fear? The LORD is the strength of my life; Of whom shall I be afraid?" (Psalms 27:1 NKJV)

Zeal quoted, "Do not worry or have any anxiety about anything, but in every situation pray and make your requests known to God with thanksgiving. And God's peace which surpasses all understanding shall surround your hearts and minds in Christ Jesus." (Philippians 4:6, 7)

The Holy Spirit reminded Jeremiah and Zeal of this verse: "Watch out, brothers, lest any of you have an evil heart of unbelief causing you to withdraw from the living God." (Hebrews 3:12)

The Holy Spirit reminded Jeremiah and Zeal of this verse: "But if you have bitter jealousy and rivalry toward one another in your heart, stop boasting and lying against the truth." (James 3:14)

Zeal struck the cave on her side with her Sword and shouted, "I will not give into my fears and take things into my own hands, but I will trust in the Lord. 'He is my refuge and my fortress; My God, in Him I will trust.'" (Psalms 91:2 NKJV)

Jeremiah bludgeoned the cave on his side while shouting, "I will not give in to unbelief but I will put my trust in the Lord, Who is my refuge and my strength, a very present help in times of trouble.'" (Psalms 46:1)

Zeal said, "The Lord is a shield to all those who trust in Him!" (2 Samuel 22:31)

Zeal said, "I will not allow my fears to terrify me, but I will be a true daughter of Sarah, submitting to my husband." (I Peter 3:6)

Jeremiah said, "I will be a servant leader, loving and cherishing my wife as my own body. I will not seek to dominate or manipulate, but I will treat her as an equal partner knowing that we are heirs together of the grace of life." (1 Peter 3:7)

Jeremiah said, "I will dwell with my wife according to a right understanding of what she needs, and I will not allow bitterness or resentment in my heart toward her." (1 Peter 3:7) (Colossians 3:19)

Jeremiah and Zeal realized that Instead of giving into fears they could rely on God's love, and as this love was perfected in their hearts, it would drive away their fears. (1 John 4:18)

Chapter 32

"Yes," said Mr. Clyde, "the love of God is the answer. It's really hard, but Jesus commands us to be loving our enemies, to be blessing the ones who curse us, to be doing good to the ones which hate us, and be praying for those who mistreat and persecute us." (Matthew 5:44)

Grandma Pearl nodded in agreement. "Nowadays we have young people who want to blame everyone and everything around them for their own sin. Sin is ultimately against God, and it is rebellion toward His rule in their life.

There are no excuses before God. He is completely just and fair." (Psalms 51:3, 4)

Chapter 33

Pastor James preached from these verses: (1 Corinthians 13:4-7)

Chapter 34

The Holy Spirit reminded Jeremiah of the time when Elisha was surrounded by a great army, and how Elisha reassured his servant by showing him that they were surrounded by an even greater army. (2 Kings 6:16, 17)

Jeremiah walked back to Grandma Pearl and Zeal. "These people are not on the Quest. They've been kept under darkness and in chains since the day they were born." (Galatians 4:8, 2 Corinthians 4:4)

Pointing toward all those who were in chains, Jeremiah said, "Look out unto the fields, for they are white and ready for harvest. For truly the harvest is plentiful, but the laborers are few. Pray to the Lord of the Harvest that He would send laborers out into the fields to gather in his crops." (John 4:35) (Matthew 9:37, 38)

Grandma Pearl nodded. "For whoever calls upon the name of the Lord will be saved, but how shall they call upon Him Whom they have not believed, and how shall they believe on Him Whom they have not heard, and how shall they hear without a preacher?" (Romans 10:13-17)

Chapter 35

Pastor George said, "Marriage was created by God to unite one man with one woman, representing the relationship between Christ and the church." (Ephesians 5:32)

Pastor George read, "For this reason a man shall leave his father and mother and be joined to his wife, and the two shall become one flesh." (Genesis 2:24) (Matthew 19:5) (Ephesians 5:31)*Each of these is a quote from the NKJV

ABOUT THE AUTHOR

I have a passion for teaching God's word and making it relatable to anyone who wants to learn. I believe that understanding and applying the words of God is the key to success in all areas of life.

Walter Cantrell

www.ingramcontent.com/pod-product-compliance
Lightning Source LLC
Chambersburg PA
CBHW020725210626
46807CB00016B/81